Cyndi

Thank you for all the support.

Forgotten Fighters

Kirk Raeber

&

Mario Acevedo

I really Enjoy working with your. You Are A GREAT RN

Enjoy the story

JK

Kirk Raeber/Honey Rock View Publishing
www.theforgottenletters.com

Cover design: Nick Zelinger, NZ Graphics

This is a work of fiction. Names, characters, places, and incidents are a product of the author's imagination. Locales and public names are sometimes used for atmospheric purposes. Any resemblance to actual people, living or dead, or to businesses, companies, events, institutions, or locales is completely coincidental.

Forgotten Letters/Kirk Raeber -- 1st ed.

ISBN 978-0-9972638-0-0 Print Edition
ISBN 978-0-9972638-1-7 Ebook Edition

For Linda

1

April 1980

My parents' rental home in Franklin Park is just as I remember it. Unfortunately. Old. Dilapidated.

I want the house to have changed, to be a symbol of transition, of progress, a launch pad from the misfortune that piles around me. Instead it ties me to a past and a present that I want to shake free.

Last year, Mother was diagnosed with leukemia. Father died of a stroke shortly after hearing the news. His passage accelerated her condition, and they died ten months apart. He was 64, she was 59.

But I don't just grieve for them, I also grieve for myself. One month after we laid Mother to rest, I learned that my husband Eric cheated on me. Our marriage had been under a lot of pressure, mostly because of finances. My way to cope was to draw inward. His way was to find comfort with someone else. Now, ironically, with the passing of my parents and the inheritance that has come my way, our money woes have eased. But Eric and I are still convulsing in the throes of remorse. We need an escape from our shared, self-inflicted misery.

Unlocking the front door to the house, I push it open to a bloom of stale, musty air. What a dying marriage smells like, I tell myself.

My brother Ichiro lingers behind me on the porch steps. He does a lot of that: Lingering. Hesitating. Stalling. Sadly, he's 25 years old and hasn't yet finished college or had a decent job. It's like he's got an anchor stuck in the mud and won't break the chain, preferring to drift in circles as the tide of life shifts around him.

I know the reason. He hates being Japanese, and he's meandered through life like he's trying to find his true soul. When he was in elementary school, playground bullies made fun of his name and nicknamed him Itchy. Now he insists on being called Kyle. Says it makes him sound like a true-blue American. Then as the Vietnam War raged, which happened during his childhood, other boys taunted him with "gook" and "dink" even though he doesn't have a drop of Vietnamese blood and is half American. Plus every Pearl Harbor Day brought another round of insults. Despite Ichiro having been born here with no memory of Japan, Mom wouldn't let him forget where his roots came from. She would only converse with him in Japanese and taught him how to read and write using kanji.

"Kyle," I say, "come on."

He lifts one earpiece of his Walkman, asking, "Huh?" like he has no idea what we are doing here.

"Inside," I insist.

The small foyer opens to a large front room. Filmy light beams through dirty windows. Faded rectangles on the dingy walls mark where pictures once hung, and wispy cobwebs dangle from the overhead lights.

Ichiro trails at my heels, heavy metal buzzing from his headset. He nods and taps his fingers to the rhythm. In their will, my parents divided the estate between Ichiro and me, but they wisely named me as the executor.

Pad and pen in hand, I wander about the first floor and the basement, cataloguing what needs attention before we list the house for sale. More than a decade of assorted renters have left their mark. Mismatched paneling and skewed electrical outlets show sloppy repair work. Stained and spongy drywall indicates plumbing leaks. Abandoned junk lies piled in the basement. The house *has* changed since we lived here, but the changes are all in the wrong direction.

Thinking back to our times here I want to sink into a state of reverence, to let memories swirl around me. But resentment over Eric eats me like acid, and I'm not a Pollyanna to ignore that my marriage problems are leaving me hollow with anguish.

Ichiro doesn't do much but trail behind me. We make our way to the steps leading upstairs. Dust bunnies scatter around our feet.

He mashes the Walkman's off button, yokes the headset around his neck, and brushes long bangs off his forehead. A loose black *The Deviants* t-shirt shrouds his gangly frame. With his shaggy raven hair and high cheekbones, he looks so much like Mom, except for his gray eyes—our father's gem-like eyes. Meanwhile I have inherited a bony Irish-Norwegian frame. Thank you very much, Dad.

Ichiro's eyes sparkle with surprising curiosity. "We really have to sell this place?" He stares at the empty front room, no doubt imagining where to drop a thrift-store sofa for his deadbeat buddies to crash on.

"We don't have to do anything," I snap. "But unless we do something, nothing will ever get done."

Ichiro raises his hands and retreats a step. "Fumiko, chill already. You got problems, don't take them out on me."

Point taken. I loosen my bitch armor and climb the stairs.

Halfway up, Ichiro says, "Hey, Sis..."

I retighten my armor. The only time Ichiro starts with, "Hey, Sis," is when he wants to mooch cash. He's already received his half of our father's insurance—minus Mom's medical bills. Even though Ichiro is as indifferent to his finances as he is to his appearance, I can't believe he's already squandered forty thousand dollars.

Clenching my jaw, I refuse to turn around and look at him. The steps sag and creak beneath me. Damn, more repair work to get done.

"Sis," he continues, "do you think Mom's cancer had anything to do with Hiroshima?"

Stunned, I hitch a step, then proceed to the top of the stairs. His question treads into forbidden ground, for our parents rarely mentioned their wartime experience.

We knew Mother was at Hiroshima. Every August, she received a paper origami crane, folded inside an envelope with a letter from the Japanese government to the survivors of the atomic bombings. Her eyes would mist and without explanation, she placed the crane on a bookshelf. Ichiro or I would play with the crane until it was reduced to a smudged, limp mess, then it and the envelope and letter disappeared.

We were like all kids, focused only on life as it unraveled before us. Even though I was fluent in Japanese, I never bothered to read the letters. I sensed they were something private. Besides, whenever Ichiro or I asked either Mother or Father about the war, their answers became vague and evasive. If our parents wanted their past hidden, it stayed hidden, remote. So remote that when Mother was diagnosed with leukemia, none of us bothered asking if it might be related to her exposure to the A-bomb's radiation.

"Well?" Ichiro insists.

I stop on the landing and gaze at him. "I don't know."

His expression dulls, perhaps disappointed because I—always Miss Smarty-pants with something to say—have nothing.

He gives a resigned shrug. "I guess it doesn't make a difference, does it?"

"I guess not."

We stare at each other, hesitating, uncertain. I feel like my brother is drawing me into his world. I snap my fingers. "Let's get back to work."

I inspect the second floor and note with dismay the battered doors, threadbare carpet, and cracked bathroom mirror. Now that I've done with my chores of inspecting the house, nostalgia presses heavily on me. Memories tug at my heart, and the loss of my parents seems again fresh and painful.

I look for Ichiro. As usual, when there is work to be done, he has ditched me. I am about to call for him when he clatters up the stairs, a stepladder perched on one shoulder.

"What are you doing?" I ask.

He slips the ladder off his shoulder and drags it to the middle of the hall. He points up to a trapdoor in the ceiling. "The attic."

Yep, I missed it and am astonished that Ichiro noticed.

He glances at his watch and says, "I know it's late but let's take a quick look-see."

I study the trapdoor. "Depends on what we find, it might take a while."

"Whatever." He steadies the ladder.

"Why don't you go first?" I ask.

"You're the oldest. And you have the flashlight."

"All right." I hand him the pad, then climb the ladder until I can touch the trapdoor. I ascend another step for leverage. The door budges on the first push. I lift and swing it aside to reveal a dark, spooky void.

Raising my head, I first look for spiders and anything that can jump on me. Deciding I am safe, I aim my flashlight, but the gloom swallows the beam. A wooden spool hangs on a cord just over the opening. Climbing another step, I clasp the spool and give a tug. A switch clicks, and a bare bulb ignites.

The bulb's yellow light turns gray as it extends into the reaches of the attic. I scramble up onto the floor and stand, careful not to bump my head on the slanting rafters. Ichiro joins me, and as we slough dust from our pants, we scope out the boxes and junk heaped against the walls.

He approaches a pile of antique table lamps. Picking one up, he whisks its tasseled shade and glass base. He puts the lamp down and examines the others, stroking his chin as he thinks. "Vintage," he says. "Authentic art deco."

His pronouncement surprises me. I didn't think my brother cared about anything except getting by with as little effort as possible.

I pan a disapproving appraisal at the rest of the clutter. Even if Ichiro is right in assuming we have some treasure here, I'm not willing to spend a lot of time rummaging through these abandoned odds-and-ends before calling it quits for the day.

Calling it quits. The thought whipsaws through my brain until it congeals into an image of Eric and me. I don't want to quit our marriage but the space between us is a minefield of recriminations and pain. What can I do? How can I forgive?

Tears threaten my eyes, and I squeeze them with my fingers.

My sadness ebbs, and when my mind returns to the present, I see Ichiro sorting through an old wooden carpenter's box filled with rusted tools.

"I'm tired," I say. "If you want to pick through this stuff, we can come back tomorrow."

Ignoring me, Ichiro makes his way around the periphery of the attic, halting to inspect whatever catches his fancy. I approach a dresser pushed against the far wall. I have a friend who restores furniture and she might like this piece. Searching the drawers, I find only old receipts, coupons, notes, broken pens. Behind the dresser rest cardboard boxes stacked on a footlocker. I pivot the dresser aside and peek inside the boxes. They are filled with moldy newspapers and *Life* magazines, sprinkled with mouse droppings.

"What have you got?" Ichiro looks over my shoulder.

"Trash," I answer.

We set the boxes to one side, and he drags the footlocker out of the shadows. It thumps heavily across the floorboards. Because the battered locker is olive green, I'm ready to declare it military surplus and packed with God-knows-what-crap until I read what is written on the lid. Stenciled in faded white paint is: Robert S. Campbell, Captain, U.S.A.A.F.

Ichiro stares. "This was Dad's?"

Dad didn't talk about his military service. "Seems to be. He was in the war."

"A.A.F? He was in the Army Air Force?"

"I guess." Taking a knee beside the front of the locker, I try the catch but it's either locked or frozen.

Ichiro leaves my side and returns with a hammer and a large flat-tip screwdriver from the toolbox. Crouching in front of the locker, he jams the screwdriver into the keyhole and twists. Nothing. With the hammer, he pounds on the back of the screwdriver, then levers the screwdriver until the lock clicks. The hasp springs open.

He drops the tools, undoes the end latches, and lifts the lid. We both lean in to see.

After so much effort on Ichiro's part, I imagine he expects to be rewarded with the dazzling glow of jewels and golden coins. But inside rest more newspapers and a large manila envelope, marked with handwritten script: Campbell, R.S. CPT. 20th Air Force.

The envelope contains typewritten military orders, many on brittle onionskin. The newspapers—*Chicago Daily Tribune,*

Los Angeles Herald-Express, Asahi Shinbun—are copies dated from 1946 through 1965.

Beneath the newspapers lay two garments wrapped in paper. I open the first. It's a precise rectangle of fabric that I unfold into a kimono of cream silk with red brocade and embroidery.

I blink at the kimono, astonished that it still exists. I last saw it the day Mother married our father, before Ichiro was even conceived.

"What is it?" Ichiro nudges me.

I wake from my reverie and say, "Mom's wedding kimono."

"Oh," he mumbles. "It's pretty." He runs his hand across the textured silk.

When I open the second package, out wafts the faint odor of mothballs. I unfold a uniform coat, in olive-drab wool. Sewn to the left shoulder is a round blue patch embroidered with yellow wings and a small red circle inside a white star. The metal insignia on the lapels and shoulder straps are tarnished, but the colorful ribbons above the left pocket remain bright as new. Pinned above them is a large set of wings, the silver black with age.

Ichiro takes the jacket. He fingers the wings. "Dad was a pilot?"

Another detail that I don't know. I shrug. This is like excavating a sarcophagus, brimming with mystery and wonder. We discover framed photographs. One is in black and white, of my pretty mother in a western dress, her belly swollen with Ichiro, me in a dark skirt with a white petticoat, white gloves, and a matching hat. My handsome father, dashing in his pinstripe suit and spectator shoes (why don't men dress like this anymore?), leans over Mom's shoulder to smile at the camera. The kanji script along the bottom reads *Matsuda Photography Studio*. The memory of that day crashes though my mind, and I swoon and catch myself before I topple over.

If Ichiro noticed my reaction, he doesn't show it. Instead he rises and slips his arms through the sleeves of the jacket. It drapes baggy, past his hips. On Dad it would've hung to his waist and fit snug around his muscular shoulders. Ichiro leaves the jacket unbuttoned and twists from side to side. "Whaddaya think?"

The contrast between the magnificent jacket and his Converse high tops and his thin legs in their frayed jeans makes him look childish and ridiculous. But I answer diplomatically. "I've never seen you this dressed up."

He kneels back down, and we continue to dig through the footlocker, unearthing more and more of our parents' past.

"Careful," Ichiro warns. "I have a friend who poked through his parents' stuff only to find Polaroids of them at swinger parties."

I blush. Though certain our parents were not wife-swappers, I now have questions as to why they kept so much of their lives stashed away.

Another photo. One of Dad in sweat-stained khakis, a headset draped around his neck, its cables dangling down the front of his shirt, pilot's wings pinned above the left pocket. Smiling, he stands with three other aviators huddled in the shadow beneath the wing of an enormous airplane.

My parents' history is such an enigma. I remember glimpses from my early childhood, but not enough to piece together what I'm finding.

In one corner of the locker I discover a box about the size of two shoeboxes placed side by side. Red foil covers the box, the top secured by a white silk ribbon squashed flat. Surely, it contains special secrets. But who keeps a box of such secrets?

I lift the box out of the footlocker and center it on old newspapers to protect it from the gritty wooden floor. I tug at the knot until the ribbon falls away.

Ichiro presses close as I remove the lid. Inside lay rows of letters, yellowed and stained.

The letters are in random order. I thumb through them, admiring the variety of stamps. The earliest postmark is 1931. I pick one with a postmark dated April 1952. The return address is in Japanese and English, from Makiko Asakawa—Mother's maiden name—in Yokohama. It's addressed in both languages to Robert Campbell, to his parents' home here in Chicago.

Delicately, I open the flap, slide the letter out, and unfold the stationery.

The script is in Japanese, written in faded blue ink.

I read aloud, "Dear Robert..."

2

March 1924

Robert Campbell stood beside his parents, Pastor Jack and Sarah Campbell, along the passenger deck railing on the steamer *SS Amanda Rogers*. They watched with fascination as the details of Yokohama harbor materialized in the haze. The cold breeze pinching Robert's face did not dampen his excitement of at last reaching their new home. His father clasped the brim of his fedora to keep it from flying away. His mother clutched the scarf knotted at her throat. The wind tugged strands of hair spilling from under her hat. Finally, fifty days after leaving San Francisco, they had arrived in Yokohama.

Last October a mysterious man wearing a fancy suit had visited his father's chapel back in Oglesby. After worship service the man introduced himself as someone from the main church in Chicago. He was then invited to their home for Sunday dinner. Nothing important was discussed over the meal. But even at eight years old, Robert recognized small talk when he heard it.

Later, when his parents and the stranger sat out on the porch, Robert snuck under a juniper bush to lie close by. From this hidden spot he eavesdropped on the serious words his folks and the man passed between them. Seemed an earthquake had damaged a town called Yokohama in the faraway place of Japan. Lots of fire and many died. An American Methodist missionary had been hurt badly and was sent back home.

The man said the main church wanted Robert's father to consider traveling to Yokohama and rebuilding that church. Robert and his mother would go along.

To Japan? Robert didn't even know where Japan was. It wasn't close, that was for sure. Plus he'd have to leave his friends, and he didn't know when he'd see them again.

But as his parents and the man kept talking, Robert pushed aside his thoughts and listened. He was certain his father would say what he usually said when faced with a big decision. That he would pray and ask for the Lord's guidance. His mother and father spoke among themselves, discussing something Robert didn't understand. Robert wished he could see their expressions but he didn't risk moving.

But the way his father answered with Scripture, announcing in his confident preacher voice, *"Behold, I am doing a new thing; now it springs forth, do you not perceive it? Isaiah 43:19,"* Robert knew that soon he'd be living in Japan.

The news made him a celebrity at school and while he could pick out Japan and Yokohama on a globe, he wasn't quite sure how far away everything actually was. It was as fantastic as planning a trip to the moon. Sure, it was a piece away, but how far? When asked how they'd get there, "by boat partways," he replied, even then he wasn't sure. Maybe they'd go by airplane or maybe a railroad bridge crossed the ocean from California to Japan.

Robert blinked, returning to the present. The change in the vibration beneath his feet told him the ship's engines had altered speed as the *Amanda Rogers* churned toward the cargo pier. Fishing boats bounced through the chop to clear the shipping channel in the middle of the bay. A giant city spread before them, the jumbled confusion of buildings spilling down the hills to the wooded shoreline.

"A bit challenging to take it all in," his mother said as she draped her arm across his shoulder.

"It's been quite an odyssey so far," his father replied, "and it's only the beginning."

***

Robert's legs jittered with anticipation. He clutched his mom's hand for the strength to hold still. The other passengers jostled against them in the corridor leading to the disembarkation station. His mother carried a suitcase in her other hand. His father hauled two large suitcases. Robert dragged a small valise. Over his woolen shirt and pants, he wore a corduroy coat and his Chicago Cubs ball cap.

He was ready to bolt off this ship and see what new adventures waited for him. His apprehension about moving had vanished long ago, what with the flurry of getting rid of so many of their belongings, then the goodbyes, the wonderful trips by train, and onto the magical steamship, so huge, so amazing. So much more fantastic than anything he could have dreamed of.

If it had been up to him, he would've ended this trip in Hawaii. The island was picture-book perfect, and had he told his pals back in Oglesby about the water full of fish and crab and shrimp, they would have called him a liar. Everything about Oahu—the clean air, the mountains green as spring moss, the endless opportunities for poking around—convinced him this was what heaven must be like. Forget the streets of gold and all those angels with their harps and singing.

The *Amanda Rogers* next sailed to the Philippines. In Manila, the confusion of languages and the people jamming the streets and markets made the city seem as lively as a county fair.

The ocean voyage had opened to his eyes to how big and wondrous the world actually was. And something else sparked in him. At first he had resisted his parents' insistence that he study Japanese from their primers and the record on the portable Victrola, but once they left Manila he decided that learning a new language might be fun. Besides, he enjoyed reading and studying. Now as he waited in the passageway to disembark, Robert counted to himself, "*Ichi. Ni. San...*"

A commotion rippled through the crowd, and passengers shuffled forward. His mother pulled him along. The queue advanced a few steps, then stopped, then advanced again. Suddenly, the pace quickened and Robert hustled to keep up with his parents, his valise banging against his leg. Sunlight poured through the broad hatch in the hull; his father pivoted to the left, then his mother, then Robert. A ship's officer waved and smiled.

Just like that, Robert and his family were marching down the gangplank to the pier. Sea gulls glided past like bits of wind-blown paper through the afternoon air. Yokohama stretched all around them—smelling of ocean and coal smoke and diesel exhaust—bustling with people and boats and cranes and trucks like he was peering inside a gigantic machine. A small crowd waved from the dock.

At the bottom of the gangplank the line of passengers turned to the right and formed three queues at an open-sided shed. A white sign was covered in Japanese script with English lettering: *Official Port of Entry. Please to reveal your passport.*

They waited in the middle line. The customs official, a stern-faced but polite man with a tiny mustache and a blue uniform, thumbed through their passports and stamped them. His father led Robert and his mother down the pier.

Robert glanced back to the *Amanda Rogers.* The cranes were already extending over the cargo holds. "What about our trunks?"

"They go through a separate customs inspection," his father answered. "I'll have to come back tomorrow and get them."

Luggage in hand, they joined the others proceeding from the customs office. The scene overwhelmed Robert with the weirdness of being in such a different country. Though some Japanese wore western-style clothes, most wore strange garments: robes, high-water pants, socks with tall wooden sandals, the men's hair gathered in topknots.

A big, fancy car nosed through the crowd.

"Pastor Campbell," a man shouted, his English distorted by a Japanese accent.

Robert waited for the car to stop, certain it was their ride. But it continued past them. From behind the car a man and a woman appeared beside a wooden wheelbarrow. The woman carried a small girl, her hair arranged in ribbons. Besides her large eyes, what Robert noticed was her plump lower lip.

"Pastor Campbell?" the man repeated.

Robert's father waved. "That's me."

The man and the woman wore quilted coats, canvas pants gathered at the cuffs into thick socks, and those odd sandals. They were both short. The breeze ruffled his shiny black hair and the scarf covering her head. He was the taller of the two, slender, with the dark tan of a man who spent a lot of time in the sun. She was stockier and bore a complexion almost as fair as Robert's mother Sarah.

Her daughter was wrapped in a quilt, which was gathered into a sling looped over the woman's shoulder. The girl stared wide-eyed—fascinated by the Americans, especially Robert—and giggled.

The man grasped the handles of the wheelbarrow and rolled it close, the woman keeping to his side. She clutched the child tight against her chest. They halted and bowed stiffly from the waist. "*Ohayou gozaimasu.*"

Jack and Sarah set their luggage on the ground, bowed similarly and repeated the greeting. Robert bowed as well; he and his mother had rehearsed the introduction.

Hand extended, the man stepped around the wheelbarrow. "It is an honor to at last meet you, Pastor Campbell."

"Pastor Jack, please," his father corrected.

Hiro said, "I am brother Hiro Asakawa from the Yokohama Free Methodist Church. This is my wife, sister Yumi." She gave another bow.

Robert wasn't sure if he had heard right. The man's name was "*Hero*"?

The girl was their daughter, Makiko.

Robert's father continued the introductions. Hiro shook hands with Robert's mother, then with him. Hiro had a firm, calloused grip. Yumi studied his face, smiled, then said something to her husband.

He said, "My wife apologizes for not knowing enough English. She admires your son. He will grow up to be big and strong. A man of decision and duty."

Robert's mother cupped the back of his head and gave a playful shake. "Perhaps. Hopefully. But he's got a way to go."

Hiro helped Jack pile their luggage on the wheelbarrow and then lashed the bags into place with a rope. When his father reached for the handles, Hiro stood in the way. "No, please. It is my duty," he protested, "you are guests."

He lifted the handles and pivoted the wheelbarrow to point away from the dock. Yumi adjusted the sling so Makiko rode high on her back. The group assembled around Hiro and started walking.

Yumi hooked her arm into his mother's and the two women walked side by side. Robert trailed behind Hiro, fascinated by how easily he and Yumi walked on their stiff sandals with thick wooden cleats. Little Makiko squirmed in her quilt to watch him with her large dark eyes.

"How far are we going?" his father asked.

"To the church," Hiro answered.

"Which is how far?"

"I imagine," Hiro said, "you didn't get much exercise on the ship."

"That's true."

"You're going to make up for it now."

"What about your wife?" Sarah asked. "Makiko is no infant. She will get heavy."

Hiro commented to his wife, and she answered in Japanese. He translated, "She says she will manage."

"Forgive me for sounding condescending," Robert's father said to Hiro, "but your English is quite good."

Hiro offered a quick bow. "Thank you. The pastor before you, Eldridge Jacobs, prepared me to be the lay minister. He had me read the Bible aloud in English for one hour every day and then quizzed me. Was not an easy task."

He led them out of the wharf district and into downtown Yokohama. Robert didn't think it was possible he would ever see a city as busy as Chicago. Much reminded him of America: the brightly colored signs, the advertisements for cigarettes and refreshments, the cars. But the complicated Japanese scripts made everything seem so bizarre. They shoehorned through clumps of pedestrians and paused at a rail line to let a trolley car pass.

Robert watched it rumble along. "We could ride that."

"Would not be helpful for our efforts," Hiro replied. "The trolley into our neighborhood remains damaged. So we must walk."

Robert had forgotten that the city had suffered earthquake and fire. Ruin extended for blocks in every direction. He noticed buildings wrapped in scaffolding with parties of men hard at work. Some men carried bricks or lumber in cradles on their backs. Others pulled handcarts or pushed wheelbarrows. Trucks of all types motored past. Occasionally, a black sedan bulled through traffic, the driver honking its horn.

The Asakawas and the Campbells continued past block after block. Some people glanced at them, others gawked, especially at his father who towered over the locals. The farther they walked from the pier, the more obvious the stares and after a while, Robert knew that his parents felt the same as he did, like an alien from a different planet. After a long hike down a central boulevard, Hiro steered around a corner and they headed up a packed dirt road.

Coal smoke drifted on the breeze. The air turned cooler, and the sky darkened. Robert's stomach growled with hunger.

Heaps of rubble spilled onto the road. Long, blackened paths cut through the neighborhoods. Robert remembered how the city had been burned and he was astounded by the devastation. His dad helped Hiro lift the wheelbarrow over a large crack in the road. Robert followed the crack and saw that it ran underneath the rubble of a wrecked building.

People dug at the remains of other buildings with shovels, picks, and pry bars. They stacked whatever they salvaged—bricks, lumber, pipe, doors, odd pieces of furniture—on the sidewalk. Everyone worked hard but looked sad.

"Were many people killed?" Robert asked.

"Many, yes," answered Hiro. "The earthquake was named the Great Kanto. Entire families were lost. Whole neighborhoods as well."

Robert wanted a number. A hundred? Five hundred? A thousand? But a warning glance from his mother told him to keep quiet.

The street zigzagged up the slope. Robert looked back to see how far they had gone. Unfortunately, the city landscape blocked his view of the ocean.

And still they kept walking. Though it had turned cold, Hiro had unfastened his jacket and paused occasionally to flex his hands and wipe the sweat from his brow.

Robert's father reached down and clasped the wheelbarrow handles. "Let me try for a bit."

Hiro looked relieved. "A bit. Yes. But only for a bit."

The street opened into a broad intersection. The husks of smashed buildings surrounded them, and people picked at the remains. Robert realized that he hadn't seen anyone his age.

"Where are all the kids?"

"In school," Hiro replied. "We take our studies very seriously."

"What time will I see them?"

"Later in the afternoon."

Robert didn't know how much time had passed, but he got hungrier. Yet they continued to hike up the winding road. People queued at an outdoor spigot to fill wooden buckets, large bottles, and jugs with water. Around them stood damaged brick buildings and lots of wooden structures, all with crooked walls and broken roofs. Some had been gutted by fire and looked like blackened, rotten teeth. And everywhere, people scratched at the ruins and slowly turned the destruction back into order.

Hiro offered to take over the wheelbarrow. He rolled it diagonally across the street toward a heavy door along a broad wooden wall. He halted outside the door and fished a key ring from his pocket. Unlocking the door, he started for inside when Robert's father reached for the wheelbarrow.

"No, leave for now," Hiro said. He disappeared inside.

Yumi loosened her sling and carefully let Makiko slip free. The little girl reached for the ground with her short legs and then stood. She wore a small quilted jacket and baggy pants tucked into socks. She chattered in Japanese and Yumi answered. Yumi ushered Robert's mom and Makiko through the door. Robert stayed outside with his father.

A couple of Japanese men in what looked like robes and pajamas strolled by and stared in at Jack and at Robert. Looking different was something he was going to have to get used to.

A gate to the left swung open. Hiro stepped through and retrieved the wheelbarrow. Robert and his father followed him into a small courtyard paved with flat stones. To the right, Yumi opened the shutters that revealed a small kitchen. "My home," Hiro said. To the left stood another door, which he opened. "This is the rectory. Your home."

Robert's father removed his hat and went in. Robert stayed close, curious about their new dwelling. Hiro followed them over the threshold. He removed his sandals and walked on stockinged feet. Robert and his father did likewise.

He knew their house in Oglesby had been small, but it was a mansion compared to the rectory. The first room wasn't much bigger than their cabin on the *Amanda Rogers*, with barely space for a narrow cot, a dresser, a desk and chair, a bookcase with books, and a washstand with a mirror, all tidily arranged on the wooden floor. A thin mattress was rolled against one end of the cot. Jack eased himself onto the cot and set his hat down. The cot had such short legs that his knees angled upward. He considered the small dimensions of the bed. "I take it my predecessor was a bachelor?"

"Yes," Hiro answered. "No wife. Yumi tried to find for him, but Pastor Jacobs was always too busy. He said that being without a woman allowed him to accomplish much."

Robert's father stood. "Or not enough."

Robert took off his cap, rolled it tight, and tucked it into a coat pocket. He looked about the room and wondered where he would sleep.

"And the chapel?" his father asked.

Hiro crossed the room to another door. "This opens to the sanctuary."

He led Robert and his dad inside.

One wall of the chapel had a splintered gap large enough for a man to step through. Several of the ceiling beams had been shored with long poles. Roof shingles drooped through a hole above. The wooden floor beneath was stained and warped from where rain had pooled. The chapel looked like it had room for fifty people. The pews had been covered with tarps and pushed away from the hole in the roof. Robert guessed that the door at the far end was the entrance from the street.

Jack stuck his hands into his trouser pockets. He looked worried, and now Robert worried too. Before this trip had started, his father kept talking about the sacrifices the family would have to make. Robert now understood what those "sacrifices" were going to be. A lot of work. A loss of space and possessions. Much-different foods. And the hardest of all, trying to live as strangers in this strange land.

His father said, "I was told you had thirty families in your congregation."

"We now have twenty-six," Hiro replied. "We lost four in the earthquake and fire."

"My condolences."

Hiro gave a quick nod and muttered, "*Kawai sou desu ne.*"

"What do you do for work? Your vocation?"

"I am a carpenter."

"A handy skill. You must have plenty of work."

"Plenty of work, yes. Plenty of people who can pay, no."

Voices hailed from the courtyard. Hiro hustled to them. Robert's father slowly turned after him, his eyes lingering on every detail of the chapel as if measuring the time and expense needed for repair.

"Jack, Robert, come here," his mother called out.

Robert and his father rushed to her.

She was standing in the courtyard, surrounded by Japanese men and women. Many of them carried bowls wrapped in towels. Some wore western attire, the rest local traditional clothes. As one, they bowed. "*Ohayou gozaimasu.*"

Robert and his father bowed in reply.

Hiro gestured to the group. "Part of your congregation. They have arrived to wish you welcome."

Jack answered, "I'm touched and gratified."

Hiro said, "Let us go into the chapel. As the Book of Matthew says: *And day by day, attending the temple together and breaking bread in their homes, they received their food with glad and generous hearts.*"

"Very good," Robert's father said. He tweaked his son's ear. "When are you going to learn Scripture that well?"

Robert pulled away. Maybe when he didn't find Bible study so boring.

The group filed out the gate and into the street. Robert's father led his mom and him through the rectory. She dragged an appreciative touch over the meager furnishings. They met Hiro in the chapel. The front door was open and the other congregants bunched inside.

The dishes were set on a table in front of the altar. Yumi and Sarah brought stacks of small bowls, cups, and a large teapot. Makiko tottered after them.

Hiro motioned to the pulpit. "Pastor Jack."

Robert's father blinked and Robert could see in his eyes what he was thinking. These people in this strange place were his new flock.

His father shrugged off the coat and folded it over a chair behind the pulpit. Hiro handed him a Bible. Jack set it unopened on the pulpit and recited from memory, "From the Book of James. *Every good gift and every perfect gift is from above,*" he paused to point to the hole in the ceiling, at the darkening sky, "*coming down from the Father of lights with whom there is no variation or shadow due to change.*"

Hiro led the congregation with an "Amen."

Yumi whispered to her husband. He said, "Pastor Jack, perhaps you would like to offer a sermon, a few words to our congregation?"

"How about this?" he replied. "A blessing for this food, which we'll share while still warm, and that will give me time to collect my thoughts."

Hiro translated to the group. They nodded and repeated, "*Hai. Hai.*"

Robert's mother stepped beside her husband. She shot Robert a stare that commanded him to join her. The congregation reached to one another to clasp hands and their new pastor led them in prayer. Robert stood between his mother and Yumi. Makiko broke into the circle and grasped Robert's hand.

With the *Amen*, the women uncovered the dishes. Aromatic steam lifted from bowls of chicken, fish, vegetables, or heaps of brown rice.

Hiro said apologetically. "Please overlook our discourtesy. Honored guests must be served white rice, but it is expensive and the work to repair our homes and businesses has consumed our finances."

Robert's father shook his head and told him the meal was more than good enough.

Yumi and Sarah passed out bowls ladled with food. Rather than sit in the pews, everyone sat on the floor. Robert removed his coat, folded it, and sat on it like a cushion. He watched the

Japanese use chopsticks to whisk food into their mouths and then tried clumsily for himself. Makiko sat in Yumi's lap and ate from her mother's chopsticks.

The chapel echoed with friendly introductions and the rattle of dishware. The day's excitement faded and Robert wanted to lie down and sleep. But he was content. What new adventure waited for tomorrow?

Bang! The entrance door to the chapel burst open. Everyone jumped, and all eyes turned to see. Makiko stared, her eyes brimming with surprise.

Four policemen stormed in, dark blue uniforms, white armbands and gloves, long bamboo poles, and fearsome scowls. They advanced down the middle of the sanctuary. Though they were as short as the other Japanese, to Robert they seemed menacing as gorillas.

Robert's father set his bowl down and rose to his feet. Hiro also stood.

"Who are they?" Sarah asked, worried.

Robert watched, chopsticks clutched in one hand, and suddenly afraid.

"The *Tokko*," Hiro said, quietly. "Special political police."

The policeman leading the group barked an order.

Hiro gave a quick, obedient bow.

The policeman swung his pole across the group and aimed it at Robert's father. He in turn glared at the policeman, face flaming, hands balled into fists.

The fright inside young Robert chilled into terror. He had never seen his father this red, this angry, this close to exploding.

His mother stood and clutched his father's arm.

"What's the meaning of this?" He towered above the policeman. "What are you doing here?"

The policeman growled his words. Hiro translated as the man spoke. "You are on notice. You and your foreign devilry are not welcome in Japan. We will be watching you. Always. Everywhere. Step out of line—" He whacked the pole on the floor. Yumi and the other Japanese women cried out. "...and we will smash your heads like clay pots."

Jack took a step toward the policeman. "I don't care who you are. This is a place of peaceful worship. I will not have you intimidate me, my family, or my congregation." Sarah pulled him back.

The policeman advanced a step and shouted at the Japanese congregants. They turned pale and lowered their heads, cowed. Then he glared at Robert's father, uttered a short message, then let his hard face ease into a grin. He nodded to his men, barked an order, and they stomped out.

"What did he say?" Robert's father asked.

"He said," Hiro explained, "'Consider my visit as your official welcome from the Emperor of Japan.'"

3

April 1924

Robert spent his days helping his father and Hiro repair the chapel and make improvements to the rectory. In the first weeks he was here, he had slept in a storage room in the Asakawas' home while an addition was built to the rectory. When his father announced that the space was to be Robert's new room, he asked in surprise, "Why so big?" There was enough space for a regular-sized cot, chairs, a desk, bookcases, and an armoire.

His father mussed his hair. "You're growing up. Soon, you'll be as tall as me."

Robert reflected on the comment. He was years away from being a teenager, and even more years away from being anywhere close to as tall as his dad. If his father and mother had made his new room that large, and just because of him, then they expected to remain in Yokohama for a long, long time.

He hadn't thought about that when they arrived in Japan. He figured it was a short, temporary arrangement, living here. How long would it be until he was over six feet tall like his father? Ten years? He couldn't imagine being that tall, and he couldn't imagine remaining in Japan all that time.

"Now get on with your chores." His father nudged him out the door.

Robert stayed busy the rest of the afternoon, sweeping sawdust and wood shavings off the chapel floor and the indoor scaffolding.

His mother and Yumi announced that dinner was almost ready. His father had bought a rubber ball at a nearby market, and he and Robert tossed it back and forth in the courtyard. His father quizzed him about the rules of baseball, preparing Robert for when he finally got to take the field. The English-language Tokyo newspaper didn't carry much news though it did report both Japanese and American games, which his father read to him. An encouraging surprise was learning that the Japanese enjoyed baseball as much as Americans did.

As the sun settled below the roofline, a sharp chill cut through the air. Another surprise was discovering how cold it could get in Yokohama. In every picture he had seen about the Orient, people strolled or lounged in light, summery clothes beneath the shade of palm trees. But Japan could get every bit as freezing as Illinois.

Hiro watched Robert and his dad play catch. Declining an invitation to join them, he sat on a wooden stool and passed the time using a whetstone and strop to sharpen his chisels and carving tools for the next day.

Dinner was fish with steamed rice. Their dining area was a large space that opened when Hiro pushed aside a sliding door, a *fusama*, to make the kitchen and the front room into one common area. They sat on tatami mats around a short table. Makiko stabbed at an empty bowl with her chopsticks. As a treat, Robert's mother had cooked fried sugar dumplings, which they ate as dessert.

After dinner they lingered in the kitchen and practiced Japanese with Hiro and Yumi. Robert was surprised how fast he was picking up words and stringing them together. He practiced with Makiko, who in turn mimicked his English. But for Robert, reading Japanese—*kanji*—was another matter, with its confusing assortment of symbols. During the day, Yumi would listen patiently and offer encouragement as he struggled to read any Japanese text: food labels, articles from magazines, the Yokohama newspaper.

"In one year," she had said, smiling to his mother and father, "his Japanese be better than my English."

"And her English," Sarah pointed to Makiko, "will be better than my Japanese."

Rain hissed on the roof and poured from gutters onto the front sidewalk. Hiro jerked up as if he had remembered something. He brought a finger to his lips and approached a front window. He cracked open a shutter. Robert joined him.

They gazed across the street. Under a lamppost, a man loitered. He clutched the collar of his coat. Rain dripped off the sagging brim of his fedora.

The stranger was a policeman from the *tokko*. One of them was always watching, usually from that same lamppost, and always in civilian clothes though it was obvious who they were.

"He's as miserable as a wet cat," Hiro whispered.

Yumi stepped between Hiro and Robert to peer through the window. "Poor thing. He'll catch cold." She turned about and headed into the kitchen. She emptied leftover dinner into a cone she made from a newspaper. She wrapped the still warm teapot in a thick towel and cradled it in her arm.

"Robert," Yumi asked, "you wish help?"

"What are you doing?" his mother asked.

Yumi started to reply in English, then in frustration explained to Hiro. He translated, "If the spy's imbecilic bosses can't take care of him, we will."

Robert welcomed this break from the evening's routine. Yumi asked him to carry the cone and a wooden cup. His mother and Hiro draped straw mats over their shoulders to use as rain capes and fastened conical grass hats over their heads.

Makiko wanted to go and pouted when Yumi told her stay put.

Hiro opened the front door to the roaring splatter of rain. Yumi and Robert hustled across the street, their *geta* splashing through the puddles, and the cold water wetting their *tabi* socks.

Yumi announced their approach. "*Konnichiwa.*" The policeman jerked his head up and pushed away from the lamppost. She bowed and said in Japanese, "We brought you something to help you pass the time more pleasantly."

The policeman considered them in the rain-filtered light of the lamppost. He looked young, maybe 20.

Yumi opened her cape to show him the teapot. Robert handed him the cup.

The policeman nodded graciously and took the cup. Yumi filled it, the tea steaming, rain drops plopping.

"Those bastards that I work for," the policeman said. Robert had picked up much Japanese, including words he wasn't supposed to know. The policeman continued, "Not only sent me to watch you in this shit, they didn't even bother to feed me. I'm lucky to get paid."

Robert offered the cone.

"What's this?" The policeman gave the cup to Yumi, took the cone, and unwrapped it. "Ah, most kind." He scooped the rice into his mouth and ate it all. He wadded the newspaper and handed it back to Robert.

"I wish my boss was as thoughtful as you. Son-of-a-bitch sends me out on a night like this while he and his sergeants bring geishas and sake into the barracks. And I don't mean proper geishas, either."

Robert knit his brow in confusion about what the policeman meant.

Yumi refilled the cup, which the policeman gulped down. He returned the cup. "Thank you much, the two of you."

Yumi and Robert acknowledged him with a deep bow. She said, "We do this in service to the Emperor."

The policeman replied with a bow of his own. "To the Emperor."

Yumi and Robert headed back to her house. She laughed.

"What's so funny?" he asked.

"Such an attentive policeman. You were standing right in front of him and he never noticed that you are not Japanese. The poor man could see nothing but his own self-pity."

***

Robert seldom ventured beyond the confines of the rectory, the chapel, the Asakawa home, and the courtyard. He looked forward to the trips with his parents and either Hiro or Yumi to downtown and the wharf. And always, a man would appear to shadow them.

He learned that the Japanese were tidy and resourceful about everything. Maybe it was that everyone felt so packed in and that the land crowded against them.

An example of the Japanese tidiness was their bathing rituals. For these, his chore was helping Yumi heat water for the *ofuro*, a square tub two feet deep and barely large enough for either of his parents to sit in without drawing their knees up. The bathing area was behind a shoji—a sliding paper screen— in the Asakawas' front room. But one didn't wash in the *ofuro*. The ritual was to sit on a short wooden stool beside the *ofuro* and ladle warm water from a bucket over one's body, then lather up with soap, and rinse. The water would disappear down a drain by the stool. Only when one was clean were they allowed in the *ofuro*, where they would sit and relax. As guests, Robert's father and mother would go first, taking turns, then emerge wearing robes. Hiro and Yumi followed. As children, Robert and Makiko went last. The Asakawas weren't at all shy about undressing Makiko in front of everybody. But Robert wouldn't strip to the altogether, and he protested against bathing with her.

After each bather, Yumi would scoop hair and debris from the water. At the end of the bathing session, she would cover the *ofuro* with thick boards to preserve the heat. When the *ofuro* had been used twice by everyone, his mother and Yumi would transfer the bath water with buckets to scrub the courtyard's tiles.

On May 14, Robert's birthday, his father announced a special surprise. First he asked that Robert help him open one of the big steamer trunks. Jack made a fuss of searching through bundles of clothes and pulled out a package wrapped in paper and string. He handed the package to Robert. He untied the string and unfolded the paper to find a pair of fielder's mitts and a baseball...a real baseball. The baseball looked new but the gloves were stained and scarred, and the laces frayed. Still, they were real fielder's mitts.

"I've been waiting a long time to give them to you," his father said.

"Both mitts?"

"In case you meet a friend. You can loan him the second glove."

Robert slipped on one of the gloves. It swallowed his hand, but he'd grow into it.

"It's a beautiful day," his father said, "let's go play catch."

Robert handed the other glove to his dad. He took the ball and smacked it into the pocket of his glove. He felt older, more capable. He put on his Cubs cap and followed his father to the courtyard.

Hiro, Yumi, and Makiko waited. His father smiled and hid something behind his back. He showed Robert another gift, a baseball bat. "Hiro carved it for you."

Robert took the bat and admired its smooth lines. He gushed thanks to Hiro, then tucked the glove and ball under his arm and swung the bat. Its heft let him imagine hitting home runs.

Jack asked Hiro, "You want to join us?"

Hiro shook his head. "I have to complete work for a customer."

Robert and his father started to leave when Makiko protested that she didn't want to be left behind. Jack hoisted her to his chest. The three of them left the courtyard through the gate onto the street. A few pedestrians glanced at them curiously. They walked past the end of the block to a vacant lot. The *tokko* policeman at the lamppost appeared conflicted. Should he stay and watch the house or follow Robert and his father? He shrugged and decided to remain by the lamppost.

Once at the lot, his father set Makiko down and then he scratched a batter's box in the dirt. A tumbled wall of bricks served as a backstop. He tutored Robert on the basics of a batter's stance and how to read a pitch and when to swing. He paced off a distance to the pitcher's mound and faced Robert, who lifted the bat off his shoulder and set his jaw.

His father wound up and launched the ball. As it whisked by Robert, he swung...and missed. The ball smacked the dirt, ricocheted against the wall, and rolled back toward them.

"Don't just swing the bat," his father admonished. "Keep your eye on the ball. It's an important lesson, and not just in baseball. Always, keep your eye on the ball."

***

Life as a preacher's kid was more than baseball and school lessons. Robert helped his father and mother prepare the chapel for the Sunday service, sweeping the floor and placing hymnals and bulletins in the pews. A few of the families brought children but they were much younger than Robert, and eager to leave the chapel once the service was over.

Robert accepted his duties in the church; this was what he'd done all his life. But he missed his schoolmates and the long hours playing outside.

His mother made him write letters to friends and relatives back home. Robert protested, arguing that he had nothing to say. Actually, he had plenty to say, but it was about baseball and how much he missed snagging catfish and spooking horses and stealing pies cooling on windowsills. But he didn't know how to write about these things, or that he should. Writing letters was about saying important things and Robert couldn't think of anything important to say. So his mom told him what to write.

The letters he received were always written on cheap pulp paper, and he could tell that the authors had been dictated to. Random spots of ink and smears showed where the nib had leaked.

A typical letter read:

Dear Robert,

I hope this letter finds you in good spirits and in better health. We had a rainy spell and the Vermillion River flooded it's banks and wipped out the dock at Sherman's Landing. Things at church are going well. My cousin Agnes is about to be married.

If you remember Cooter James. He fell off a horse and broked his arm. Lefty Crimes is no more plying his trade on the river. The revenoors caught up to him and sank his boat. I'm sure we'll find him joining his brother in the Joliet prison. We spend a lot of recreating time watching baseball. Next year I hope to play on a team. I wish you could be here then.

My mother asks that I mention her best wishes for you and your family.

We sorely miss you. Zeke as well.

With the Blessing of Jesus.

Daniel Rollins

Aside from baseball, Robert's favorite pastime was accompanying Yumi to the produce market five blocks toward downtown. Makiko toddled along with them as best she could. She clung to Robert's fingers. When she tired, Robert would carry her piggyback.

As Robert kept to Yumi's side he felt people stare at him, but he could no more hide himself in the crowd than a giraffe could lose itself in a herd of zebras. Now that he knew more Japanese, he was able to understand what was said about him behind his back.

"That hair. Brown as a horse's."

"He is so big. He looks like a boy but is as tall as a teenager." Robert was aware of his growing stature. His mother had let out the waistband of his trousers and would soon have to buy him new pants.

On the way home with Yumi, he cradled a paper sack with a jar of cooking oil, boxes of matches, a large bar of all-purpose soap for the clothes and bathing, corn meal, and teas. Yumi carried Makiko in the sling.

They found a note in the kitchen. It was from Hiro, and he wrote that he and Robert's parents had left to visit a member of the congregation who had fallen sick.

Robert stored the cans of food on an upper pantry shelf. Makiko helped him. Something jumped past his hand, and he pulled back, startled. It was a spider, a large one, with legs that could've straddled a bottle cap. The spider floated to the floor on a web strand. Once on the floor, the spider paused as if to get its bearings. Robert and Makiko crouched to study it. The spider scurried along the bottom of the pantry, then sensing it was trapped, raced across the floor to the door.

Robert grasped a newspaper, rolled it, and raised his hand to club the spider. He was drawing a bead on the doomed bug when Yumi shrieked.

"Don't kill it!"

Robert held his hand still. What was the fuss over the spider? Back home, they squashed dozens of them in a day.

Yumi used her foot to herd the spider under the door and outside to safety. "Robert, Makiko, you must learn how to respect all life. Even the lowliest of spiders has a place in the universe. Remember, all life is precious."

4

For the longest time, Robert thought much about what Yumi had told him about the spider. He understood her compassion for the poor creature; it hadn't threatened him and was only trying to escape. He felt guilty for all the other little critters he and his friends had delighted in killing. Bugs whenever they found them. Crawdads. Frogs. Snakes. Using sharp sticks. Slingshots. Firecrackers. What had been play before was now very wrong, and he felt the burn of shame.

He daydreamed being hunted and killed for sport, imagining himself in bed and awakened by a fierce shaking. Then the roof above his head was ripped apart, and a gigantic monster loomed over him. Robert cowered in a corner of the room, like a trapped mouse. The monster reached in with immense claws, and Robert recoiled with a quite real, sickening fear.

Later that week, during a morning break helping his father in the chapel and before he was to start his daily school lessons, he asked, "Is it okay to kill?"

His father was sipping coffee, a luxury he and Robert's mom found they couldn't do without. He set his cup down. "You know the Commandments. Which one talks about killing?"

This was one of the reasons Robert didn't like raising such questions with his dad. Rather than get a straight answer, he'd get quizzed first. "The Sixth Commandment," Robert answered. "*Thou shall not kill.* But we do kill. Animals."

"The Bible was referring to people."

"But is it okay to kill animals?"

"You've hunted. Fished," his father replied. "Why are you asking about this?"

Robert didn't want to answer. Yumi's lesson about not killing the spider seemed so trivial he was embarrassed to share the story. "I dunno. Was something I was thinking about, that's all."

His father mussed his hair. "Okay." He again sipped coffee and glanced about the chapel. At the ceiling that still needed painting. To the floor that needed repairing. To the cracks in the wall. The exposed electrical wiring. Sometimes a few of the parishioners helped, but people had jobs. Besides, a lot of the work depended on getting new materials and that strained an already thin budget. So it was he and Hiro doing the work when they could. But Hiro had to make money as well, so Jack did many of the tasks alone. Maybe by the end of the summer the chapel might be finished.

He looked back at his son. "We're animals, Robert. God's special creatures but animals nonetheless. We have to eat. And eating means killing."

Robert had thought about this. Yumi didn't seem reluctant at cooking chicken, fish, or pork, but she hadn't killed these animals herself. "But is it right?"

"Is it right to go hungry?" his father replied.

Robert had read stories of starving, snow-bound pioneers who ate their leather belts and saddles to survive. And that was after they had eaten the last of their horses and dogs. And he had also heard of people going so mad with hunger they became cannibals.

"What about plants?" his father asked. "We eat them and they are also living creatures. Think about it, apples and peaches are the children of trees."

Robert stared at his feet, feeling foolish for bringing the subject up.

His father said, "I guess the answer you're looking for is, don't be cruel. Don't kill for the sake of killing. I'm sure a fish doesn't like the idea of being caught. Think what you're doing to him. Poke a stringer through his mouth and out his gills." He mimed the scene, sticking a finger into his mouth and then pretending to draw it out the side of his neck. "Then you slice him open, clean him, and into the frying pan he goes."

For some reason Robert thought fish didn't feel pain, but now he was certain they felt everything: dread, terror, the agonizing end.

"But killing that fish for the sake of killing him," his father continued, "that would be wrong. Same for any other animal. Remember what Genesis says. *And let them have dominion over the fish of the sea and over the birds of the heavens and over the livestock and over all the earth and over every creeping thing that creeps on the earth.* Dominion means stewardship, and stewardship means care."

Back in Illinois, Robert had helped his father and mother slaughter chickens for dinner. Every boy and girl in every family did the same chore. He had never thought it was wrong to kill poultry. In fact, he watched fascinated when a headless chicken scurried around the yard spraying blood out the stump of its neck before falling dead. And afterwards they feathered and cleaned the bird. Then cooked and ate it. He'd watched hogs and turkeys get killed and butchered. And during hunting season, seemed there wasn't a tree in Oglesby without a gutted buck hanging from a branch.

"How about a mouse in the pantry?" Robert asked. "Even Mom kills them. And we aren't going to eat them, either."

"A mouse in the field is minding its own business. A mouse in the kitchen is a different matter. It will eat our food and soil everything. It brings disease. If we trap the mouse and let it live, it will only come back. Killing such a mouse is a matter of survival. We have to defend ourselves against threats, no matter how small or big."

Robert knew this. Deputy Sheriff Duncan once shot a stray bitch, a mangy cur with mangled ears that had bitten one of the Belleview sisters. No one once uttered a word of pity for that dog. Robert felt foolish asking the question about the mouse, but it still bothered him that he had to kill. "What about foxes and mink?"

"You've killed a fox?"

"No, sir." That was true though once, he, Dan Rollins, and Dan's uncle had gone into the woods with a .22 rifle. When it was Robert's turn to plink at some tin cans, a fox had jumped from the brush in front of them. Dan and the uncle shouted excitedly for Robert to draw a bead on the fox. He managed one quick shot and missed. The uncle scolded him for wasting the bullet and, more importantly, for letting that damned chicken thief get away. At the time, Robert was embarrassed and felt clumsy for missing the shot, but now he was glad the fox had escaped.

"What about bugs?" he asked.

"Depends. I don't imagine there'll ever be a shortage of flies. But other bugs like praying mantis and butterflies, they won't harm you."

"And spiders?"

His father laughed. "What's gotten into you with these questions?"

Robert shrugged. "Just been thinking."

His father finished his coffee. "Son, don't let my humor discourage you. It's good for a person to ponder these matters. As for an arachnid, I'm sure God will forgive you for squashing a spider that fell out of your shoe or one that jumped on your pants."

Robert now regretted bringing the subject up. He was no closer to an answer than he had been. He thought about war, which was all about people killing people. He recalled the veterans he'd seen around Oglesby and in Chicago, young men from the recent Great War and older, bearded coots from the Civil War, many of them with either an empty sleeve or a trouser leg pinned up. The older men often let their eyes mist as they shared stories of battle. Places like Chickamauga.

Vicksburg. Antietam. They spoke of buried friends and lost brothers, clouds of musket and cannon smoke, of confusion and carnage. But to kids like Robert, even the stories of misery and deprivation sounded romantic and adventurous. The old vets always ended their tales of combat with, "Just be glad you weren't there, son."

For their part, the younger men never talked about their war against the Hun. These veterans regarded the world with a troubled, faraway look, like their minds remained snagged on the barbed wire in No Man's Land. Most of them stayed drunk all day. Robert once asked why the Civil War veterans didn't drink so much. One of them answered, "Bunches of us did and they done drank themselves to the grave. Give these young soldiers a few years and the bottle will kill many of them, too."

***

The newness of living in Japan dulled into a routine. Robert's days consisted of morning chores, school lessons, then more chores. On Sundays, he played catch with his dad and practiced his swing, that was, when his father was not tending to his duties as pastor. He spent time tutoring Makiko in English with his picture books. Twice, Hiro and Yumi had taken the Campbells to the Yokohama trade university and watched the home team take on rivals from Machida and Fujisawa. The games thrilled Robert and he was glad that maybe, he'd soon have the chance to play baseball.

With Yumi's help, his Japanese improved. Robert had plenty to keep him busy but he missed spending time with friends his age and doing nothing. Everything the adults wanted him to do had to have a point to it, a purpose, and he just wanted to play and goof around. And with adults around him always, he had to be careful with what he did or said. He couldn't just be silly.

The last time he had accompanied Yumi to the market, he was confident enough to ask and pay for the produce and sundries. The clerks and shopkeepers acted surprised and responded with exaggerated courtesy, as if Robert had done them a great honor in learning their language. So when his mother and Yumi were in the middle of preparing the lunch meal and Yumi commented that she was low on cooking oil, Robert volunteered to go to the market on his own.

"Are you sure?" his mother asked, her voice heavy with concern.

"I'll be fine," Robert answered. "I'll be there and back before you can sneeze."

Yumi pretended to sneeze. "Are you back already? Where's my cooking oil?"

"Okay, I'll need a few more minutes than that."

Yumi handed him two silver yen coins, which he tucked into a pocket of his trousers. At the front door, rather than slip into his *geta* sandals, he put on his regular shoes. Makiko watched from the table, having been told she was to remain home. He stepped outside and turned to his left, toward the market.

He'd been down this route so many times that people no longer seemed to notice him. It was only when he reached the market that people stared. He passed by the vegetable stalls, the booths offering kitchen utensils and tools, and newsstands crowded with newspapers and magazines. He saw ducks and chickens in wooden pens, fish in tubs, all waiting to be taken away and cooked.

Robert entered the narrow mercantile belonging to Mr. Watanabe, a friendly moon-faced man with a wispy mustache. His white apron was frayed around the edges but starched and immaculate, with a pen and a pencil tucked into the front pocket. Besides cooking oil, he sold bagged rice, canned goods, boxes of crackers, and items like nails and light bulbs. Robert made his way between the shelves and selected a liter can of the cooking oil Yumi always bought, *Marigold Promise*. He set the can on the front counter and placed the coins on a tray. Watanabe wrapped the can in old newspaper and took the money. He then dropped the coins into an open cash box, marked a ledger book, and smiled at Robert, much like the shopkeepers back in Oglesby used to do.

Robert cradled the package with the cooking oil. He bowed, "*Arigatou gozaimasu*," and left the store.

He tucked the sack to his side and made his way out of the market. He had walked a couple of blocks when he heard a commotion in a side alley.

Boys yelled in Japanese.

"Eater of rats and dogs!"

"You son of a dirty witch!"

He halted and stared down the alley. Four boys about his age had forced another against a wall. They whipped the fifth boy with switches made of tree branches.

"Cry, you filthy Korean," the tallest of the boys shouted. "Cry like a baby monkey. A little Korean monkey."

One boy fighting another, that Robert could understand, but a group ganging up on another, there had better be a good reason. Maybe they had caught him stealing or he had picked on one of the other smaller boys?

The boy with his back to the wall held up his arms to ward off the switches. Red marks crisscrossed his forearms. His eyes glistening with tears, he stared defiantly at the tallest boy.

Robert stepped closer. He didn't hear a reason for the boys to be picking on the other. No accusations of wrongdoing. Just taunts about being different.

One of the smaller boys noticed him and shouted, "Atsuto, watch yourself."

The tallest boy spun about and faced Robert. The other boys followed his example. Even the boy at the wall gawked at him. They seemed confused by Robert's appearance, and this led him to believe they had never seen an American before.

The tallest, Atsuto, squared his shoulders and said out the corner of his mouth, "What an ugly stranger. I suppose if he gets nosey, we'll have to teach him a lesson, too."

"Teach who a lesson?" Robert replied.

Atsuto winced, astonished by Robert's Japanese. He flexed his grip on the switch. "So you know Japanese, foreign toad? How about we give you some lessons in Japanese fighting."

Robert wanted to say that he was ready to punch Atsuto but as he never had occasion to use such words—he didn't even know the word "fists"—he said, "For you I have hands of unpleasantness."

Atsuto laughed. "Hands of unpleasantness? Where did you learn how to talk? Well, I'll also have to give you a lesson in our language."

Keeping his eyes fixed on Atsuto, Robert crouched to set the sack with the can of oil on the ground. He stood to his full height and measured the others. Atsuto looked older than him, maybe he was 11 or 12, but he wasn't any taller. One of the others was a little shorter than Robert, and the other two were both younger and smaller.

Atsuto muttered an order, and he and the others advanced on Robert. Atsuto came straight at Robert, while the second tallest circled to the right, and the two shorties circled to the left. They halted three feet from him and waved their switches menacingly, expecting Robert to retreat or cower.

Robert had been in enough schoolyard scrapes to recognize the strategy. They would outflank him. One of the smaller boys would lunge at him, get him to shift his attention from the leader. At that instant, Atsuto would strike.

So Robert did what they least expected. Go for the big one first. He pounced and socked Atsuto in the mouth. Head reeling, Atsuto staggered backwards and fell. Robert danced alongside, hands clenched.

But the other boys didn't attack; they only gaped at Atsuto. He pushed to his hands and knees. He released the switch, sat back, and cupped both hands to his mouth. He drew them away and grimaced at his bloody fingers.

Robert raised his fists. "I have plenty for the rest of you. Who is next?"

The other three boys dropped their switches and retreated from the alley. Atsuto brought himself upright. Blood foaming on his lips, he glowered at Robert and stumbled after his buddies. They assembled in the road. The peewee of the group shouted a curse, and then they sprinted from view.

Robert turned to the boy who leaned against the wall. He rubbed the welts on his arms and the one on his left cheek. The boy looked Robert's age and was a little shorter and just as skinny. A mop of black hair draped over the dark eyes of his narrow face. His trousers were patched at the knees and his tattered shirt looked a size too small. Robert figured the boy's parents didn't have much money. "Are you okay?"

The boy nodded.

Robert couldn't think how to ask *Why were they picking on you?* Since he'd never had the occasion for that question before, he now asked awkwardly, "Why were they bunched to fight you?"

The boy furrowed his brow for a moment as if he didn't understand the question. "I am Korean."

Robert recalled the "Korean monkey" comment by Atsuto. He offered the boy his hand and pulled him from the wall. "They attacked you because you are Korean?"

The boy nodded, embarrassed.

Robert stared in the direction Atsuto and the others had fled. It saddened him that the Japanese could be as stupid and mean as folks back in Illinois. Once, boys in his school had pelted Noah Abraham with onions and called him "a dirty Jew," "a kike," and "Christ killer." Then another time, in a pool hall, somebody had knifed "Dutchy" Hess for being a "kraut-head bastard."

"What's your name?" he asked of the boy.

"Kaito Satake."

"That sounds Japanese to me."

"It is. My father is Japanese, but my mother is Korean, so that makes me Korean."

"And that is why Atsuto and his friends attacked you?"

"The Japanese hate Koreans. They consider us trash and bad luck and blame us for everything that goes wrong. They say we are thieves and robbers. They accuse us of poisoning wells and bringing the earthquake that destroyed Yokohama." Kaito swept his hand to point at buildings that remained damaged.

"Seems that if you could start earthquakes, the Japanese would want to be nice to you."

"I don't think about those things. I only want to be left alone."

Robert offered his name, and Kaito repeated it with difficulty. "*Roh-baht Cahm-beru*. It's a funny name."

"No funnier than Kaito Satake." Robert bent down to retrieve the sack with the cooking oil. He was lucky none of the other boys had kicked it out of spite. He explained that he was living with his parents, missionaries from America.

"New York America?" Kaito asked.

"Not New York. I am from Illinois."

Kaito frowned to show he didn't know where Illinois was. "Cowboys?"

"No cowboys," Robert replied. "Farmers."

"Ah." Kaito sounded disappointed. "How about baseball?"

"Yes, lots of baseball."

"I like baseball," Kaito said. He lunged and pumped his arms. "*Sutoraiku.*"

Now it was Robert's turn to be puzzled. "You mean, *strike?*"

"Yes, *sutoraiku*, what I said."

Robert pointed to the left. "I live that way. Three blocks."

"I can walk with you," Kaito said. "Then I have to go that way. We live by the wharf." He gestured south.

Robert headed toward the street. "Let's go."

Kaito hesitated. "What if the others return?"

"Then they have the two of us to fight."

Kaito smiled. "All right then. We'll walk as friends."

"Yes," Robert grinned. "As friends."

5

August 1924

Robert stood with his mother, Yumi, and Makiko on the edge of the sidewalk. They had been out shopping when a mob abruptly took over the street and pushed everyone to the curb, a mob of men: young, teeming with pious rage, and wearing *hachimaki* headbands decorated with slogans. Some tooted bugles or banged drums. Others brandished home-made signs denouncing the government and calling the Diet a den of fools and cowards. The buildings of the commercial district echoed with the cacophony of their angry chants.

"Down with foreign capitalists. Usurpers of our destiny!"

"Manchukuo belongs to us!"

The oppressive, frenzied anger added another layer of discomfort to a day already suffering under a hot sun and miserable humidity.

A frightened Makiko pulled at Yumi's sleeve.

Sarah asked, "Why is everyone so angry?"

Before Yumi could reply, a fierce-looking man blew a whistle. Bugles played an off-key tune. Drums pounded a martial beat. The men assembled into a ragged formation and began marching as they sang. "We serve the Emperor and live to honor his name, our blood is ready to water the blossoms of the homeland."

Thuggish men along the sides of the column wielded long batons and prodded the bystanders. One of them halted close to Robert and jabbed a nearby man in the chest. "Sing, damn you."

His expression hardening, the man stared at the thug and sang half-heartedly. The thug scowled, displeased with the bystander's lack of enthusiasm. The thug drew the baton back and looked ready to deliver a blow when he noticed Robert and his mother. Relaxing the hold on his baton, the thug tramped in front of Sarah and shouted the lyrics into her face.

Robert tensed, afraid the thug might drag her away. She groped for Robert's hand and clutched it.

The thug whacked the baton against the curb. Robert and his mother winced. Makiko shrieked. The thug laughed and resumed marching alongside his comrades.

The parade continued down the street. The singing, the blare of bugles, and beat of drums faded into a dull roar, and a collective sigh breathed through the crowd. A few released mutters.

"I'm as patriotic as the next man, but dammit, I can't afford to go parading like this. I've got a living to make."

"And taxes to pay. Those troublemakers would be better off learning a trade or working."

"I'll bet these so-called patriots are headed straight to the sake parlor."

Yumi shared an embarrassed look with the Campbells. "I am so sorry," she said. "When men join these mobs they become mindless animals."

Robert's mother responded with an understanding smile. "In America, we also have our share of hot-headed fools."

Robert was glad that his father wasn't here. Preacher or not, he would have punched that thug in the face, and then the situation would have become much, much uglier.

The street returned to its usual bustle, but the disturbing, combative mood of the parade lingered like smoke after a fire. It didn't help anyone's spirits to read the large banners hanging from the sides of office buildings, obscuring the advertisements underneath for cigarettes, tea, and rice crackers. The banners pictured brooding men primed to respond to an insult, the captions applied in angry, staccato strokes demanding immediate action. *Communist agitators, do not tread on us! Honor, duty, and self-sacrifice forever! Japan will always prevail!*

Yumi led Robert and his mother through the market, and they bought supplies to replenish the pantry back at home. The day was sunny, and Yumi wiped sweat from her brow.

Sarah eyed a bench shaded by a maple tree. "Let's take a break."

Yumi agreed and walked to the bench, set her bag of groceries on the ground, and eased herself and Makiko into the seat. She kicked off her *geta* sandals and wiggled her toes. Sarah sat beside her and cooled herself with a folding fan. Her sack of groceries remained cradled in her lap.

Robert decided to get back to the house. "How about I carry the groceries home?" he offered. "That way you and Yumi don't have to hurry." He squinted at the sun to emphasize the heat.

His mother replied, "I'm fine."

But Robert was already lifting her sack of groceries. She relented with a nod and kept fanning herself. He looped the handles of Yumi's shopping bag over one wrist and pulled it up.

"So strong boy," Yumi said.

Robert wasn't expecting a compliment but the comment pleased him. Taking the initiative of carrying all the bags made him felt mature and more capable.

Makiko slid off the bench. "I want to go with Robert."

"It's a long walk home," he said, "and I won't be able to carry you."

"Maybe she will carry you," his mother rejoined.

Makiko smiled, said goodbye, and led Robert from the bench. After traveling for several blocks, they reached the alley where he had rescued Kaito from Atsuto and his gang of pint-sized bullies. Robert eyed the enclosed space warily, worried that Atsuto might be waiting with a pack of older boys. Though the alley yawned empty, Robert hurried Makiko along and they continued home.

***

Saturday. Robert's father organized an outing for Robert and his mother to visit the wharf. Although they were good friends with Hiro and Yumi, sometimes each family needed time alone.

The Campbells had wandered through downtown Yokohama and paused on an open street corner to admire the vista. They stood on a rise that sloped to the coastline about a hundred yards distant. At their left, freighters and passenger ships cruised with stately majesty through the harbor. Fishing boats bobbed in the sun-dappled water, their crews drawing nets. Smoke plumed from the stack of a ferry plowing across the bay.

Between the wharf and where the Campbells stood, the rows of warehouses became a jumble of sheds, and along the slope below them, the sheds gave way to crude shacks erected in dirt lots between stone outcroppings and clumps of scrub trees. From the corner, one street narrowed to a rutted trail that continued to the shacks and to a rickety pier beyond. A dirty, oily surf churned around its pilings. Garbage tossed on the waves and collected on the rocky shore on either side of the pier.

Clothes hung from lines stretched between the shacks. Men in loose shirts and shorts lounged beside the husks of discarded skiffs, metal barrels, and other junk. Smoke feathered from the chimney pipes of outdoor stoves. To Robert, this collection of hovels resembled the hobo camps he'd seen along the rivers or under bridges back in Illinois.

Robert's mother gestured to cafés and stores along the street, busy with shoppers. "Let's get something to drink. Maybe some sweets."

Robert brightened. His father approached the cart of a peddler and bought a small packet of *yokan*. He peeled the paper wrapping and doled slices of the sweetened bean paste, giving one to Sarah and keeping one for himself before handing the rest to Robert. He grinned and was nibbling his second slice when shouts and curses echoed down the street.

The commotion jarred his nerves. It seemed there was no relief from the restless agitation that could erupt like a fever. He made sure his mother and father were close, and that they were safe.

A man jogged down the sidewalk. He brandished a newspaper, the *Yokohama Nichinichi Shinbun*, and it screamed a headline in bold: *Chinese Bandits Murder Japanese Soldiers*.

"Those beasts," he shouted and hustled away.

Robert's father turned toward the newsstand. A stack of the *Shinbun* lay in a row with other newspapers and magazines. Robert sidled beside his father to read the article beneath the headlines, which they helped each other to translate aloud. "Kieto Station, Manchukuo. Two soldiers of the Development and Prosperity Force were killed when their unit was ambushed by a gang of Chinese bandits. The fallen men, Corporal Yoshito Kakitani of the Ninth Prefecture and Private Makoto Uchida from Nagano, were part of a survey team bringing telephone service and clean water to—"

Robert was pushed aside, and he nearly dropped his yokan. A group of men rushed past to gather at the corner. More men joined them, braying and shouting.

"Death to the Chinese dogs!"

"Revenge for our murdered brothers!"

Down at the shacks, those men rose to their feet and faced the ruckus. Now Robert understood. That was a Chinese labor camp. Even at this distance, Robert sensed their anguish and fear. They gesticulated up the slope and scattered like spooked deer. Some raced through the brush in the direction of the wharf. Others hid in their shacks.

More Japanese men collected at the street corner. Passing cars were flagged down and surrounded by the growing mob. One man climbed on the hood of a sedan. He held the *Shinbun* over his head, the newspaper spread to display the headline. His neck corded and livid, he hollered, "Vengeance, brothers, vengeance! Let's teach a lesson to those Chinese bastards."

A truck with policemen arrived. Robert expected them to form a barrier between the mob and the Chinese men below. Instead the policemen dismounted and fanned behind the crowd, as if to channel it onto the trail leading to the camp.

Robert's throat drew tight and his stomach became queasy with dread. Even if he forced himself to eat the rest of his yo-kan, he would probably retch it back up.

"I can't eat this," he said.

"Just dump it," his father replied sourly.

Robert reluctantly dropped the remaining treat to the curb.

The crowd seethed like a mad dog clawing at a fence. His mother said, "We should go."

Robert and his father looked for a way out that didn't require them to push through the mob, and so they were trapped on the corner. The only path from the crowd was down the hill, and that only put them right in harm's way.

The mob suddenly roared, a gruesome howl that sent Robert teetering backwards on his heels, his pulse hammering in alarm.

The men charged down the hill, shrieking and cursing, gaining momentum with every stride. In another situation they were regular citizens—students, clerks, mild-mannered nobodies—but here it was as if their character had turned inside out, and the inner monster sprang free, unleashed.

They swarmed around the shacks, wild with fury, and tore the flimsy structures apart. The mob resembled an army of ants raiding a rival's nest. They grabbed men from inside the shacks and hoisted them aloft. In their dingy white clothes, the Chinese men writhed like captured larvae clutched in the mandibles of their hunters. The men were pitched to the ground, and the mob swallowed them with a flurry of kicks and swinging clubs.

Bystanders drew around the Campbells, everyone both curious and horrified. Like his parents, Robert couldn't tear his gaze from the grisly spectacle.

Another man bolted from the other side of a shack and raced toward the water. A pack of Japanese men broke from the mob and chased him. To escape he ran to the pier and dove off. His pursuers halted at the water's edge, where they laughed and pitched debris at him as he flailed haplessly in the foul water.

The wail of a siren made Robert turn his head. A fire truck had arrived. He expected it to advance down the slope. Perhaps the firemen would use their hoses to disperse the crowds and stop this madness. But the fire truck halted. The firemen removed their helmets and watched the riot as if it were entertainment.

His father trembled and started down the hill. Sarah grabbed his arm and pulled him back. "They'll only kill you."

Voice quaking with rage, he said, "I must stop this." His glare settled on two nearby policemen. They smoked cigarettes and had their caps tilted back as if on break.

He approached them and demanded in halting Japanese, "You must do something."

The policemen returned his glare, astonished to find a white foreigner addressing them. They mumbled to one another, deliberating until one replied, "What business is this of yours?"

Jack pointed to the riot. "You can't let this happen. Would the Emperor approve?'

The policeman's face collapsed into a maroon scowl. He threw his cigarette to the ground. "Do not dare take the Emperor's name in vain! Who are you to remind me of my duty?"

His partner sneered, a cigarette hanging from his lips.

"You either hold your tongue and keep back," the first policeman scolded, "or I'll kick your ass down the hill where you can stand beside your precious Chinese scum."

The mob parted to let men drag the bodies of three victims, limp and bloodied like sides of butchered beef. The bodies were heaped together. One of them squirmed and that invited the mob to attack with bricks, stones, and sticks. Someone brought bedding from a shack and tossed it over the bodies.

Someone else brought a can of kerosene and upended it over the pile. Then a flame, a whoosh of fire and smoke.

The mob howled in delight and backed away.

The firemen donned their helmets, and the fire truck started.

Smoke billowed from one shack. The mob tore apart the adjacent shacks to make a firebreak and contain the flames. They found another Chinese laborer cowering in the debris and beat him until he was another bloody ragdoll to be tossed on the pyre.

Robert became weak-kneed and nauseous. It was worse than watching hounds tear a fox to pieces. He had heard of the lynching of blacks and had seen photographs of broken corpses hanging from poles. But those images were so alien that he had to think hard to understand the horror. Now that he had seen it firsthand, he still couldn't understand.

The mob retreated from the burning bodies, their blood-lust satisfied. The policemen at last brought a semblance of order when they forced a gap in the mass of Japanese men to let the fire truck through. The firemen readied a hose and directed a jet of water onto the pyre. Its flames died with a burst of steam. The force of the jet tore through the pile and the scorched corpses flopped across the puddled water like blackened, rubber puppets. The firemen next turned their attention to the burning shack until it was a smoldering ruin.

The bystanders at the street corner began to melt away, grim and sober-faced. Robert's father pulled him and his mother back toward downtown. The two Japanese policemen followed their retreat with disapproving stares.

For the next week, Robert read the newspaper for word about the murder of the Chinese laborers. It was never mentioned.

***

Robert and his father stared at the entrance to their chapel. Brush marks of crude graffiti defaced the walls and the front door.

White devils, return to your home.

We do not need your garbage ideas.

The windows had been smashed and a dead cat tossed inside.

A policeman examined the damage, but he acted bored, unconcerned.

"What are you going to do about this?" Robert's father asked.

The policeman had just lit a cigarette. He tossed the match onto the broken glass on the sidewalk. "Perhaps," he said, "if you minded your business, this would not have happened."

Though Robert didn't recognize this particular policeman, he knew by the comment that word about his father's protest at the riot had spread. His name was on a list.

***

Robert and Jack arrived at the office of their municipal ward captain, Hiroshi Nagatomo. He was a prim man who wore a tall starched collar and a suit with a four-button coat, clothes that had gone out of style twenty years ago. He sat behind his large desk, remaining stiff and expressionless. Framed certificates and photographs crowded his office walls. Electric fans drew air through the open windows and rustled papers on his desk. He did not rise from his seat to greet his American visitors.

The Campbells had come alone. Even if their mastery of Japanese wasn't quite adequate for the purpose, Robert's father didn't want to draw Hiro or Yumi into this confrontation with the local authorities. He halted three paces from the desk and bowed deeply. "I am honored that you have taken the time to grant us an audience. I have brought my son to learn and appreciate the Japanese ways." He had practiced what he intended to say with Hiro, but he knew that at one point in this discussion he would run out of Japanese vocabulary.

Nagatomo nodded.

Both Robert and his father also wore suits, clammy and sweaty in this humidity. His father handed an envelope to the ward captain. Nagatomo perked an eyebrow and considered the envelope.

"Open it, please," Jack said.

From the envelope, Nagatomo slid black-and-white stills into his hand and shuffled through them. "What is this?"

"Those are photographs of the most recent vandalism to my church. I took them because the police sergeant said," Robert's father paused to remember the words, "that I have no proof that any damage had been done," another pause, "even though his own men had walked the scene and taken my statement."

Sweat collected along Robert's collar; the heat bothered him, and he knew his father felt more uncomfortable by what he could not say. What he wanted to bring up was the massacre of the Chinese laborers, although the riot had occurred in another ward and was outside Nagatomo's jurisdiction. The vandalism of the church was inconsequential compared to those public killings. But the riot played on long-standing hatreds, part of the rotten fabric inside any country, and to mention the dead Chinese would be to sting a raw nerve and cause his Japanese hosts to withdraw, ears covered, eyes shut tight, and deny everything. Americans did the same thing about the casual murder of blacks and Mexicans.

Nagatomo returned the photographs to the envelope, which he placed on the edge of his desk. He splayed his fingers across the desk blotter as if tidying some invisible paperwork. "You must understand, that in Yokohama, much like any city in the United States, we cannot stop every act of random violence."

"This is not random. This is deliberate."

"What is your proof?"

Robert's father pointed to the photographs. "The graffiti always looks the same. It is obviously the work of one individual or the same group of people."

Nagatomo didn't bother to acknowledge the photos again. "This is a matter for the police."

"Then my apologies, Mr. Nagatomo. I am disappointed in myself for bothering you. I will write home and tell everyone that the great city of Yokohama is no better than the worst slums of Chicago, and the authorities are helpless to make improvements."

The ward captain twitched his upper lip, his pencil mustache shifting up and down. He wondered how connected this holy man was back in America. Perhaps his report would filter into the international press and back to Japan. And then Nagatomo would be brought and humiliated in front of the mayor for bringing disgrace to the city.

The Campbells bowed again to dismiss themselves.

"Wait," Nagatomo announced.

Out the corner of his eye, Robert saw his father halt in mid-bow. He was looking up at Nagatomo through his lashes.

Nagatomo chafed at his father's ploy, the subtle jab at his honor. How very Japanese of his guest. If he as the ward captain did nothing, then he was admitting that he was a superfluous tool. He placed his hand on the envelope. "I will pursue this."

Jack completed his bow. "Whatever you can do will be appreciated."

Nagatomo nodded curtly.

The next morning, the undercover policeman who normally spied from across the street was replaced by a uniformed cop who walked his beat in front of the chapel.

The vandalism stopped.

6

April 1929

Robert and Kaito Satake raced down the hall of District Four Intermediate School Seven. They each shoved a push broom, wielding it like a lance.

Their teacher, Daichi Ishihara, clapped his hands and shouted, "Easy now. Let's not be reckless."

This was Robert's second year as a student in a Japanese school, after three years studying at home with Hiro and Yumi. Though Robert enjoyed school and learning, when he first enrolled, it scared him plenty. The language differences intimidated him. And the customs. His fellow students were from poorer neighborhoods, where the families couldn't afford to pay tuition at a private school. But it reassured him that kids were kids. Some studied hard and came to class prepared. Others goofed off. Forgot their homework. Threw spitballs. Some even slept in class. He figured many of the kids came to class dead-tired because of working late hours, helping their families put food on the table.

Robert and Kaito reached the end of the hall, stopped, and shouldered their brooms. They retrieved their school satchels from their classroom and joined the other students filing out of the building. Many of them carried buckets of trash to be emptied in garbage bins behind the school. Two older boys started mopping the hall floor from the far end and made their way to the exit. One of them was Hideki Matsui, a husky thirteen-year-old and captain of the *yakyu*, the school's baseball club. A rough-and-tumble kid, he parroted his father's working-class prejudices, mostly against foreigners and especially the Koreans.

Once outside, Robert and Kaito knocked lint and dust from the broom bristles. The students with the trash buckets rinsed them under a tap and shook the water out. Everyone lined up in formation, satchels slung over their shoulders, brooms, buckets, and mops presented like military weapons for their teacher's inspection. In their dark-blue uniform shirts, the group resembled an army platoon.

Ishihara proceeded down the rows, saying, "Very good," or "Why can't your homework sparkle like this bucket?" He circled to the front of his class. "Everyone—"

Every student braced at attention.

"You are dismissed." Ishihara walked to the school's *kura* and opened the padlock securing the shed's door. The students queued up to store their implements.

Robert and Kaito were hanging their brooms on wall hooks inside when Kaito cried out, "Ow."

Robert whirled around to see what had happened.

Hideki stepped away with his mop, the end of its handle swinging past Kaito's head. Hideki faked a sheepish apology. "Sorry. I was careless."

He was always too careless around Kaito, and so Robert's Korean friend was frequently tripped, or accidentally knocked on the head or across his back.

"You need to be less careless," Robert warned. He squared his shoulders and kept his hands loose. Japanese bullies weren't different from American bullies.

Hideki tightened his grip on the handle of the mop. Considering the tight confines of the *kura*, he couldn't manage a decent swing, and Robert would be right on top of him.

"You won't always be around to protect Kaito," Hideki grumbled.

"But I'm here now," Robert replied, eyes leveled on Hideki.

"Is there a problem in there?" Ishihara asked.

"No problem, sir," Robert replied, though he kept his gaze on Hideki as he whispered, "Is there?"

Hideki held Robert's glare even as he propped the wet head of the mop against the wall.

Ishihara clapped his hands. "Outside then. Now! Except you, Hideki. Get the equipment bags."

Hideki barked the names of some of his friends, other players from the baseball team.

Robert and Kaito sprinted around the corner of the school for the grassy field on the south side. Now for the best part of the day: baseball practice.

The baseball field stretched across a barren lot between the school and a warehouse. The infield was a rough dirt surface, with plenty of rocks and divots to make a ball skip into the air. The outfield didn't have much grass and was just as likely to make a grounder ricochet in all crazy directions. But they had a backstop and a pitcher's mound. Faded chalk lines connected the bases.

They crowded with other boys into a dugout, actually a bench behind a short wooden fence that shielded them from wild foul balls. They dropped their satchels and whipped off their shirts, bony adolescent torsos glistening in the sun. They replaced their shirts with faded, baggy jerseys yanked from their satchels. The club couldn't afford practice uniforms, so the boys were issued hand-me-down jerseys and cleats from the club's upper division team. Each boy shucked his school shoes and slipped into his cleats, so worn that toes stuck out the sides. Everyone donned his prized team ball cap, in gray wool with the English letter "T" embroidered on the front of the crown: T for Tigers. To Robert, the name Tigers recalled the Detroit Tigers.

Besides his job as schoolteacher, Ishihara also coached the team. He had changed out his school clothes, and his slender physique was draped in a complete baseball uniform, gray woolen jersey and matching pants with red trim, team cap, and polished cleats.

Hideki and his crew arrived at the dugout, huffing as they dragged canvas bags filled with bulky equipment. They upended the bags in front of the dugout, bats clattering out and fielding gloves, balls, and a catcher's mask spilling across the dirt. Hideki yelled out more names, and as they were summoned, the boys ran to him to retrieve base bags that they then arranged on the diamond. Hideki trotted from base to base with a hammer and spiked the bags into position. When it was time for these chores, he never called on Robert, or Kaito, nor the other two Koreans on the team.

Ishihara winced at Hideki's shunning of the other players. Whatever Ishihara's opinion about the Koreans, he kept it to himself, mindful that as a teacher and a coach, he had to be careful about expressing thoughts counter to the prevailing political attitude. Which was, Koreans were at best merely tolerated.

When the base bags were in place, Ishihara shouted for the team to form up. The boys ran past second base into the outfield and gathered into three neat rows. Hideki recited the roll. He barked out the commands for warm-up exercises.

"Toe touches. Hands overhead. Arms straight. On one... One, touch your toes. All the way down."

After calisthenics, Ishihara ordered two laps around the field. Here Robert showed off his greater speed, and he grew faster day by day. He was the tallest and the lankiest. However, some of the other boys were quicker and with their sharper eyes and reflexes, managed better batting averages. Still, once Robert connected with a ball, it rocketed deep into the outfield. If the ball wasn't caught, he at least managed a double every time.

Ishihara assigned players for batting drills. The others collected gloves that were shared from player to player. Kaito played shortstop and Robert rotated from third base to left field.

Once practice started, the animosity that Hideki and his clique displayed to the Koreans fell away. Everyone had to earn their spot on the roster, and while Hideki didn't like the

Koreans, those on the squad were good players. Even he had to appreciate their skill. To win games, teamwork was paramount. Besides, after a victory, Hideki would taunt the losers, "We whipped you bums, and we even had Koreans on our team!"

Robert was by now familiar with the Japanese versions of baseball terms, and they sounded comical to his American ears. "Boru" for *ball.* "Hitto endo ran" for *hit and run.* But playing the game was serious business. Fun, serious business. He loved the crack of a bat as it connected, the blow stinging his hands. The satisfying thwack of a fly ball snagged in the pocket of his glove. The way his heart pounded with nervous energy as he debated stealing a base, then the explosive release of tension when he sprinted forward. Even if he was tagged out, his spirits sang with happiness.

After practice, Robert and Kaito helped their teammates collect equipment and stuff it back in the bags. Hideki and his crew dragged the bags back to the *kura.* Like the other boys, Robert and Kaito changed back into their school uniform shirts and regular shoes. They headed down the street toward their *chome,* their trousers dusty from sliding into base and chasing grounders. This late in the afternoon, their bellies rumbled.

Robert asked, "How come you don't talk much to Yohie and Ryo?" They were the other two Korean players on the team.

Kaito answered, "Because I don't want to be seen as Korean."

"But you are. Half anyway."

"Half Korean is the same as all Korean. I want to be all Japanese." Kaito explained, "You're lucky that you are an

American, so you don't have to put up with the insults and always watching over your shoulder for trouble."

Because of the way he'd seen the Koreans and Chinese treated, Robert understood, unfortunately. This was knowledge he'd rather not have.

"I wish my parents were like yours," Kaito said. Robert had brought his friend to the house a few times, where he had also met Yumi and Hiro. "They ask about your schoolwork. They show real interest in what you do. Maybe with that encouragement I might do better in my studies and have the chance at a good trade school."

Robert knew Kaito's mother worked in a laundry, and his father was a day laborer who was often gone for weeks chasing jobs along the coast and on the farms.

"My mother's Japanese is not very good," Kaito added, embarrassed. "She only hangs around with other Koreans and that's all we speak at home."

Robert wanted to ask Kaito to study at his house tonight but didn't. First of all, they would arrive at the dinner hour and Kaito would be another mouth to feed. Plus, Robert's mother served him meat and extra portions of fish (vegetarian meals won't do for a growing boy, she would insist), an expense the family couldn't share with Kaito. After dinner, Robert had his own chores, and then study time. Plus, Kaito had his duties at home to help his mother earn a little extra cash.

Kaito tapped his cap. "But we get to play baseball."

Robert pushed his friend. "And win games."

The street passed through a neighborhood shop district. Three older teenagers in white shirts and baggy western-style pants stood outside a corner market. They smoked cigarettes and gave off an air of being tough guys.

Kaito slowed and dipped his head to peer from side to side as if glancing for another way forward.

"What's the matter?" Robert asked.

"I know these boys."

"Hey, Kaito," the largest of the toughs called out. "Yeah, you. Son of a Korean whore."

Robert's guts knotted. He sensed a fight coming on, and it was too late to turn around. If they did, the boys would only chase them.

The other two toughs chattered. "What are you doing here? Shouldn't you be at home? Eating garbage?"

The toughs snickered. One of them flicked his cigarette to the curb. The head tough kept his smoke clamped between his lips. He approached Kaito and Robert and moved with the confident grace of a tomcat among kittens. His buddies trailed at his heels. The older boy wore suspenders over his shirt, its sleeves rolled past his elbows. A wispy mustache barely darkened his upper lip. His gaze roved from Kaito to Robert, sizing him up, then back to Kaito.

"Hello, Kaito," the tough mumbled around the cigarette.

"Hello, Takuya."

"We don't want trouble," Robert said. Takuya was taller, but not by much. Robert was certain he could take him, but not all three.

Takuya swiveled his eyes back to Robert. "I've heard about you, American. You speak Japanese. And speak it well. You must be a smart guy."

"He can't be smart," one of the others rejoined. "Not if he hangs around that Korean shithead." The third tough snickered.

"Like I told you, I don't want trouble," Robert repeated. He felt like he was jamming the brakes on a train but its momentum kept hurtling him toward disaster.

"We won't give you trouble," Takuya replied. "It's this scumbag," he thumped Kaito's chest, "that we want to talk to. Remind him of his place."

"So we won't give you any trouble," the second tough said, a pudgy, square-faced fellow. "Not if you stay out of the way between us and this Korean bastard."

Robert glanced to his friend. The breath whistled from Kaito's nostrils. His face reddened and he was tense as a compressed spring. Robert also felt the anxiety cinch his nerves. He tipped between anger and rage, blaming Takuya and his two moronic chums for not only picking on Kaito, but that their hatred ruined what had been a good day.

"Back away," Takuya growled, his tone stoking an already fiery mood.

Robert lifted his chin. "No."

Takuya did a double take, as if he didn't believe what he had heard. Grinning, he looked back at his comrades. "This guy is more stupid than the Korean. Kaito can't help but be an idiot because he was born a stupid Korean monkey. But you, American, the smart thing would be to keep walking."

Takuya knocked his hand against the brim of Kaito's cap and sent it flying. Robert thought his friend would've swung at the bully, but Kaito remained rigid, eyes glassy with shame and anger.

Tough number two picked up the cap and handed it to Takuya, who set it on his head.

"Give the cap back," Robert said, temples pulsing so hard he was seeing red.

"It's mine now," Takuya smirked.

"You want a cap, join the team," Robert said.

"Why do that when I already have this cap?"

"Take your cap back, Kaito," Robert insisted.

"Let him keep it," Kaito replied.

"Did you hear that?" Takuya exclaimed. "He gave it to me. Your friend is generous because he's a coward."

Robert loathed bullies. If it were possible, he would hit Takuya so hard that every bully in the world would feel the hurt and stop pestering other people. He reached for the cap.

"Don't touch it," Takuya said, icily.

He and Robert traded glares. Robert slowly extended his hand for the cap's brim, knowing the instant he touched it, the fight would start. Takuya grabbed his hand and yelled, "Get him. Get him."

Robert seized Takuya's wrist and swung him around. The second tough brought his arm up, hand clenching a short wooden club.

The third tough and Kaito crashed into each other, fists a blur.

Takuya lunged to head-butt Robert, who turned his head and let his shoulder absorb the blow. He broke free of Takuya's grip and punched him one, two, three in the face. Takuya staggered backwards, shook off the pain, and lunged back to Robert. They grappled, feet shuffling as they tried to knock each other down.

Pain exploded across Robert's back and his muscles locked tight. Takuya let him go and Robert stumbled, twisting in pain. The second tough raised the club, and all Robert could do was look up at it through the corner of one eye and wait helplessly for the next blow.

A large man in a shop apron appeared behind the second tough and grabbed him from behind. The man reared back and lifted the tough off his feet. Another man yanked the club from the tough's hand.

Takuya smoothed his hair as he panted hard. Blood stained his teeth. Kaito and the third tough had separated. Both breathed hard and red marks spotted their faces. Takuya raised a finger at Kaito. "It's that Korean son-of-a-bitch who started this."

"Well, I'm ending it," the man with the apron said. "You boys bring nothing but trouble. If you're not shoplifting, you're starting fights." He dropped the tough and pushed him away. "Now go on. All of you."

Takuya and his crew ran down the street, cursing and vowing revenge.

The man turned to Kaito. "So you're Korean?"

Kaito gathered his cap and set it on his head. "Yes, sir. And thanks."

"Get lost," the shopkeeper shot back. "If your kind hadn't come into this country, none of this would be happening."

Kaito backed away, meek as a scolded dog.

Robert straightened and felt sparks of pain shoot from where he'd been struck.

The shopkeeper eyed him. "Are you okay?"

Robert swallowed the pain. He nodded. "I'm fine. He barely touched me." Which was not true. The club had hit him square across the back of his rib cage. He started for home, limping, Kaito at his side. He kept quiet, as if there wasn't enough room in his body for breath and the agony.

At the corner where their paths typically separated, Kaito asked Robert if he wanted him to walk him home. Robert shook his head and continued alone.

When he arrived at home, he tidied his appearance, hid his limp and acted as if all was well. Still, his mother fussed over him. "Look at you. You didn't wear those filthy clothes to school, did you?"

"No, Mom. They got dirty during baseball practice."

Her motherly eyes studied him. "And you're hurt."

"It's nothing. Somebody hit me with a ball. It was my fault, really. I should've been more careful."

Yumi and Makiko watched from beside the kitchen basin, their gazes questioning. "I'm all right," Robert said to her and his mom. "After I get something to eat, I'll be a thousand times better. By morning, I'll be okay like nothing happened." If he told his mother the truth, she would make him quit the team, maybe drop out of school altogether. Then he'd be forced to stay home all the time.

The next morning Robert woke up feeling like the bones in his lower ribcage had turned into scorched wood. Before he left his bedroom, he examined his back in a mirror. He'd taken the blow right on the large circular birthmark on his lower back. Normally a bright red, the birthmark had turned purple and was surrounded by inflamed skin. Worried that a rib was broken, he faked that he was okay and went to school as usual. He practiced with the team and stoically endured the shards of pain clawing his back.

Three days he suffered. The swelling in his back eased, but instead of feeling better, pain began shooting down his legs. When the other boys lapped past him during baseball warm-ups, Ishihara asked Robert if there was a problem. Robert replied that he didn't feel well because of stomach flu.

On the fourth day, Kaito walked him home. Robert ambled stiff-legged and dreaded telling his parents of his injury. When he and Kaito entered through the gate into the courtyard, Yumi was watering the bonsai trees along the back wall. Makiko jabbed a stick in the mud around each tree. Yumi's eyes widened and she set her watering pail on the ground. She scurried to Robert, and Makiko ran behind her.

"Robert, what is the problem?"

He braced against Kaito. "My back."

"Ah," she said. "The injury you suffered five days ago, right?"

He nodded and bit his lower lip to hold back the pain.

"Let me see what I can do," she said, and added knowingly, "while your parents are not home." She ordered Kaito, "Help him inside."

With Kaito propping him upright, Robert hobbled into Yumi's house where he was led to the front room.

Yumi pointed to a chair and said, "Take off your shirt and sit backwards on the chair."

Robert did as she instructed. After days of unceasing pain, he wanted to hope the agony would soon stop.

For some reason, Kaito stared at his back.

"What is it?" Robert asked.

"I have to leave." Kaito's gaze lingered on Robert's back as he stepped out of the room. "Get better. I'll see you soon."

Yumi knelt beside Robert to inspect his back. He flinched when she first touched him and braced himself so she could press her fingers into his bruised skin. She noted, "Your ribs are not broken, that is good."

She brought a jar from the bureau. She unscrewed the jar's cap to release the fragrance of eucalyptus and spices, and gooped liniment into her hands. "Hold still." As she rubbed his back, the pressure sent needles of pain through his nerves, but with each deliberate stroke, the pain settled into a tolerable ache. The lotion felt cool, pleasant. At last, he could feel his muscles loosen and relax.

"Let me do this," Makiko said.

Yumi stepped back and let Makiko slather liniment across Robert's back.

"Robert," she said, "I will help fix you."

Her fingers glided over his skin and then pushed into his flesh. Strangely, her hands on his bare skin affected him differently than had Yumi's. This was the first time anyone other than an adult had touched him like this. Whereas Yumi's massage had been careful and attentive, Makiko added a tenderness that both warmed and unsettled Robert. He knew that

Makiko liked him and now realized this attraction had risen to a level he was not familiar with. He glanced toward Yumi and it embarrassed him that she watched. These thoughts confused him enough to make him push against the chair and start to rise. "Thanks, Makiko."

"I have something to show you." She wiped her hands on a towel, retrieved a hand mirror, and positioned it for Robert to see his back.

All he saw was his birthmark.

Smiling, Makiko moved the mirror away but kept it aimed on his back. "Now what do you see?"

He saw the red mark surrounded by smooth pale skin. "My birthmark?"

"Look again," Yumi said. "A red circle against a white background. Doesn't it look like the flag of Japan?"

Robert had to agree. "Yes, it does."

"Then that's good," Makiko said. "I'm sure that's what Kaito saw as well. The flag of Japan is a good-luck symbol. This will protect you."

7

September 1930

Robert sulked as he made his way home, his feet heavy,
his mood grumpy. Kaito walked beside him and kept an
equally brooding silence. Their high school team, the Nishiya
Comets, had lost 9-4 against the Nogata Wildcats, which accounted for the gloomy attitudes. After continuing for several
blocks, the two boys parted ways without speaking.

Robert reflected on his life in Japan. Had it been seven
years? Now 15 years old, he was by far the tallest boy on his
team and a novelty because he was an American, but that alone
didn't guarantee him a spot on the roster. His fellow players,
especially his competitors, were tough, quick, and agile.

When Robert first learned that his dad had been offered
the job as missionary, he had no idea where Japan was. Now
he was fluent in the language and earned high marks, as a
student in a Japanese school no less. He got along well with
everybody—discounting the occasional bullies—although he
regarded Kaito as his closest friend. Robert had plenty to be
thankful for. However, he felt pangs like he was missing something. A yearning he couldn't quite name. He thought about

his friends back in Oglesby, though it had been years since they last exchanged letters. Where were they? What were they doing?

His parents tried their best to acquaint Robert with Japan beyond Yokohama, a challenge considering their meager budget. They had taken jaunts along the southern and eastern coasts of the main island, journeying by train to Hiroshima, Okayama, Kobe, Kyoto, Shizuoka—where they picnicked and admired Mount Fuji—and continued north to Tokyo and Sendai. His favorite destination was the fishing town of Miura, at the end of the peninsula south of Yokohama, where he watched ships passing through Uraga Channel as they cruised in and out of Tokyo Bay. The steamers sailing to all points of the globe reminded Robert that he lived in a small but crowded corner of the world.

He continued toward home knowing that a slate of chores waited. His father's congregation had grown to sixty and to accommodate them, Robert had to help Hiro finish and stain a new set of pews. Plus climb on the roof and replace shingles. And sweep and mop the sanctuary.

His wool uniform itched and he couldn't wait to take it off and wash off the dirt and humiliation of defeat. On the way through his *chome*, neighbors smiled and greeted him. He tipped his head politely and strolled past.

When he arrived home, Makiko ran circles in the courtyard, a puppy scrambling at her heels. "Look at him, Robert," she squealed in English, "he will be a good hunter." The furry, rust-colored puppy yipped and wagged his curly tail.

Robert couldn't help but smile. "Where did he come from?"

"My father brought him."

"Does he have a name?"

"I've just chosen it," she said. "*Sutōkā.*" Stalker.

"That's a lot of name for such a small dog," he replied.

"He's a Shiba Inu so he thinks he's big. Besides, look how fast he can run." She sprinted across the courtyard, bare feet slapping the pavers, and Sutōkā chased her.

Robert dropped his satchel with his glove and cleats beside the gate. He crouched and beckoned Makiko. She herded the puppy to him. He brought it to his chest, where it squirmed, pawed his shirt, and licked his chin. The puppy's playful enthusiasm soaked into Robert and erased the ache of today's loss to the Wildcats.

"Makiko," Yumi called from the kitchen, "you've been playing with that dog long enough. Come inside and help me clean the house."

As she grasped Sutōkā into her arms, Makiko mumbled in Japanese, her voice low so only Robert could hear. "Why is the house never clean?" She carried the puppy inside.

Yes, why are our chores never done? thought Robert. He headed into the rectory. Its entrance was open for ventilation. He expected to see his father in grubby work clothes and covered in sawdust or splotched with paint. Instead he sat hunched over a desk in one corner of his bedroom, occupied with ledgers, assorted loose papers, and an open Bible. He wore regular clothes and they were clean, which meant Robert had his father's share of chores to complete.

Smoke curled from Jack's pipe. He scooted back in his chair. "You're smiling. You must have won. What was the score?"

The question brought back the sting of the loss, and Robert's frown returned. "We got whipped. I did terrible at bat. Never even made it to first base."

"Remember what the Bible says," his father replied. "In 1st Corinthians, verse 9. *Do you not know that in a race all the runners run, but only one receives the prize? So run that you may obtain it.*"

Robert wasn't in the mood for Scripture. "Thanks, I'll keep that in mind."

His father tapped his pipe over an ashtray. "Hiro left to buy lacquer and stain. He's going to need help with the pews."

"Dad, I haven't forgotten." Robert continued to his room. He kept his door open to circulate the warm summer air. After removing his jersey and shoes, he sat on his bed and relaxed, thinking that he would like something to eat before he had to work.

A car rumbled to a halt in the street. Doors squeaked open and footfalls tramped on the pavement. He heard Yumi addressing someone. The exchange was animated and urgent. Curious, Robert rose from the bed and stood where he could see out the rectory door and onto the courtyard. Yumi appeared in the doorway and announced, her voice strained with worry, "Pastor Jack, you have a visitor."

Robert's father rose from his desk and walked into the courtyard. Robert followed, still dressed in a t-shirt and his dusty baseball pants.

Hiroshi Nagatomo, in a formal suit—high starched collar, vest and tie, white gloves—waited by the open gate of the courtyard. His neatly-parted and slicked hair glistened in the sun. Round, wire-rimmed spectacles captured his forlorn stare. A thin mustache decorated his upper lip. His white, gray, and black ensemble made him look like a pigeon, though there was nothing flighty about his somber demeanor. The corners of his eyes crinkled nervously. He cleared his throat. The man did not bring pleasant news.

Two stern-faced soldiers in khaki uniforms stood at the threshold of the gate. A dark sedan waited on the street. The more dour of the two soldiers wore the insignia of a first lieutenant and carried a leather message pouch slung over one shoulder. The other soldier, a lance corporal, rested the butt of his rifle on the ground and clicked a bayonet onto its muzzle. If that gesture wasn't alarming enough, the sleeves of both soldiers were blazoned with the crimson arm badge of the *Kempeitai*—the military police corps, who acted as secret police and were more ruthless than even the dreaded *tokko*.

Robert's mother watched from the kitchen door of the Asakawas' home. Food stains spotted her apron. Squinting anxiously, she asked in English, "Jack, what's going on?"

Robert's father gestured to the man in the suit. "This is Hiroshi Nagatomo, our ward captain."

Upon hearing his name, Nagatomo bowed stiffly, formally.

Yumi bowed and held it, her gesture docile and subservient. Makiko, looking apprehensive and confused, stood beside her, Sutōkā cradled in her arms. She bent forward and kept her gaze on the visitors.

Robert's father bowed, as did his mother, and Robert followed their example.

The lieutenant and his corporal did not bow; they only glowered.

As one, the Campbells stood straight.

"Enter, please," Jack said in Japanese. He began to make introductions. "This is my wife, Sarah. My son—"

"We know who you are," the lieutenant bellowed, his declaration cracking the air like a whip.

Nagatomo once again cleared his throat. He coughed. "I have been sent by the prefecture's military commission." Another cough. "You and your family," Nagatomo cleared his throat again, "are suspected of being American spies."

Robert felt his eyebrows rise. He stifled a laugh. In the last months, the ultranationalist screeds about foreign threats had become more and more paranoid, and more and more ridiculous. Posters, pamphlets, radio announcers repeated the same loony ideas. *One mind; One will; One Japan. Make Japan pure. Cleanse our culture of foreign pollution.* Koreans and Chinese had been harassed, attacked, even murdered, but aside from the one episode of vandalism long ago, the Campbells and their church had been left alone.

Robert's father did not share his son's bemusement. Cheeks enflamed and brow furrowed, he advanced a step toward Nagatomo.

The ward captain flinched. As a bureaucrat he was certainly used to having a big desk between himself and his constituents. The two soldiers scowled menacingly and took positions on either side of Nagatomo. The corporal brandished his rifle.

Makiko whimpered. Yumi wrapped an arm around her daughter's shoulders and pulled her close.

The lieutenant offered a cruel bitter scowl. "We have proof you are spies."

"Proof, what proof?" Jack demanded.

The lieutenant opened his leather satchel, reached in, and tossed newspapers to the ground.

Robert and his father regarded them. *The Chicago Tribune. The Chicago Daily News. The New York Herald Tribune.*

"So that's what happened to my copies," Jack said. "I haven't received any in weeks. If you had asked, I would've gladly shared, provided I got to read them as well."

A smirk creased Nagatomo's lips.

But the comment only darkened the lieutenant's expression. He jabbed a boot toe toward the newspapers. "These are nothing but lies that slander Japan."

"How do you know? Can you read English?"

The lieutenant's mouth pruned into a sour, wrinkled line.

Jack added, "You can't hold me responsible for what is printed in them."

"As a foreigner, a guest in my country," the officer explained, "you are responsible for the information that feeds this reckless propaganda."

"I can't vouch for what was written, but I doubt anything was intended as slander. It was either the truth or someone's opinion. Besides, slander is not the same as espionage."

"Do not play word games," the lieutenant shot back. "Those newspapers also report on Japanese manufacturing and industrial processes. Information of strategic value to our enemies."

"That was probably public information provided by your government. Go arrest them."

"Your flippant attitude will only get you in more trouble," the officer retorted.

"What trouble? What have I done?" Robert's father raised his open hands.

"You are agents of a foreign government."

"We are Christian missionaries, you know that."

"Your church is simply a cover for your espionage."

"That's a lie." Jack leveled a hard gaze at the officer.

Nostrils flaring, the lieutenant drew his lips back and bared small, yellowed teeth. "You have been in this country for six years and yet you have not learned proper manners." The officer then glared at Yumi as if this lapse was her fault.

Robert's father replied, "Proper manners belong to those who deserve them."

Sarah hustled from the kitchen, and her *geta* sandals clattered on the courtyard's pavers. She scolded in English, "Jack, please. Keep that temper of yours under control."

Robert's father smoothed his hair and shook his head as if to clear away his anger. "Okay. Fine." He switched to Japanese. "My apologies."

The lieutenant kept his scowl. "By order of the National Committee for Safety and Good Order, your church will be shuttered and the congregation disbanded."

Robert's father clenched his fists into hard knots. "That will not happen."

A shiver of fear electrified Robert's spine. His father teetered on the verge of attacking that windbag lieutenant. If he did so, then whatever predicament they were in would only get much, much worse. If his father and the lieutenant came to blows, that corporal would join in and probably club his father with the rifle, or worse, skewer him with the bayonet. Robert couldn't let these soldiers harm his father. His insides trembled with fear that he might have to jump into a fight, regardless of the consequences.

Sutōkā's raspy barking echoed within the courtyard. Makiko tried to hush him.

Nagatomo frowned, not at the pastor, but at the officer. "You are exceeding your authority, lieutenant. You let me handle this."

The officer kept his stare locked with Jack's. He groused, "Then handle it."

The ward captain cleared his throat and lifted his chin. "We have alternatives. The church will be allowed to remain open. But on the condition that you, your wife, and your son leave Japan."

Robert felt the ground shift as if this announcement were an earthquake.

His father countered, "I will not abandon my congregation."

Nagatomo answered, "The government is being lenient in allowing you this way out."

"Out?" Robert's father raised his voice. "What if we don't want to leave?"

"If you choose to remain," the lieutenant replied, "your status as a religious man will not shield you from justice."

"So I'm a spy?" Robert's father presented his wrists. "Then arrest me. Here. Now."

His mother put herself between his father and the soldiers. "Jack, calm down."

He shouted over her shoulder, "No, take me to court. Put me on trial. I want to see this evidence. Show me your justice."

The lieutenant snarled, frustrated. "Your theatrics impress no one, holy man. If this were up to me, I would've enacted *hijoji (martial law)*, thrown you in prison, and dynamited your so-called house of worship. Perhaps that will happen, and soon."

At the moment the officer stopped talking, Sutōkā started barking again as if in rebuttal to the lieutenant's bluster.

The lieutenant glared at the little Shiba Inu writhing and barking in Makiko's arms. He boiled over and he shouted, "Either silence that stupid little mutt or I'll do it for you."

Makiko clamped a hand over Sutōkā's muzzle and retreated behind Yumi.

Robert noticed with relief that a grin had softened his father's expression. A puppy had gotten the better of that loud-mouth idiot from the *Kempeitai*.

"When are we expected to leave?" Jack asked, still cross.

Nagatomo cleared his throat. "I do not know but I advise you to get started on your preparations." He stiffened and started to bow.

Robert's father pointed a finger at the ward captain. "If you think this is over, it's not. I'm taking this matter directly to the prefecture governor. And I'm going to the American embassy. You, Mr. Nagatomo, are not going to wipe your hands of us so easily."

The lieutenant stepped forward and knocked Jack's hand aside. Robert worried that his father would give the officer a well-deserved punch in the face, but miraculously, Jack yielded and kept his hands at his sides.

"You will adopt a civil tongue when addressing a representative of the authorities," the lieutenant said. "If you wish to complain, then you will do so from jail."

His mother pulled his father back and stroked his arms to keep him calm. He pulled free of her and bowed, still defiant. Nagatomo bowed in return.

The two soldiers escorted the ward captain to the sedan. They climbed in and drove off.

Robert's father blinked back tears. He squared his shoulders and turned to consider the rectory and the church. Years of hard work he would soon have to abandon.

***

Robert and Makiko sat on the floor inside the Asakawas' home. Rain pattered on the roof. He had the day off from both school and baseball so he remained here to play with the puppy. Makiko sorted through a stack of Robert's books that she read to improve her English. Sutōkā nipped at Robert's feet.

Hiro sat in a chair beside a reading lamp and thumbed through a stack of magazines. Yumi and Sarah watched the puppy from the kitchen. Yumi asked in jest, "Why did I allow you to have that dog? He's nothing but another mouth to feed."

"He'll feed us," Makiko answered. "We'll take him to the woods where he'll hunt rabbits and quail."

The front door opened abruptly. Robert's father entered, looking bothered and unsettled. Ever since receiving the ultimatum from Nagatomo, he had stewed as he contemplated a response to the government. Robert knew his father did not want to cave in to the *Kempeitai*. But if he stood his ground, he not only risked more trouble for himself, but also for Sarah, Robert, and the Asakawas. Perhaps even for the church's congregation. His protests and refusals to cooperate would only entangle him further in the government's web of repression.

He sloughed water from his raincoat and draped it on the coat rack. Removing his hat, he whisked the brim and hung it over the coat. He replaced his wet shoes with slippers and walked into the front room, stoop shouldered like he carried the weight of the world.

He sat by the kitchen table. Yumi poured him tea, which he sipped to warm up. Color returned to his face but his expression did not soften.

Sarah fixed him a bowl of rice and vegetables. He reached into a shirt pocket and withdrew an envelope, from which he removed a folded telegram.

Hiro left his chair and sat beside Robert's father.

"The main church in Chicago finally replied," Jack said. The government had suspended telegram delivery to foreigners, and so they were forced to guess when they had messages waiting. If any had arrived, they had to sign for them from the *Kempeitai*.

"What did they say?" Sarah asked, though it was obvious by his subdued manner that he had nothing encouraging to share.

He answered, "The main church told me to comply with the government's demands." Sighing, he then added, "If there is any consolation to this mess, most of the Christian mission-aries have received similar orders."

"Most?" she asked. "Not all? Then why us?"

"I guess we're first in line. The government is kicking out foreigners as fast as it can."

"For what purpose?"

"Paranoia. Stupidity. The rhetoric from the ultranationlists has forced the government to follow through with their de-mands, otherwise it's perceived as weak. I imagine every mis-sionary will be chased out within the next few years."

Yumi cupped her face with both hands and shook her head in disbelief. "What happens to the church? Our congregation?"

Robert's father looked at Hiro. "You'll have to be the new pastor."

Hiro rubbed his forehead and dabbed his eyes.

Makiko gathered Sutōkā into her arms. Her moist, hurt eyes settled on Robert. "You're leaving us? When?"

Leaving? How was this possible? Robert's cheeks turned cool as the blood emptied from his face.

Robert's father answered, "Maybe within six months."

Sobbing, Makiko hugged Robert and squeezed the puppy between them.

Jack rested a hand on Hiro's shoulder. "The burden rests on you, my friend."

Hiro nodded to acknowledge his duty. "*Hai.*" He added, "At least the chapel is finally in good shape."

8

April 1931

Jack Campbell took his place as pastor for the last time at the pulpit of the First Free Methodist Church of Yokohama. He delivered his sermon from 1 Corinthians 2:5, *That your faith should not stand in the wisdom of men, but in the power of God.* As he spoke, the women and men in the congregation dabbed their eyes. Some wept openly. Hiro sat in one of the chairs behind the pulpit. His eyes grew shiny and he grimaced in the effort to remain stoic.

Robert occupied his usual spot for the worship service, the front left pew. Makiko sat between him and Yumi. Aside from the Asakawas, Robert had never grown close to anyone else in the congregation. But as the sobbing washed over him, he was drawn into their collective sorrow. Until now he had been focused on his own private sadness of being uprooted, of leaving his mates from school and baseball. He realized that everyone shared this heartache. Tears made him squint.

Besides the painful goodbye, Robert was aware that his family's forced departure was more evidence to the congregation of the problems ripping Japan apart. The country was crumbling into chaos and fear even as the ultranationalists pushed for order and unity. After the Campbells left, the church's difficulties with the authorities would not be over.

Makiko squirmed in her seat and looked back across the sanctuary. Yumi nudged her to hold still. The girl brought her red, moist gaze to Robert. He placed an arm across her thin shoulders and smiled. Leaning against him, she grasped his wrist and held tight.

His family's impending departure felt like a vise squeezing his heart. Tomorrow, he and his mom and dad would finish packing. The day after that, they would journey to the pier, board a steamship and return to America.

What most troubled Robert was that he hadn't yet said goodbye to his best friend Kaito. They had planned to meet today, at the ball field by the rail yard, 2:00 PM, and Robert feared something might happen to detain either one of them. Tomorrow Kaito was also to leave Yokohama with his father, so today was their last chance to exchange farewells.

An "Amen," lifted from the pews and broke Robert from his mournful reverie. His father stepped back from the pulpit and Hiro took his place to assume the duties as the new pastor. Hiro asked the congregation to rise for the Benediction. After the prayer, Robert's mother played "Amazing Grace" on the piano. His father and Hiro walked down the center aisle. When Hiro opened the entrance door, sunlight washed into the sanctuary. The congregation filed out, Yumi, Makiko, and Robert following.

Out on the sidewalk, his father and Hiro chatted with parishioners and shook hands. A breeze of fresh air seemed to have lifted the despair. But across the street, two *tokko* police-men watched, a reminder of the government's heavy heel.

Yumi tugged on Robert's arm and said in Japanese, "We have work to do." With Makiko in tow, they reentered the sanc-tuary and walked through the rectory and into the courtyard. His mother was helping the elderly widow Mrs. Yunekura, who had tended warming dishes during the service. Yumi re-turned from her kitchen with a tray of cups and bowls that she arranged on a table.

Robert's mother assigned him ladling duties. He removed his suit coat and hung it on a post nail. Donning an apron, he stood behind the line of warming dishes and took his place by a large pot of rice wrapped in a towel.

Families trickled into the courtyard. When the entire con-gregation was finally present, Hiro climbed on a bench and asked everyone to hush for the Blessing. A quiet fell over the courtyard, disturbed only by Sutōkā who yipped and yapped from his cage inside the Asakawas' home.

At the conclusion of the prayer, Robert lifted the lid off the pot of rice. A cloud of delicious-smelling steam enveloped his face. A lively conversation bloomed as people queued by the table with the cups and bowls.

Robert ladled rice into the bowls of the people filing by. When he had first met many of them years ago, he was still a young boy. Since then, thanks to his American heritage, he had sprouted upward, and he noted how much taller he was than most of the adults. Knowing that he would probably never see them again, he made it a point to address everyone politely and sincerely.

"Mr. Aragaki," he said as he ladled rice, "you're looking well. And Mrs. Aragaki, what a beautiful kimono."

Mrs. Aragaki covered her mouth to hide a giggle. "Robert, you can be so charming. We will miss you."

Their son Takeshi held his bowl up for Robert to fill. Takeshi made only fleeting eye contact. He acted bothered by having to attend church, and although he and Robert were close in age, he'd never showed that he wanted to be friends.

The Aragakis continued down the serving line. Robert greeted the Watanabes and their teenage daughter Masami. Like Takeshi, she showed no interest in making friends with him.

He noticed that his mother had given up her duties at the serving line. Looking pale and worn out, she had retired to the bench along the back wall. Lately she'd been feeling weak, and she spent several hours of the day resting.

Worried for his mother, Robert covered the pot of rice and approached her. "Are you all right, Mom?"

She fanned herself with one hand. "I'm fine."

"You don't look fine."

She forced a smile. "Quit making a fuss over me. I was raised a farm girl. I'm as sturdy as a mule."

Robert's father brought a cup of tea. "It's the stress of moving."

"It's not even that," his mother replied. She thanked him for the cup and sipped. "Now everyone," she whisked her fingers, "go mingle and have fun. That's an order."

Robert returned to the serving line. The bowls were filled and people milled about the crowded courtyard. As the dinner progressed, the congregation separated into two groups, the women who gathered around his mother, and the men who clustered around his father.

Yumi led Mrs. Aragaki to his mother. Mrs. Aragaki carried a small box wrapped in decorative paper. Curious to see what it was, Robert stood behind the women and rose on tiptoes. His mother opened the box. She unfolded a colorful silk scarf and held it up for all to admire. It was a modest gift but much appreciated, considering the strained finances of the congregation.

The women clapped their hands and began singing. Sarah wrapped the scarf around her neck and joined them. Color returned to her face and she beamed in gratitude.

His father bellowed a laugh from a corner of the courtyard. Towering above the other men and smoking his pipe, he appeared jovial and jaunty. Hiro cracked a joke and the men answered with laughter.

But Robert didn't share the good cheer. He had to get away and see Kaito. But he couldn't simply go. After days of dreary funk, the festivity was a welcome relief. Even his mother had brightened.

He felt guilty for wanting to leave, for abandoning his family at a time when smiles and laughter had replaced frowns and quiet tears. But to Robert it felt like his insides had turned into an hourglass and the sand was draining out. He slipped away to read the wall clock above his father's desk. A quarter to two. It would take him fifteen minutes to reach the ball field. If he was to rendezvous with Kaito, he had to leave now. But he couldn't just go; he had to tell his parents where he was going.

The problem was that his mother looked genuinely happy, the first time he'd seen her that way in days. He didn't want to spoil her mood by telling her he had better things to do than celebrate with her. Same for his father. Besides, how long would Robert be gone? A couple of hours at most. If his parents got after him when he returned, what was the worst that could happen? Make him wash dishes and clean the courtyard? Those were chores he was going to do anyway.

Robert ducked into the rectory and from his room, collected his fielding glove and a ball. He didn't risk changing out of his Sunday clothes, otherwise he'd signal that he had other plans. He tried to slip out the front of the church, but the door was locked. He froze, thinking he was trapped. He returned to the courtyard, acting nonchalant, and eased out the gate.

Nerves tingling, he walked up the street in the direction of the ball field. At any moment he expected his father to shout for him. When he turned the corner and no one had yet called his name, he relaxed and let his thoughts turn inward.

During his years in Yokohama, he kept wondering if and when he would return to America. He'd been gone a long time and those recollections of Illinois were like faded pictures, while his memories of Japan were in fresh vivid color. This was his home now.

He removed his tie and stuffed it in a back pocket. Though he knew the moment ahead would be bittersweet, he looked forward to seeing Kaito. Jogging to make up for lost time, his mind swung like a pendulum between keeping track of where he was going and his thoughts about all the changes in his life.

Something furry and rust red flashed by his ankles. Startled, Robert halted. It was a Shiba Inu. Because of its size, color, and blue collar, the dog had to be Sutōkā. It must've escaped the courtyard and followed him. He took stock of where he was. More than halfway to the ballpark. Either Robert had to take the dog with him, or he had to turn back. The problem was, he had no leash and like all Shiba Inus, Sutōkā would run off after whatever suited him.

"Stupid dog," Robert said, angrily. "Why did you leave home?"

Turning around, he crouched to grab the dog's collar. When he looked up, he saw Makiko running toward him.

"Robert," she exclaimed. "You got him."

He clutched Sutōkā. "How did he get away?"

She reached him and halted, her chest heaving. "I was about to put the leash on him," she gasped, "when he ran out the door."

Robert frowned. "I keep telling you, put the leash on him first, then you open the door."

"I'm sorry," she replied.

"Where's his leash?"

"I...I... I left it behind." She stared at her hands as if realizing they were empty. "I wasn't thinking." Her chin began to quiver. "I just wanted to be with you."

Robert handed her Sutōkā. "Take him home."

She struggled to hold the puppy. "Where are you going?"

He stood and stepped back. "I have something to do."

"But Robert," her voice cracked, "don't leave me. I want to spend time with you."

"We'll have tomorrow."

"But what about now? You're leaving us and I want to spend every minute with you." Her eyes dewed over. The dog yipped and squirmed to get free of her arms.

Robert knew that Makiko liked him, and he liked her as well. He knew that the attraction between them was deeper than friendship. But he had important business. Hearing the clock in his mind tick away the minutes, he turned and started up the sidewalk.

Makiko followed at his heels. "Robert, don't you want to spend time with me?"

He turned to face her. She stopped in place, her expression going pale.

"Look, we will," he said. "Just let me do this." He continued on his way.

Makiko scurried after him. "Do what, Robert? Why can't I go with you?" She began to cry.

"Because it has to be just Kaito and me."

Her sobs lashed at him. He was torn enough as it was, and now she was making him feel cruel.

He quickened his pace but she remained right behind him. "Robert. Robert."

Whirling about, he glowered at her. "Stop it, Makiko. Just go home. Let me be for now."

She stared back, her eyes sad and heavy with tears. Robert had many things to share with her and heartbreak wasn't supposed to be one of them. "Go home. Now."

He spun around and ran up the street. When he reached the next corner he slowed to glance back. Makiko remained where he had left her, looking hurt and betrayed.

Tears blurred his eyes. Why was she forcing him to be so mean? He turned his back to her and dashed up the sidewalk. Faster and faster he ran, the rhythm of his pounding feet seeming to hammer the anguish deeper into his soul. At the next block, his throat burned and he had to stop to give his heart and lungs a rest. He bent forward and propped his hands on his knees. Staring down the street he had run, he wondered if Makiko would appear again, scuttling along on her slender legs as she cradled Sutōkā. The image made him smile and lightened his mind. She was that stubborn, so he wouldn't be surprised.

A minute passed. Makiko never showed up. Behind Robert, a train rumbled into the rail yard. He started for the ball field, now two blocks away. He approached through the outfield, its perimeter marked by weeds, and glimpsed Kaito waiting by the backstop. He wore loose work clothes and was chucking rocks at tin cans along the fence.

Waving his glove, Robert sprinted across the outfield, heart pounding in joy. He yelled, "Kaito!"

His friend turned to greet him.

Robert cocked his arm and launched his baseball as hard as he could. Kaito snatched his glove from the dirt and sprinted toward the ball. He raised his hand and the ball landed with a proper *thwack* in his glove.

Robert sprinted to first base, his glove ready. "Stop the runner."

Kaito flung the ball and ran to third. Robert snagged the ball and fired it at Kaito, who made a diving catch.

The two boys darted from base to base, saying little except for prompts to explain the play.

"A double."

"A pop fly. Tag the man at second."

"A grounder and stop the runner stealing home."

On and on they played until the long shadows of late afternoon crept across the field. Thirsty, hungry, Robert and Kaito plopped beside each other in the dirt. Swaths of dust covered Robert's white shirt and his dress shoes were scuffed and filthy. He didn't care. All that mattered was that he had spent this precious time with his good friend.

Now to say goodbye. Without having to ask, he knew what Kaito was thinking. Why was life so unfair? What were they to the big important men who ran the world? Why did they have to suffer?

Sorrow welled in him, a pressure he couldn't hold back. He bent forward and collapsed into sobs. Kaito draped his arm across Robert's shoulders and also sobbed.

Shame stung Robert. Men weren't supposed to cry. He couldn't imagine his father grieving openly like this for anything. So what that Robert and Kaito were parting ways? It had to happen eventually. But why did it hurt so much?

Robert caught his breath and composed himself. He wiped his eyes and pretended he didn't see Kaito wiping his as well.

Train cars banging into one another echoed across the ball field. A locomotive blew its whistle, and the melancholy sound drifted across the landscape of dingy warehouses and empty streets.

Robert had made plenty of acquaintances but made only one true friend among the boys his age: Kaito. Try as hard as they could, Robert and Kaito could never blend in completely and maybe that was why they bonded. The Japanese would always regard them as foreigners.

The first stars began to peek through the darkening sky. Robert had to start for home, hours late and facing a scolding.

"I'm going to miss the team," he said.

"Well, maybe with you gone," Kaito replied, "we might have a chance at winning."

The sudden humor relieved the sadness. He punched Kaito on the upper arm and laughed.

"Here, take this." He handed his baseball to Kaito.

His friend clasped the ball and stared at it. "Are you sure?"

"Yeah, I'm sure."

"Thanks, but why?"

"Because now you owe me. Someday, you'll have to return the favor."

***

The day before the Campbells were scheduled to leave Japan, Robert invited Makiko to join him for a walk to the nearby park. She brought along Sutōkā, and he trotted regally ahead of them. Gray clouds hung low in the sky, and the air smelled like rain was coming.

Upon reaching the park, Robert selected a clear spot among the cherry trees and poplars. He and Makiko sat cross-legged, she in a yellow print blouse over monpe pants. Both of them wore canvas slippers instead of the usual getas. Sutōkā lay beside her and kept watch on the other visitors in the park.

Robert removed the canvas pouch he had slung over one shoulder and set it on his lap. Inside the pouch he had gifts for Makiko. He didn't want this last time together to be marked with sadness and tears, like what had happened with Kaito. He was torn between leaving behind Makiko and her parents, but at the same time looking forward to returning to America and seeing what he had missed. You could always be sad about something, or happy about something else, and it was better to look for reasons to be happy. Otherwise you would be sad all the time.

He sensed that Makiko was waiting for him to set the mood. She pulled a handful of grass and tossed it over Sutōkā, who sneezed and shook off the leaves.

"I'm glad it's just you and me," Robert said. "This will be our last time alone together."

She frowned. "I hope not."

"You're right. I hope not, too." The question was, when would they ever meet again?

From the pouch he pulled out a coloring book and handed it to her. The book's title was *Animals of the World*, and a giraffe, a bear, and an eagle decorated the cover.

Makiko's eyes lit up with wonder. She studied the cover and slowly flipped through the pages. "How did you get this?"

"I saved some money." Robert reached back into the pouch and retrieved a small box that he gave to her. She emptied the contents—five wax crayons in bold primary colors—into her hand and admired them as if they were a treasure. Then her face abruptly dulled.

"What's the matter?" he asked.

"I feel bad because I don't have something for you."

"But you will." Robert had this figured out.

Makiko's delicate features bunched up like she didn't understand.

"Aren't you going to write me letters?" he continued.

"Of course."

"Well then, when you finish coloring a page, mail it to me." She grinned. "I'll start now." Rolling to one side, she propped herself on one elbow, and began thumbing though the book until she found a tiger. "I'll color him because you used to play for the Tigers, remember?"

"You have a good memory."

She arranged the crayons in the grass and selected yellow to begin filling in the tiger's fur.

As Robert looked at her, thoughts stirred emotions he had no words for. He was 15, old enough to appreciate the differences between girls and himself. He noticed women and their curves. Makiko was only ten, and even so, he could tell she was going to become a beautiful woman. But more than that, he knew she was as attracted to him as he was to her. And he knew this attraction was deeper than being friends. But there was no way to express this infatuation other than through small acts of affection, and above all, he had to keep these thoughts to himself.

Raindrops spattered on the coloring book. Makiko slapped the cover closed and jerked up. She clutched the book to her chest and looked up. "Oh no."

Sutōkā sensed her alarm and sprang to his feet.

"Here." Robert opened the pouch for her to slide the book and crayons inside.

The rain grew heavier, and they scrambled for cover beneath the wide branches of a poplar to stand with their backs against its trunk. Sutōkā sat at Makiko's feet.

The cloudburst drenched the ground with a loud hiss. Raindrops spattered down the leaves, and the air brought a moist chill. Makiko huddled against Robert. Her touch made strange feelings percolate inside of him. She grasped his arm, draped it over her shoulder, and pressed even tighter into him. He expected those feelings to turn uncomfortable but instead they melted into something that warmed him. He wanted to hug Makiko and never let go. Though he had promised himself to remain cheerful, leaving her was going to hurt, and he blinked back tears.

The rain moved on as quickly as it had arrived. A heavy mist settled over the wet ground and a steady *drip, drip* from the leaves broke the silence.

Makiko let out the slack of Sutōkā's leash, and he trotted onto the muddy grass. Following him, she tried to step around the puddles but gave up. She grimaced at her slippers, now soaked and dirty.

"Come on, Robert." She splashed her feet and splattered mud. "Let's get home so I can finish that tiger. I want to put it in the mail so my letter will be waiting for you in America."

9

May 1932

Robert opened his most recent letter from Makiko and slid a folded sheet of thick paper from the envelope. Since he had left Japan, correspondence between them crisscrossed the Pacific.

He had reread this letter so often that he had memorized its contents. The letter had been written on the last remaining page from the coloring book he had given her. He knew this because she had jotted *This is it No more* in English across the top of one side. The crayons had been worn to nubs months ago and she colored these drawings—an ostrich and a sea otter—with washes of watercolor that left the pages wrinkled.

Using her neat and careful script, Makiko had penned notes in the margins on both sides. As in her previous letters, she related only passing details about her family life, switching from kanji to English as the mood suited her. *Father and Mother were holding the church together. The lack of money caused a lot of anxiety. Sutōkā was proving to be a good mouser.*

What interested him even more than the letter was the photograph of herself she had included, a small black-and-white portrait. She wore her school uniform, a dark apron smock over a white blouse, her long hair pulled back and neatly parted down the middle. Her face had lengthened, but her eyes, and that pouting lower lip, were the features that he most remembered. She held a slight smile like she was hiding a secret.

Makiko had grown to the age where it was difficult to tell how old she was. In this picture she could pass for 16, though she was only 12.

He was 17, which meant there were five years between them, and that gap was a taboo he couldn't dare cross. But thinking forward, when he was done with college, *she* would be 17. At that point, if there was anything serious between them, then he could express himself. He knew of couples in his father's congregation where the husband was at least ten years older than his wife. So the older Robert and Makiko became, the less relevant the difference in their ages.

Robert folded the letter around the photo and tucked them both in the envelope, which he pushed into an inside coat pocket. He next picked up another letter from the end table.

He was waiting in the parlor of his family's home. From the armchair he occupied, he glanced to the clock on the mantle and wondered, when would his parents return? The time was quarter to five in the evening. Each tick-tock ratcheted his distress.

When he had left for school in the morning, he knew his father would be driving his mother to the clinic for more diagnostic testing. Robert was certain that when he returned from school they would already be back. Hopefully with good news.

But they weren't.

Perhaps he was making too much of their tardy arrival. Perhaps they had stopped for groceries.

He was still dressed in his school clothes: a sport coat and an open-collar shirt, no tie. Nervous, he tapped the second letter against the knee of his trousers. What was sealed in the envelope was another source of distress. He had an announcement to make, one that his parents might not understand.

When his family had arrived back in Illinois, he was certain he had left behind the kind of turmoil and misgivings that had marred his final days in Yokohama. As a reward for his father's missionary service in Japan, the church had offered him the pulpit of a nice congregation in Wheaton. Besides a higher salary and the prestige of ministering to a large prosperous congregation, the church had also provided Jack's family with this nice house and a new car. America may have still been in the throes of the Great Depression, but compared to Japan, they were in the Land of Plenty.

But life's problems found you no matter where you lived.

He shifted in his chair and held the envelope still. The letter had been addressed to him. The return address: the Springfield Cardinals, a team in the Missouri minor leagues. Upon his return from Japan, Robert had elbowed his way onto the varsity roster of his high school baseball team. Though the team had not advanced past divisional championships, his personal triumphs—MVP and a .402 batting average—must have caught the eye of the farm-league scouts. If the Cardinals had written to him, it was to show their interest.

A car rumbled into the driveway. A bright light flashed through the living room window, probably from the sun reflecting off the Plymouth's windshield as it turned the corner. Robert remained seated. The car halted and its engine died. Seconds later, a car door squeaked open, then closed. He imagined his father walking from the driver's side and around the sedan. A second door squeaked open and a moment later, that door closed, only more gently. Another moment later, steps shuffled on the front stoop and shadows fluttered in the small window of the entrance. The latch clicked and the door swung open. His father reached over his mother's shoulder to hold the door.

Robert rose from the chair and strode across the parlor floor to meet his parents.

Using a cane, his mother shambled over the threshold. Despite the warmth of a late spring afternoon, a wool shawl covered her head and a dark housecoat hung over her stooped form.

He could remember how tall and robust she once walked. While others succumbed to colds and fever, she bragged that because of her tough prairie stock, her constitution was as tough as oak. But for the last two years, a mysterious ailment whittled at her health and left her bent over, complexion pale, hair thinning, joints aching.

Robert took his mother's arm. She turned from the door and ambled across the carpet. Tenderly, he helped her onto the sofa. She leaned against the cane and her frail hand clasped his wrist. She lay back on the cushions and stared at the ceiling, her rheumy eyes swimming in disturbed, viscous pools.

His father took the cane and grasped her ankles to swing her legs over the end of the sofa. Her housecoat fell open and revealed a simple dress underneath, baggy and rumpled. Before this sickness, she would have never left the house without presenting herself as a proper lady.

Robert had grown as tall as his father and when he looked directly in his eyes, he saw despair behind the stoic mask. His father had for over two decades shepherded members of his various flocks through their troubles, but providing that same strong shoulder to his wife seemed to daunt him.

She pulled the shawl from around her head. Robert's father took the shawl and placed it on an end table. She eased her head against the arm of the sofa and releasing a sigh, slowly blinked her eyes.

Her hesitant movements reminded Robert of an old and withered cat settling into its bed. Old and withered were not the words he wanted to describe his mother. Where had her youth gone? That fluid, confident ease of her movements? Her vigor? Her smile? With each passing month he saw her diminish a little more. It was as if he was watching his mother die in increments.

Tears pushed against his eyes. "What did the hospital say?"

"The tests remain inconclusive so the surgeon scheduled more tests. *More tests!* Like your mother hasn't been studied and probed enough." His father added with a dismissive bark, "Bah, so much for the miracles of modern science. We'd be better off sending your mom to a witch doctor."

Considering his father's irritation, Robert debated sharing the news contained in the letter. But he was delaying the inevitable and tomorrow might not present a better time, either. He waved the letter. "I've heard from the Springfield Cardinals."

His father jerked toward him. His mother lifted her head. When Robert saw the anticipation in their expressions, it stung him because he was only going to let them down.

"What did they say?" his father asked, his voice lifting with hope.

"I dunno. I haven't opened the letter yet."

"Well, get on with it, son." Jack pulled a chair close to the sofa and sat. He reached for Sarah and laid a hand over hers.

Robert fished a penknife from his pocket and sliced the envelope open. He unfolded the letter and read. The news was exactly what he feared. He kept the emotion from his voice as he said, "They've invited me to summer tryouts."

Beaming, his father hopped from the chair. He shook Robert's shoulder. "Congratulations, son! Next stop, the St. Louis Cardinals."

"It's only an invitation to try out. Not a sure thing."

His father let go. "You seem awfully cool about this." His brow knit, suspicious. "I thought you'd be doing jumping jacks on account of that news."

Robert's mother motioned for the letter and he gave it to her. She turned it to catch the light and her eyebrows twitched as she read.

Robert shuffled his feet. If the letter had said the Cardinals had passed on him, then this announcement would've been easy. He knew what to say but the words remained a tangled knot in his mouth. At last he forced them out. "I have other plans."

"Oh?" his father asked, his tone lacquered with disappointment. His mother peeked over the top of the letter.

"I want to study engineering. Get into aviation."

His father retreated to the chair and sat. "Oh," he repeated, as if he were churning Robert's words in his mind.

"Well, I'm not surprised," his mother said. She handed the letter to Jack. "You've started looking at airplanes the way other boys look at girls."

"That's not true, Mom," Robert replied, flustered. Though he spent most of the spring and summer months playing ball, he had managed to hang around the local airfield, where biplanes fluttered to and from the grassy pasture. His friends spent that time courting the young women from school.

Whenever he could, he'd visit Elmhurst and the Chicago Air Park to admire the newest airplanes, like the sleek Northrop Alpha and the big Ford Trimotors. Day by day, his dreams of playing baseball were overtaken by his desire to fly and make airplanes. On the walls of his bedroom, clippings of baseball heroes had been overlaid with photos of his favorite flying machines.

Working odd jobs, he had saved enough to buy short hops on a Jenny. Once aloft, he was mesmerized by the magic of flying. The bird's eye perspective of the world, the ability to soar over earthly boundaries with the grace of an eagle. The wind in his face. His chest rumbling from the engine, its oily exhaust filling his nostrils. His guts swaying and pitching as the airplane banked and wheeled in the sky.

But it wasn't magic; it was physics and technology. He knew Bernoulli's Law accounted for the lift beneath the wings. And it was the thrust of the internal combustion engine through the propeller that pulled the whole contraption up and forward. The airplane represented man's ability to unlock nature's secrets and harness her power to do his bidding. He would attend college and learn the mathematics and science behind those secrets.

Robert's father took the letter and his eyes tracked over the words as if they contained a message his son could not see. "You've come far as a baseball player. Sacrificed much for your success. Springfield wouldn't have sent this letter unless they thought you had the potential to compete as a professional." He breathed heavily, betraying the weight of dismay. "Think how many boys would jump at this chance."

"Dad, please, I've made up my mind."

"Son, you're turning down an opportunity that I wish I'd had. I don't regret answering God's call to witness, but I would have loved to have been a professional baseball player, even on a farm team like the Cardinals." His voice slumped. He sat back in the chair and took Sarah's hand.

Robert mulled over his father's reaction. As a preacher and a husband he couldn't let himself give in to misgivings over his wife's declining health, but as a father he was free to agonize over his son's decisions.

Sarah shivered from a chill that only she felt. She bunched the front of her housecoat and looked at Robert's father. "I never thought you'd be disappointed by your own son wanting a college education. As an engineer, no less."

Jack shook his head. "College is expensive." He turned to Robert. "How will you manage?"

Robert knew this question was coming, and he had his answer memorized in a way his father would appreciate. "Like it says in the Book of Matthew. *Therefore do not be anxious, saying, 'What shall we eat?' or 'What shall we drink?' or 'What shall we wear?' For the Gentiles seek after all these things, and your heavenly Father knows that you need them all."*

***

The Tribune Tower, 435 North Michigan Street, Chicago.

Robert stood in a huddle of reporters and clerks, riding an elevator to the eighth floor. It halted, pinged, and the door opened. He pushed out and headed straight down the hall.

So far, so good. A half hour ago he had convinced the receptionist in the ground floor lobby to make a call on his behalf. Now he was on his way to an interview. He had contemplated this move for weeks now, and he was astonished that it was unfolding just as he had imagined.

At the first left, he turned through a set of double doors, propped open. As he stepped between two large electric fans on either side of the entrance, the blasts of air tousled his hair and batted his collar. Men and a few women sat hunched at desks, many of them clutching telephones between their jaw and shoulder as they banged away at typewriters. Ribbons of cigarette smoke twisted from ashtrays scattered about the large, open room.

He walked down an aisle toward a row of offices, names and titles painted on the frosted windows. His destination was straight ahead: the office of Warren Simmons, Associate Editor, City News.

Robert halted at the door and listened. He heard a man inside speaking. A one-sided conversation so Robert assumed the man was on a telephone. When he heard the handset rattle into its cradle, Robert knocked and announced himself. When he was invited in, he opened the door and stepped through.

Warren Simmons was a large, soft-looking man, dressed in a tailored white shirt. A suit jacket hung from a nearby stand. His physique filled his chair like dough settling in a pan. Owlish eyes peered from behind round glasses. A yellow bowtie with blue stripes clung to the front of his thick neck.

Framed articles and photographs from the *Chicago Daily Tribune* lined the walls. Stacks of magazines and newspapers towered on cabinets. Freshly typed articles lay on his desk, the pages scratched through with a red pen. Behind Simmons, a fan swiveled on the sill of an open window.

Robert extended his hand and introduced himself. "Miss Tully said she had called you."

Simmons stared as if thumbing through pages of memory. Strands from a comb-over lay across his pink scalp. Perspiration stains mottled the edge of his shirt collar and his armpits. He pointed a finger. "Robert Campbell, right? Said you were looking for a job? That you're fluent in Japanese?"

Robert nodded. "That's right."

Simmons gave him the once-over, as if incredulous that this tall, Midwestern young man could speak that language. He indicated that Robert take a seat. "Okay, educate me. Give me the abbreviated version of why you're here."

Robert explained about his father's assignment as a missionary to Yokohama, that he had attended a Japanese school, and even played baseball over there. What he didn't share was any detail about Makiko. He added that his family had been forced out of Japan and that he was a freshman at Northwestern University, studying engineering. He wanted a job that would keep him fluent in Japanese.

Simmons mugged an appreciation for the story. He opened a desk drawer and pulled out a section snipped from a Japanese newspaper, the paper yellowed with age. "Here's your chance to impress me. What does this say?" He placed the clipping in front of Robert.

He perused the article. It had been clipped from the *Toshima Shimbun* and was dated 1928. Coincidentally, considering his baseball experience, it was from the sports section and he read aloud—in Japanese—the report of a double-header between the Nakano Dragons and the Koto Fish Merchants. He then paraphrased a translation.

Simmons listened, nodding. "I know a smidgeon of Japanese from a stint with the merchant marine. I said I wanted you to impress me and damn if you didn't." Simmons took the clipping back and slipped it into the drawer. "Obviously you're here for a job, but what can you do for us?"

"I could translate Japanese newspapers and magazine articles."

"We already get reports from Reuters and the Associated Press."

"Do they tell you everything?"

"Probably not."

"There you go," Robert replied in a confident flourish. "I could read whatever you provide. Then your reporters

working the foreign desk could quiz me about whatever top-
ic. If I had read something pertinent, I could help fill in the
blanks of what they want to know."

Simmons let his gaze range across the confines of his
cramped office. He brought his eyes back to Robert. "Got another job?"

"I load trucks at a dairy. I don't mind the hard work but I'd
rather work here."

"It'll only be part time, and you'll be at the bottom of the
pay scale."

Robert nodded. "That'll be good enough for now."

Simmons leaned to one side of his chair. It squeaked beneath him. The fan rustled papers on his desk. He stroked his
chin. The phone rang, but he ignored it. When the phone quit
ringing, Simmons plucked a sheet from a pad on the desk blotter. "Gimme your address. It's going to be a couple of weeks,
but I'll make it happen. You won't be working for me so we
gotta figure all that out. In the meantime, don't throw your
back out loading those trucks."

Robert gave him the address and telephone number to his
boarding house on Erie Street. Simmons folded the note and
tucked it into his shirt pocket. He stood and offered his hand.
"Welcome to the *Tribune*. We'll see you soon."

Elated, Robert sauntered out of Simmons' office and made
his way back to the elevator. He was certain that once he
proved his worth, he'd get a bump in pay and more hours. In
the meantime, he faced more of those dreaded early-morning
wakeups and hundreds of crates to lift and load.

He walked out of the lobby and down the sidewalk for a streetcar to the boarding house. Passing a coffee shop, he made a detour inside and sat at the counter. He ordered a Coca-Cola.

Digging into his pocket, he withdrew his latest letter from Makiko. Though he had read and reread the letter since it had arrived three days ago, each time he looked at her words it was as if she were so very close.

Although she preferred to practice her English, she had written in Japanese, because she and Robert had learned that the *Kempeitai* censors would delay any correspondence they couldn't immediately read. The government was so paranoid that even a letter from a fourteen-year-old wasn't above scrutiny.

The bulk of her letter contained an upbeat assessment about life in Yokohama, and included a paragraph about Sutōkā and his humorous exploits chasing cats.

At the bottom of the letter she had included a poem. It described chrysanthemums and swallows and ended with the line, "Look down, past the words you see, and find the hidden message."

Robert sipped his drink through its paper straw. He had pondered what that line meant, since it differed in tone from the rest of the letter. Was this a riddle? Maybe Makiko or Yumi had included another message in the letter. But where? He turned the stationery and held it to the light, looking for a watermark. Nothing. He did the same with the envelope. It had been handmade from kraft paper, and he couldn't see through it. He held the top open and peeked inside. Along the bottom he noticed faint pencil scratches, markings he hadn't noticed before. *The hidden message?*

Robert hurriedly searched his pocket for his knife. He carefully sliced the envelope apart and laid it flat on the counter.

Now he understood Makiko's clever clue. Faced with mountains of letters to process, a censor would only open the envelope and read the letter. He might shake the envelope to make sure nothing was stuck inside. What was the chance that a harried government slug would take the initiative to examine each corner and crevasse of every piece of correspondence?

The message had been written along the bottom fold in faint pencil. Only four terse lines, two on one side of the fold, two on the other.

Church closed for good. Older boys from congregation drafted into the army.

Mother not doing well. Medicine hard to find.

Hiroshi Nagatomo, the ward captain arrested by the army. Disappeared.

Father works in new factory, making wooden wheels for ammunition carts.

That was all. A few words that spoke volumes about what was happening in her world. He wished he could bring the Asakawas to America and spare them such heartache. The Japanese would always be welcome here.

What about Kaito? It had been a year since Robert had heard from him. His friend was now old enough for the military draft. As a Korean-Japanese, Kaito had suffered indignities all his life because of his mixed heritage, but that might now be a blessing. Robert was certain the Japanese army wouldn't trust

Kaito with anything more dangerous than a shovel. Hopefully, Kaito would serve in a labor battalion where his most dangerous enemy would be boredom.

Robert finished his drink and placed a nickel beside the empty glass. He gave Makiko's letter another read and tucked it back into his coat pocket. The more he longed to be with her, the more helpless he felt. But that only stoked his hope that they would meet again.

10

December 1941

Robert studied Makiko's photograph. She sat for a formal portrait in traditional Japanese garb, a kimono, her hair piled into soft rolls decorated with beads and jeweled sticks. Truth was, he would've preferred her in another pose, something less stiff, more casual. In keeping with the expectations of her culture, she wasn't smiling, but he suspected that she fought hard to keep her playful manner from breaking the taut set of her mouth. The wallet-sized photo was her last correspondence to him, having arrived in October in an envelope dated August 24, 1941. Judging by the size of the envelope, he guessed she had included a letter but the *Kempeitai* must have confiscated it. If they had, he hoped whatever she had written didn't cause her any trouble.

He turned the photo over to read her kanji.

I have started medical school. Mother and father are fine.

Pink blossoms fall from
the cherry tree, spinning, but
always drift to you.

Makiko

That poem was the only time she had admitted a romantic longing for him. She was now 21 years old and if she were here, he wouldn't hesitate crushing her against him.

Robert slipped the photo into a small manila envelope where he gathered all of her pictures, a catalog of her maturing from girl to teenager to young woman. In every image, she regarded him with those lively searching eyes and that pouting lower lip. She was quite striking, and he mused: If after they finally connected, would people stare at them and wonder what she was doing with him?

During the intervening years, he had sent photographs of himself in his letters to her. Some were formal portraits, others snapshots of him in his baseball uniform, or outside his father's church, or in his school clothes. Hopefully she enjoyed looking at him as much as he did at her.

He kept every one of her letters, presently safe in a cardboard box with his other belongings, and in quiet lonely moments, he would pick one at random and comfort himself with her words.

Robert promised himself that he would return to Yokohama, but first he had to get his degree, and then a job, which he had done. Meanwhile, his mother's multiple sclerosis kept getting worse. The strain of caring for her pressed down on his father like a relentless screw, and Robert felt obligated to watch over him as well.

He stared out the window of his railcar compartment at the bleak winter landscape scrolling past. Gray upon gray no matter which way he looked. The train rolled through prairie and wooded fields and belts of industrial parks. Smoke and steam plumed from stacks picket-fenced across the horizon. Another unremarkable Sunday in December.

The conductor announced that the train was about to arrive in Chicago's Grand Central Station, Robert's destination.

A businessman hustled past Robert's compartment. Robert heard only a snippet of what the man uttered. "Did you hear? The Japs have attacked Pearl Harbor."

Robert's thoughts plunged into disbelief and horror. If true, then the world war had just swallowed America. Returning to see the Asakawas was a task he had left for tomorrow, and it seemed he had run out of tomorrows.

When the train pulled into the station and halted, Robert wasted no time rushing from his car, suitcase banging against his leg. He wanted to shake free of this terror that had clamped onto him. He couldn't believe, didn't want to believe, that reality had slammed shut any chance that he would ever see Makiko again. And worse, if and when the U.S. attacked Japan, Makiko could very well end up on a pile of corpses. The image sickened him and he slowed to tamp down the nausea. Once outside the terminal, Robert paused by a newsstand but the newspapers were sold out. "What's this about the Japanese attacking Pearl Harbor?" he asked the clerk.

"You know as much as me, Mac."

Robert turned away. He spied a crumpled *Chicago Daily Tribune* in a sidewalk wastebasket and pulled it out, smoothing the front page and scanning the headlines. Nothing about any attack on Pearl Harbor or any other American base. Of course, if the attack happened earlier today, then it wouldn't have yet appeared in print.

Frustrated, Robert jammed the newspaper back into the trash. Desperate for news, he scoped the mostly deserted streets. Passengers spilling from the terminal had scattered and disappeared into the neighborhood like ants through a pantry. At the end of the block, a group of people had clustered outside a coffee shop. All faced the door and shared the same stunned expression. Some looked down, morose and pensive. Others kept staring at a large radio perched in the open transom above the entrance.

Robert drew close and nudged his way to the radio. The announcer was saying that the defense forces on both coasts had been put on high alert, and this news made Robert weak with dismay. He set his suitcase down and whispered to a man beside him, "What are we listening to?"

"WGN. They were broadcasting the game between the Bears and the Cardinals and then interrupted to announce the attack."

So it was true. Robert closed his eyes and sighed, feeling sick.

"...the office of the Chief of Naval Operations issued a statement that the air attack on Pearl Harbor inflicted numerous casualties and a number of ships were damaged." The announcer sounded like he was adlibbing from wire reports. "No word yet from Army headquarters at nearby Schofield Barracks. American air and sea patrols in the Pacific have been stepped up. General Smith of the—"

"When I got up this morning," a woman said, "I didn't even know there was such a place as Pearl Harbor. Hawaii is halfway around the world. Now it seems the war is down the street."

The woman's comment aside, Robert was aware of the vast distances across the Pacific Ocean. He remembered the weeks of sailing the 2,400 miles from San Francisco to Oahu, followed by the trip from Oahu to Yokohama, another 3,900 miles and more weeks at sea. Then he and his family had repeated the journey, in reverse, for the trip back to America.

How had the Japanese caught our Navy by surprise? The announcer had mentioned an air attack. From where? The Japanese had no long-range bombers. Even if they did, where had they launched them from? *Japan?* Impossible. The latest American prototypes couldn't manage those distances. *Aircraft carriers?* Did Japan have any? From what Robert knew about Japanese aviation, even their most modern combat aircraft were antiquated, copycat versions of British and Italian machines.

Realizing he wasn't going to learn anything useful, at least not for a while, Robert decided to go about his business. He grabbed his suitcase, returned to the terminal and stood at the taxi pickup point, for the moment deserted. The day was warm and he unbuttoned his long coat and adjusted the set of his fedora. As he waited, his thoughts zinged in dozens of directions, like the day's events were yanking on every nerve. His mind looped in wild circles, anxious about what was going to happen to him, to this country, to Hiro and Yumi, and most important, to Makiko.

The toot of a car horn brought him to the present. A yellow Chevrolet taxi had pulled to the curb. Robert cracked open the right rear door to look at the driver. He appeared not much older than Robert. His gray cabbie hat was tipped back to reveal a broad forehead and a pair of thick eyebrows.

"St. Luke's Hospital?" Robert asked.

"Get in."

Robert shoved his suitcase onto the rear seat and scooted beside it.

The cabbie set his meter and cruised forward. "I'm sure you heard the news."

"If you're talking Pearl Harbor, I have."

"Roosevelt finally got his war," the cabbie said. His gaze caught the tattered poster of the America First Committee glued to a passing fence. "I suppose this kills it for them. No way can we sit on our asses spouting non-intervention. Not after this. Whaddaya think?" The cabbie's eyes flicked to the rearview mirror.

Robert ignored the glance. He wasn't in a mood to argue politics.

"Where are you from?" the cabbie asked.

"Here."

"So you're coming home? Why are you going straight to the hospital? You a doctor?"

"No. I used to live here. I'm traveling from Santa Monica."

"California?"

"Yeah."

"I heard it's beautiful out there."

"It is."

"What brings you here?"

"I'm on vacation. My mom's not doing well."

"Sorry to hear that. Whaddaya do?"

"I work for Douglas Aircraft."

"You guys will be raking it in now," the cabbie said. "Soon you'll be churning out airplanes like they were donuts."

For our war. Robert stared out the window, too melancholy for conversation. He felt the cabbie's gaze on him, expecting a response.

After a minute the cabbie said, "I guess it was bound to happen, the war I mean. Though I was expecting the Germans to hit us. You know, on account of the Neutrality Zone, and us leaning toward the British."

Robert agreed with the cabbie, though he remained quiet. In the days after Hitler's attack on Poland, President Roosevelt had declared the western half of the Atlantic Ocean as neutral territory, enforced by patrols from the U.S. Navy and the Coast Guard. Last September, the Coast Guard had raided and destroyed a German weather station on Greenland. Then in October, U-boats torpedoed two destroyers, damaging the *Kearny* and sinking the *Rueben James*. Undaunted by American interference, the German submarines kept sneaking into the Neutrality Zone to send transport ship after transport ship to the bottom of the sea.

"How long you figure fighting the Japs is gonna take?" The cabbie studied Robert through the rearview. "A couple of weeks? Months? I mean, what have they got compared to us? We got MacArthur in the Philippines. We can launch our Flying Fortresses out of Manila and pound Tokyo to rubble. Those sneaky Japs bit off more than they can chew, and they're going to choke on it."

Robert's queasiness returned. The world's nations seemed engulfed with a murderous fever like they hadn't learned a damn thing from every previous war. The German blitzkrieg had smashed the Allies in western Europe, accomplishing in weeks what years of trench warfare had failed to do during the First World War. France had collapsed. The British Army barely escaped annihilation and retreated to England. Norway had been done in by that turncoat Quisling. After carving up Europe between themselves, Hitler turned on Stalin, and Nazi armies closed in on Moscow. Meanwhile, Japan had ransacked Nanking. Starting today, it was America's turn to wade into this global bloodbath.

Sooner or later, Robert was certain, the Americans were going to hit Japan. Hard. Though not with B-17s. Not yet anyway. As big and capable as those bombers were, they couldn't fly from Manila to Tokyo and back on one load of fuel. Neither could the newer B-24s. But when the U.S. did strike, they'd certainly target Yokohama to destroy its railhead and shipyards. Hopefully, Robert prayed, the Asakawas would have fled the city for safety in the countryside.

The taxi approached the hospital and parked along the front sidewalk. Robert peered out his window at the brick edifice and wondered where he'd find his mother.

The cabbie swiveled around and hooked an arm over the top of his seat. "What are your plans?"

Robert furrowed his brow, puzzled by the question.

"The war, I mean," the cabbie explained.

"I'm not sure. I just heard about the attack."

"I got classified I-B," the cabbie said, "*limited military service* on account of some stuff I've done, legally-wise."

"I'm II-B," Robert replied. Deferred for war production. Fit for unrestricted military service.

The cabbie's expression faded, and he turned wistful. "Not sure what I'll do. Enlist. Or not. Wait for Uncle Sam to come get me. Driving a cab might not seem glamorous; then again I don't get shot at and I get to go home at the end of my shift. The thing seems for us is to go *rah-rah* for God and country and all that. But I had an uncle who fought in the first one. He didn't come back. Everybody talks about him doing his patriotic duty, but given the grand schemes of things, I wonder if that's something we tell ourselves to make sense of the loss, cuz war don't make no sense."

"That's the challenge," Robert said. "To find meaning in this madness."

The cabbie grinned. "I knew I'd get an opinion out of you, sooner or later." He glanced to the meter. "That'll be fifty-five cents."

Robert dug three quarters from his pocket. "Keep the change." He climbed out of the cab and suitcase in hand, trudged along the sidewalk for the hospital entrance. He was yoked with two enormous worries, his mother and the war. The cabbie had been correct in claiming that Douglas Aircraft would be raking in a fortune. Robert could use his deferment and ride out the war from the safe confines of a desk on the production line. Uncle Sam did need airplanes...and tanks and trucks and ships, but those were useless without men.

Men—soldiers—willing to put themselves in harm's way. Men willing to sacrifice themselves if that's what it took to beat the enemy.

He entered the hospital, removed his hat, and approached the receptionist's desk. Though everything looked normal, he sensed the heavy mood bearing down on everyone.

A prim older woman with a white nurse's cap greeted him from behind the desk. He asked for his mother's room number, which she gave, and he asked if he could leave his suitcase at the desk. The receptionist agreed.

He rode the elevator to the third floor. Along the way, his thoughts detoured to Makiko and his musings suddenly turned grim. He imagined her and Sutōkā dashing for the sanctuary of an air raid shelter. Around them, Yokohama lay in smoking ruin. In his mind's eye, Robert could only watch, helpless, as Makiko and the little dog ran like hunted prey, bombs falling around them, bullets raking the ground. She scrambled into the shelter and in the dim light of a candle, he saw her pull a grotesque gas mask over her beautiful face. He cringed in terror and pinched the bridge of his nose to clear away the gruesome picture.

What could he do to help her? Nothing. As a civilian he would help make weapons to quicken the destruction of her homeland. By the time the last cartridge was fired and a dazed, wounded world limped back into peace, hundreds of thousands if not millions more would be dead. He pictured heaps rotting in the sun. Tears bit his eyes and he prayed, *Please dear God, spare Makiko and her family.*

All of his life, Robert had heard about the Hand of God and how It lay on a person's shoulder with Divine Guidance. But Robert had never experienced it. Things happened because... they happened. Most of his decisions he made on the spot. The tough ones he deliberated over, and frankly—though he would never tell his father—he had quit praying years ago for God's intervention, because the line between him and Heaven seemed like a one-way conversation.

But this time Robert was flooded with a profound clarity, as if God *had* spoken to him, and the decision came so resolutely that it jolted him.

A line from the book of Jeremiah came to mind. *Call to me and I will answer you, and will tell you great and hidden things that you have not known.*

Robert would volunteer. He would fight. Somehow, some way, in whatever crazy naive scheme that would unfold before him, his efforts as a soldier, or airman, sailor—he hadn't decided which service yet—however miniscule, would help save Makiko and her family.

The elevator reached the third floor and the door pinged open. His father was sitting in a stuffed chair in the foyer. He put down his newspaper and rose haltingly from his seat.

"Dad, how have you been?" Robert had last seen his father in the spring and in the seven months since then, he had aged half a decade, the lines on his weary face deepening, his hair thinning and turning white.

"Fine, considering." His father's shoulders remained hunched and the mass of his torso sagged toward his middle.

"Where's Mother?"

Jack gestured down the hall. "She's doing about as expected." Code for, she was getting worse. He raised his arm for
Robert to step close for a hug.

Afterwards, he pulled away just enough to lay a sad gaze on
Robert. "How are you, son?"

"I'm fine. I got plenty of rest on the train."

His father clung to his arms. "That's not what I meant. I'm
talking about the war. There's no escaping it now."

Robert hesitated. He had to tell his father he was going to
enlist, but he knew the news would wreck his heart. His father
was suffering enough.

Jack's eyes bore into his, searching, and they crinkled with
painful realization. "You have something you want to say?"

Robert tried to keep steady, but he flinched.

"If you have something to tell me," his father said, "better
that you tell your mother at the same time so you won't have to
repeat yourself." Jack let go and started up the hall.

Robert stayed behind and kneaded the brim of his hat. If
his decision pained his father, it would torture his mother.
Robert prepared himself and continued up the hall.

His mother had a private room. She lay propped up in bed,
her skin wrinkled and papery, eyes shrinking into their red
sockets. Robert smiled, both to let her know he was happy to
see her and to keep himself from dissolving into pity.

He opened his coat and sat beside her on the bed. Red and
purple lesions spotted her face and neck. Her arm rose toward
him, its skin wormed through with varicose veins. She laid a
palsied hand on his sleeve. When he leaned to kiss her temple
he could see her waxy scalp through dry wisps of hair.

Robert told her about his job as an aircraft engineer and how different life was in Santa Monica compared to Chicago. He said, "Someday soon you'll have to visit," though unless a miracle happened, that wasn't likely.

"Have you heard from the Asakawas?" she asked.

"Makiko's last letter arrived two months ago. They seemed okay. She couldn't tell me much, with their censors and all."

She withdrew her hand and stared at the wall. "I'm worried about them." She swiveled her eyes to him. "And you as well."

"Robert has something to tell us," his father said.

The moment settled on Robert, heavy with dread like he was betraying them. *Out with it then. Stop being a chicken.* "I've decided to enlist."

His father gasped and closed his eyes. "Why, son? I thought you told me you had a deferment."

"Everybody has to do their part."

"The government has millions of other men to draw from."

"I know, Dad." How could Robert explain himself? He was catapulting into a fool's errand. His intentions may be noble but once he was in uniform and sent overseas, what happened to him would be more luck of the draw than anything else.

"You're twenty-six. War is a young man's game."

"According to the government I'm young enough. I still had to register for the draft."

"What will you do?" his mother asked.

"With my degree, I'm sure I can serve as an officer. Plus I know Japanese as well as anyone else. I can work for Naval Intelligence. The State Department."

"That's what you say but I know you," Jack replied. "You'll volunteer to be on the front lines."

"Dad, I'm not even in uniform."

"Yet." His father hunted for a chair and eased into it, slowly, like he was afraid his bones would break apart and he'd clatter like a discarded marionette to the floor. "This war is going to take so many from us, and I don't want it to be you. I don't understand why you're doing this."

His mother patted his arm. He glanced at her touch, then met her eyes. The mucus film seemed to have lifted from them and they studied him with a piercing sharpness he hadn't seen in a long time.

"Be careful, son. And give my regards to Makiko when you see her."

11

June 1944

Robert wondered how any place could be so dry and yet so humid at the same time. Having perspired through the starch in his khakis, his uniform clung to him like damp rags. Sweat trickled from under his service cap and he wiped his temples with a handkerchief.

Thankful for his aviator-issue sunglasses, he gazed across the airfield, at the rows and rows of parked airplanes shimmering in the heat like mirages strewn across the flat prairie.

The sky trembled from dozens of B-24 Liberators lumbering above. One flew directly over him and for an instant, its broad wings blotted out the afternoon sun. Ground crews jokingly referred to the big airplanes as aluminum overcast.

He was done for the day, having just landed from his training mission. A six-wheeled Dodge truck waited beside his B-24 to take the crew back to squadron operations, but first they had to complete the post-flight inspection and debriefing with the instructor. On account of an appointment with the squadron commander, Robert had to leave early. He looked around for another vehicle to bum a ride but none were close by. Since the appointment was in twenty minutes, he had no choice but to grab one of the airfield bicycles scattered about.

He wondered what the old man wanted. These career brass hats loved mystery. Robert never knew if they offered good news or bad news. Maybe they would be passing along word about his mother. Last time he had talked with his father, she seemed okay, considering she was only getting worse, day by day. Maybe she had passed on.

Or maybe the roster for Duty Officer had changed and instead of accompanying his buddies on a three-day pass to Lincoln, he was going to spend the weekend twiddling his thumbs beside a battery of telephones in headquarters.

He hoped the duty roster hadn't changed. He had been looking forward to time away from this dog patch of a military post. Bruning Army Airfield, Nebraska, II Bomber Command. 510th Army Air Force Base Unit.

Before the war: Bruning, population five hundred. Maybe...when the fair was in town. Then with the start of the war, seemingly overnight—as happened in countless locales all over the U.S.—fleets of military trucks convoyed here and within weeks, a city of wooden barracks sprawled across the arid emptiness.

Now that America had marshaled its people and industrial might, and sent a million fighting men into this terrible war, the tide had at last turned. Earlier this month, the Allied armies had landed in Normandy. Rome had been retaken. In the Pacific, the U.S. had invaded New Guinea and pried yet more islands from Tojo's grasp. The Philippines were next. The American military was grinding forward on all fronts.

But the end of the war was still far from certain, and many more thousands of Americans would die to secure that peace.

Robert hadn't shirked from hoisting himself to the task. What kept him from getting deployed sooner was that he'd been too good a pilot. Once posted to B-24s, he was groomed as an aircraft commander, and with that came the responsibilities of honchoing a crew of ten and melding them into a team of flying warriors.

A trio of AT-6s cruised above. Beyond them, a formation of twin-engine types, too far away to identify the type. The sky was so crowded with airplanes it looked like migration season.

A deuce-and-a-half rumbled past him toward a row of P-47s, the truck's tires lifting dust from the dirt trail worn into the flat grass. A placard on the side read: DANGER AMMO; it was probably delivering fifty-caliber ammunition for gunnery training.

Above the horizon, a gaggle of B-24s queued up to land at the far end of the main runway. Although Robert had worn his pilot's wings for a year now, he remained fascinated with aviation in all its forms and venues. He imagined himself in the cockpit of the first Liberator as it wallowed toward the ground like a reluctant goose. The spinning propellers from its four engines caught the sunlight and gleamed like silver disks. He mimed instructions as if he were the instructor pilot evaluating the crew. *Line up on the runway. Wings level. Flaps ten degrees. Airspeed steady at 160 knots. Trim for crosswind. Gear down and locked. Ball turret retracted. Cowl flaps closed. Intercoolers open. Booster pumps on. Superchargers set and locked.*

The first bomber touched down on the concrete, dirt puffing from beneath its fat rear tires. The nose wheel settled with another chirp of dust. As soon as the B-24 reached the end of the runway, the second bomber in line skimmed its wheels across the threshold. To a new bomber pilot, the ten-second intervals seemed recklessly quick and intimidating, but overseas, with squadrons of aircraft returning to base after a mission—damaged, low on fuel, and with wounded aboard—urgency was a priority.

Robert became aware of the passing of time and checked his watch. Now he had fifteen minutes to make his appointment. Hurriedly, he selected a bicycle from a pile and climbed on. He screwed his service cap tight to keep it from being blown loose by a sudden breeze or by a fighter pilot beating up the airfield in an unauthorized high-speed, low-level pass. He pointed the bicycle toward the distant airfield headquarters complex and started pedaling, the fierce sun beating down on him.

In the weeks after Pearl Harbor, he had volunteered for pilot training and chose the Army Air Force. At every turn in his training it was another roll of the dice about what he'd fly, where he'd go. He could have been shuttled to pilot cargo planes, most likely C-47s or C-46s. Or gotten B-25s, B-26s, A-20s. If he had been assigned to B-17s, then Europe would have been his destination. But as he'd been tapped to fly B-24s, the chances were even-Steven, Europe versus the Pacific.

Maybe, the squadron commander would be informing Robert that he'd been reassigned to one of the big new B-29 Superfortresses. That would mean the Pacific for sure. But he didn't know how flying a B-29 could help the Asakawas or

Kaito, since being at the controls of that heavy bomber meant he would be raining destruction on their heads. It was a scenario he tried not to think about.

He circled through the gravel parking lot in front of the headquarters building. Amid the rows of sedans and coupes painted OD, he spotted a Chevy Fleetline Aerosedan, conspicuous because of its navy-gray color. He steered the bike behind the hangars and between barracks. Signs and painted rocks marked boundaries between different units and commands.

Reaching the area for his training squadron, he dismounted and stashed the bicycle in a heap of other bikes. If he was going to see the commander, he had better look presentable even if he had just spent three hours wilting in the sweatbox of a cockpit.

His shoes...well...they looked like they had been on the flight line climbing in, on, and around his airplane. He crouched and spit on one shoe. With his handkerchief, he wiped off dust and buffed out the worst of the scuffs, then repeated the process with the other shoe. Standing, he checked himself in a nearby window, adjusted his tie, his gig line, and ran the cuff of a sleeve across the brass buckle to buff it up a little. Lastly, he checked that his pilot's badge was in place, that the end of the pin hadn't fallen loose so that his wings dangled like a limp windsock.

He stepped through the entrance to squadron headquarters, removed his sunglasses, and tucked his hat under his left arm.

The commander's orderly, a corporal, sat behind a desk and banged at a typewriter. A Negro sailor in a white jumper sat backwards in a chair next to him. Both men smoked cigarettes and were chuckling at some joke. When the men noticed Robert, the sailor pushed away from the chair and rose to his feet. The orderly stopped typing and removed the cigarette from between his lips. "Can I help you, sir?"

Robert said, "I have an appointment with Colonel Garza." He was certain the sailor was the driver of the gray sedan outside, but the question was, what was the Navy doing here?

The orderly glanced at a clipboard beside the typewriter. He tapped his cigarette over an ashtray and resumed typing. "Go right in, sir." The sailor sat back down.

Robert walked around the orderly's desk to a door stenciled, "Lt. Col. Emmanuel Garza, Squadron Commander." He smoothed his hair and knocked on the door.

A voice answered, "Come in."

Robert opened the door and marched in. Garza waited behind his desk, wearing khakis. A receding hairline drew attention to the widow's peak on his prominent forehead. A trim pencil mustache looked like a painted line across his upper lip. A row of service ribbons, *fruit salad*, occupied the space between his command pilot wings and the left breast pocket. Among his decorations were the Distinguished Flying Cross and a Purple Heart. He had paid his dues in this war.

A second officer in khaki sat beside Garza. His leathery, ruddy cheeks peeled from a sunburn. Gold aviator wings identified him as a Navy pilot. He wore silver oak leaves as did Garza, but these were different, the Navy version.

Robert halted smartly three steps from the colonel's desk and saluted. "Captain Campbell reporting as directed, sir."

Garza saluted in return. "At ease, Campbell." He pointed to his left, at the Navy officer. "This is Commander Gerald Miller. U.S. Navy."

Miller stood abruptly and reached to shake Richard's hand. "A pleasure." Miller's grip was firm, his hand calloused. He had the compact build of a wrestler. He returned to his chair.

"Equally, sir." Robert considered Miller and Garza and what they wanted from him. The military could be maddeningly circumspect about revealing information, from the most grave to the most trivial. But Robert took comfort with the fact that if a naval officer was here, that meant this meeting didn't involve breaking unfortunate news about his mother.

Garza flipped open a personnel folder on his desk and let his eyes drop to the first page. "I should be angry with you, Campbell."

Robert felt his shoulders tighten. *What have I done wrong?*

Garza nodded to Miller. "The commander brought me this information about you." Garza tapped the folder and raised his eyes to Robert. "I want to know why you didn't declare your facility in Japanese when you listed your relevant military skills."

Robert hunted for a reply that he could easily explain. "I wanted to fly, sir," he responded. "I felt that if I declared my fluency in Japanese, I would've been pigeon-holed doing intelligence work. I wanted to contribute more."

Garza suppressed a chuckle. "There are a lot of men who would give good money for a posting where all they did was read the enemy's mail."

How could Robert have answered? *It's about a Japanese girl.* While he was thinking about the Asakawas, what he saw in his mind was Makiko's pretty face. So what if she was Japanese? The differences between them were a function of geography, not politics. But the truth was, even if Makiko and her family had been in the U.S., it was doubtful he could've seen them anyway. They'd be stripped of their property and locked away in an internment camp, branded as enemies regardless of their true loyalties.

Miller asked, "Do you remember Warren Simmons?"

A roly-poly face came to mind. "He was an editor at the *Daily Tribune*. In Chicago."

"I got your name from him," Miller said. "He and I met last month when I was at the Glenview Naval Air Station."

Miller paused and in the silence, with both sets of the senior officers' eyes fixed on him, Robert felt obligated to say, "Yes, sir. I know where that is."

"He works there part time as a civilian translator," Miller explained. "In passing I mentioned to him that I was looking for a bright young man for my outfit. Someone fluent in Japanese. Someone...American. At the time I thought it was wishful thinking. Anyone with those credentials would've been snapped up by the war effort. Then he suggested your name on the off chance that you hadn't yet been drafted."

Robert braced for bad news.

Miller smiled warmly. "He couldn't say enough good things about you. Judging by examples of your work for the *Tribune* that Simmons shared with me, you're easily a superior translator compared to anyone I've yet run across."

Robert gulped. He was nervous about what Miller wanted and nervous that he was showing that he was nervous. As the pilot commander of a B-24, he was expected to be the epitome of cool under the worst kind of pressure.

"Relax, captain." Miller fished a packet of Lucky Strikes from a breast pocket. "It's no secret that we're closing the noose on Japan. Any day now, Superfortresses will begin bombing Tokyo. Hell, they've already hit the steelworks at Yahata. Aircraft carriers are also launching attacks. By the end of next year, the Marines and the Army will be hitting the beaches of the Japanese mainland."

Robert clenched his teeth. By that time, most of Japan would have been smashed to ruins.

Miller offered a smoke to Garza, who refused. He held the cigarettes out to Robert, who also turned them down. Nonplussed, Miller dug into a trouser pocket for a lighter and lit a cigarette, puffing clouds of smoke as he did so. "Our boys have sacrificed a lot and in the process, we've flattened mountains." The commander smiled at Robert, proud at what destruction the Navy had heaped on the Japanese.

Robert didn't see any great victory, only Makiko holding her red Shiba Inu, waiting for him, or for the terrible end, whichever arrived first.

Miller released a jet of smoke. "What's the matter, captain? You're looking a little green in the gills."

"It's because I don't know what you want from me, sir." Robert glanced at Garza, hoping for a clue. But the colonel only steepled his fingers and rocked back, judging him.

"I've worked hard to get this far," Robert said, "and I don't want to be robbed of my chance to do my share."

Miller hunted for a place to flick ash from his smoke. Garza pushed a tin can to the corner of the desk. Miller dumped the ash and said, "Belay your worries, Campbell. One of the quandaries in this war is getting the services to share information on a timely basis. To streamline our operations, and most particularly, to expedite intelligence to the appropriate headquarters, I've been tasked to organize a special composite, air-reconnaissance unit. Our job will be to collect intel on Japanese defenses as we prep for the invasion. We'll be flying Privateers, the Navy version of your Liberators. While the ground crew will all come from the Navy, half of the aircrews and the operational staff will be Army Air Force, the rest, Navy. This is theater command's way of ensuring that all the interested parties have a finger in the pie."

Robert stared at Miller, who after a long drag on his cigarette asked, "Do you understand what I'm asking?"

Robert nodded. "Yes, sir. You're offering me a position in your unit. But as what?"

"As a pilot. Or a co-pilot. In any case, you'll have your hands on the aircraft's controls."

"And my Japanese?"

Miller exhaled smoke. "Your primary duties will be helping us analyze Japanese radio traffic. Some will be from recorded transmissions. Others while you're airborne. You're going to give us the edge we need."

"Before you accept," Garza rested a hand on the personnel folder, "I have orders posting you to the 98th Bombardment Group, Fifteenth Air Force."

Italy, Robert thought. *A long way from Japan.*

Robert at last smiled. He had to acknowledge the irony. All this time he'd kept his knowledge of Japanese a secret lest it sidetrack him. Now that his secret was out, it was taking him exactly where he felt he had to go.

"So it's my choice?" he asked.

"Not really," Garza replied, smugly. "It's the needs of the service, but I thought I'd give you the courtesy of at least going through the motions of making the decision."

Robert squared his shoulders. He stared at Miller, then at Garza. "Sir, I'll go with the Navy. To the Pacific."

12

July 1945

"What do you think?" Commander Miller asked.

Robert bent close to the stereoscope and peered at the twin black-and-white images beneath the lenses. He and the commander were in the photographic interpreter's office, inside the wing's heavily guarded reconnaissance processing center on Okinawa. Two petty officers from fleet operations watched. Outside, the air rumbled from dozens of aircraft as the business of war continued. Even before the entire island had been secured, SeaBees and Army engineers wasted no time bulldozing new airfields and laying acres of Marsden Matting.

Robert heard the rustle of cellophane. Miller had retrieved a packet of Lucky Strikes from his shirt pocket. He fumbled with the pack, nervous, frustrated, because smoking was forbidden in the office. One errant match and weeks of crucial intelligence material could go up in flames. Normally, the old salt acted as if nothing in the war bothered him, but on the eve of every combat mission he tended to smoke like there was no tomorrow—because there might not be.

Miller commanded a unit of PB4Y-2s: VD-151, Heavier-than-Air Reconnaissance Squadron One-Fifty-One—the Black Crows—with the mission of electronic warfare: detecting and disrupting the enemy's radio and radar. The outfitting of troublesome top-secret gear in the bellies of the big Privateers had delayed the squadron's deployment to the Pacific by half an aggravating year, and Miller was itching to make up for lost time.

"Well?" he asked, still crackling the cellophane.

Robert's eyes wandered across the image. The stereographic effect gave the illusion of three dimensions and aided in sifting through the ground clutter. Even though a technician had earlier written "Yokohama" in white ink across the bottom of the photos, Robert had no trouble recognizing the coastline and the wharf...what was left of it, anyway. Now months into combat, he had made himself numb to the sight of familiar landmarks and neighborhoods blasted to rubble. Baseball stadiums, some of which he had played in, with their easily discernible fields were common aiming points for bombing attacks. He tried to forget the memories.

But this time he wanted to maneuver the stereoscopic image to its most northern edge and see how close the war had come to ravaging the neighborhood of his early youth. Mercifully, the image didn't extend beyond the downtown ward, many blocks away.

While Miller had tapped Robert for his Japanese language skills, in the last few weeks Robert hadn't done much with them, other than eavesdrop on radio transmissions while on patrol or translate captured enemy technical documents. He spent many hours doing what he was doing now: staring in dismay at pictures of a modern Armageddon.

Feeling the prodding gaze of his commander, Robert focused his attention to the center of the image. The squadron's priority was to find evidence of Japanese radar and then assign surveillance missions to verify the existence of such radar. Once that was done, headquarters would task bomber or fighter units to home in on the radar units and destroy them.

On the street between two buildings (where his father had first bought him yokan) he spied a rickrack outline, the telltale shadow of a radar dish antennae but of a design he hadn't seen before. "I see an antennae but I don't recognize the radar type." Robert looked up from the eyepiece.

"What you're looking at is an Army Tai-Chi Mark 24," Miller explained. "It's one of the newest sets, mobile, and can detect both airborne and sea targets. That will greatly improve their ability for advance warning of an invasion. The Jap army has been deploying them along the coasts."

Miller jammed the Lucky Strikes back into his pocket. "I got to hand it to these bastards," he said with begrudging admiration. "For all the pounding we've been giving them, they keep cranking out new weapons and gizmos. Each new radar is a bit more advanced than the previous model. We can't afford to rest on our laurels until the last damn Nip cries uncle or falls dead."

The problem was, the Japanese didn't surrender so that meant kill them all. Other armies beat their chests about fighting to the last bullet, to the last man, but only the Japanese clung to that suicidal philosophy. German prisoners of war numbered in the hundreds of thousands, Japanese in the hundreds, most of them starving, living skeletons too weak to fight. The Japanese sacrifices became more desperate the closer the Americans advanced on the home islands. Fleet headquarters wouldn't admit this, but kamikazes were the deadliest weapon the enemy had yet unleashed against American ships. And despite the already horrendous toll of soldiers and sailors, the enemy still retained a deep reservoir of men willing to lay down their lives for the Emperor.

"You lived here, right?" Miller pointed to the stereographs.

"Close by," Robert admitted. "But I can't get my bearings," he lied. "That was a long time ago and much has changed. Aside from the damage."

"Do you remember anyone from back then?" This was the first time Miller had broached the subject.

"A few," Robert answered.

"So we're killing your former neighbors." Miller regarded Robert. "Hell of a thing, war, isn't it?"

"I try not to think about it." He remembered Yumi's admonition that all life was precious. And here they were massacring their fellow humans with less regret than stepping on a spider.

Miller said to the petty officers, "We're done." One of them gathered the stereograph and tucked it into an envelope stamped SECRET. Miller gestured to the door, and he and Robert stepped outside. They paused between two Quonset huts in an area marked with a placard: SMOKING. Mounds of cigarette butts filled gallon-sized tin cans.

The afternoon sun hovered low over the mountainous, serrated horizon. On the other side of the barbed wire perimeter enclosing the intelligence center, their Privateer waited for tonight's mission. A Corsair was parked alongside, its cowling removed. Ground crew clustered around both aircraft like worker bees tending to their queens.

Miller checked his watch and fished the cigarettes from his pocket. Robert checked his watch as well, an Army Air Force issue Elgin A11. They had a half hour before evening mess, then pre-flight their airplane, attend their final mission briefing in operations, followed by takeoff. They should arrive over Sagami Bay at one in the morning.

Miller struck a match and lit a Lucky Strike. "Robert, let me share a secret."

Robert pricked his ears. The commander was not one to open up about anything, so what he was about to share had to be noteworthy.

"My family's original name was Mueller. That's right, German."

The Corsair's engine coughed to life and its roar echoed over them. Miller and Robert turned their backs to the din. Miller raised his voice. "My grandfather anglicized it during the First World War. You can imagine I still have plenty of kin in the old country. The bombing of Cologne, Hamburg, Berlin, has probably wiped most of them out. For their sake it's good that the Nazis finally threw in the towel, though I'm sure the misery will continue for a long time."

Miller's admission surprised Robert. The commander had always been a charge-forward-don't-look-back kind of a man.

He had never lost a moment in introspection. Robert didn't know how to respond so he said simply, "Like you said, sir. War is a hell of thing."

Miller puffed hard on the cigarette, drawing the ember halfway down its length, as if he wanted to consume the entire thing with one breath. He released the smoke in a long blast from his lungs.

The Corsair's engine died in a gasp and for a moment, the silence seemed unreal.

Miller glanced about and leaned close to Robert's ear. "You didn't hear this from me, but I got a whiff of a rumor from operations. Based on the reception our boys received here on Okinawa, the upper brass has estimated American casualties for the invasion of Japan as *one million men*. God knows what they predict for the Japanese. This last fight is going to be a bloodbath that will make every other battle of the war—Midway, Normandy, Leyte Gulf, hell even Stalingrad—look like a goddamn misunderstanding."

Miller took a final drag from his cigarette. "Our job is far from over, captain. We shirk from our duties, and too many good men will die."

***

The Privateer's four Pratt & Whitney engines droned relentlessly, reassuringly.

Robert peered out the co-pilot's side windows. The world was layered in shades of dark grays, the sky a dome of black velvet pierced with stars. Ghostly clouds outlined the horizon.

An oily black sea reflected the glint of the stars and the thin blade of a crescent moon.

He thought of Job 10:21. *A land of darkness, as darkness itself; and of the shadow of death, without any order, and where the light is as darkness.*

The darkest, most forbidding of the blackness was the land, a ragged, torn outline that bounded the water. As they trolled for enemy radar, their course had taken them over Sagami Bay and straight up Tokyo Bay. Within the last few months, B-29s had incinerated square miles of city across southern Japan. What remained was shrouded in a blackout.

Miller clasped the control wheel. His face shined with a dim glow from instrument lights and the fluorescent panel lamp. The radar repeater mounted on the center of the instrument panel illuminated the ground's contours for navigation. Though the navigator was responsible for keeping them on course, Miller kept track with the chart spread across his lap.

Robert sat to Miller's right, in the co-pilot's seat. Besides helping fly the big Privateer, Robert's job was to monitor the instruments and translate when the radiomen patched him into a Japanese radio transmission.

Behind Miller and Robert, across the rest of the flight deck, sat the engineer and one of the radiomen. And behind them, the forward dorsal gunner rotated his turret to scan for enemy interceptors. Three men occupied the nose compartment: the forward turret gunner, the navigator, and the second radioman, who also operated the special electronics.

The Privateer's crew of twelve kept quiet. Miller didn't put up with chitchat, but no matter; the anxiety pressing upon the men kept them wrapped tight.

Someone keyed a mike, and the buzzing over the interphone interrupted the nervous ennui. "Checkpoint 22," Paulson the navigator announced.

Miller and Robert glanced at the radar repeater. It showed the outline of the coast. They were now over dry land. Miller read the instrument clock and penciled a tick mark on his chart. Robert scanned the fuel gauges and compared them to his estimates. They were right on, and he said, "Fuel, check."

Miller gave a thumbs up. He started a bank to the left to fly directly over Tokyo. Tiny, random lights flickered below them, too scattered and too small to be of any concern.

They flew at nine thousand feet, well above machine gun and 20-23mm automatic cannon fire. Larger antiaircraft guns could reach them, but not at night, not firing blindly. The enemy needed searchlights or radar to pinpoint their targets, and tonight the Japanese appeared to be playing coy.

Minutes passed. They approached Checkpoint 17, a large bridge over the Tone River in Saitama. Miller again turned and headed southwest, toward Yokohama and the last sighting of the Tai Chi radar unit.

They droned on for more long minutes when one of the radio operators called over the interphone. "I've detected the signal for the Tai-Chi radar. It swept us but didn't lock on."

Miller replied. "Thanks, McPhearson. Well, they know we're up here. Everybody, keep your eyes peeled. The radar may have passed our location to night fighters. Emery,

Philips—" the gunners in the waist blister turrets— "stay alert for an interceptor sneaking under our belly."

"Roger," the gunners acknowledged.

"McPhearson," Miller said, "did you get a fix on the radar?"

"Negative, skipper. It went on, then off."

"Let's see if they ping us again." Miller banked the Privateer to the right, on a northwest course. When the airplane rolled wings level, Harold said, "They're painting us. I've got a good read. Bearing two six eight off our nose."

Miller passed the controls to Robert so he could refer to his chart. "The radar seemed to have moved further east. Unless it's another set." Miller took back the controls and banked left, after the radar. He dipped the nose to lose altitude and gain airspeed. "Are they still tracking us?"

"Just blinked off," McPhearson replied. "They know we're on to them."

Robert reflected how the roles between them and the enemy radar flipped back and forth like a game of hot potato. Hunter, prey, hunter, prey. The loser dies.

He gazed out the windshield, then to his rows of instruments, to the orange face of the repeater, to Miller. Robert's guts clenched, and his mouth went dry like he'd swallowed dust. He fumbled for a canteen and slaked his thirst.

Miller adjusted the throttles and began a climbing turn to the right. *About time*, Robert thought, worrying that flying at any one altitude in any one direction only let the antiaircraft guns draw a bead on them. Miller leveled at ten thousand five hundred feet.

"Skipper," McPhearson said, "I've got another sweep. Bearing two nine four. I've got a good fix on the map."

"Mark it," Miller said. "Let's get the hell out of here. We'll follow the coast back to Sagami Bay and see what else we can find."

An explosion bucked the aircraft. The blast dazzled Robert. Another explosion slammed into the Privateer. The antiaircraft guns had found them.

Heat slapped Robert, followed by the rush of outside air. Red warning lights blazed on the instrument panel. Panic surged over him, and he instantly sloughed it off. Without hesitation, Robert grabbed his control wheel and looked at Miller.

The commander slumped in his seat harness, headset askew. Robert shouted and grabbed Miller's right arm. He didn't respond. Robert beat his hand against Miller's chest and discovered that the commander's Mae West rubber vest had been shredded. Robert withdrew his hand and it was slick with blood.

The Privateer groaned like a wounded animal and began to yaw and pitch. Robert's stomach rose in his belly as if he were in a falling elevator.

If Miller needed help, he had to wait. Right now, Robert had to control the aircraft before it thrashed itself to pieces. The radio compass spun right-left-right. Staring at the attitude indicator as he worked the rudder pedals and control wheel, he wrestled the flying beast to hold steady, wings level, nose pointed at the horizon. Altitude, nine thousand feet. The instruments showed both port engines were on fire. His eyes cut to the pilot's windows and saw them painted with yellow flame.

Robert yelled to Hayes, the flight engineer. "Engines one and two, fuel off!"

Hayes didn't reply. Robert mashed the interphone button and again shouted. Maybe Hayes was wounded or dead, or maybe the interphone had been severed.

He glanced behind him. Sparks and flames silhouetted the crewmen scrambling in the smoke-filled flight deck. Strips of the airplane's aluminum skin fluttered from holes in the shrapnel-riddled fuselage. Robert yelled to his men but the wind buffeting the cockpit swallowed his words.

No matter, Robert had to keep the Privateer from burning and exploding. He feathered the propellers of the stricken engines and shut off the booster pumps. He opened the cowl flaps and yanked the release valves of the fire extinguishers. The fire out the port window dulled to orange and faded. According to the temperature gauges the engines were still raging hot, but at least the flames were out.

The altimeter's needle dropped past eight thousand feet. With two engines gone the Privateer was sinking. The port wing dipped, and the airplane began a slow bank to the left, toward the bay. Maybe, with luck, if he arrested the loss in altitude they could reach the Pacific Ocean and ditch close to an American ship. The other two options were to bail out over Japan and fall right into their hands, or stay with the airplane until it crashed.

Someone grabbed his shoulder. It was Paulson, his overalls shiny with blood. He shouted, voice cracking, "Hayes, Alvarez, Smith, they're dead. Emery and Phillips are pretty tore up."

"What about Johnson and McPhearson?" The two crewmen in the nose compartment. "Beardsley and Evans?" The gunners in the aft dorsal and tail turrets.

"Bleeding, shaken but okay."

Paulson let go of Robert and examined Miller. Grimacing, Paulson turned back to Robert and shook his head. Four dead out of the crew of twelve.

White tracers arced past the airplane's nose. The Privateer had lost enough altitude to put it in range of smaller antiaircraft guns that now used its smoldering outline as an aiming beacon.

A string of detonations hammered the fuselage. Robert locked his muscles as if the exploding antiaircraft shells were punches directed right at his guts. The aircraft bucked and renewed its slow roll to the left. Paulson latched onto Robert's seat to keep from toppling.

Robert braced his feet and heaved against the wheel to straighten the wings. But the airplane circled from the bay and back around toward the mountains northeast of Yokohama. Smoke seeped from under the instrument panel, and it brought a pungent odor that added to the terror.

He read the instruments and decided the aircraft was doomed. Two engines burned to junk, two engines straining to keep the Privateer aloft. Fuel and oil pressures dropping. They were in a three-way race between being shot down, blowing up into a fireball, or smashing into the earth. For years he had dreamed of returning to Japan, and his plans had instead coiled like a treacherous snake to strangle him. How did he ever think it possible that he could return to Makiko in the middle of this war? What about her parents and Kaito? But he couldn't muddy his thoughts with self-pity; as aircraft commander he had to save the crew.

"Paulson," he yelled, "make sure the radio codes are destroyed. Then tend to the crew and get them ready to bail out."

Paulson slapped Robert's shoulder, "Aye, aye," and turned around to leave.

Robert advanced the throttles of the starboard engines, pushing their tachometers toward the red, sacrificing the engines to buy altitude and time.

He doubted Smith had managed a distress call. As far as the squadron would know, this airplane had vanished. He re-engaged the autopilot to help fly the airplane. Hesitantly, he let go of the control wheel to mash the IFF Destroy buttons. The autopilot—George—didn't falter. Robert opened the bomb bay doors. The airplane buffeted and slowed. He pushed the Auto-Destruct button for the electronics in the bomb bay and pulled the Jettison handle. The airplane bucked upward with the loss of weight. The engines strained and the altimeter lingered at five thousand seven hundred feet. The nose pointed on a bearing of 331 degrees. Reluctantly, Robert reached to the pilot's side of the center console and placed his hand on the alarm button. This was it. Their survival depended on the mercy of a pitiless enemy. He pushed the button six times. Six sharp trills to alert the crew to prepare for bailout.

The engines hiccupped. For an instant he feared losing them, but they seemed to have found their second wind.

Robert began Psalm 23:4, a scripture recited so often during the war that he was surprised it hadn't been worn out. *Yea, though I walk through the valley of the shadow of death, I will fear no evil: for thou art with me; thy rod and thy staff they comfort me.*

He punched the alarm on a long steady tone. *Everyone, bail out!*

More smoke rolled from beneath the instrument panel. Then flames. Robert held the airplane steady for a ten count. A tongue of white heat lashed across the cockpit, singeing his face and hands. Sparks scorched through his overalls and he slapped his clothing to keep them from burning.

The engines wheezed as if to warn him that they had done their all. Slowly, Robert released the control wheel. George was in charge now. Robert tossed aside his headset; the roar of the dying engines and the shriek of the wind lashed his ears. He unfastened his seat harness and climbed free of his seat. As he staggered to the rear of the flight deck, his parachute pack bounced against his back. Smoke stung his eyes. All the men were gone. Paulson had probably hoisted the dead out and let them parachute to earth. It was too late to give Miller that courtesy.

Robert ducked under the forward dorsal turret and through the hatch in the bulkhead aft of the flight deck. The roaring wind tore at his clothes. Blinking the smoke from his eyes, he groped onto the walkway over the bomb bay.

An uncertain mosaic of forbidding land scrolled between the open bomb bay doors. Loose wires and cables whipped spastically against the inside of the empty bay. He jerked the straps of his parachute harness until it fit snug. Grasping a length of structural tubing, he positioned himself at the rear of the bay, looking into the void. He took a deep breath and tensed his legs. He sprang forward and curled into a ball as he fell.

The Privateer bucked in its death throes. The fuselage pitched and slammed its belly against Robert, twenty-five tons of disintegrating airplane colliding with a one hundred seventy-pound man.

13

July 1945

Thirst. The sensation overwhelmed Robert as he regained consciousness.

Robert couldn't remember being this thirsty. His throat was so parched, swallowing was like grinding broken glass.

He was lying on his back, mind swimming in confusion. Where was he? What had happened to him? He flexed his legs to sit. Barbed pain shot up his right hip. When he placed his hands on the ground, his fingers stung like he had pressed them against hot metal, and he jerked them away.

The misery was too much. He let go trying to figure out where he was and returned to his delirium.

Hazy, jumbled memories flashed through his brain. The chaos on the Privateer. Fire. Smoke. Shrapnel ripping through the airframe. Instrument needles dancing as the engines failed and the big airplane wallowed in its death throes. His arms straining at the controls. Desperation. Men scrambling through the cramped hatchways. Fear. The night-shrouded earth yawning before him. A leap downward. The slap of the wind. Something slamming into him like he'd been hit by a bus. Then being lifted and floating through the air like a bubble.

Then...then...

Robert cracked open his eyes and through the blur of eyelashes regarded an expanse of blue above him. Daylight. Clouds. The sky seemed so familiar, so serene. He could have been back in Oglesby, Illinois, with the Rollins brothers. They'd be staring at the sky from the bank of the river, a stringer of fish beside them. Or he'd be lying on the grassy commons at Northwestern University. Or in the dugout with his baseball teammates.

But he wasn't. The thirst returned. Keen as a knife, cruel as the lash from a sadist's whip, reminding him of reality.

He was in Japan. Enemy territory. He closed his eyes. His mind fumbled with pieces of memory and he sorted through the puzzle as it took shape. The PB4Y-2. Lost, destroyed. Miller, Alvarez, Hayes, Smith, dead. What about Paulson? The others? Robert hoped they had safely bailed out.

He tried to pinpoint where the crew had abandoned the airplane. He imagined the Privateer tracing over the aeronautical chart. About twenty miles northwest of Yokohama was where he had sounded the alarm to order the crew to parachute out. From the time he issued the order to the moment he had jumped clear, how much time had passed? A minute? Two minutes? Three?

Three minutes at an airspeed of a hundred and fifty knots. How far had the crew scattered? Over a track of five miles? Seven? Ten?

The thirst tortured him. He groped at his clothing and took inventory. The parachute harness still bound him. The Mae West was gone. Somehow it had been ripped away. He retained his pistol belt, its small pouch with extra ammo, but his holster was empty. On the left front of the belt, he touched a pouch containing his compass. In his upper left pocket he felt the cylindrical outline of a waterproof match container. Aside from that, no canteen, no first-aid kit, no rations, no map. Nothing except thirst and pain.

Robert again tried pressing his hands against the ground to help him curl upright, to see where he was. But it hurt to extend his fingers, to put pressure against his palms. Pain drilled into his right hip, scolding him to remain flat. The best he could do was to swim through the delirium and lift his head to consider his surroundings.

He was on the side of a rocky slope studded with pine. A breeze murmured through the trees, a soothing sound incongruent with his misery. The air smelled fresh and tantalizingly moist. Water had to be close by.

The thirst, the pain from his hands, and the throbbing ache in his hip gnawed into his thoughts. Eyes fluttering closed, the sun warming his face, he sank back into a trance of despair.

The snapping of twigs teased him to semi-consciousness. Voices chattered excitedly. Footfalls approached and stopped. Shadows blotted out the sun.

A woman asked, "*Konohito ikiteru?*"

"*Wakaranai,*" another woman answered.

They were speaking in Japanese. *Japanese!* Robert pictured Hiro, Yumi, Makiko, and Kaito huddled around him. For a moment, the pain whisked from him, and he was bathed in friendship and hope.

Yes, I'm alive, thought Robert. "*Kokoni iru,*" Robert's words croaked from his lips. "*Kaette kuru to ittadaro.*"

"*Kaette kuru?*" one of the women asked. "*Nani itteruno?*"

He blinked at the two silhouettes leaning over him. "*Kaette kuru,*" he repeated. His words faded into a moan. "*Kaette kuru.*"

***

Hiro sat on a bench in the shade of a thatched-grass awning. He reviewed the list of tools needed to repair the rice paddy canals: shovels, pick axes, hoes. He would never have believed that it was possible to wear out something like a shovel, but they had. Handles splintered and broke. Rivets fell out. The metal rusted through. And replacements were rare. Because of the war, everyone had to learn how to improvise, to make do. Even tea leaves were saved and reused until the brew was nothing but tinted, flavorless water.

To spare his family from the American bombings, Hiro had brought Yumi and Makiko with him to Honshu Farming Camp 27, a collection of huts and sheds along the Tama River. Although he had never farmed rice, as a carpenter he was an experienced handyman and was put to work mending roofs, sheds, and the canals.

He set the list aside and let his gaze range beyond the bench. Their hamlet sat above the river, which flowed wide and flat across the valley toward Tokyo Bay, dozen of kilometers distant. Steep wooded hills crowded the valley, which was segmented into muddy parcels for rice fields.

Modest *nōka* homes straddled a rutted path connected to the dirt road that ran parallel to the river, which connected them to the rest of the prefecture. The river ran too fast for easy travel upstream, and every trip downstream was pretty much one-way unless you hitchhiked back on the road or in a motorboat. They had no telephone or electricity, which made the war seem far away but not far away enough.

Despite the remoteness, they found enough to eat, at least enough to dampen the pangs of hunger. Besides what they pilfered from the government rice stocks beyond their allowance, they foraged for berries and roots. They fished and trapped game and added that to their gruel. Hiro considered them all lucky for these meager provisions. In other parts of Japan, people wandered the forest like starving, abandoned donkeys and ate bark they stripped from pine trees.

People everywhere were short of food, of medicine, of clothing, of both luxuries and necessities. The rice crop had failed, depleting already diminished reserves. Life had deteriorated into a bleak, relentless march with no end in sight.

And the reason for all that misery was the war. Young men had been taken away by the tens of thousands, and few returned who were not crippled and mangled. Fleets of American airplanes roamed the skies like a plague of demons, to ravage entire cities. And still the militarists talked of victory. Of honor. Of doing one's duty for the Emperor. So much was invested to kill and die, so little invested to live. Madness.

Two thoughts kept Hiro sane. Love and hope. Love for his family. They needed him, and he needed them. And he nurtured hope, like a candle inside his heart, shining outward, promising a tomorrow without fear, without deprivation, without this constant anguish. Some day, some way, this ordeal would end.

A voice called, "Hiro. Hiro." Azusa sprinted down the path from the woods. The young teenager shouted, "We found an American."

An American? It had to be an aviator who had parachuted from his stricken airplane. Hiro eased from his stool. Aches punished his weary joints. "Where?"

Azusa stopped and panted. She carried her wooden clogs and had run barefoot. Her work blouse and monpe pants hung baggy on her slim frame. She pointed back up the path and when she caught her breath, the words tumbled out. "About a kilometer that way. Kozue and I were collecting firewood when we found him. He was still wearing his parachute. He's hurt."

"How bad?"

Azusa shook her head. "I don't know. He's got burns on his face and hands. And I think his legs might be broken."

With those injuries the American would have to be carried here. Hiro had to summon medical help, and that would take hours to arrive. He said, "Go find Nahomi and Aya." They were the two older women—war widows of the farmers drafted to fight—who leased the rice fields. "Tell them to summon the other girls." Hiro was the only man in the village, but with his arthritis was in no shape to help carry a litter.

He surveyed the interior of the shed for materials to make a stretcher. He hobbled to a stack of bamboo poles and selected a stout pair. He lacked canvas but thought he could improvise a stretcher by threading the poles through empty rice sacks.

How big should he make the stretcher? The only Americans he had known personally were the Campbells. The preacher Jack was tall and muscular, compared to the average Japanese man. If the airman was anywhere near his size, Hiro would need at least four of the strongest women to hoist the stretcher.

He turned and saw Azusa staring at him. "Why are you still here?" he scolded. "Go do what I just told you."

"He spoke Japanese," she said incredulously.

"What do you mean?"

"I mean he spoke Japanese."

"Are you sure he was an American?"

"As sure as I know you are Japanese."

Hiro pondered this revelation. "What did he say?"

"It was strange, jibberish at first. But he said, 'I'm here. I told you I'd come back.'" Azusa cocked her head in puzzlement. "What does that mean? Is it code?" Her voice softened. "Is he a spy? An infiltrator?"

"I don't know what he is, child." Hiro shooed her away. "If the man is hurt, he needs attention, so quit dawdling."

An hour later Hiro rested on a log where the path to the woods forked. He massaged his legs and waited for the litter party to return with the airman. Word of the American had electrified the village, and the workers gathered for news. Hiro asked Yumi to collect bandage materials and prepare food and tea. Makiko was still gone with her dogs, hunting food. Hiro organized the litter party, which had climbed up one fork of the path, Azusa leading them to where Kozue watched over the fallen American.

An airplane buzzed close. Hiro checked to make sure he was deep within the shadow of a maple tree. Early in the war, at the sound of an airplane, people would rush out and wave. Now they hid with almost superstitious fright because every airplane seemed to be American, and they strafed anything that caught their attention. For a moment he worried the airplane might spot the litter party, but the tree canopy was thick, and the rocky, undulating landscape provided plenty of cover.

The drone of the airplane receded, and Hiro breathed easier. He drank from a wooden canteen in his haversack.

Up the slope, branches snapped. Feet scrambled for purchase. He made out several figures clambering down the hill. They waddled side by side and leaned toward each other, burdened by the weight between them.

Megumi and Nobuko struggled with one end of the stretcher. The soles of a large pair of boots faced Hiro from the stretcher. Aya and Nahomi carried the far end. Grimacing and gasping, the party made its way along the trail. Their faces glistened with sweat and strands of moist hair dangled from their headbands. Azusa and Kozue followed, toting the olive-green parachute and harness between them. The taller of the two, Kozue also carried the airman's web belt, with pouches and a holster, draped over one of her thin shoulders and across her chest.

With a volley of whispered commands, Megumi guided the party onto the main trail, toward Hiro. The stretcher's bamboo poles sagged to contain the American's heavy frame. Even unconscious and wounded, the man was a formidable physical specimen.

Azusa fluffed the loose folds of the parachute in her arms. "Look, silk, as if we needed more." She pulled away from Kozue to stretch lengths of cord. "And rope. This we can use."

Megumi led the team to the shade around Hiro where they lowered the stretcher to the ground. Each of the women stepped away and massaged her lower back. Hiro passed around his canteen.

He leaned on his cane and studied the American. Scorch marks and burn holes marred his khaki overalls. A bandage of parachute silk was wrapped around his face, forming a mask with slits for eyes and a hole for breathing. Tufts of brown hair spilled from the top of the bandage. His hands were also wrapped in loose silk.

"Did the flier say anything?" Hiro asked.

"He's been quiet as a dead cat," Megumi replied with gallows humor.

"Did you search him?"

"We only took his harness and belt to make him comfortable." She used her sleeve to wipe sweat from her face.

Hiro saw that the holster was empty. "Where's his pistol?"

Nahomi shrugged. "I guess it's lost. None of us saw it."

Hiro noticed a gold watch on the flier's wrist. He thought about taking it, but changed his mind. He didn't need a watch and besides, it might be a treasured memento. With so much bad karma swirling because of this war, why not indulge in generosity and let the American retain this keepsake?

"What's going to happen to him?" Nobuko asked.

"He's a prisoner of war," Hiro answered grimly. "The military will do with him whatever they wish."

"What kind of a reward will we get for turning him in?" Nahomi asked.

"Plenty of cooking oil," Aya replied. "Some soap would be nice. Sugar. Tea. Maybe a wool blanket or two."

Hiro reflected that the aviator's misfortune was their gain.

Megumi narrowed her eyes at the American. "Why does he live when my husband had to die? And yet I find myself carrying him, the enemy."

Aya stroked Megumi's arm. "He has family, too. Most likely a wife he's left behind."

"Perhaps, but that doesn't ease my heartache." Megumi blotted her eyes.

The women stood silent in the cool stillness, acting reluctant to resume hauling the stretcher to the village still hundreds of meters away. The two girls, Azusa and Kozue, played a game where they whirled in a circle and tried to trap each other with the parachute cords.

After several minutes passed, Hiro said, "The village isn't getting any closer."

Megumi shot him a glare but didn't gripe because he couldn't help with the load. On her command, the women gathered around the stretcher, lifted and began the awkward trek to the village.

Yumi was waiting on a stool beside the doorway of her home. She coughed into a handkerchief. Bracing her frail body against the wall, she stood and raised her other hand to shade her face. When the litter party drew near, she stepped close and upon noting the wounded American, her expression wilted in pity.

Hiro led them through the narrow door into the *doma* of their home. Kozue dropped the web belt on a chair. She and Azusa prepared sleeping mats, and the stretcher with the airman was laid on top. Hiro tugged the bamboo poles free and leaned them in a corner.

Azusa brought a steaming teakettle and a stack of wooden cups from inside the house.

Hiro, Megumi, and the other women waited until each had a cup. They prayed for Yumi's health, and toasted each other for retrieving the airman, and added, "To the Emperor."

Makiko appeared in the doorway, face flushed from running. The strap of a satchel hung across her chest. Two Shiba Inus tugged at the leashes clasped in her hand. She stared in wonder at the airman. "I heard you found an American."

Hiro offered a half-hearted military salute. "He is our prisoner."

"Leave those dogs outside," Yumi warned, "they'll bring germs and infect the American."

Makiko rolled her eyes and cinched the leashes to a post outside the door. She returned inside and crouched beside the airman. "Bring something to cover him."

Azusa explained how she and Kozue discovered him and described the effort to carry him here.

Makiko leaned over the American and canted her head. "I need to look at his wounds." She had been a student at Tokyo Medical College and interrupted her schooling to help take care of her mother. After the war, hopefully she'd resume her studies to become a physician.

"I don't have much to help him," Yumi said. "Some balm. Some herbs."

"Why bother?" Megumi remarked sourly. "The army will take care of him. We've done enough bringing him down the hill."

"When he comes to, we should try to feed him," Makiko said.

"With what?" Megumi protested. "We've barely enough for ourselves."

Makiko reached into the satchel and withdrew a dead rabbit. "My dogs caught four. We'll manage."

"Azusa. Kozue," Hiro said. "You must go to Okutama and report to the army depot that we've found an American airman." He limped on his cane to the chair with the American's belt. He opened the pouches and fished out a compass and two magazines of ammunition. "Take these as proof. I will write a note with the details." The depot was three kilometers away, so the trip there and back would take until late afternoon. "Makiko, prepare bento boxes for them to take along."

In his plan to repair the canal, Hiro was going to have the two girls dig out mud that clogged the main sluice gate. Now he had to haggle with Megumi to have other women do that chore.

"Father!" Makiko shrieked.

Hiro pivoted on his cane to face his daughter. She was sitting back on her heels, her aspect pale with shock. Strips of stained bandages looped around the airman's exposed head. Spots on his face glistened red like raw skin inside a blister.

Makiko held a pair of metal tags on a beaded chain. "It's Robert," she exclaimed. "It's Robert Campbell!"

14

July 1945. The next day.

Makiko kept vigil beside Robert, kneeling beside him as she waited for him to wake up. In midmorning, his eyelids cracked apart. When his eyes struggled to open, her heartbeat quickened. When his eyelashes at last parted, revealing his blue eyes, she placed a hand on her chest and let herself breathe in relief.

Robert blinked as if still confused. His gaze focused on the ceiling, wandered about the room, then swiveled to her and narrowed as if he didn't believe what he was seeing.

She stroked his hair, careful to avoid stressing the tender skin of his forehead. "Robert, it's me, Makiko," she said in Japanese.

***

Makiko. The name burned through the fog of Robert's confusion. He had found her; rather, she had found him. They were together. Her hand on his chest seemed to draw the anxiety from him. His pains faded, and his heart lifted. Every shred of pessimism evaporated. He wanted to leap up and wrap her in his arms. For one beautiful moment, they were together, radiant with happiness. The years of separation vanished in a flash; there was no war, only elation and the anticipation of a wonderful life together.

But when his muscles flexed, the pain stabbed him, holding him down like cruel chains. Slowly, the optimism ebbed, replaced by a despairing reality. He was behind enemy lines and his presence here put Makiko in great danger.

"Yes, I know," he replied, also in Japanese, his voice thin.

***

Makiko expected a smile. A chuckle of surprise. Of joy. Something besides a bland appraisal of his circumstances. Her expression softened in disappointment. "Aren't you happy to be alive? And to see me?"

"Very much so," he answered with a labored rasp. "But I know where I am, and I wish I wasn't here."

Makiko lowered her gaze, agreeing that although Robert was alive and with her, the worst of his problems still loomed ahead.

"Makiko, I've dreamed for so long to see you again, but not like this." He licked his lips and tasted the shiny balm she had applied earlier. "Sooner or later, the army will come for me."

He reached for her and winced. He looked down the length of his battered body.

"You're going to heal okay," she said.

"Are you a nurse?"

"Actually, I was studying to be a doctor, but when my parents came here I had to leave school so I could be with them. Mother has tuberculosis."

"I'm sorry to hear that."

"With luck, we might have her transferred to the sanitarium in Hiroshima."

"Hiroshima," Robert repeated. The city had yet to be targeted, so it remained possibly the safest place to wait out the war. He then asked, "Where are we?" He lifted his head and sniffed. "Smells like we're in the country."

"We're in my father's house at Honchu Farming Camp 27. It's a tiny village on the Tama River."

Robert's eyes became withdrawn as if he were reading a map in his mind. "Then we're north of Yokohama?"

"On the other side of the mountains."

"Your father is here as well? And your mother?"

Makiko nodded. "Father is busy with chores. Mother is in the other room, resting. We live on a small farm. We grow rice and vegetables."

The whiskers on his grizzled jaw caught the light from the door. His hair fell over his forehead in a tousled wave. Despite his weather-beaten appearance, he looked so American. So cowboy. So Hollywood. The teenage boy she had been infatuated with had come back as a ruggedly handsome man.

During the years they'd been apart, she wondered how she would react to their reunion. Would they regard one another with curiosity and greet each other as long-lost friends? Or would they be cool and realize that despite shared memories from a distant childhood, they had little in common? But that was not the case. Her heart ached for him, and she rested her head on his chest and strained to hear his heartbeat. He stroked her hair. They were so close, and yet much separated them.

Her hands trembled, her emotions straining for release. If she tried to speak, her quavering voice would reveal too much. Her mind grasped for a distraction. Lifting her head, she said calmly, "I have something to show you." She rose from the cushion and hustled out. The door was open but a gauzy curtain hung over the threshold to keep flies out of the *doma* and offer privacy. Her two Shiba Inus lay in the shade along the house. At her approach, they stood. She untied their leashes and brought them inside, certain they would cheer Robert. Curly tails wagging, the two dogs sniffed at him.

He propped himself on his elbows. The heavy concern on his face evaporated into a grin. "Sutōkā? And who else is this?"

"Sadly, Sutōkā died two years ago. He grew tired waiting for your return." Makiko snapped the leash of the larger dog. "This is Yoshi. Sutōkā was his father." She tugged the leash of the smaller one. Swollen teats hung from its furry belly. "This is Takara. Yoshi's mother. She recently birthed two puppies."

Makiko pulled the dogs to her side as she returned to the cushion, and they lay on the edge of the comforter.

Robert's gaze strayed to a short table beside his bed, past a washbasin and towel, and fixed on a cup and teapot. "I'd like a drink. Please."

She filled the cup and held it to his lips. He slurped the tea and gulped it down. She expected him to settle back but instead he used his arm to slide the comforter off his body. The motion disturbed the dogs, and they sprang away.

Robert sat up, moving stiffly, grimacing and favoring his left hip.

"I don't think you've broken anything," she offered. "You must have jammed your hip when you jumped from your airplane or when you landed."

He acted like he wanted to massage his hip with his hand but decided against it. He regarded his bare feet and saw that he still wore his flying overalls and his watch. He noted that his boots, with the socks tucked inside, rested by the adjoining wall. Scooting off the sleeping mats and away from her, he said, "I'd like to walk around."

"It's better that you rest."

He coughed self-consciously and whispered, "I have to relieve myself."

Makiko pointed to a bedpan beside the mats.

He shook his head. "I'd like some privacy."

She stood and pulled Yoshi and Takara to their feet. "Then I have to leave."

"I prefer to go outside."

"Father says that you shouldn't."

Robert furrowed his brow. He looked to the curtain over the doorway. "Who knows I'm here?"

"Everyone in the village. It was such news when we found the 'American.' Father was going to send word about you to the garrison at Okutama. But when he learned that it was you, he decided to keep the news quiet."

"Until when?"

Makiko shrugged. "I don't know. Perhaps until you're better? Until the war ends?"

"The end of the war? I wish. But I don't see how you can manage that. Sooner or later someone will get suspicious. Someone will talk."

The truth yanked at Makiko like a snagged anchor. Robert was the enemy, and she and the village had a duty to render him to the authorities. Plus, they could use the reward from his capture. It was selfish for anyone to put the village in danger and deny them what goods they could get. Or was it more selfish to only think of themselves and not give in to this act of humanity?

She started for the door. "Use the scraps of silk I've left for you to wipe."

"Silk?"

"Paper tissue is impossible to find, but we have plenty of silk." She parted the curtain over the door. "Do your business, and I'll dispose of the bedpan."

Robert demurred, embarrassed.

"I worked in a hospital," Makiko remarked, chagrined that this American warrior was ashamed by such a simple, necessary bodily function. "I've emptied the bedpans of ministers and generals. Of my mother and father when they fell ill. Don't think what comes out of you is that special."

***

Afterwards, Robert slept for most of the day, through the night, and on the second day, during the morning, he awoke to see Hiro and Yumi on a bench facing him. A blanket draped Yumi's shoulders. She looked gaunt, her eyes anguished. She coughed into a cloth and managed a smile.

Hiro cradled a tray with a covered pot, a small teapot, and a cup. "I've brought you something to eat."

Robert sat up and looked at Yumi. "You didn't have to come see me. I would've gone to you."

"I'm not so sick that I can't make time for a good friend." She motioned to the tray. "Please, eat."

At the mention of food, Robert's stomach rumbled. Thanking Hiro and Yumi he took the tray and set it on his lap. He removed the pot's lid and steam lifted into his face. Using chopsticks, he ate rice, vegetables, and an unknown meat.

"How are Jack and Sarah?" Yumi asked.

Robert gave them a summary but wasn't sure how to approach the subject of his mother's health. Hiro and Yumi listened, nodding.

"I'm glad that when your father returned to America he was rewarded with a large church," Hiro said, his hands resting on a cane. "Jack was a good man. Strong. Forceful. I learned much from him."

"He misses you, as well," Robert said.

"And Sarah?" Yumi asked.

"Mother is not doing well," Robert replied reluctantly. "She has..." He couldn't think of the Japanese term for multiple sclerosis, so he said, "a disease of the nerves."

Yumi coughed. Hiro gripped her hand. "We will pray for her."

The bowl empty, Robert poured tea into it, swished the tea around to gather the remaining grains of rice, and drank. He set the bowl on the table. "What happened to your church in Yokohama? We did so much work to improve it."

Hiro's expression turned gray and somber. Yumi coughed again. He said, "We had to disband. But it wasn't just us. Every church of every denomination has been closed. Even the Shinto temples have been shuttered."

"Why?" Robert asked.

"Paranoia," Yumi answered caustically. "The government is afraid of anything they can't control. It's a symptom not of their strength but of their weakness. We even have a Thought Police so what's in your head is also suspect."

"Where do people worship?"

"In their homes or private gatherings." Hiro pointed with his cane to the small shrine of family ancestors in the corner of the room. A simple Christian crucifix hung on the wall above.

"How have you been healing?" Yumi asked, to change the subject.

"Getting better, thank you." Robert extended his fingers and clenched his fists and repeated the gesture to demonstrate his progress.

"Good," Hiro remarked. His expression cooled as if he was hiding something from Robert. Yumi coughed. She closed her eyes and knit her brow.

"What is it?" Robert asked.

"You can't stay here, my friend," Hiro replied. "In this house, I mean. I'm afraid the army or the police could arrive unannounced, and if they found you, it wouldn't go well for any of us. I've asked the others in the village to cooperate with me in hiding you, and they've promised, for now. But should you be discovered, I will take responsibility."

Guilt stung Robert at the thought of others punished because of him. "I will go, that is not a problem."

"You don't have to leave. We have a place for you to hide." Hiro leaned on his cane and pushed himself up. "Makiko will show you where."

Late in the afternoon, Makiko and the two teenagers, Azusa and Kozue, carried Robert's bedding to a large shed behind the house. Just in case an outsider was present, they set up a look-out so no one would spot him when he left Hiro's home.

The front of the shed housed a chicken coop. Hens and adolescent chicks scratched and poked at the dried grass and wood shavings on the floor. Feathers and down clung to the wooden bars of the cages. Makiko entered and brushed the chickens aside with her foot. They darted away, clucking in protest. The coop stank of chickens and chicken shit. The smell reminded Robert of the coops he and his friends used to raid for eggs back in Oglesby.

Makiko dragged a crate with nests on top from the back wall. She fussed with a section of boards and placed it to one side to reveal a small doorway. She was the first to duck through. Azusa and Kozue filed after her with sleeping mats and pillows. Robert handed through the door his comforter and a metal pail filled with supplies Hiro had provided, and then limp-crawled to join them.

They entered a narrow room hidden behind the false wall. The sun's last rays slanted through cracks under the eaves. In the gathering darkness, Robert counted three wooden animal crates against the far wall, under shelves heaped with empty bags for rice and soybeans and wooden boxes filled with junk. The Shiba Inus were in two adjacent crates; the third one was empty. Takara looked up from where she lay inside her crate. Two puppies suckled from her. Yoshi circled in his crate. The chicken odor from the coop masked the kennel smell.

Azusa announced, "I'll keep watch," and crawled out the door.

Keep watch? Robert thought about the secretive arrangements to enter the room. "Why are you keeping the dogs here?"

"Pets have been outlawed," Makiko replied. "Every morsel of food must go to the war effort."

"So the dogs and cats starve?"

"They don't live that long," she answered, and with those words Robert knew that family pets were now considered rations. She added morosely, "Even our cherished Shiba Inus are not spared from the stew pot."

Robert considered the shiny black eyes and the grinning countenances of the fluffy red dogs and felt ashamed. "I'm in good company," he said. "One false move and I'll also feel the knife."

Kozue left and returned with another pail, this one containing rice balls and a bottle filled with water. Robert arranged his bed in the narrow space between the door and the dog crates. Makiko filled one of the pails with dried grass for him to use as a chamber pot.

"I have to leave." Makiko attached Yoshi and Takara to a pair of leashes. "I'm taking them out for fresh air. With luck, we might bag a rabbit or two, but even those are becoming scarce. I'll return with dinner."

Robert didn't want her to leave, at least not yet. In this small room, with its chicken odor, this was the first time he had Makiko all to himself.

She was the grown-up version of the little girl he had left behind. Tall (for a Japanese) and fair, she had grown into a woman more beautiful than he had imagined. It would have been easy to forget her, or pigeonhole her memory, but she remained always in his mind, like the awareness of the coming spring. Why did he think they would meet again? Why did he think it was inevitable?

Yet it happened.

Incredibly, he found himself aching for her, and aching at cruel fate. They were together, like survivors touching fingers, each of them on their own life raft. At any moment the storm of war would yank them apart as if to mock their hopes. He fought the sadness and kept quiet as she and Kozue left with the dogs and set the door back in place. He heard them drag the crate back into position. He sat still for several moments until the ache ebbed into sadness. Carefully, he crawled to the crate with the puppies and drew them into his arms. They squirmed and nipped at him, and Robert was amazed that such wonderful little creatures could exist in a world filled with so much cruelty and hatred.

***

During the next two days, Robert did little but rest, heal, and remain as still as a mouse surrounded by cats. He listened as people passed by the shed but never caught a mention of him or the dogs. If the dogs were with him, he would stare at them, and they at him, looking resentful for not being able to run free. He could rub his hands together without them smarting. But his face remained too tender to shave. He raked his fingers over a coarse stubble and wondered if he resembled a hobo. At night he was kept company by the pain in his hip. He slept in fits, dreaming of America, of hot food and comfort, of Makiko in a place of sanctuary and peace.

At the start of the day, Makiko and one of the girls would bring him and the dogs food and water. The girl would take the pail he had relieved himself in, empty it, and return. On the second morning Makiko brought a pile of outdated gazettes, and was about to leave with the dogs to go hunting and give them exercise.

Since this was his time to play with the puppies, Robert poked at their cage. "Do they have names?"

Makiko shook her head. "Not yet. When they get a little older then we can decide on something suitable." She turned to leave but didn't.

Robert felt a mutual pull between them like their hearts were magnets. When she was gone, the anticipation of seeing her once more caused his insides to screw tight, and when she did arrive, there was a release of joy. But that joy was shadowed by the realization that he remained confined behind the chicken coop with even less freedom than the dogs.

"I want to stay," she said. "But the others are talking. It's enough of a risk for the village to keep the dogs. With you here, who knows what will happen? And they resent that I spend time with you at the expense of my chores."

Robert didn't know what to say. Neither did Makiko, and she excused herself with a weak smile.

Alone again, the ennui wore on Robert. He lost interest in the gazettes and he could only play for so long with the puppies. Fearing that if captured, he'd be stripped of every possession, he decided to safeguard his watch. The Elgin was no heirloom, but it chafed him to think it might get confiscated. He wanted at least one souvenir of his service in this war. So he stashed the watch in a hole he had dug along one of the corner posts.

That afternoon, when Makiko returned with the dogs from their second daily hunt, her expression was clouded with bad tidings.

"What is it, Makiko?"

"Sit, please," she said ominously. She cradled a shoebox.

He lowered himself on his bed mat and tried to keep his mind from flying wild after imagined fears. She knelt in front of him and opened the box. Inside stood the letters he had sent her.

"I've kept them all," she said.

He thumbed through the envelopes, recognizing his handwriting on the front of each. The stamps and postmarks brought back memories of when he had mailed them. He remembered every stroke of his pen on the paper, the taste of each envelope when he sealed it, the faces of the mail clerks when he slid the letters across the counter to be weighed and stamped. He used to worry that he had read too much into her correspondence, but this trove confirmed she had thought about him as much as he had of her.

"I've kept yours, too," he said.

"There's something else," she continued. From behind the row of envelopes she produced a small, rectangular package wrapped in silk. She unwrapped the silk to a layer of paper and unwrapped that as well. She showed Robert a framed photograph of a young Japanese sailor. He was young and handsome and gazed back at the camera with a stern expression brimming with patriotic fervor.

"Who is he?" Robert asked, though his heart already told him.

"His name was Kosuke Uchida. We were betrothed in 1943."

Robert was in primary pilot training at the time. "Oh," he said simply. He suspected that a comely woman like Makiko must have had many suitors. And she and Robert had made no promises to wait for one another. How old was she now? Twenty-five? Well into marrying age. How long did he expect her to remain alone?

"He was a wonderful man," Makiko said.

Robert felt no jealousy. If anything he pitied her for losing someone that dear to her.

She wrapped the photo in the paper and the silk. "He's dead. He was assigned to a cruiser and it never returned."

Robert didn't ask if she retained feelings for Kosuke. It was obvious that she did, and it was also obvious that she had feelings for Robert as well. Makiko remained still, the silk package on her lap.

"Psst, Makiko," Azusa called from outside. "Megumi is calling for you."

Robert placed his hand on Makiko's. "We have all lost much in this war."

She didn't lift her gaze and only responded with a curt, sad, "*Hai*." She tucked the package behind his letters and closed the box. With it in hand, she rose and crawled out of the room. The door and the crate sliding into place sealed Robert up with his thoughts.

***

The next day, Makiko brought a sewing kit and swatches of khaki-colored material to mend his uniform. After she left, Robert removed his overalls and repaired the holes and rips. As he worked the needle and thread, thoughts about Makiko tumbled in his brain.

Why was he foolish enough to think that now, during this terrible war, as a fugitive among vicious enemies, his reunion with Makiko would be like gold at the end of the rainbow? Was God toying with them? Give them what they want, but only during the worst of circumstances. Perhaps, like the fable about the genie, Robert should have been more careful about what he wished for.

He was well aware of what would happen to him as a captured airman. Torture. Starvation. Execution. Japanese officers were especially fond of beheading prisoners with their samurai swords, and for one to lop the head off an American would give him bragging rights.

His mind veered into the macabre. If he was captured, would the soldiers force Makiko to watch as they chopped off his head? Through his mind's eye, he saw the moment in all its gruesome detail. Her tearful face stretched in cries of mercy and pity. Or would she watch, stoic and hard? He would kneel, head bowed, neck arched to receive the blow. It would be a quick death, for Japanese officers prided themselves on their swordsmanship and the keenness of their blades.

Robert would feel the quick burn as his head was sliced free, then the world would tumble around him, and his head would land on the dirt, in the pool of his warm blood, and perhaps, most cruelly of all, stare at Makiko as his vision dimmed and he slipped into blackness.

His imagination got the better of him, and Robert began to sob.

As a Christian, he believed in the Bible and the Almighty, but now he had his doubts. For civilians, death was a haphazard yet inevitable fate. Everyone died, but usually old and at the tail end of life. In this war, people were butchered deliberately, wholesale. He thought back to the time when Yumi admonished him about stepping on a spider. *Who scolded God about stepping on us mortals?*

If God was the Wise and Merciful Creator, how could He, their Father, let this happen? Robert kept repeating the verse from Matthew 27:46. *My God, my God, why have you forsaken me?*

15

July 1945

Five days after he'd been shot down and taken under the protective wing of the Asakawas, Robert finally got to shave. His face had finally healed enough to let him use one of Hiro's straight razors. Robert had also washed his overalls and underclothes in a bucket and let them air-dry in the shed. Hiro brought him a kimono to wear so that he wouldn't have to lounge about naked while waiting for his clothes to dry.

Light piercing the cracks of the shed traced across the kimono's lustrous fabric. It was a luxurious garment and played up the irony that the Japanese had plenty of expensive silk but little else, especially food.

Robert spent the day doing what he usually did, pacing back and forth inside the shed, playing with the puppies, lying on his sleeping mat, and thinking. Thinking. Thinking.

Thinking about his prospects should he be taken prisoner. Escape from Japan was practically impossible. Here in the mountainous interior, he could remain undiscovered as long as the police or army didn't wander into the village. The coast was a different matter, for the Japanese military knew an invasion was forthcoming. Every yard of beach would be under surveillance, so an attempt to escape by water was courting suicide.

Robert also thought about the war. The big picture. The grand strategies in play to smash Japan. He hadn't been privy to any specific invasion plans—those would be top secret—but he knew the American juggernaut was gathering steam to launch the last great battle of the conflict.

He thought about his comrades in the reconnaissance squadron and about the executive officer writing letters of condolence to the kin of the Privateer's crew. Would Robert be counted as among the dead? No, not yet. His status would be listed as Missing in Action until they found him or his remains. This made him stew in guilt for the anguish he was causing his mother and father. He hung his head, closed his eyes, and prayed for them.

And he spent a lot of time thinking about Makiko. Finally, he was close to her, only to hide behind a smelly chicken coop like a common outlaw on the run.

He also thought a lot about food. Steaks. Hamburgers. Pie. His stomach rumbled but all he could do was wait for Makiko to bring him dinner.

When his clothes were dry, he slipped into them and tied his boots back on.

Late in the afternoon, Yoshi and Takara stood in their cages and stared at the door into the shed. Chickens in the coop clucked irritably. A moment later, the crate on the other side of the wall was dragged away and the door shunted aside.

Makiko peeked her head through the opening and crawled through.

She smiled and they exchanged greetings. She wore a fancy yellow silk blouse over dark blue short pants. In contrast to the elegant blouse, her canvas shoes were stitched and patched together to get just a little more use out of them. A satchel was draped over one shoulder, and her conical *sugegasa* dangled behind her neck.

In better times, Robert wouldn't have hesitated to draw close and show her how he felt. But these were not better times, and the circumstances from the war—the fear, the de-privations—carved a moat too wide and too deep for him to act on those feelings.

Makiko patted the satchel. "I brought us dinner. I thought that we could take a walk away from the village and go up the hill."

"Is it safe for me to walk around?"

"Would I be asking if I didn't think it was safe?"

He chuckled and spread his arms to take in the confines of the shed. "Then I would like that. If the war doesn't kill me, the boredom will."

Besides hunger and his longings for her, misgivings rang in his heart, ominous, foreboding. He knew that sooner or later he'd be discovered and taken prisoner. And the longer he stayed here, the deeper the trouble for Makiko and her family. What was the point of opening up to her and kindling those feelings if he was only to be wrenched away? And besides the anguish of losing her, what about the punishment she would receive for not turning him in?

If Makiko had similar thoughts, she wasn't sharing. She reached into the satchel and fished out a small bundle wrapped in silk. Opening the bundle, she palmed a handful of meat scraps that she fed to Yoshi and Takara. The puppies pawed at their cage and Makiko scratched their furry little heads.

She opened Yoshi's cage and he scampered out, head up, tail curled, to rub his head against her leg. After she tied the leash to his collar, she looked at Robert. "Since we're leaving, I can get you civilian clothes. If someone sees you in that uniform, they'll know you're an American."

"They'll be able to tell that by just looking at me. And if I wear civilian clothes, then I can be shot on the spot as a spy. This way," he waved at the patchwork decorating his overalls, "there's the chance I will be treated as a legitimate prisoner."

"Are you allowed to wear a hat?" Makiko pulled on the ties of her *sugegasa*.

Robert dragged a hand through the hair of his bare head. He had worn an overseas cap during the mission but forgot how and when he had lost it. "I suppose a hat would be okay."

Makiko rummaged in the shed and brushed dust from a *sugegasa* she found on a shelf. Robert tried it on and Makiko stepped close to adjust the cloth ties. Her fingers caressed his neck as she fussed with the ties, and her nurturing, delicate touch made him want to grab her hands and crush her against him. But he resisted, knowing that to give in to passion would be dangerous.

He decided to act silly. Hands on his hips, he struck a pose. "How do I look?"

"Like a rice farmer. A very tall rice farmer." Her large, dark eyes held his, and in the moment, Robert felt the spark of desire jump from him to her.

Shaking her head as if to clear her mind, she turned to watch Takara in her cage nursing the puppies. Makiko grasped Yoshi's leash and announced, "Let's go."

"One more thing," Robert said. He crouched by the corner post where he hid his watch. He swept aside the layer of dried grass and wood shavings that had drifted from the chicken coop and used a stick to dig. The watch was folded inside a scrap of cloth. He slipped it on his wrist and said, jokingly, "So we don't violate the curfew."

Makiko led Yoshi through the door and out of the coop. She set her *sugegasa* on her head and kept lookout as Robert crept out, his hat in hand. When he stood in the sunlight and away from the chicken odor of the shed, he paused for a moment to secure the *sugegasa* back on his head and to appreciate the humid fragrance from the river.

They sneaked out of the village and hustled up the trail. Robert enjoyed stretching his legs and the respite from hours of doing nothing. They were in such a hurry to reach the sanctuary of the woods that he didn't have the opportunity to look back at the village or the river. They walked at a fast clip uphill and Yoshi trotted alongside, ears folded back and his nose pointed straight ahead as if on urgent business.

"He seems to know where he's going," Robert said. "Why don't you let him go?"

"Shiba Inus are bolters. You have to keep them on a leash until you spot something for them to chase."

The trail proceeded up an uneven incline. Occasionally, Robert's boots slipped on loose pebbles. He caught himself from falling and slowed to appraise the rough, steep ground. "The women from your village brought me down this trail?"

"It wasn't the Shibas," Makiko quipped.

He shook his head in disbelief and admiration.

They continued to the clearing where Kozue and Azusa had found him. He studied the area for evidence of the exact spot where he had touched down, but didn't find anything. He stood on a large flattened rock in the center of the clearing and surveyed the tall pines around him. The clearing was about a hundred feet in diameter and half of its area was in shadow from the setting sun. Seen from this angle, the clearing appeared large enough, but from the air, and at night, it would've been an impossible target.

He had been unconscious during the descent so it was providence that he had landed here. The chances were greater that he should have snagged a tree and impaled himself on its branches. Or he could have splashed into the river and drowned. Or landed where the Japanese Army would have found him.

He kicked the rock beneath him and considered its unyielding surface. He realized that his hip hadn't hurt for days. He had jammed his hip upon smacking this rock, and again, considering that he might have broken his ankle, or leg, or hip, he thought himself very lucky.

Yoshi strained on his leash and whined.

"I think he's spotted something," Robert said. He was eager to see the dog chase and catch something.

"Not up here," Makiko said. The sun's low rays daubed her with yellow light. Whenever she moved her head, the curved shadow from her hat's brim slid up and down her face. "And not so late in the day. If I let him loose now we'll spend the rest of the night looking for him." She tugged Yoshi's leash and they resumed the hike up the hill.

The trail narrowed so they walked in single file, Yoshi at point. Robert let the gap widen between him and Makiko so he wouldn't step on her heels. He couldn't help but appreciate the muscular calves of her trim legs as they flexed and relaxed beneath the hem of her short pants. The sun disappeared below the trees and twilight gathered around them. They negotiated switchback after switchback as the trail continued without end. "Just how tall is this hill?"

"Tall enough, I suppose," Makiko replied. "Not as tall as the others and easier to climb." She added with a wink, "It was the one I thought you could handle."

Robert enjoyed the teasing, but the more they walked, the hungrier he became. They reached a rocky knoll and Makiko finally halted. She tipped her *sugegasa* back until it slipped off her head and hung behind her shoulders. Yoshi sat on his haunches. "The trail ends here." She pointed up the slope. "The summit is that way, about a hundred meters."

"This is good enough," Robert said, glad for the excuse to stop. "If anyone asks, we'll tell them we reached the top."

"Fair enough," she replied, grinning.

Robert took in the panorama before him. The bare spot on the hill faced north. From this vista, the curve of the slope and the wall of trees kept him from seeing the village or the adjacent river. But to the left and right, where the hills gave way to the flat valley, the Tama River shimmered like plates of pewter in the approaching gloom. The first stars peeked through the darkening sky and their reflections sparkled like flecks of sugar on the river's undulating surface.

Makiko tossed her *sugegasa* on the ground, then slipped the satchel off her shoulder. She looped the end of Yoshi's leash over a short gnarled stump poking from a patch of hard dirt. She squatted beside a crack in the ground about a foot wide and several feet long. Removing a quart-sized tin can from the satchel, she set it inside the crack, where it rested below the surface.

Robert watched her work. Triangular holes had been punched in the sides of the can, along the top and the bottom, and he recognized it as an improvised stove.

"Back in America," he said, "we called that a hobo stove," then explained what "hobo" meant.

Makiko stuffed paper through a square opening in the side of the can. "That's what this war has reduced us to. A land of hobos." She said this with a trace of humor, but the truth of her remark bit deep and drained the comment of its levity. "I'm going to make tea. Go find twigs and wood for the stove."

Robert took off his *sugegasa* and used it to carry the wood he collected. When he returned to Makiko she was tending to a small flame inside the can.

Orange light flickered through the can's holes, but the illumination was confined within the crack in the ground. Makiko laid out the contents of the satchel. A canteen. A small metal teapot. Two wooden cups and two wooden bowls. Chopsticks.

A bento box. She filled the teapot with water and set it on the stove.

He dumped the wood from his hat into a pile. Crouching beside her, he cracked the wood into smaller pieces.

She said, "People used to come here in the summer and spend the night. The air is cool and there's hardly any humidity. They would light fires you could see up and down the valley." She waved at the open ground, now shaded with twilight's gloom. "But that seems so long ago. Now we can't even boil water for tea without hiding."

She opened the bento box and held it to him. "I brought rice with vegetables and stewed rabbit mixed with egg." She used one set of chopsticks to scrape half of the box's contents into one bowl, then the rest into the second bowl. Yoshi perked up at the smell of a meal. The tea had finished brewing and Makiko poured it into the cups.

They sat opposite each other, the food and teapot between them.

"It's quite the banquet," he said.

"I suppose considering the circumstances," she replied, "it is."

Holding the bowls close to their chins, they plucked at their food with chopsticks, and ate. The meat portions were small but that didn't stop Robert from sharing with the dog.

"Do you think we can keep this up?" she asked. "Hiding you, I mean."

Her question brought a chill to the warm evening. "Let's count our blessings while we can. As for the bad, that will happen in its own way and so there's no point wasting time thinking about it."

They finished eating. "You wouldn't have seconds, would you?"

She upended the satchel and gave it a good shake. She looked inside and shrugged. "I think I left any extra food at home."

Of course, they didn't have any extra food, and he admired her ability to joke about that.

She doused the fire in the stove with a splash from the canteen. Night shrank around them. She tipped the can over and swirled the dying ashes with the stick.

They sat side by side facing down the slope, looking south out of the clearing, and finished what was left of the tea. The landscape was dark as the bottom of a well save for the stars' reflections on the distant river.

Through a gap in the mountains, he saw red and white dots arcing above the distant horizon. Random explosions blossomed in the night sky. Antiaircraft fire. Guessing on the direction from the hill, Robert was certain it was an air attack on Yokohama.

He read his watch by the light of the moon: 9:24 PM. Early for a night attack.

More explosions silhouetted the bottom of a billowing cloud of smoke tinted blood red. He waited to hear the explosions but the fighting was too far away.

Makiko let go a deep sigh. The distant explosions traced sparks in her glossy eyes. "Luckily, my family and I were here during the big attack on Yokohama last May."

Robert's squadron hadn't supported that mission, yet he burned with shame. "I'm sorry about this, Makiko."

"Why? You didn't start this war. We're all just doing our duty."

"I'm sorry that it's happening at all. Big men in high places make these decisions and we at the bottom pay the price."

Makiko sprang to her feet, and at first Robert thought he had offended her. She gathered the picnic items and arranged them in the satchel.

"Are we leaving?"

"Not yet," she replied. "Let's forget the war and do something else." She pulled a thin blanket out of the satchel and extended her hand to him.

Robert took it and levered himself to his feet. He gave her fingers a gentle squeeze and they squeezed back.

"What about Yoshi?" he asked.

"Leave him."

She led Robert by the hand to the periphery of the clearing, where the leaves and pine needles on the soft ground crunched beneath their feet. Along the way, Robert's thoughts floated as though unmoored from the world. Makiko glided before him, half real and half dream. Turning abruptly, she drew him close. In the darkness, her eyes still glistened, weighed with sadness, as if this moment was the most she could steal from the heartache and hardships around them.

Robert wrapped his arms around her torso and brought his hands to the back of her head. She dropped the blanket and brought her hands up to cup his head. She rose on tiptoes and this time her eyes shined brighter, the sadness gone, replaced by yearning.

Their lips met, a soft initial greeting, brushing against one another. Then their lips parted, the air holding still between them as if the world had stopped.

Then another kiss, this one deep and hot, a flame of passion. Her hands pulled at his neck while his hands traveled up and down the length of her back. They traced over her buttocks, and his fingers splayed across her taut flesh, gripping, kneading.

She let go and crouched to spread the blanket over the ground. She sat on the blanket and loosened the buttons of her blouse.

Robert sank to his knees and clutched her for another probing kiss.

Makiko melted beneath him, pulling him down, and guiding his body on top of hers.

16

July 1945

Robert and Makiko lay naked next to one another, their clothes spread about them. He pressed against her and appreciated the warmth where their bodies molded into each other. Her head rested on the biceps of his left arm. His right arm was hooked over her side, across the curve between her ribs and hip. His hand cupped her belly.

A late-night breeze murmured through the trees, and a stray current of cool air blew over him, light as a whisper. It raised goose bumps across his exposed, sweat-moistened skin.

"I can tell you're cold," she drawled sleepily. "I should have brought another blanket."

He kissed the back of her ear. "I'll manage."

"I can tell you've done this before," she whispered.

"You mean lie naked outside and freeze?"

She rubbed the back of her head against his cheek. "No, silly. I mean spend the night with a woman."

He kissed the back of her neck. "I don't want to think about them."

217

"Good," she replied firmly. "I don't want you to think of them, either."

"Deal."

Her breathing relaxed like she was falling back asleep. Then she firmed up and said, "On the other hand, if you'd never had a lover, I'd be disappointed. A woman prefers a man who knows what he's doing."

"I'll keep that in mind," he replied.

"So?"

"So...what?"

"How many?"

"Two."

"Two?" she huffed ambiguously. "Girlfriends?"

"Just women I met. When it was over, they went one way, I went another."

"Do you miss them?"

"I can't even remember their names."

She grabbed his wrist. "Will you remember my name?"

"Of course. It's Misaki, right? No, Mayumi."

She pinched the back of his hand. "You bastard."

Robert pulled his hand free. "I've gone through all this trouble just to have you talk to me this way?"

"If you don't like it, then behave yourself."

"Like this?" He set his hand on her breast.

"Mmm," she purred.

They remained silent, inhaling and exhaling until their breathing synchronized. After a moment, she shrugged free and extended her legs. Her hand drifted to his and, fingers interlaced, they rolled onto their backs.

Lacy clouds traced across the star-filled bowl of the night sky. A partial moon bathed the landscape in a silvery light.

Makiko raised her free hand and groped upward. "The stars look close enough to touch."

"I'd rather touch you."

She lowered her arm and turned her head to face him. Her large eyes reflected the gloss of the moon. "It feels odd to lay out here naked, doesn't it?"

"I'm not used to it," he said. "We'll have to try this again in a more civilized setting."

She raised her head. "Poor Yoshi, tied there all alone."

Robert sat up and looked at the dog. Yoshi lay where he had been tethered to the stump, a stoic sentinel, his furry head and back outlined by the moon's glow.

Makiko brought herself up and pressed against Robert's side, her longing pulsing into him. He draped an arm over her shoulder and drew her closer.

Robert thought about the respite from want and fear that this night with Makiko had brought. Soon the moment would be gone, extinguished like a candle's flame. They would return to the village and accept whatever bad tidings the day would bring. If not this day, then the next. Or the next. The best Robert could do was clasp tonight's memory with all its jeweled instances and tuck it deep in his heart.

He wondered if Makiko was thinking the same thing. "You're too quiet," he whispered.

"So are you," she replied. "If we're not going to talk, then we might as well keep busy doing something else." Her hand slipped over his thigh, sliding through the tangle of his pubic hair, and fondled him. Aroused, he turned on his hip to lean against her. Their lips melted together. He brought his body over hers and she parted her thighs to accept him.

The tenderness gave way to athletic heaving, their gazes locked. Spent, he collapsed on her, shuddering and gasping. She wrapped her legs around his and stroked the back of his head.

After that, the night blurred. He remembered the awkwardness as they got dressed, then the hike back to the village, Yoshi straining at his leash. One long kiss before they left the gloom of the woods and entered the village, quiet as thieves. The houses were dark, without so much as a tiny lamp to greet them. They snuck through the chicken coop and once in the shed, crumpled together in an exhausted heap on his sleeping mat, where he barely had the energy to drag a blanket over them.

***

Robert awakened with a start. He blinked at the rays of sunlight slanting through the shed. What had startled him from sleep was the bark of a man's gruff voice, the squeak of brakes, and the raspy idle of a poorly tuned motor.

He took stock of his situation. He was alone in the shed. Yoshi and Takara were gone from their cages. He checked his watch. The time was 8:22. Makiko must've taken the dogs for their morning hunt.

His stomach rumbled but his hunger mattered little. What mattered, what disturbed him, what dragged icy claws down the back of his neck, was the presence of the man and the truck. As the questions about them blossomed in his mind, his nerves buzzed with misgivings and dread.

Robert eased cat-like from his bedding and on his hands and knees approached the shed's wall. Staying low, he peeked through a crack.

An army truck straddled the road in front of the Asakawas' home. Its engine died with a cough and a rattle. His breath caught in a painful lump, and those icy claws raked deep along his spine.

Why was the army here? He fought the impulse to scurry away and escape. In the hours and days he had spent alone, he'd thought about where to hide should the army or police close in. But he knew there were no good options.

If the army was looking for him, then something about this situation didn't seem right. The fear ebbed enough for him to swallow.

Five women in drab civilian clothing sat crammed with an assortment of crates in the open bed of the small truck, not much larger than that of a Ford Model A. They looked resigned, as if they'd just been plucked from their chores and assigned a more unpleasant task. But they didn't appear like a search party hunting for stray enemy aviators.

Three soldiers wandered into view between the back of the truck and the house. At the sight, Robert tensed and his mouth turned dry as the dirt beneath him.

The soldiers were dressed in field garb with canvas webbing and cloth puttees. Two of the soldiers—boys actually— wore helmets that teetered on their heads like washbasins.

Rifles with fixed bayonets sagged from their shoulder slings. The third soldier however, with his stern countenance and mustached, leathery face, projected the demeanor of a grizzled veteran. An officer's insignia adorned the collar of his tunic and the front of his soft field cap. He carried a ledger in one hand and barked commands as women from the village formed a ragged line in front of him.

From his angle, Robert couldn't see the entire line. He recognized the women from his time observing from the shed, though he couldn't put any name to a face.

Hiro appeared from his home, limping on his cane.

"What is the meaning of this?" he asked.

Robert pricked his ears to hear the exchange.

The officer motioned with the ledger. "I have a list of women who are to report for military duty at Sawai. From there they will be transported to the coastal defense command."

"Military duty?" retorted Hiro. "They are needed here. The rice fields have been neglected to ruin. The harvest keeps getting worse and worse, and without the needed labor, it'll only get worse."

The officer's face compressed with displeasure. "Do not use this as an excuse for your failures, old man. These girls will be impressed into service where and as the Emperor wills it."

Hiro bowed sharply at the mention of the Emperor. He said, "I doubt that His Majesty specifically requested these girls. I only ask that whoever interpreted the Emperor's wishes should reconsider. If we're to fight, the army needs food. To grow food, we need workers."

"I didn't come here to argue with you." The officer faced the truck and snapped his fingers. A woman in the truck handed one of the soldiers a long bamboo pole with a papier-mâché cone on one end. The wide end of the cone faced away from the shaft, and three wooden prongs jutted from the cone's circular base. The soldier hefted the pole as if it were a lance, the prongs pointed forward.

"The women have been called to begin training with this," the officer explained as he waved at the pole. "It is a practice simulator of a lunge mine, our new decisive weapon, which has been especially developed to destroy enemy tanks. The cone contains an explosive charge that will blow a hole through the thickest armor. The soldier will leap from hiding..."

The soldier assumed a ready stance and hopped forward, jabbing the pole.

"And lunge at the enemy tank." The officer gestured to the prongs. "When these smash into the target, the charge will detonate and destroy the enemy."

"And the soldier?" Hiro asked.

"He," the officer swept an appreciative grin toward the women, "or she, will make a most glorious sacrifice to the Emperor." The officer grunted a new command, and the soldier handed the lunge mine back to a woman on the truck.

A suicide bomb? Robert choked back dismay. The Japanese had already thrown wave after wave of kamikaze airplanes at the American fleets. While some of the suicide airplanes had made it through the gauntlet of air defenses and inflicted serious damage, most of them had been swatted out of the sky by American fighter planes and antiaircraft fire. In ground combat, the Japanese had also used lunge mines and, even more simply and equally diabolical, had infantrymen hide inside camouflaged holes, legs wrapped around an artillery shell while waiting for an American tank to roll over them. At the precise moment, the Japanese soldier would smash a rock on the fuse, detonating the shell, blowing up the tank, and of course, killing himself. On Okinawa, the U.S. Navy discovered kamikaze torpedoes, fitted with a cockpit and controls for a human operator to ride and steer at a warship.

And now, on the eve of the great invasion, the Japanese were so desperate they were planning to attack with girls using these primitive lunge mines, in the fanciful hope of bleeding the Americans dry and driving them home, defeated.

"When your name is called, come forward." He opened the ledger and recited names. Two of the younger girls strode to his side, their smooth faces devoid of emotion.

He asked, "Where is Yumi Asakawa?"

"My wife?" Hiro replied. "She's in bed coughing blood."

"What is her problem?"

"She has tuberculosis."

The officer jotted a note in the ledger. He then announced, "Makiko Asakawa."

Robert's heart thumped. Hiro grimaced.

But no one stepped forward.

"Makiko Asakawa," the officer repeated, impatiently. After a moment passed and no one answered, he glared at Hiro. "She is your daughter, no?"

"*Hai.*"

Where is she?"

"Busy with chores."

"Then summon her." The officer stamped his foot. "Now!"

Robert considered that Yoshi and Takara were gone. Makiko was with them, hopefully far off in the woods. *Please stay away*, he prayed.

"I don't know where she is," Hiro said.

"Then go look for her. Stop wasting my time." The officer advanced and jabbed the ledger against Hiro's chest. "Unless you are hiding her."

"How can that be?" Hiro asked. "I had no idea you were arriving."

"You are full of nothing but excuses and disrespect." The officer kicked Hiro's cane, and the old man toppled to the ground.

Robert's hands clenched with the desire to throttle that sadistic excuse of an officer.

As Hiro pushed up from the ground and dusted himself, the officer taunted, "Get up, you geezer, and do your duty. The enemy is at our doorstep because of shirkers like you." The officer turned his ire on all the women, those of the village and those on the truck. His tirade boomed like a chorus of war drums.

His harsh words made the puppies squirm and yelp. Worried that the soldiers would hear them, Robert crawled to their cage. He gathered the little dogs and stuffed them inside his overalls. Hugging their shifting, soft bodies, he whispered to comfort and quiet them.

Outside, a dog barked. Robert said to himself, *No. No*, and scooted to the wall to look.

Yoshi sprinted across the road, his paws lifting tufts of dirt. He growled and barked at the officer.

Wheeling about, the officer cried out in astonishment. "What is this?"

Makiko raced down the path from the woods, Takara running beside her on her leash. "Yoshi! Yoshi!"

The officer glared at Makiko. He pointed at Yoshi, who circled out of reach, still growling, the fur on his back grizzled in warning.

Makiko slowed to a trot, then a walk, a shuffle, and halted about thirty feet from the soldiers. With every step, her face lost more of its color, and her shoulders drooped lower and lower.

"Why do you have these animals?" The officer stabbed a finger at Yoshi and Takara. "Dogs. Cats. All pets have been outlawed."

Makiko and Hiro remained mute and blanched with fright.

The officer's face turned livid, his neck corded in fury. "How dare you divert precious food for these animals, when people go hungry." He shouted at his soldiers and they snapped to attention. "Collect these dogs and put them in the truck."

The two young men started for the dogs.

"Where are you taking them?" Hiro asked.

"To the garrison at Okutama," the office gloated. "They'll be on tomorrow's menu."

"No!" Makiko shrieked. She scooped Takara into her arms and stumbled backwards.

The officer shouted a new order. His men unslung their rifles and closed upon her, bayonets menacing. Teeth bared, Yoshi snarled at the officer.

"Get your dog to heel," he commanded. He placed one hand over the holster on his belt. "If not, I'll kill him now."

Makiko sank to her knees and in a quaking, tearful voice, pleaded, "Yoshi. Come here."

The dog lowered his head and tail and crept to her, still wary of the soldiers. Makiko drew him into her arms and pressed him against Takara.

The officer kicked dust at Makiko. "Stupid, foolish girl. All over Japan people are sacrificing themselves by the thousands to defend the Empire. And you sob over a couple of dogs?" His mouth pruned in disgust. "Perhaps there is more that you're hiding? Perhaps you're hoarding rice?" He stared at the coop. "Eggs? Chickens?" His voice dipped. "More dogs?"

Makiko wiped her eyes and shook her head.

"Load them on the truck," the officer demanded. When his soldiers stepped forward, he barked, "No, not you." He pointed at Makiko. "You. Put the dogs on the truck."

He paused and his scowl gave way to a knowing smile, evil and malicious. "I take it you're Makiko?"

She tipped her head with a humble nod. "*Hai.*"

"Then you're coming with us. I'm turning you over to the magistrate because of your insolence and disregard for the law. Perhaps time in jail and prisoner's gruel will improve your attitude. And then, off to fight the Americans."

Robert's heart plummeted. Makiko was about to be arrested. And Yoshi and Takara taken away to be cooked. The thought nauseated him. An image flashed of a mess hall cook butchering these beautiful dogs. He saw their severed heads sitting side by side on a platter.

Robert could see only one solution. He would offer this martinet a greater prize and hopefully distract him from Makiko and the dogs. That prize would be himself. He would surrender.

That might give her time to hide the dogs somewhere else. It was a tiny victory, but in this war of wholesale, inhumane sacrifice, it would have to do. And maybe, the fickle decision that had singled out Makiko for suicide duty would move on, and she would be spared.

Carefully, Robert returned the puppies to their cage, hushing them. He stroked their backs until they lay quiet. They regarded him with their small, shiny eyes, ignorant of the disaster that threatened to take them away from their mother and their master.

Slowly, he retreated from them. He crouched by the post and buried his Elgin. He gazed at the inside of the shed to memorize its layout in the tattered hope he would return and reclaim the watch.

His spirit sagging under the weight of doom, he crept out of the shed and tiptoed through the coop. Chickens clucked softly and hopped out of his way.

He had to divert suspicion from the Asakawas that they had been complicit in hiding him. Keeping the coop between himself and the soldiers, he back-stepped to the edge of the woods and disappeared into the foliage. Threading his way around the weeds and brush, he made his way behind the houses and circled back to the road, where it curved up from the river.

The officer's voice carried to him, one long, unintelligible harangue.

Robert emerged from the brush and walked past the last house. His feet turned into lead, and his body argued against the decision of his surrender, aware that soon, it would be suffering greatly. An ulcer of fear gnawed his insides. His throat parched until it hurt.

Heart pounding, he stepped onto the road, in view of the soldiers and the women. And Makiko. At bayonet point, she was cradling both dogs in her arms as she walked toward the truck.

When Makiko noticed him her face turned white. Her lips formed an "O" of disbelief. As Robert advanced, hesitant step by hesitant step, she shook her head.

Arms raised, he avoided her eyes and kept advancing.

The officer caught Makiko's expression and followed the line of her gaze. His eyes speared Robert, then widened in astonishment.

"I surrender," Robert said in English.

The officer slapped the ledger across one soldier's back. "Forget Makiko and the dogs. Get him. Get the American."

The two young soldiers charged at Robert, scowling as fiercely as their smooth, unshaven faces allowed. He kept his hands raised and eyes fixed on a point in the woods.

"On your knees, American murderer," one of the soldiers shouted.

Robert acted as if he didn't understand.

The soldier slammed his side with a rifle butt. The blow jolted pain through Robert, and he folded to his knees.

The officer tossed the ledger into the bed of the truck. Pistol in hand, he ran to Robert.

He straightened his shoulders and said, "My name is Robert Campbell. Captain, United States Army Air Force. Serial number—"

"What is he saying?" the officer interrupted. He turned to face the women. "Does anyone speak English?"

Makiko nodded meekly. "*Hai.*"

"Then drop those dogs and get over here." The officer trained his pistol at Robert's head.

Robert looked only briefly at Makiko and in that instant, a torrent of impending loss and regret gushed between them. He then averted his eyes and said in English, "Tell him that I've been hiding in the woods."

Makiko translated as he spoke. The officer's scowl softened in wonder.

"I saw the truck down the road," Robert motioned with his chin toward the river, "and followed it here." He hung his head. "I wish to surrender."

The officer circled behind him. Robert froze at the prospect that the officer was about to shoot him in the back of the head. Instead the officer laughed and kicked him square between the shoulder blades. The wind knocked out of him, Robert crumpled against the dirt. His lungs struggled for air, and he reeled in terror of suffocating. As his breath returned, he sucked at the air filling his throat.

"Surrender? *Coward,*" the officer spat the word. "You kill our women and children and then think you can simply surrender to take advantage of the Emperor's mercy?" He kicked Robert in the side. Eyes clenched, Robert grunted and curled to absorb the pain. He wanted to look up for a final glimpse of Makiko, to capture her image like a snapshot, something to bring him warmth in the cold, terrible days ahead. But he didn't. He couldn't risk betraying that they knew each other.

The officer kicked him again.

One of the soldiers said, "Sir. Our orders are to take all prisoners at once to the nearest military intelligence center."

The officer glared at him.

The soldier kept his eyes locked forward as he added in a discreet tone, "We cannot mistreat them. We are to keep them healthy for interrogation."

The officer stomped toward the soldier and slapped him. "You must never correct a superior." He returned to Robert, grabbed him by the hair, and shook his head. "Aren't you lucky? I must let the experts take care of you."

The world swam like a painful delusion before Robert's half-opened eyes. The vision through his dust-caked eyelashes reduced Makiko to a blurry, formless silhouette.

The officer shoved Robert's head into the dirt. "Everyone, off the truck. And forget those stupid dogs. Change in plans. I'm taking this shameless wretch to the garrison at Okutama. There he'll face his reckoning."

17

July 1945

Robert knelt on the concrete floor of his prison cell, arms trussed behind his back and cinched to a bamboo rod. A headache pounded the inside of his skull. The sting from the last volley of beatings ebbed into ache and nausea.

He tried to take solace in Scripture from the First Book to the Corinthians. *No temptation has overtaken you that is not common to man. God is faithful, and he will not let you be tempted beyond your ability, but with the temptation he will also provide the way of escape, that you may be able to endure it.*

Light from a single overhead bulb filtered through the blur of sweat across his eyes. The floor sloped to a small circular grate in the middle, and from it bubbled a dank sewer stench.

His interrogator, Major Taishi Ogihara, stood between Robert and a stool and small table pushed against the cell's far wall. Ogihara's assistant, Corporal Ueda, waited beside Robert. The corporal's chest heaved from exertion as he stood bamboo cane in hand, ready to administer another round of beatings at the major's word.

Robert's stomach knotted. He had retched and retched but as he had eaten nothing since the day before yesterday, he could only cough up phlegm and yellow bile. He curled forward to endure the agony, to collect it, to push it away, to keep from breaking.

This last beating had been punishment for being flip. When he commented that Ogihara's English was quite good and then asked where he had studied, Ogihara responded by shouting, "Do not patronize me," and ordered Ueda to cane Robert across the back and kick him in the stomach.

From the first moments of his interrogation Robert stuck doggedly to providing only his name, rank, and serial number. But if he didn't give Ogihara something more, the military might return to where he had been captured and try to fill in the blanks between when he had been shot down and then surrendered. Should the army poke around the village, they might discover that the Asakawas had given him shelter. To protect his friends Robert had to start dribbling crumbs of information, but he had to be careful. If he conceded information too readily, the major might become suspicious.

Robert had another worry. What he could not reveal was to have his captors suspect that he knew Japanese. They would conclude he was an intelligence officer and then really dig into what he had done during his time as a fugitive. Things would only get worse for himself and the farming camp, the Asakawas—Makiko especially.

More Scripture came to mind. Exodus 14:14. *The Lord will fight for you, and you have only to be silent.*

Ogihara shifted weight from foot to foot. The overhead light gleamed across his polished boots. Like his fellow countrymen, Ogihara was short by American standards, but he was as compact and fierce and cunning.

He pulled the stool forward and eased onto it. "Again, what was your mission?"

Robert answered, "Robert Campbell, Captain, United States—"

Ogihara chuffed in disgust. He barked, "Hit him."

Robert heard the swish of the bamboo cane. The blow landed across his lower back. The jolt of pain made him buck forward and the corporal grabbed his collar to rein him in place.

"What airplane did you fly?" Ogihara asked.

"Robert Campbell, Cap—"

Whap!

Eyes clenched, Robert doubled forward. The corporal let go, and Robert melted to let his forehead press against the concrete. Through gritted teeth he sucked at the meager spit in his mouth. On the major's order, Ueda yanked Robert by the hair and pulled him back to his kneeling position.

Ogihara lifted an army-issue canteen of water from the table and filled a tin cup. He said in Japanese, "Ueda, you must be thirsty from working so hard." Robert followed the cup as Ogihara handed it to the corporal, who accepted with a nod. "Thank you, sir." He guzzled the water and returned the cup to the major.

"And you, my stubborn American friend?" Ogihara taunted, switching back to English. "Are you thirsty?" With chameleon-like deftness the barbed rancor in his eyes softened into pity.

Robert was aware of the game between the major and him. To accept any kindness from Ogihara was to obligate himself, which he couldn't grant. But his body ached for relief from its torment.

He lowered his gaze and whispered, "I am."

"Ha!" the major burst out in mirthful Japanese. "Our monkey speaks." He refilled the cup and crouched in front of Robert. He waved it an inch from Robert's mouth. "Tell me, what was your mission?"

Robert stared at the cup. His parched mouth longed for a quick taste. Never had the promise of release been so simple. His body screamed, *Take it. Take it.* His mind joined the chorus, *Take it. No more misery.* But his spirit asserted itself. He raised his head and locked gazes with Ogihara. "Robert Campbell, Captain—"

"Enough!" Ogihara muttered in Japanese. "Stubborn jackass. Corporal, give this moron another lesson."

The cane swished through the air and smacked Robert across the soles of his feet. The explosion of pain made him jerk forward and twist to one side.

"Ueda, again please. On his torso."

The cane swatted hard against Robert's chest, once, twice. His vision turned dark; it was as if the air had turned into black oil and he was drowning. He gagged and coughed.

Ogihara mumbled something. Ueda grasped the bamboo restraint and wrenched Robert back to his knees.

"Why do you do this?" the major implored in a hurt, pleading voice. "I am not a bad man. I don't want to hurt you. I ask you simple questions." Still clutching the tin cup, he sat back on the stool. "Okey-dokey, how about this? You were trained not to divulge military information, I respect that. At least grant me this. Give me something for my superiors and then we can stop this useless exercise. Tell me again, where were you shot down?"

Now the game was getting more subtle, more treacherous. By varying his questions, Ogihara sought to thread together the circumstances that led to Robert's capture, to weave a cloth of details, to be picked apart for truths and lies.

"I don't remember."

Ogihara's sympathy disappeared with a snarl. Ueda reached forward and slapped Robert's face. As the sting ebbed, he tasted blood seeping around his loosened teeth.

"I was unconscious," he admitted.

"Finally," Ogihara praised. "Tell me more."

"When I came to, I wasn't sure how many days had passed."

"I'm no physician but I doubt you would've been unconscious for more than half a day." He brushed the cup against Robert's lips. It smelled heavenly. "Here, take a drink."

Robert kept his lips pressed tight. He would make the major work to give him anything.

"It's no reward," Ogihara said. "Drink, as a favor to me."

Please, Robert's body begged. *One drink. One tiny drink.*

He parted his lips, and the major tipped the cup. The water, cool and refreshing as any Robert had ever tasted, trickled into his mouth. His body clutched at the respite from anguish, but he knew the drink was only to keep him going, to have him endure more torment. "Thank you," he whispered, then added pointedly, "much appreciated."

Ogihara set the cup back on the table. "After you awoke, how many days and nights passed?"

Robert nodded as if he were counting. "Three."

"Three? Then explain something. I'm getting the impression that you were shot down for a while. Let's go with the three days as you say. Look at me."

Robert raised his head.

Ogihara cupped Robert's chin and dragged the back of his fingers across the light stubble on the aviator's cheek. "Then why is your beard so smooth?"

Deep in his head Robert went *Shit!* But he kept his face as gray as the concrete around him. "I stole a bag."

Ogihara's eyebrows canted upward. "What kind of bag?"

Robert waited, then drawled, "A small bag. It contained a shaving kit."

"You were behind enemy territory and you shaved?"

Robert paused. "Another drink, please."

The major obliged him.

Robert suppressed a smile and relished inwardly the tiny victory of manipulating Ogihara. He said, "It made me feel better."

Ogihara replied with a soft grunt of approval. "And your uniform? How did it get mended?"

Another wait. "The bag also contained a sewing kit."

"Where was this bag?"

Wait again. "On a boat."

"What boat?"

Robert coughed to buy time. "A boat on the river."

"Why did you steal the bag?"

He cleared his throat. "I was hoping it had food. I was hungry."

Ogihara rotated on the stool and scribbled notes across a writing pad on the table. "Corporal Ueda, watch the prisoner." Ogihara stood and walked around Robert to exit the cell. An iron door creaked and clanged shut.

Robert wondered the reason for the major's sudden departure. Was Ogihara reacting to what he had said? Or was there another agenda at play?

The minutes passed, and Robert relaxed in the sweet absence of pain.

Ueda leaned against one wall, looking bored. He poked Robert with the cane and said in Japanese, "You're fortunate Ogihara is your interrogator. The other one, Major Hosogai, loves to pull fingernails. That man is a real sadistic bastard. Once I've seen him use a vise to squeeze an Australian pilot's ball sack until it burst. Like a ripe plum."

The gruesome image poured from Robert's mind and funneled straight to his groin, which withered in horror. He fought the urge to squirm in revulsion and kept stone still.

The corporal tapped the cane against Robert's side. "So you're a lucky, lucky man, Prisoner Number 112." He screwed the end of the bamboo cane into Robert's ear and then traced the cane across the back of his neck. "Until you're beheaded."

Robert let the taunt pass. He had no say in what the Japanese would do to him. All he could do was endure and cling to the pledges he had to honor—his oath as an American fighting man and his promise to protect the Asakawas. He pushed aside his misery and brought into focus memories of what was good in life, what his captors couldn't take away.

Moments sparkled from his childhood. He warmed himself with his mother's smile, the approving nod from his father, the thrill of hitting a home run, and above them all, that brief and tender time he had spent with Makiko. He could feel her skin, her moist kisses.

Footfalls echoed in the hall and approached the cell. Ogihara had returned. Robert tried to cling to his daydream but it dissolved from his mind like smoke through fingers. The major sat back on the stool and unrolled a map on the floor between himself and Robert. He placed large pebbles on the corners to keep it from curling. Curious, the corporal leaned over his shoulder to observe.

Ogihara tapped a pencil on the map, a topographical depiction of the Tama River Valley. He dragged his pencil across the mountains north of the river. "Five days ago we found an American Navy Privateer that had crashed here. Was this your airplane?"

Robert kept quiet. If he admitted that he was aboard the Privateer then Ogihara would ask why an Army Air Force captain was crew on a Navy airplane. He had to think through his answers by planning moves ahead and avoid getting boxed in.

"And we found a B-29 here," Ogihara said. "Which of these was yours?"

Robert considered saying the B-29, but in POW training he had been taught to keep his stories as simple and close to the truth as possible. The interrogators would study your words and it was best not to be caught in a lie.

So Robert said, "The Privateer."

"Oh," Ogihara replied enthusiastically. "Why is an Air Force pilot on a Navy airplane?"

He answered, "I was an observer."

"Simply an observer? Why?"

A pause. "The Army Air Force is interested in the Privateer. I was on board to see how it handled."

"And...how did it handle?"

Robert drew a breath and released an extended, regretful sigh. "It could have done better. We did get shot down."

Ogihara laughed. His face went plain again. He rested the pencil point on a spot along the river. "This is where you were captured."

The major had raised the ante. If Robert betrayed one sliver of a clue, it could mean disaster for Makiko. What he had to do was to nudge the major's attention from the village. He remembered the road where it led from the river.

"To the west," Robert said.

Ogihara scrutinized the map. "Where was the boat?"

"Which boat?"

The major grunted and Ueda whipped the cane across Robert's back.

He stiffened until the pain eased. "The boat I stole from?"

"What other boat are we talking about?"

"It was someplace along the river. Along the northern riverbank. I don't remember exactly."

Ogihara's pencil hovered ominously over the village. "Why did you choose this place to surrender?"

Robert stared at the spot. The fate of many hung on his words. "I saw the truck and followed it. I was hungry. I was tired of hiding."

"In the three days between when you were shot down and then surrendered, did anyone see you?"

"I'm guessing not. Otherwise they would've turned me in."

"Back to the boat. What color was it?"

"I don't remember."

"How big was it?"

Robert blinked and blinked to mime that he was trying to recall. "It was a small boat. Something for two people."

"What did you eat?"

"I found rice balls in the bag. And apples."

"How did you shave? Where did you get the hot water?"

"I made a small fire."

"With what?"

"There were cigarettes and matches in the bag. I found a tin can to heat water."

"Quite a camping trip for you. A real holiday. A regular picnic." Ogihara's eyes went sly. "Didn't meet any friendly Japanese girls, did you?'

Terror slashed through Robert. He clutched at Makiko's memory. What did Ogihara know?

"No one saw me."

"Ah," Ogihara clipped. He sighed heavily, the schoolmaster disappointed with his headstrong pupil. "I'm afraid there is much you're not telling me." He gathered the map and stood abruptly. The stool scraped backwards across the floor. He marched around Robert, stepped out of the cell, and shouted in Japanese, "Sergeant Aoyama. Come in here and help Ueda soften the prisoner for more interrogation."

Robert gulped. *Soften the prisoner.* More beatings. His heart labored to prepare him for the ordeal.

Sergeant Aoyama entered the cell. He was a stout man, with a bear-like torso and thick arms. He projected no special enmity for Robert but carried himself like a stevedore reporting for some lengthy, heavy lifting.

He grunted orders to Ueda. Together they loosened the bamboo rod across Robert's back. The surge of blood returning to his shoulders and arms brought a welcome tingle. They hauled him to his feet and spun him to face the wall. They yanked his arms up and bound both hands with rope to an eyebolt high on the wall. Ueda kicked his legs apart and then lashed his ankles to either end of the bamboo rod.

Robert complied without a struggle like an animal led to slaughter. What else could he do? He lacked the strength to fight against his tormentors, and whatever energy remained he would need to survive the forthcoming nightmare.

Aoyama grasped the collar of Robert's overalls and ripped it apart. They peeled off his undershirt and threw it aside.

"Ah, look," the sergeant noted. "His birthmark. It will make a splendid target."

The two soldiers stood behind Robert. One of them planted his boot on the rod and bore down, fixing Robert's feet to the floor. They took turns beating him with Ueda's bamboo cane, working him over with methodical resolve.

Blow by blow, the pain grew into a howl—intense, terrible—until it consumed Robert like he was roasting inside a raging furnace. He bucked and writhed and tore at the ropes binding his wrists and ankles. He peed and fouled himself.

He collapsed and hung by his arms, his face scraping against the concrete wall. Blood wept down his back, piss and diarrhea trickled between his thighs. "No more," he muttered in English. "Please, no more."

"What's he saying?" Ueda asked.

The sergeant sniffed and deadpanned, "Probably that he crapped his pants."

Cold water splashed across Robert's back. He squirmed and grunted as the water gnawed at his welts and lacerations. The pain lifted and brought a nurturing coolness to his naked skin. Gulping, he rested against the wall, grateful for the surcease from agony.

The downward pressure on his ankles relented. Gruff hands worked at the rope binding him to the eyebolt. The rope went slack, and he crumpled to the wet floor. His ankles were untied, and his legs stretched open. His eyes fluttered as he floated on the edge of unconsciousness. Aoyama and Ueda blocked the overhead light and their shadows slid over him. The cell door creaked open and clicked shut. Their steps retreated down the hall.

Robert curled into a fetal position facing the door. He kept his eyes closed and let his mind withdraw to a safe place deep inside himself.

Another set of footfalls approached.

"Prisoner Number 112," the man said, a fresh soldier.

Robert remained still, unwilling to stir from the sanctuary of his mental cave.

The soldier unlocked the door and entered. He stepped around Robert toward the table. The soldier's footsteps abruptly halted.

Robert sensed that something was wrong. He turned his head as much as the pain allowed and through bleary eyes regarded the man. Robert squinted but the stranger remained a hazy, indistinct silhouette.

The soldier gasped, "That birthmark." He crouched beside Robert and lifted his head. "Robert Campbell?"

The question sounded incredulous, hopeful. That voice, like a distorted echo from a long-lost past.

"Yes," Robert croaked, "I am Robert Campbell."

The soldier brought his face close to Robert and smoothed his hair back. "It is me, your friend Kaito. Remember?"

18

July 1945

Kaito knelt beside Robert. His face collapsed in distress as if he was the one suffering torture. Grasping the back of Robert's neck, he leaned over his American friend and stroked his head. Kaito repeated in English, his voice breaking on the edge of sobs, "I'm so sorry."

Robert was too weak to lift his arms and greet Kaito with an embrace. But his heart, which had been withering in misery and despair, now inflated with joy and hope. Robert closed his eyes and let himself sink into the moment. How was this possible? Kaito—his childhood friend from Yokohama—was here? Was Robert hallucinating?

Kaito eased Robert back against the floor. Robert let his eyes creep open, fretful that he was dreaming. Instead of Kaito he might see Ueda and Aoyama looming over him like a pair of gargoyles, ready to tear into him again.

But it was Kaito, his face long and gaunt, creased with anxiety, a wispy mustache coloring his upper lip. He wore a Japanese Army uniform with the insignia of private first class on its collar. Not rising from a crouch, Kaito scuttled to the table and returned with the canteen and tin cup. He filled the cup. "Take it," he said in Japanese.

A black thought shadowed Robert's mood. What if his interrogators knew more about him than Major Ogihara had let on? What if Kaito was part of their ruse to coax information out of him, to get him to betray his fluency in Japanese? He hated to think this but maybe Kaito had been forced into making a bitter choice, to pick a lesser form of treachery at Robert's expense. Was Kaito honest or was he a sell-out?

"Thank you," Robert said in English, guardedly. He tried to sit up but he was too fatigued to hold himself upright, so he scooted against the wall. Moving gingerly, he rested his naked, lacerated back against its surface and inventoried his wounds as each touched the cold concrete.

Kaito placed the cup in his hands. At first Robert sipped the water, then guzzled it. Kaito refilled the cup and Robert emptied it again. He returned the cup to Kaito, who refused with a shake of his head. "You keep."

Kaito sniffed and wrinkled his nose. Robert cringed with embarrassment because Kaito smelled that he had fouled himself.

Kaito stood and cracked open the cell door. He tipped his head into the hallway and looked right, then left. He whispered, "I'll be back right away." He eased into the hallway, shut the door, and hustled to the left. His shadow traced behind him on the wall and disappeared from view.

Robert set the cup down, groped for the canteen, and uncorked it. He tipped the canteen to his lips and poured directly into his mouth. His thirst slackened, he splashed water over his head and let it cascade cool and refreshing down his face. The water ran over his lips and it was salted by his perspiration. Water trickled down his neck and he sloughed it angrily across his chest. Glowering at the cell door, he fumed with loathing at his jailers, damning them.

Save for Kaito.

A friend? Here?

Yes. Thankfully.

Robert shook the canteen. Not much was left. He drank the remainder and let the canteen fall to his side, where it clunked hollow against the floor.

Feeling better, he closed his eyes and tried to sort his thoughts. Reality settled over him. He was still a prisoner and still faced more torture. He hurt, inside and outside. A headache gnawed at his brain.

He wanted to trust Kaito, to believe in miracles, that somehow the immutable laws of the universe had shifted just enough for Robert to slip through the cracks of his circumstances and be spared.

He gave a prayer, from Acts 24:3. *In every way and everywhere we accept this with all gratitude.*

Footfalls approached. Robert reeled in his hopes, resigned that his tormentors might have returned.

But it was Kaito. He carried an army knapsack and a courier's pouch made of canvas. He rested the pouch on the table. Kaito dragged the stool close to Robert and sat with the knapsack between his boots. From the knapsack he produced a bundle of rags and a canteen. He moistened one of the rags and gave it to Robert. "Here, so you can wipe yourself."

Embarrassed again, but grateful for the chance to clean up, he loosened his overalls from about his waist. He took the rag and painfully twisted from side to side to slide the overalls over his hips. Kaito looked away, and Robert appreciated the gesture. He blotted the gummy stink from between his legs. Kaito handed him a fresh rag. Robert gave his legs another pass and scrubbed the insides of his overalls as best he could. Carefully, he slipped his arms into the sleeves and buttoned the front. The wet backside of his overalls clung to his buttocks.

Kaito gave him the last rag and tipped the canteen over Robert's cupped hands. Robert wiped and cleaned them. He balled the rags and tossed them half-heartedly into a corner. He relaxed against the wall and took measure of his weariness and pain.

"What are you doing here?" Robert asked in a low voice, still careful to use English.

Kaito waited with a bento box on his lap. He handed a rice ball to Robert. "First, eat," he whispered in Japanese.

Robert bit the rice ball in half. He chewed and stuffed the rest into his mouth. Though meager, the food was like kindling igniting inside a cold furnace. Robert's heart lifted with warming optimism. Kaito shared the canteen and the remaining contents of the bento box: another rice ball, some crackers, morsels of seaweed wrapped around bean curd, and wonder of wonders—slivers of dried apricots. Both the seaweed and apricots were gamey and tough, and they made Robert aware of his loosened teeth. Hopefully he wouldn't lose them. Even so, the meager provisions made for a delicious, sumptuous banquet.

He took a pull from the canteen to wash down the food. Kaito motioned for the canteen, the gesture intimately familiar. Robert imagined the two of them in a dugout, watching their team play during a double-header, the scene so simple and yet fantastically idyllic and dream-like.

Kaito dropped the empty canteen and bento box back into his knapsack.

"What are you doing here?" Robert asked again.

Kaito shrugged. "The war started. I was drafted. What else was there to expect?"

"But you're Korean?" Robert asked hesitantly.

"Half Korean. The army needed troops. At first, I was certain that I'd be assigned menial duties. But when I reported to the induction center, my school records showed that I knew English, so I was assigned to this," he tapped the black stripe on his sleeve, "military intelligence."

"You're an interrogator?" The idea that Kaito abused and tortured revolted Robert.

"No." Kaito shook his head as if he was equally disgusted by the implication. "I'm still regarded as Korean, which means they don't trust me completely. I only review transcripts and process documents."

"At least you're here in Japan and not on some battlefield."

"Only recently. Most of my service was in Korea, where we interrogated Koreans. It was very bad. Now because of my English, they brought me here." His gaze dropped to the floor. He wrung his hands. "I watched our soldiers do many terrible things to the Koreans. Then again, the Koreans would kill us every chance they could. The hatred came at me from all directions. The Japanese hated me for being Korean, and the Koreans hated me for wearing a Japanese uniform."

Kaito's eyes misted and he wiped them dry. "Oh Robert, why does the world have to be a complicated, terrible place? I'm just one man with simple ambitions and what would it matter if I disappeared? Does the fate of this war and Japan's destiny hinge on what happens to me?"

Robert didn't know how to answer. What words could ease Kaito's anguish?

The minutes passed, the stillness unbroken until Kaito tapped his boot against Robert's foot. "And what brings you here?" He phrased the question with an impish smile that seemed as out of place here as a rose blossoming in a swamp.

"Bad luck, I guess."

Kaito chuckled. "We all have too much of that. It's been years, Robert."

"It has."

"I could've imagined a more pleasant reunion," Kaito said.

"I'm sorry I stopped writing," Robert said. He had penned his last letter to Kaito over a decade ago.

"It wouldn't have mattered. The government confiscated all the mail coming from you. Imagine their fits of suspicion when they studied correspondence between an American and a Korean? Even though we were boys, our letters could only have been coded messages of intrigue and sabotage."

Robert smiled at that observation.

"What about your father," Kaito asked, "the preacher?"

"He's still preaching."

"And your mother?"

"Getting older."

Kaito kept quiet, deep in thought. Robert hoped he wouldn't ask the next question, which he did anyway.

"What about the family you stayed with in Yokohama?"

The Asakawas. Not even Kaito could know the truth. Robert replied with a smirk of pretended disappointment. "I haven't heard from them either."

"I thought for sure you would keep in touch. Especially with the girl."

The remark came at Robert like the deft twitch of a scalpel. Was Kaito probing for information?

"I lost track of them the same time I lost track of you," Robert lied, paranoid, frightened that his friend might just be his worst enemy. He added a shake of his head to emphasize regret. To distract Kaito, he asked, "What about your mother?"

"Still employed as a laundress. Mostly for the military."

"And your father?"

Kaito's eyes became pools of despair and loss. "He was assigned to a unit that rescued people trapped in bomb-damaged buildings. One collapsed and killed him."

With this admission Robert let go of his misgivings. Guilt chilled the camaraderie between him and Kaito. Fellow American aviators had been responsible for killing his friend's father. "I'm sorry to hear that."

"This war is giving us plenty of reasons to feel sorry for a great many things."

Robert nodded. *True.*

"Perhaps, my fortunes will change for the better."

"What do you mean?" Robert asked.

"I'm being transferred. I leave the day after tomorrow to Nagasaki to reinforce their garrison. The rumor is the American invasion will strike there first."

Robert reflected on this. Perhaps it was a good thing, for now. As far as he knew, Nagasaki ranked low on the list of American targets for air attack and it was not where the Americans planned to invade. He had pondered the same good luck when he heard that Makiko's mother would be sent to Hiroshima. At the moment, Nagasaki and Hiroshima were the two safest cities in southern Japan.

Kaito retrieved the courier bag. He acted circumspect about what it contained. As he was opening it, someone approached. He jumped to his feet and snarled at Robert in Japanese. "You will learn proper manners, American dog. You will be held accountable for your heinous crimes against the Emper—"

Corporal Ueda halted outside the cell. "Private Satake, what's going on? Is the prisoner giving you trouble?" Ueda glanced menacingly at Robert.

"No, corporal," Kaito answered, "I have everything under control."

Ueda shifted his gaze and narrowed his eyes at him. "What are you doing here?"

Kaito presented the courier pouch. "Major Ogihara sent me to tend to the prisoner. I have to get him ready for transport."

Ueda mulled the words. "Very well. Continue."

Kaito replied, "*Hai*," and nodded. He kept his head tipped until the corporal vanished down the hall. Kaito's shoulders sagged in relief. He sank onto the stool, unfastened the straps of the courier pouch, and pulled out a sheaf of papers. He whispered in a flat voice, "Major Ogihara has consigned you to execution."

The words doused Robert, leaving him cold and empty. He felt weightless, insignificant, like a bubble waiting to burst and become nothing.

Kaito continued, "You'll be taken to the Kofu barracks at Camp Number 7 for more interrogation and then shot." He raised his hand. "But don't despair, please."

And then shot? How was Robert not supposed to despair?

From the courier pouch Kaito hurriedly removed a small tin of ink and a pen and set them on the floor. He arranged the papers on his lap and selected two forms. He held still for a moment, listening wary as a mouse when a tanuki prowls nearby. He unscrewed the lid from the tin and dipped the pen. Staring intently at the forms, he began writing. He wrote carefully, deliberately, then stopped to study his handiwork.

"What are you doing?" Robert whispered.

"I've changed your destination to the Nagoya No. 3-C Branch Camp. It won't be a pleasant place but at least you'll live."

"Won't anyone notice?" Robert asked, suddenly worried about the motives prompting Kaito's risky subterfuge.

"I will," Kaito chirped. He winked. "It is my job is to check the prisoner manifest when they board the trucks to leave."

"But won't someone catch the mistake?"

"I doubt it. Major Ogihara and the adjutant have already approved these forms. Besides, with so much disruption caused by the air attacks, if anything manages to work half of the time, we're lucky."

Kaito capped the tin of ink. He blew across the pages to dry them. Satisfied, he slipped them back into the pouch and cinched the straps.

"I appreciate this, Kaito. But why are you doing this? If you get caught, it won't go well for either of us."

"I must try, Robert. After all, I have a debt to settle."

"With who?"

"You," Kaito answered. Again holding still, he remained alert, as if listening for the most trivial of noise. Satisfied they were alone, he reached back into the knapsack. Drawing his hand out, he was clutching a baseball.

"Remember that last day in Yokohama?" he asked in a hushed tone. Robert strained to make out the words.

Kaito handed him the ball. "When you gave me this?"

Robert took the ball in one hand, astonished that Kaito had not only remembered the ball but had kept it these many years. He studied the ball, squeezing it, and ran his fingertips over its scuffed surface. The leather was stained, and the threads frayed from heavy use. The ball's presence was surreally incongruent with their surroundings, like its existence was a mistake of nature, and a triumph over the gloom of war.

The recollection of when he had given the ball to Kaito came to him in a burst of color. Everything about that moment blossomed in microscopic detail, especially the sadness of their impending separation. But that sadness had been grounded in brotherly love, and that affection now shined brightly inside Robert.

He returned the ball, smiling. "I remember. This is a fine baseball."

Kaito palmed it, savoring its heft. "The best. The other boys were so jealous of me. It was the cause of many black eyes when I caught someone trying to steal it." He returned the ball carefully into the knapsack as if it were a delicate treasure. "When you gave me the ball I said I owed you."

"You didn't owe me a thing, Kaito. Back then you did as much for me as I did for you. And now with what you've done, it is I who owe you."

Kaito shook his head. "You are the kindest and dearest friend I've ever had. I promised myself that I would someday, somehow, return the favor, no matter the cost to me." Kaito patted the courier pouch to acknowledge its promise of salvation. "This is it, Robert. Hopefully, I've saved your life."

19

Late July 1945

Robert arrived at the Nagoya No. 3-C Branch Camp and
was hustled off the cargo truck. He was led into a holding area within the barbed-wire encirclement of the prisoner
compound. A sergeant barked at him to stand at attention,
and Robert did so. He remained motionless but let his eyes
range over what he could see.

Before him stood crude barracks, wood siding daubed with
mud; nine shacks as far as he could tell, arranged in a square.
Ragged tarpaper and sheets of canvas served as roofs. Men
congregated around the open doors of the closest barracks,
and they watched with curiosity like a pack of emaciated, feral
dogs.

Barbed wire was strung between tall poles spaced about ten
feet apart. The compound yard was dirt, which made Robert
fear what a hellish mud pit this place would become during
rainy season.

To his right, beside the gate into the compound, stood an
observation tower. In the shadow beneath its squat pyramid

roof, he caught the silhouette of two guards and the menacing shape of a heavy machine gun.

The late afternoon sun hovered above his left shoulder. Robert hadn't sipped water or eaten since before starting the six-hour journey here. He hoped he hadn't missed dinner, though he expected the meal wouldn't be much. His injuries didn't hurt as bad, a minor blessing. He had been issued an American fatigue uniform of mismatched shirt and pants to replace his tattered overalls. His socks had worn out and he wore his boots over bare feet. He carried no belongings.

He waited, his sanity shielded behind a wall of numbness. He didn't allow himself to think about anything except what he needed to get past the next few minutes.

Flies buzzed his head. They landed and crawled across his brow and face. Their feet skittering across his skin made his nerves crawl, but he resisted brushing them away. Tired as he was, he couldn't help but let his posture sag. At the approach of footsteps from behind, he locked his knees and stood rigid.

The sergeant had returned. His face had the aspect of an apple left too long in the sun, and like its juice had turned to vinegar. Two more soldiers took positions behind Robert, at his left and right.

The sergeant barked at Robert in guttural Japanese, "From now on, when we ask for your identity, you will answer, Nagoya Prisoner Number 112. Understood?"

He scowled as he waited for Robert to acknowledge. The Japanese made no allowances if a prisoner didn't understand their language. Robert remained circumspect about revealing his fluency of Japanese; then again, if he didn't reply with what the sergeant wanted to hear, he risked a beating.

Robert nodded curtly, "*Hai*," and recited clumsily, "*Nagoya shūjin hyaku-juni ban.*"

The sergeant chuffed, acting neither pleased nor disappointed by the reply. He pointed to the shacks. "Private Imura, take him to the officers' barracks."

The guard on his left prodded Robert across the back with a stick. Its touch stung his wounds, but he remained stoic and started forward. The second soldier paced alongside.

Three prisoners at the door of the barracks watched, their eyes smudged sunken pits in skeletal faces. Robert met their stare. Threadbare dirty clothing hung from them like rags on stick dolls. Tiny scabs dotted their hair follicles. One of them puffed on the stub of a cigarette, made of book paper and reeking of eggplant. Even so, it was the only indulgence Robert had yet seen granted to a prisoner.

He was pushed forward, and Imura said, "We'll see you at roll call tomorrow morning, prisoner 112."

The three men at the door parted to let Robert pass. He shuffled into the shadowy interior. The air was stifling and oppressive, like the inside of a stable that needed mucking. Planks of sunlight slanted through one wall and illuminated low wooden bunks facing a center aisle. Men lay corpse-like on several of the bunks.

Several other prisoners stood in the aisle, waiting side by side in a semblance of a military staff. As Robert's eyes became accustomed to the murk, he recognized one of the men, sandy-haired and the tallest in line. At the same instant, the man announced, "Robert! Captain Campbell. It's me. Randall. Lieutenant Paulson."

At the sound of the familiar name, the despair constricting Robert's heart eased a bit. He leaned forward, hand thrust out. Paulson snatched his hand and gave it a hearty squeeze. He announced, "The captain here was the co-pilot of my Privateer."

The man in the center followed Paulson's example and took Robert's hand. "I'm Colonel Steven Mancinelli, U.S. Army." The colonel was short with an oversized head, which might have looked okay on a stockier build. But here he resembled a puppet made of discarded parts. A swarthy growth of beard colored his wide face. Like the other men, patches of black soot and grime stained what remained of his uniform. Instead of service boots, he wore crude sandals woven from jute cord.

Mancinelli offered a weak smile. "It is my dubious distinction that I'm the prisoner commander. I won't say welcome, considering the circumstances, but at least you're not dead." He grasped Robert's shoulders and sized him up. "You don't look too bad."

"Trust me, colonel, I've been better."

"Haven't we all." Mancinelli introduced Robert to the other men, eight total, all officers—Army, Army Air Force, and Navy.

After shaking hands, Robert asked, "You wouldn't have something to eat? And some water?"

Mancinelli shook his head. "Dinner, if you can call it that, was an hour ago. You'll have to wait until morning."

Someone tapped Robert's arm. It was Paulson presenting a tin can that had been fashioned into a cup. "About the only thing we get plenty of is water. The Japs let us boil it so it's reasonably safe to drink."

The water might have been potable but it still tasted brackish. Paulson showed him where to hang the cup on a pole above the drinking bucket. A board covered the bucket to keep the bugs out.

"So you were shot down with Paulson?" Mancinelli inquired. "That was thirteen days ago. Where have you been?"

Thirteen days? Robert had lost track of time. He studied Paulson and regarded how wasted he appeared. The man looked like he had been tormented and abused for thirteen years.

"I parachuted near Okutama and foraged for as long as I could," Robert said. The memory of his time with Makiko hovered dreamlike in the back of his mind, a thought he would savor in a better moment. "Then I was captured somewhere along the Tama River and spent the next few days at the interrogation center in Kofu."

Mancinelli looked at Paulson, then back at Robert. "Since you two know each other, you'll help Lieutenant Paulson keep track of supplies."

Robert didn't think the prisoners owned anything except for the rags on their backs. "Supplies?"

"Sometimes we get extra blankets, castoff uniforms, needle, thread, pieces of soap, matches, a tin can that's been left around. Whatever any of the men finds or is issued, he has to turn that over to you. Then we, my esteemed staff—" Mancinelli gestured to the officers beside him, "decide who gets what. I, of course, get final word."

The colonel paused and amended, "Actually the Japs, and especially Major Tanaka, the camp commandant, has the final word on everything around here."

"What's Tanaka like?" Robert asked hopefully.

"A real bastard. As is Sergeant Uchimi. You've already met him."

Robert asked, "And the supplies? Is there a list?"

"The Japs won't let us write anything down." Paulson tapped his temple. "You'll have to keep the inventory up here." He gestured to an empty bunk. "That one's yours. The last occupant was our one Marine officer. He died three days ago. Dysentery. His name was Lieutenant William Ericson. Ring any bells?"

"No. Never heard of the man." Robert noticed the worn tatami sleeping mats and blankets spread flat and neat over the bunk. "What happened to his body?"

"We dumped it in a pit past the lumber shed. Where all of them go," Paulson replied. "The Japs don't allow us to grieve over a body so we have to mourn their passing in private."

"I suppose the guards don't let you keep a list of the dead."

Paulson brushed away the flies. "That's right. We've lost sixteen men since the camp was started eight months ago. You'll have to memorize their names. Several of the other men also keep a list in their heads so when the time comes for the reckoning, we should be able to compile a thorough accounting."

"How many men in the camp?"

"With you, thirty-two."

Paulson showed him the rest of this barracks. Just more bunks on the dirt floor. The only amenities were: the bucket of drinking water; at the back of the barracks, the piss pots and a pair of shit-squatters (toilets made from the bottoms of rusted fifty-five-gallon drums with sitting boards on top); and near them, crude slabs of concrete that lined the opening to a deep hole.

"The air raid shelter," he said. "When you hear the alarm, duck in here as fast as you can and stay down until you get the all clear. The Japs have their own shelter and when they come out, if they catch you in the open first, you'll be shot on sight."

More men filed into the barracks, among them Petty Officer Emery, one of the turret gunners from the Privateer.

Robert remembered him as a cheerful, beefy sort. Now the skin hung off his bones like his flesh was melting from within. His complexion was jaundiced, and while his eyes sparkled at seeing Robert, they couldn't hide the underlying misery.

After the initial handshakes and back slapping Robert noted, "There's you and Paulson. Anyone else here from the Privateer?"

"Chiefs Phillips and McPhearson landed with us. But McPhearson was pretty tore up in the guts with flak shrapnel. He didn't live past morning. A patrol captured us soon after."

"So where is Phillips?"

Emery shrugged. "From interrogation he got sent to another camp. God help him wherever he went."

"And the others? Evans? Beardsley?"

"No clue."

They sat on Robert's bunk and chatted, mostly sharing tips about how to survive the camp. When night fell, Emery and the enlisted men returned to their barracks. A piece of tarp was pulled over the doorway. One of the officers retrieved a homemade tin-can lamp from under his bunk. After placing the lamp in the middle of the aisle, he lit it with a match. Kerosene-scented smoke curled from its small sputtering flame.

Eight officers sat on bunks facing the lamp, eight faces etched with woe and anguish, eight pairs of eyes studying the flame, glistening with dreams of hope and salvation, mesmerized by the dancing lick of fire. One of the men produced a cigarette and it was passed around.

Four other officers remained in their bunks, too stricken by scurvy, dysentery, and starvation to move.

Heavy steps tramped close. A guard shouted in Japanese, "Lights out," and banged the wall with a stick. The owner of the lamp blew out the flame, and as darkness swallowed the prisoners, the reality of their situation returned fully upon them, hot and sticky, like slime from a sewer. The guard continued to the other barracks, shouting and banging the walls.

"If you need to talk," Paulson cautioned, "then whisper."

Robert had nothing to say. His belly ached from hunger. He arranged his bunk, removed his boots, and lay down. At least he had the blessing of being among comrades.

Mosquitoes buzzed around him. He pulled one of the thin blankets over his head for protection. Fleas emerged from the mats and crawled along his skin, seeking his armpits, crotch, and head. He scratched them, carefully at first, then angrily. He had to be careful though. Scratch too hard and he risked tearing his skin and getting infected.

Thoughts of home and Makiko drifted into his mind, the images soft as clouds, but he pushed them away.

***

The days unfolded with dreadful regularity. At six every morning, a soldier in the guard tower clanged a bell. The prisoners shambled into the washroom in the center of the square. In the dim light of morning, men crowded around large concrete basins arranged down the middle. They stripped out of their shirts to splash cold water on their faces and their bony naked torsos. Every third day, the guards brought straight razors and the men were forced to shave as best they could with the dull, chipped blades.

They filed out of the washroom and gathered along the walls of the barracks fronting the yard, and waited. Outside the gate, the Japanese soldiers assembled into formation.

Time for *Tenko*.

The prisoners formed four neat rows, with Robert and the other officers in the front rank. Mancinelli stood at the front center, facing the gate.

A squad of soldiers hustled into the compound and took positions along the fence. They carried rifles at port arms, bayonets fixed. Other soldiers circulated around the prisoners, glowering, bamboo truncheons at the ready.

Major Tanaka led an entourage into the yard, a samurai sword hitched to his side. Because of his paunch, the dark circles around his eyes, and his thin beard, the prisoners nicknamed him the *Raccoon*.

Mancinelli called the garrison of prisoners to attention and reported, in his mangled Japanese, how many were present and accounted for, which could fluctuate day by day. Within a week after Robert had arrived, the last two of the Dutch prisoners had died as well as the one civilian, an American businessman who had been interned when the Japanese captured Manila. Yesterday, four survivors from a downed B-29 had been added to the camp's roster.

Mancinelli bowed, and the prisoners took his lead. They held the position for a long time. The guards with the truncheons charged through the formation, smacking the backs and legs of prisoners not showing proper respect.

Tanaka mumbled something, and Mancinelli straightened. Every morning, he recited his spiel in Japanese. "I humbly resubmit my request for our Red Cross packages. Nine of our men need medical attention."

Robert was tempted to intercede and make the request in proper Japanese, but he decided against it. Better that he kept his proficiency a secret for as long as possible.

And every morning, Sergeant Uchimi (nickname: Itchy-face) pounced on Mancinelli to slap and kick him. Mancinelli would drop to his knees, and head lowered to the ground, ask again.

Then Tanaka—*Raccoon*—would lecture in his gruff voice that the prisoners were awarded luxuries—bunks, blankets, running water, regular meals—that Japanese soldiers on the front lines were doing without. And every lecture ended the same. "Request denied."

Tanaka and his staff marched away. Itchy-face shouted for the assorted morning details to fall out. Men dragged the shit-squatters and urine pots to the sludge pond on the eastern side of the compound. Other men followed guards to a hand-cart that brought kettles of food to a long table under a shed. Prisoners queued up, tin cans in hand to receive breakfast— a watery, saltless stew consisting of coarse brown rice and a maize-like grain, both of which passed through the intestines undigested. Occasionally they might get bits of boiled white radish. Rarely were they offered morsels of fish or squid.

Breakfast finished, the prisoners were separated for the day's work details. Some men worked the sludge pit, drawing the foul goo to fertilize the prison gardens. Others were put to work around the camp, digging out stumps, filling in potholes, dragging lumber, stirring and pouring concrete. For those without chores, the guards would lead them in hours of pointless calisthenics.

Robert and twelve of the men were marched to the foundry in the village up the road from the camp. They shoveled slag and coal into wheelbarrows and within a half hour were black with soot. They toiled under the watchful glare of the guards, only allowed to speak if it contributed to the task at hand. "Move that pile here." "On three, push."

Robert passed the time mentally reciting his list of dead prisoners.

At noon they rested for a half hour in whatever shade they could find. Sometimes they were given water but were never served anything to eat.

In the middle of one afternoon, Robert noticed that Paulson was missing. Robert steered his empty wheelbarrow next to Emery and grabbed a shovel. When the guard turned away, he whispered to Emery, "Have you seen Paulson?"

Emery adroitly spaded the slag in a circle, furtively glancing up and around, then sidled beside Robert. "No, sir. He came out here with us but I haven't seen him since morning."

Robert wondered what had happened to his friend. Could he have escaped? Not likely. How far could a cadaverous American get without collapsing or being discovered?

At the end of the work shift, the foundry detail was gathered. Robert noted that the guards paid no mind to Paulson's absence. The prisoners were marched back to the camp, and when they entered the wire perimeter, they found him.

Paulson had been lashed to a post on the southern end of the yard, his arms hooked over a pole fixed crossways to the post, crucifixion style. He hung bare-chested with his toes barely touching the ground, and he squirmed like a caterpillar impaled on a stick.

Itchy-face and two of the other guards—Yasuda, *Fish mouth* and Okazaki, *Onion*—walked up to Paulson and punched and kicked him.

Robert cringed in disgust. His loathing for their captors sank into the deepest reaches of hate he could imagine.

All the prisoners formed up for roll call and dinner. The menu was the same as breakfast. They were forced to look at Paulson as they ate and watch the guards take turns abusing him. The worst was when the guards critiqued one another's technique when they kicked him in the balls. Paulson's cries and moans carried over the yard, disturbing and sickening.

Itchy-face never announced what had been Paulson's transgression, but a rumor circulated that a guard had searched his bunk and found a small can of cooking oil. Since the prisoners were not issued such an item, he could only have stolen it.

The prisoners retreated to the barracks. Paulson remained, hanging from the pole like a torn, bloodied flag.

Long after lights out, Robert was awakened by a voice. It was Emery kneeling beside his bunk. "Sir, we got to help Lieutenant Paulson," he whispered. "Take him some water. Do something."

Robert sat up. The mosquitoes were especially thick tonight and that must have added to Paulson's torment. Robert looked past the gaps of the tarp over the door, to the deep translucent purple of night.

What were the chances any of them could cross the yard undetected? None.

"Negative," Robert whispered, his tone harsh. "I know what you're trying to do. But if we go out there, the Japs will have more bodies to hang and torture."

"Then sir," Emery pleaded, "I'll go alone."

"No," Robert answered, doing his best to keep his voice low. "I forbid it."

Another voice called from the darkness. Mancinelli. "What's going on over there? Who's that?"

"Nothing, sir," Robert answered.

"Is this about Paulson?"

Robert let a beat pass. "Yes, sir."

"Then stand fast," Mancinelli ordered. "There's nothing we can do for him without making it worse for the rest of us. Understand?"

Robert and Emery stayed quiet.

"This is my decision. Understand?"

"Aye, aye, sir." Emery scuttled down the alley to the back of the barracks, where he would crawl out a hole to return to his bunk.

Robert drew a blanket over his body to ward off the mosquitoes and set his head back down.

The next morning, at Tenko, the guards cut Paulson loose and his bruised and lacerated body fell to the dirt. Itchy-face ordered two prisoners to strip off Paulson's trousers and drag his naked corpse to the pit.

Robert had another name to add to his memorized list of the dead.

20

August 1945

Makiko stood over a wicker basket stuffed with her bedding, clothes, a few kitchen utensils, and personal belongings. In the bottom of the basket she had hidden Robert's letters, which were crammed into a smaller box for easier transport. Regretfully, she had left Kosuke Uchida's photo behind. He belonged in the past, and Robert was her true love.

A wicker rucksack heavy with more belongings sagged on her shoulders. Azusa and the other women of the farming camp also waited with Makiko, each of them bringing what she could carry in a basket and a rucksack. The morning was decidedly warm, and sweat sopped through Makiko's cotton blouse and the bandana tied around her brow. She waited for the order to board the pair of army trucks that had come to evacuate the camp.

Makiko thought about her parents and her friends. Where was Robert? She shut her imagination to thoughts about what the army could be doing to him. She forced herself to recall those joyful moments from their one night of passion.

Soldiers inspected the cottages and sheds, collecting what was needed for the war effort—the chickens, farm and carpentry tools, anything made of aluminum—and left everything else. Furniture. Lamps. Books. The few heirlooms the women had brought were abandoned for good.

While others grumbled, Makiko kept quiet and wiped the tears weighing her eyes. Yoshi, Takara, and the pups watched the proceedings from separate bamboo cages placed close to Makiko's basket. Misfortune had found her once more.

Yoshi pawed at his cage, but Makiko couldn't bear to look at him. The poor trusting dog had no idea what was happening, and she was certain she would never see him or the other Shiba Inus again. When the evacuation order specifically mentioned that no pets were allowed, she knew her only option to spare them was to set them free. But no one would remain in the camp to take them in, and stray dogs wouldn't last long before they ended in a dinner bowl.

Sergeant Watanabe approached her. He grasped the handles on Takara's and the pups' cages. Makiko closed her eyes and absorbed the grief.

"Don't worry," he said, his voice unexpectedly kind.

Makiko opened her eyes to see him pointing at his collar insignia. The piping was purple instead of the usual red. "I'm with the veterinary corps." He crouched beside the cages and stroked the dogs' coats through the latticework. "What beautiful Shiba Inus." He stood and brushed dust from his uniform.

He fished a note from a trouser pocket and handed it to her. "You're going to Kaichi, correct?"

Makiko nodded.

"And your mother is in the tuberculosis sanitarium in Hiroshima?"

"*Hai,*" Makiko acknowledged, now confused as well as sad.

"Your father told me," Watanabe explained. "I processed his orders when he was evacuated to Kaichi. I've given you the address of the kennel where I'm taking your dogs. It's in the same ward as the sanitarium. When you visit your mother, stop by."

Makiko stared at the note. "But how? Why?"

He picked up the cages with Takara and the pups. "The government has mandated that Shiba Inus are to be taken to Hiroshima for safekeeping. These dogs are the pride of Japan and they deserve a better fate than to wind up as soup bones."

Makiko was taken aback by this measure. It both astonished and gratified her that in spite of the chaos and ineptitude plaguing the government, someone was at last doing something worthwhile.

"I'm being transferred to the garrison there. When the situation improves—" Watanabe chuckled sardonically, "I'll try my best to reunite you with your dogs."

Another sergeant yelled orders for everyone to start boarding. Azusa and the other women glumly hauled their baskets to the other truck.

Watanabe pushed the dog cages along one side of the first truck's bed. "Come on," he said to Makiko. He pointed to Yoshi's cage and snapped his fingers.

She lifted the cage and handed it to Watanabe, who shoved it next to Takara's and the pups'. Another soldier hopped onto the truck and stacked crates of chickens.

"Wait," Makiko shouted. She wanted to touch Yoshi one last time. He poked his shiny wet nose through the gaps of the latticework. Tears came back to sting her eyes.

"You'll see him again," Watanabe said. "I promise."

She trusted his sincerity but couldn't believe him. What promises had any merit in this chaos?

Makiko lowered her head and backed away. She dragged herself to the other truck, where she was helped by a soldier to climb aboard. The women settled onto the benches on opposite sides of the truck bed, jammed tight as plums in a jar. They rested their feet on the baskets and rucksacks piled between them.

Their truck grunted to life and pulled behind the first one to start the journey toward the train depot at Hachijoi. Dust swirled over their truck and the women masked their faces with bandanas.

People began to accumulate along the road, sometimes a solitary figure, other times the remnants of a family. Kilometer by kilometer, more and more people clotted the road as it seemed like the countryside was emptying itself of humanity. Everyone resembled an animated rag doll, and shuffled listlessly in a pained, relentless procession. Women trudged along, babies strapped to their backs. Few carried anything larger than a bundle, and the road was littered with discarded items of every description. Clothes. Tatami mats. Books. Luggage. The occasional framed portrait.

They passed the blasted and scorched remains of houses and vehicles, tangible evidence of the war that threatened to strike at any time.

The truck slowed to a crawl and forced its way—horn blaring, Watanabe shouting—through the masses of the dispossessed huddled around the station platform. The truck halted and Watanabe released the tailgate. He said, "Makiko. Azusa. You are boarding this train." He gestured to his right. "Everyone else, the train to Osaka is that way. Hurry, the trains could leave at any moment."

The women disembarked and collected their baskets and rucksacks. When Makiko noticed that the truck with the Shiba Inus continued toward her train, she allowed a small smile in relief. Perhaps Watanabe's plan would work out.

People lay in forlorn heaps like they had given up on themselves. Everyone smelled like musty laundry. Others hustled with children in tow through gaps in the mob. Names were shouted. Babies cried. A voice on a loudspeaker shouted unintelligible instructions. A train bell clanged. The cacophony was a din of desperation and hopelessness.

With no time for prolonged goodbyes, Makiko, Azusa, and the other women exchanged brief hugs and blessings. Makiko and Azusa shouldered their rucksacks, lifted their baskets and proceeded in a hobbling gait, bumping and shoving their way forward.

"Which car do we board?" Azusa asked.

Makiko led them toward a soldier who had his back to their train. He pushed against the anxious, roiling crowd. She set her basket down and brandished her evacuation order at the corporal. "Where do I board?" she yelled.

The corporal snatched the order from her hand, glanced at it, and handed it back. "This train. Any car." He turned his attention to another woman.

Makiko and Azusa forced their way around the corporal and climbed aboard.

She remembered prewar train travel as efficient and glamorous. Now it was anything but. Drab military colors obscured the decorative livery. Many of the light fixtures lacked bulbs. The cozy compartments had been gutted to open the interior for cargo. They stepped over fellow passengers, tucked around baskets and crates, and situated themselves on a simple wooden bench, on which Makiko spread a quilt for cushioning.

The train lurched forward, and soon the depot disappeared into the distance. The train proceeded haltingly around the curves and hills, like it was a snake hiding from marauding hawks.

Since they had to give up their chickens, the women of the farm camp had butchered and cooked a few to prepare meals for their trip; no telling when they would eat again. Azusa pulled a bento box from her basket and shared the soybean curd and cold roasted chicken with Makiko. When Makiko noticed a mother and two small girls eyeing them, she reached into her basket and handed them one of her bento boxes. The mother took the box with effusive thanks and handed the meal to her hungry brood.

The train chugged past work crews repairing sections of cratered railroad. The view out the windows varied from bucolic vistas of green meadows and pastel-blue mountains, to horrific panoramas of bombed towns and eviscerated buildings. Lines of civilians—a parade of haggard, blackened faces, hair grayed with dust—shambled along the roads.

Why were they all punished like this? Misery after misery, humiliation after humiliation piled one on top of another. How much could they endure? Day by day what they owned kept shrinking, their possessions, their circle of loved ones. To what end? Until they were each alone in the world, with nothing, indigent, each like a weed that had been pulled out by the roots and thrown to the wind?

***

The next morning the train halted briefly in Kaichi. After hours of doing nothing but sitting and waiting, Makiko and Azusa had to hurry off their car before the train rushed to the next station.

Hiro was sitting on the edge of a bench in front of the depot office and was nodding in slumber. A straw hat shaded his head, and his hands were folded over the top of his cane. He looked like a pensioner on holiday instead of a man waiting for the world to end.

A poster on the wall behind him showed two teenage girls shoulder to shoulder with a young, fierce-looking soldier. He wielded a rifle with fixed bayonet, the girls wielded sharpened bamboo poles. The background showed hordes of enemy troops and tanks surrounding them. The caption read: *Victory in the last five minutes!*

Madness, thought Makiko. *If we couldn't stop the Americans with modern weapons, how can we stop them with sticks and knives?* But she kept the thought to herself. You never knew who was listening.

She hailed her father, and he sat up straight, suddenly startled.

"Father, how long have you been waiting?"

Blinking, he braced against his cane and stood. "As if I had anything else to do." He led them to a wheelbarrow, on which they piled their baskets and rucksacks. Relieved of their burdens, Makiko and Azusa smothered him with kisses and hugs.

"And Mother?" Makiko asked.

"Doing better, though she is worried sick about you."

"And my parents?" Azusa asked.

"I spoke with them last week when I was in Hiroshima," Hiro replied. "They send their prayers."

Excited, Makiko produced the note Watanabe had given her. "And I have a little good news. Can you believe this? Yoshi, Takara, and the pups have been taken to a kennel close to Mother." She explained what Sergeant Watanabe had done.

Hiro studied the note. Smiling, he returned it to Makiko and said, "We must be grateful for all the Lord's miracles, big and small." He tapped his cane against one of the wheelbarrow's handles. "Let's get going."

***

Life in the new farming camp wasn't much different from their previous home. Mostly they did without. The camp was populated with women and girls evacuated from the southern coast of Honshu. Being one of the oldest, Makiko was put in charge of work details.

Today she and Azusa wandered the main dirt road down the valley in search of firewood. When they found something worth retrieving, they took turns dumping the sticks and branches in one another's wicker rucksacks. The rucksacks full, they headed back to the camp. Makiko wondered about dinner. Rice was impossible to find, even on the black market, and wheat flour porridge was like eating paste. Maybe Hiro had bartered for some fish and barley.

The echo of an airplane engine throbbed over the landscape. A shiver of fear wiggled down Makiko's spine and she panned the valley in search of the airplane.

A flash in the corner of one eye snagged her attention. Something shiny darted low over the valley floor, silvery like a fish. Her feet halted and she stared.

Not one but two sleek flying machines raced over the ground. The throbbing increased to a menacing rumble. The two machines zoomed upward, suddenly dark against the azure sky. Sun glinting over their metallic silhouettes, they wheeled toward Makiko and Azusa.

Fighter planes.

Makiko couldn't identify the type but their lack of camouflage confirmed one thing. These belonged to the American Air Force. Japanese airplanes bore camouflage, but the Americans sent their warplanes into combat in polished chrome-like aluminum that reflected every ray of the sun. Rather than sneak through the sky, it was as if they were advertising their presence and daring the Japanese to come and fight.

That wiggle of fear turned into a lash of panic. It was like swimming and seeing a shark's fin slice through the nearby water. She hurried her steps, her wooden clog sandals spanking the bottoms of her feet. Terror fueled her movements. Azusa stayed close and kept her head turned toward the airplanes.

The fighters banked, tiny and toy-like. Makiko figured the airplanes were more than a kilometer away, but they could close the distance in seconds.

"I'm scared," Azusa admitted, her voice quaking.

Makiko looked for cover. They were on the open road with nothing but barren dirt and meager grass for a hundred meters in every direction. The sanctuary of trees and rocks looked impossibly far away.

The vibrato of the engines shook her guts. Makiko looked over her shoulder and saw the airplanes lining up on them.

Azusa screamed, "Run, Makiko. Run!" She shucked her rucksack and kicked off her sandals.

But Makiko thought, *What good would it do to run?* The fighter planes were closing upon them at hundreds of kilometers per hour.

Instead she dove to the ground. The rucksack slammed against her back and firewood spilled over her head. She lay still, like a mouse caught in the garden and hoping the predator wouldn't notice her. Flattened against the dirt, she managed to holler, "Azusa, throw yourself to the ground!"

But Azusa sprinted up the road, arms and legs flailing, the bottoms of her bare feet whipping behind her.

The fighter planes shrieked like murderous demons. A noise like that of a buzz saw ripped through the air. Crimson tracers rained upon Azusa, splattering, ricocheting, and she was engulfed in geysers of dust.

Makiko tried to melt into the ground, fearing that she was next.

The airplanes roared overhead, for an instant blotting out the sun, then whistled up the valley.

Makiko carefully lifted her head. Sand and dirt sifted from her face. Azusa lay in a tattered heap, dust lingering over her. A howl of despair erupted in Makiko's throat.

The two fighter planes cruised upward, the drone of their engines fading, their pilots seemingly unconcerned with the carnage they had so leisurely administered.

Makiko shrugged out of the rucksack and rose to her feet. Tears flooded her eyes and sobs racked her body. She stumbled toward what was left of Azusa.

The girl's body looked like it had been savaged with an ax. One severed leg lay off to the side. The air reeked with the stench of a slaughterhouse. Blood pooled around her mangled form, and smoke coiled from a tracer bullet embedded in her back.

Makiko collapsed. The world vanished, replaced by a vast desert of heartbreak where it was just her and her sorrow and the bloody thing that had been her friend. She reached toward the corpse, weeping uncontrollably, uncomprehending of the need or the reason for Azusa's death.

21

August 7, 1945

An hour before their usual early morning wake-up, Hiro roused Makiko and the other women and girls in the farm camp's bunkhouse. When they congregated in the dining shed, rather than eat breakfast, they were set to work cutting bed linen into square bandages.

Makiko and the others sensed from the quiet urgency and the disruption in the camp's schedule that something terrible had happened. Both Hiro and the camp director, the normally affable Shinobu Aoki, wore strained expressions but didn't share what troubled them.

As dawn's light gradually illuminated the camp, an army truck arrived and halted beside the dining shed. Makiko and three of the older women were ordered to collect barrels and fill them with fresh water from the nearby creek. The routine occupied her mind and kept her nerves from fraying. She still ached for Azusa's death but kept the grief to herself. Several of the girls in the camp were orphans, and so Makiko's pain was not anything special. Better that she focus hopeful thoughts on those who lived. Her mother. Her father. Plus Robert. And her beloved Shiba Inus, Yoshi and Tanaka.

They were loading the truck with the water barrels and wicker baskets stacked with bandages when one of the soldiers let slip: "We're on our way to Hiroshima."

The name rippled from woman to girl to woman. They dropped whatever task occupied them and rushed toward Hiro and Shinobu, asking in a terrified chorus, "Hiroshima? What's happened? What do you know? My family, have you heard from my family?"

Shinobu lashed out at them. "You'll learn soon enough. Quit being so selfish with your concerns. You're only delaying needed help."

"Help for what?"

"Get back to your chores!"

Some of the workers wept, others returned to their duties. Makiko looked at her father, but he only returned her gaze with a guarded, poker-faced stare. That he wasn't even trying to comfort her meant something horrific had happened in Hiroshima. What about her mother?

Shinobu pulled Makiko aside. "You have medical experience, yes?"

"*Hai*," Makiko replied. "But not much. I started the physician's program at Tokyo Medical College, but had to drop out to help my par—"

Shinobu interrupted. "Get on the truck."

Makiko slipped under the tarpaulin stretched over the truck bed, figuring that her destination must be Hiroshima.

She took her place on a bench and settled in for a long ride. She prayed for her mother's safekeeping.

The truck started down the road. The girls and women who were left behind, slack-jawed and somber, followed them to the main road and shuffled to a halt. The truck picked up speed and dust swirled behind it. Makiko and the others in back—three women from the camp and two soldiers—each tied a scarf around his or her face, letting only their anxious eyes show.

They traveled for kilometers and joined an impromptu column of trucks and military cars headed southwest to Hiroshima. The worry nagging Makiko ratcheted into anxiety so acute it parched her throat. In this war of escalating horrors, she steeled herself for the worst. She had pulled bodies out of the rubble in Yokohama. She had seen charred corpses stacked in heaps.

What disaster awaited them in Hiroshima? Another aerial bombardment like the one that had ravaged Tokyo? Or had the American fleet sailed into the harbor and blasted the city with its big guns?

Upon approaching the Oto River valley, a pungent smoky odor filtered through their scarves. Makiko and the other women winced at the smell. The truck slowed and lurched to a stop. They scrambled from their seats and peeked out from the shelter of the tarpaulin.

Dozens of vehicles were parked randomly on a dirt field by the railroad tracks. From the adjacent trucks, crews were unloading cargo: wicker baskets, crates, barrels, and duffle bags.

A sergeant appeared behind their truck. He pulled the cloth mask down from his mouth. "What have you brought?"

"Water and bandages," a soldier replied.

"Any medicine? Tinctures?"

"No, sergeant."

He sighed and grimaced. "Do what you can."

The two soldiers jumped out of the truck and dropped the tailgate.

Makiko loosened her scarf to ask, "Where are we?"

"A kilometer from Akiyaguchi," the sergeant replied. "Just up the river from Hiroshima proper." He readjusted his mask and trotted to the next truck.

Makiko and the women climbed out. A gray curtain of smoke and ash obscured the sun, and what should have been a bright summer day was instead dulled by a dirty film.

Makiko stared down the road toward Hiroshima. The smoke wasn't localized over one part of the city, but seemed to fill the entire sky where it was framed by the hills east and west of the river.

They piled the water barrels and baskets into a handcart and pushed it to join a procession of soldiers and civilians heading down the sloping road, also pushing carts laden with supplies. The column halted at a checkpoint staffed by marines. Some were wearing baggy overalls and all wore cloth masks. In contrast, Makiko was dressed in her usual work clothes: cotton top, baggy *monpe* trousers, *tabi* socks, and *getas*.

"Proceed to the first triage assembly point," the marine commander instructed, his voice muffled by his mask. "But beware. The rubble might be poisonous."

"Poisonous?" a voice asked. "With what? Chemicals? Germs?"

"That's all I've been told," the officer replied.

Makiko and her crew continued to a park across the street from the Akiyaguchi train station. Judging by the hundreds of bodies arranged on the ground, the park had to be the triage assembly point. Military and civilian caretakers tended to the wounded.

Most of the victims were women and children. Some rested on mats or blankets, others lay directly on the grass. Some were naked, others clothed in tatters. All suffered terrible injuries: charred flesh, mangled limbs, faces lacerated and puffy.

An Army major wearing the brassard of a military doctor approached. He said, "Do your best to comfort them."

Makiko and the others moistened bandages and went from victim to victim to wipe away the soot and dirt. They draped wet cloth on reddened skin to soothe the pain. Eyes brimming with misery blinked at Makiko, and sorrow flooded her heart. Wiping back tears, she choked down sobs and set herself to work.

More wounded kept streaming into the park, some on stretchers; others staggered on bloodied feet, some were strapped to the backs of fellow survivors. Many suffered cruel burns, as if their bodies had been subjected to a sudden and appalling heat.

A group of children, covered in soot, wearing frayed rags, waddled toward them, advancing single file like a queue of lame ducks.

Two men in smocks, their faces covered by masks and goggles, shepherded them into the assembly point. The wounded proceeded in a macabre foot-dragging gait with their arms outstretched.

With growing angst, Makiko could see that their skin was bright pink with patches of wet crimson, as if the flesh had been fried and peeled off. Loose skin hung from their outstretched arms and hands. They walked in a bizarre side-to-side rocking gait, and she noticed that skin dragged from their naked feet like tattered socks. Their eyes glared from faces peeled raw and on some of them, the ears, noses, and lips appeared to have been scraped away.

The angst hardened into a shock that paralyzed Makiko. The children shuffled past her, a procession of unfathomable horror.

Makiko awoke from her gruesome reverie when a dazed older woman stumbled into her. The woman was covered in gray ash. She led a man by the sleeve. His face and hands were swollen into what looked like grotesque black rubber bags. His puffy lips glowed bright red and curled back to reveal broken teeth.

The old woman crumpled to Makiko's feet and wept. "It was one bomb," she managed between sobs. "One super bomb! It exploded brighter than the sun and destroyed everything." She clutched Makiko's pants and cried out, "Hell opened and swallowed Hiroshima!"

The burned man watched Makiko, shiny bloodshot eyes staring from his monstrously disfigured face. A marine grasped his arm and pulled him away. Another marine scooped the woman off the ground. "One bomb," she shrieked.

One bomb? A super bomb? How was that possible? Makiko regarded what she could see of Hiroshima. Around the train station, the damage wasn't as bad as she had witnessed in Yokohama. The sides of buildings facing away from the city looked relatively unscathed. But the sides toward Hiroshima were scarred and scorched, the windows blown out. Shingles dangled from blasted roofs. But closer to the center of the city, she knew, the destruction would be much worse.

A sergeant tapped her arm. He led a group of four who carried shovels. "If you're up to it," he said, "we're going into the city to rescue who we can."

"*Hai*," Makiko replied. He gave her a shovel and they hiked down the road into the city.

Charred bodies lay everywhere. Some were alive and moving. A soldier pushed a wheelbarrow up the road, a young woman sprawled inside, her body covered in a blood-soaked blanket. Her arms, feet, and face were minced into pulp. She moaned in delirium.

The man explained, "She was giving birth when the bomb exploded. The windows of the delivery room shattered and sprayed her with glass. Needless to say, she lost the baby."

The sergeant pointed up the road. "Take her to the assembly point. She'll get help there."

But what kind of help? They had no medicine or even morphine to ease the woman's suffering. The man trundled off with the wheelbarrow and his miserable passenger.

Makiko kept up with the sergeant and his team. Debris littered the street. Block by block the devastation increased, and up ahead, Makiko could see that entire blocks had been leveled into an expanse of rubble, relieved by solitary stumps of concrete and gnarled twists of steel.

Two men in western-style suits with fedoras fussed with a tripod-mounted camera. They seemed quite unremarkable if not for their cloth masks and the carnage around them.

Makiko tried to get her bearings. "Where is Higashi-ku?"

The taller of the two men pointed toward the worst of the devastation. "The ward is over there. The bomb exploded directly above. Nothing is left but cinders and waste."

Makiko stared and couldn't recognize a landmark to note where her mother had been. Everything—the buildings, the trees, the streets—was wiped out, replaced by smoke and destruction. The ghastly astonishment slammed into her. She sucked for breath but no air traveled down her throat. "Mother," she tried to cry out. "My mother."

The world wobbled beneath her feet. Her vision dimmed, she let go of the shovel...

Hands clutched her; it was the sergeant pulling her off the ground.

A soldier gave her a drink from his canteen. Makiko sipped and gathered herself. Her gaze ranged across the ruin, and deep inside, she pushed down the terror, pushed down the despair, and made herself go numb to the grisly reality. She knotted the scarf tight around her mouth and followed the sergeant and his men into what was left of Hiroshima.

Flames licked from the remnants of shattered buildings. Blackened, withered corpses were strewn about the streets. They passed processions of people shuffling in that bizarre, side-to-side gait, arms stretched before them, skin hanging from their wrists and dragging from their ankles. Scores of naked dead huddled around community wells or fountains, leaning toward the polluted water in a macabre communion.

Makiko became like a movie camera that recorded sights, sounds, and even smells, but could process no emotion. She witnessed ruin and torment that seared her mind, the destruction so massive that it remained incomprehensible for her to grasp as one continuous narrative. Rather the images branded her memories like vignettes from a nightmare.

At the moment when she was certain that she had witnessed the most gruesome of catastrophes, yet another ghastly scene would unfold before her.

A man rushed to their party. Shabby, burned rags clung to his bony frame. "Help me," he pleaded, his blistered and soot-covered face contorted in anguish. "My sister and her baby are trapped over there." He pointed to a heap of smoking rubble.

Makiko and the soldiers followed the man, who sprinted barefoot and left bloody prints behind on the dust and broken pavement.

A voice cried from deep inside the rubble, a woman's voice labored with pain. "Help me. Help my baby."

Smoke puffed through the confusion of shattered brick and concrete as if the fire were a beast in search of its next victim.

"I feel the heat," the woman shrieked. "I'm burning."

"Koharu!" the man yelled. He flung himself onto the heap and tore at the rubble with his hands until his fingers bled. The sergeant ordered everyone to dig around a large concrete fragment that blocked an opening into the heap. Makiko and the soldiers jammed their shovels around the fragment and began scraping. Thickening smoke seeped through the detritus.

The woman screamed, "I can't see. It's hot! I'm burning! Please help me and my baby!"

The cries skewered Makiko's ears. Her eyes blurred with tears, but she pressed on, matching the soldiers shovelful for shovelful. They raced against time and the fire, knowing that to save this woman and her child would be a small victory, but a victory nonetheless against the misery and loss surrounding them.

They cleared away enough of the debris to jam the points of their shovels under the fragment. As one they heaved on their shovel handles and slowly, the fragment began to tilt out of the way. Smoke curled from around its edge and Koharu's cries rose into an inhuman shriek whose pitch climbed higher and higher, until it faded into a shrill keening that tore at Makiko's nerves. She wanted to drop her shovel and cover her ears. The keening faded. Smoke belched from behind the fragment, and they retreated, defeated, eyes stinging.

The man dropped to the rubble and squirmed in misery. He clawed the dust and ash. Makiko stared at him, wondering if he was poisoning himself as the marine commander had warned. She absorbed the man's anguish, feeling her heart compress with pity. One of the soldiers tugged at her sleeve and led her away.

They walked along the concrete embankment of a canal, its waters clogged with bodies, mostly women, mostly naked. Some were bags of wrinkled broiled flesh, others red and pink like scalded stew meat. And all were quite dead, their bodies drifting in the slimy, putrid water.

Scene after scene, horror after horror, Makiko's mind reeled until it shut down.

When she came to, as if awakening from a fever, she was sitting and swaying in the back of an army truck as it rumbled up the road from Hiroshima. Her hands, arms, and shoulders ached with cramps, and she remembered that she had spent the last two days pulling the living and the dead from the ruins.

She looked out the back of the tarpaulin. In the distance, fire and columns of greasy black smoke corkscrewed from pyres of her dead fellow Japanese, the corpses neatly stacked and immolated to prevent contamination and disease.

At one point she had asked if any American prisoners were in the city. She was told about fifty were interned at Hiroshima Castle, itself practically at the center of the explosion, and so the castle had been demolished with no survivors.

She took stock of her loss with cold calculation. If Robert had been there, he was certainly dead. The tuberculosis sanitarium was destroyed, her mother dead. The kennel destroyed. Strangely, considering all the devastation and the suffering, she wept over the loss of her dogs.

Their deaths became a metaphor for the incomprehensible woe inflicted upon Hiroshima. She tried not to visualize what had happened to Yoshi and Tanaka, but she couldn't help but see their small bodies, smoke lifting from their scorched fur, their limbs charred to stumps, where they had been roasted alive.

***

When Makiko arrived back at the camp she learned that a second super bomb had destroyed Nagasaki. How much would Japan have to suffer?

The next day, a vintage decrepit taxi rattled into the camp. Curious about the visitors, Makiko stepped outside the dining shed. A wizened old man in a moth-eaten Army uniform dismounted from the driver's side. Strands of stringy white hair jutted from under his misshapen officer's cap. He wore the rank of colonel on his collar. Several boys, the oldest perhaps 14 years of age, remained inside the sedan. They wore a ragtag mix of military uniforms and civilian clothes. One brandished an antique rifle, their only weapon.

Without saying a word, the old colonel headed into the shed. Makiko followed. Hiro and Shinobu were sitting beside a table and rose to greet him.

The colonel slapped a riding crop against his thigh. "I need to feed my troops."

"What troops?" answered Hiro.

The colonel gestured with the crop toward the taxi. "Them. We haven't eaten since we left Yatsugi."

Makiko peeked under the lid of a pot stewing on a brazier. What cooked was to be the only hot meal today for the camp.

"We don't have much. Some *nukapan* with acorns and radish. And we have hot water disguising itself as tea."

"That will do."

"Where are you going?" Hiro asked.

"To the defenses at Fukuyama."

"Just you and those boys?" Makiko asked. "You have ammunition for that museum piece of a rifle?"

The colonel didn't answer, and the way his eyes crinkled and his mouth hardened betrayed his understanding of the folly of his assignment. But he answered as all the Japanese did when so pressed. He squared his shoulders and bowed curtly. "*Shouganai.*"

"*Hai,*" Hiro replied softly, nodding.

Makiko ladled porridge into a smaller stew pot she carried to the taxi. She passed the pot and a spoon to the boys and each took a turn helping himself to a mouthful. The pot emptied, she returned to the shed and emerged with a pot of tea. One of the boys offered a military canteen cup, which she filled and they shared. They acknowledged her generosity with effusive thanks. In these desperate times, one didn't feed another without robbing from his own bowl.

The colonel climbed back into his rickety taxi. Two of the boys jumped out and pushed the old car until it grumbled to life. As the taxi clattered down the road the boys scrambled back in.

Makiko closed her eyes to the lunacy and shook her head. The Americans could incinerate an entire city with one blow, and Japan was reduced to defending itself with elderly retirees and boys armed with relics.

The camp's barley ration was cut yet again. She spent the following days helping Shantou and the others catch crickets, which they ground and added into their gruel.

***

Hiro shared an official memorandum ordering everyone to report to the village of Mukaihara. Word was the government intended to broadcast a special announcement.

In the late morning of the next day, August 15, the camp emptied and the women and girls trekked down the road. Hiro was carried in a handcart. They met with soldiers, farmers, and other refugees who clustered around the post office in Mukaihara. Everyone looked equally haggard and spent, too withdrawn for gossip.

A radio in a wooden cabinet had been propped outside, above the post office front door. Hiro expressed surprise that there was electricity to power the radio. As they waited for the hour of the announcement, people milled about in grim expectation.

"I've heard rumor about a surrender," a farmer said, somberly.

"Yes, a surrender," a young boy yelped in glee. "The Americans have surrendered. We have won the war."

The farmer cuffed the boy across the back of his head. "You dolt! The Americans are bombing us to oblivion, and they wait at our doorstep like hungry bears."

The radio played a medley of patriotic songs. Then the music stopped and when an announcer began speaking, the postmaster stepped onto a chair, reached to the radio, and turned up the volume.

Makiko clutched her chest and held her breath.

The announcer, a man with a crisp voice, said, "Everyone please show the proper and necessary courtesy. I present to you, our exalted monarch, the Emperor Hirohito."

Everyone braced to attention and bowed their heads. Out the corners of her eyes, Makiko traded looks of astonishment with those around her. *The Emperor?* Rarely was his visage seen in print, and no one had ever heard his voice.

The hiss of a record with static and pops emanated from the radio speaker. Then a slow measured voice, somewhat high-pitched, began:

"To our good and loyal subjects: After pondering deeply the general trends of the world and the actual conditions obtaining in Our Empire today, We have decided to effect a settlement of the present situation by resorting to an extraordinary measure.

"We have ordered Our Government to communicate to the Governments of the United States, Great Britain, China, and the Soviet Union that Our Empire accepts the provisions of their Joint Declaration."

The language was formal and stiff, and Makiko listened intently to cull its meaning. Certain phrases stuck in her memory.

"The welfare of the wounded and the war-sufferers, and of those who have lost their homes and livelihood, are the objects of Our profound solicitude."

The message continued, "The hardships and sufferings to which Our nation is to be subjected hereafter will be certainly great."

And finally, "Unite your total strength, to be devoted to construction for the future. Cultivate the ways of rectitude, foster nobility of spirit, and work with resolution—so that you may enhance the innate glory of the Imperial State and keep pace with the progress of the world."

The Emperor's words ended abruptly, and the broadcast continued with a hiss and pops before fading to dead air. People raised their heads and gaped in confusion. What did the Emperor just say? What did he mean?

The announcer returned and explained, "The Emperor has just allowed that Japan has surrendered."

People gasped.

"Orders of capitulation will be promulgated in due time. All military, police, and civilian entities will submit to the authority of the occupation forces. Long live the Emperor."

Makiko stared, stunned, overcome by the news. People wept.

An Army captain whispered, "Our humiliation is complete. I cannot live with this shame." He drew a pistol from his holster and marched into the woods. Shortly, a gunshot echoed.

Men and women crumpled into one another's arms. No one could comprehend what the future would bring. In its thousands of years of history, Japan had never surrendered, had never been occupied. Centuries ago, the worst threat to their sovereignty, the Mongols, had been driven back. Now the Americans were coming and everyone was certain that Japan was forever destroyed.

The years of despair, of deprivation, of tragedy, welled within Makiko. Tears pushed against her eyes, the last of her resolve drained from her, and she couldn't help but fall to her knees.

22

August 16, 1945

Robert noticed a shift in mood among the guards. The previous day, they were especially somber. Like the other prisoners, Robert had grown to read the guards' moods the way a sailor reads the weather. Some great concern seemed to hang over the guards' heads, but if that weight came crashing down, it would be the prisoners who would get squashed.

Early the next morning, Robert paced along the fence closest to where the guards rested and smoked when on break. He tried not to act interested in what they discussed, and they in turn took little notice of him because they assumed he didn't know Japanese. He overheard snippets of conversation.

"Travel restrictions are still in place."

"Rice will continue to be rationed."

"How long before we go home?"

"What now that the Emperor has spoken?"

The Emperor? Spoken about what?

Then he heard: "Who would've thought that surrender was possible?"

Surrender? When? How? But he had heard *surrender* and knew that accounted for the guards' bleak mood. Japan had lost the war. Robert's fingers quivered, and he clenched his fists to hide his excitement. He wanted to sprint to the officer's barracks and share the news. But he remained close to the fence and kept his expression plain as if he hadn't heard anything. When the two soldiers ended their break and returned to their duties, Robert strolled from the fence.

The other prisoners waited by the barracks for the morning's *Tenko*. Robert headed straight to Mancinelli.

"It's over," Robert said. The words threatened to explode from him. "Japan has surrendered."

Everyone within earshot turned and stared, dumbstruck. Eyes peeled wide in hope and astonishment.

"How do you know?" Mancinelli asked.

Robert pointed to where he had been standing and related what he had overheard.

"It's over?" Lieutenant Welles asked. He was a new prisoner, the bombardier from a downed B-29.

Men congratulated and slapped one another.

Mancinelli raised his hands, looking worried. "Let's put a damper on the rejoicing. You've all heard the rumor. If the Japs surrender, they will shoot us all to save face. Plus they've got a lot to hide for what they've done to us in these camps."

The guards lined up outside the gate, which was the cue for the prisoners to assemble for *Tenko*. Major Tanaka and his staff marched from the cadre building. Two guards opened the gates and Tanaka strutted through, samurai sword at his side, his uniform starched, his boots gleaming. His staff and guards took position around him.

Standing at attention, Robert waited for a sign from the Japanese that the war was over. But *Tenko* followed its scripted routine until the point when Mancinelli, as always, requested their Red Cross boxes.

Tanaka mumbled an order and Sergeant Uchimi sprang from his position to pounce on Mancinelli, beating him with a cane.

Robert cringed at the sound of bamboo smacking against flesh. But there was nothing he could do except watch Mancinelli wither under the blows and roll to his side like a groveling dog.

Uchimi withdrew and Mancinelli slowly rose to his feet, clutching his ribs and bleeding from his cheeks and nose.

Tanaka growled another order. Uchimi repeated it, shouting, "Everyone on their knees. Hands up and behind your head." Several of his men stormed through the prisoners, caning them indiscriminately. "*Ima! Ima!*" Now! Now!

In short order the prisoners dropped to their knees and held themselves upright, fingers laced behind heir heads.

Tanaka and his officers paced to the side. The guards formed a semicircle facing the prison yard and chambered fresh rounds into their Arisaka rifles, the sound making an ominous click-clack.

A cold panic traced down Robert's spine. Though the threat of getting gunned down was always a possibility, this was the first time the Japanese menaced them so openly with loaded rifles.

A squad of soldiers trotted into the yard, the heavy machine gun from the guard tower propped on their shoulders. The semicircle of guards parted in the center and the machine gun was positioned in the gap, fifty feet in front of the prisoners. The machine gun crew crouched beside their weapon. The gunner cycled the charging handle while his assistant gunner slid a strip of cartridges into the feed tray. The clatter of the gun's mechanism sounded like a guillotine ratcheting into place. The gunner grasped the spade grips and squinted through the gun sights as he traversed the barrel across the prisoners. All he had to do was press the trigger and he would chop them to pieces. He held the muzzle steady on Mancinelli and waited.

The prisoners watched, trembling, emaciated chests heaving, lungs bellowing their final breaths. At any second Tanaka could give the order, and the yard would be drenched with blood.

Robert had never known such terror. The muzzle of every weapon was like the mouth of a tomb ready to swallow him. His heart slammed against his ribs. His pulse thumped so hard the sound echoed in his skull.

What was the sense in this execution? The war was over. They had survived. What was the point of enduring what they had, praying day after day for salvation, then on the eve of peace to be slaughtered like rats? He would never see home again. The memory of Makiko taunted him, like he had no right to even dream of her or anything pleasant and beautiful.

Robert's world caved in on a realm of filth and hunger, suffering and despair. He was beyond tears. All he could do was let his eyes range from the machine gun, to the eyes of the gunner, then to Tanaka, Uchimi, to the individual soldiers watching them, fingers on rifle triggers. He stared at the back of Mancinelli's dirty head, closely shorn, scabbed over from scurvy.

He tried not to contemplate what awaited them, but the images came to him in gruesome sharp focus. At the moment when the machine gun opened up, the prisoners would scramble for safety, but to no avail. Bullets would mince flesh, shatter bone. Blood and gore would splatter everywhere. And where would the prisoners run to? The fence, only to get snagged on the barbed wire where the guards would use them for target practice.

Afterwards the Japanese would drag their bodies to the burial hole. Then raze and burn the camp and expunge all traces of what had happened. No one would know that Nagoya No. 3-C Branch Camp had ever existed.

The minutes passed, the tension brittle as thin glass.

At last Tanaka stirred. Without a word, he started for the exit and his staff trailed behind him. The guards relaxed their rifles, but the machine gun remained trained on the prisoners.

More long minutes ticked by. Uchimi ordered the guards to remain at ease. Then half were sent away. The men at the machine gun relaxed. But the prisoners remained on their knees, hands behind their heads, still pale with fright.

Robert's legs began to cramp. Adding to the misery, flies crawled down his collar, up his sleeves, and crept around his eyes and up his nostrils. His knees ached.

The sun burned overhead. Sweat trickled down his temples and brow. His throat burned from thirst. Out the corners of his eyes he saw men waver. One plopped to the ground. Then another. He expected Uchimi to rush over and beat them with his cane, but the sergeant remained by the gate, looking hateful and frustrated.

More prisoners fell. Soldiers left the yard. The machine gun crew sat behind their weapon, and in boredom, sipped from their canteens and fussed with rocks in the dirt.

Robert became light-headed and nauseous from heat stroke. By the sun's position overhead he guessed it was noon, and they had been suffering for five hours.

Uchimi barked an order. The machine gun was unloaded and its cartridge strips stowed in an ammo box. The crew lifted the gun and carried it out of the yard. The last of the soldiers filed out, and Uchimi told Mancinelli to dismiss the prisoners.

Hearing that, Robert released his hands from behind his head and crumpled to the dirt. He stretched his legs and flexed his fingers to restore the circulation. All around him, his fellow prisoners lay on the ground, squirming in relief. In ones and twos, they rose to their feet and helped their comrades.

Why hadn't Tanaka killed them? And what now?

They waited—confused, anxious—for the Japanese to return to their usual schedule. The machine gun was lifted back to the guard tower and the guards continued patrolling the yard. But nothing else happened. No work details. No calisthenics. No breakfast. When the sun settled over the western horizon, the prisoners gathered for dinner. Again, nothing. It was as if the guards had forgotten them.

Robert and the officers waited in their barracks, convinced that the Japanese had not fed them for why waste food on the condemned? Tomorrow, Tanaka would surely have them all killed.

That night the prisoners discussed escaping, but Mancinelli ordered everyone to stay put. Within the barbed-wire perimeter, they at least had a hope of surviving. Outside the wire, they would be shot immediately.

Robert crawled into his bunk with barely the strength to move. Desperation, the day's torment, and a starvation diet sapped his energy, but even so, he spent a fitful night fearing tomorrow.

The next morning the prisoners assembled for *Tenko*. But the Japanese cadre was led by Captain Saito, the owlish camp adjutant. Strangely, instead of rifles, the guards carried waxed-cardboard boxes, which they stacked beside the adjutant.

Robert understood what was happening. Those were the much-denied Red Cross boxes. He broke formation and proceeded to Mancinelli. Uchimi tried to stare him down but did nothing to interfere. Robert took his place beside the colonel and said, "If you don't mind, sir, let me translate."

"What's going on?" Mancinelli whispered.

"I'm not sure, but I think we're out of danger," Robert whispered back.

Mancinelli squared his shoulders and stared at the Japanese adjutant. He ordered Robert, "Ask Saito if Japan has surrendered."

Robert translated the question. Saito was taken back by his fluency and replied with an evasive, "The war is over."

"What happened to Major Tanaka?"

"The major is indisposed."

The same soldiers who yesterday manned the machine gun, now pushed the meal cart, laden with steaming pots of food. More soldiers toted wicker baskets heaped with fresh clothes and shoes and placed these beside the Red Cross boxes.

An infectious celebration rippled through the prisoners. Mancinelli turned about and shouted for everyone to remain at attention. He called his officers for a huddle.

"Tanaka has taken off and left Saito to answer for what's happened to us. It's no coincidence that they're bringing us the Red Cross boxes and food. They intend to fatten us up before we're repatriated. Tell the men to safeguard their rags and keep them as evidence." Mancinelli tugged at the tattered sleeves of his uniform and pointed to his frayed rope sandals. "I'll bet the Japs are going to make it look like this place was a summer camp instead of a hellhole."

He ordered the officers to take charge of the Red Cross boxes and distribute their contents accordingly. The boxes were of two types. Most were food parcels that contained cans of fruit, corned beef, tuna, biscuits, coffee, plus chocolate, hard candy, gum, cigarettes, and soap. The other boxes were medical parcels with aspirin, ointments, iodine, bandages, gauze, writing pads, and pencils.

While the prisoners distributed the contents of the Red Cross boxes, Saito and his men shrank out of the yard.

The prisoners spent the rest of the day eating, washing up, and tending to the sick. Now with the means to record names, Robert circulated among the prisoners to compile from memory a list of their fallen comrades. Outside the fence, the guards watched, solemn and withdrawn.

That night the prisoners lit a bonfire in the center of the yard and sang about freedom and America and promised they would never forget one another. Giddy with elation, Robert stared at the night sky, at the fire's embers floating upward, and thought of them as sparks of good fortune seeking his mother, his father, and Makiko.

At daybreak, Sergeant Jackson rushed into the officer's barracks. "They're gone," he announced breathlessly. Robert dashed outside. It was true. The guards were gone. All that remained of their presence was the machine gun in the tower, though in typical Japanese tidiness, the weapon had been left wrapped in its canvas cover.

The cadre building looked eerily desolated. Mancinelli led his officers to the prison gate, the enlisted men herding behind them. They clung to the barbed wire and stared at the camp headquarters. Robert shouted in Japanese, "Major Tanaka. Captain Saito. Anyone? Where are you?"

After moments of bizarre silence, Robert opened the gate and walked hesitantly to the building. The doors were closed but not locked. The interior greeted him with a mysterious crypt-like quiet. He continued inside, nerves on pinpoints, as if waiting for ghosts to pop out of the closets.

Everything looked in place for a normal duty day, the floors swept and mopped. The rifles were missing, but personal items like toothbrushes, magazines, framed photographs, and uniforms neatly folded, remained in place.

Robert stepped into Tanaka's office. It looked as if the major had just walked out. A telephone sat on the edge of his desk. Curious, Robert picked up the handset and held it to his ear. Expecting a dial tone, he was disappointed to find the line was dead, as if nothing existed on earth but the camp.

The other prisoners explored the building and discovered bags of brown rice and barley in the kitchen pantry. Mancinelli ordered that provisions were to be rationed and for everyone to stay put within the camp yard.

They found white paint and in an orgy of patriotic fever, daubed stars and "USA" on the barracks' and cadre building's roofs, and painted rocks they then arranged in the yard to spell out AMERICAN POWS and UNDER NEW MANAGEMENT.

Two days later the rumble of an approaching airplane drew them into the yard. A B-29 thundered close by and wagged its wings. The men cheered and waved clothes tacked to poles. The B-29 circled back, bomb-bay doors open, flaps extended. The gigantic bomber slowed and buzzed the camp. Dozens of parcels tumbled out the bomb bay, unfurling parachutes, and scattering like dandelion seeds. The men chased after them, grown men shouting in schoolboy glee.

The next day another B-29 visited, this time dropping uniforms and more food. Petty Officer Emery brought Mancinelli a note he had found in a parcel.

The typed note read:

To the Allied Force prisoner camp commander near the town of Nagoya:

*We are aware of your location. Expect an occupation force to
arrive within five days.*

*In the meantime, maintain order and military discipline.
Tend to the wounded and infirm*

as best as possible. Document your treatment by the Japanese.

God bless,
Douglas MacArthur, General of the Armies
Commander-in-Chief, US Army Forces Pacific

Mancinelli began to shake. Tears dripped from his eyes,
and his knees buckled. Robert grabbed the colonel's arm to
keep him from collapsing. Mancinelli's voice broke as he whispered, "We're going home."

Emery grabbed the note and waved it over his head as he
danced through the prison yard. "It's official, you ugly sons-
of-bitches! Next stop, America and Mom's blueberry pie."

Robert helped Mancinelli compose himself. The colonel
dabbed his eyes, embarrassed. "Sorry for losing it. General
MacArthur orders me to maintain military discipline and the
first thing I do is bawl like a baby."

Robert slapped Mancinelli's back. "Forget it, sir."

***

Everyday another B-29 flew overheard and showered them
with provisions. Like the other prisoners, Robert counted the
days until their rescue.

His belly no longer suffering hunger cramps, his body washed and wearing clean clothes for the first time in weeks, Robert let himself think about going home and, equally important, about Makiko. Where was she?

He wanted to defy Mancinelli and go searching for her. But where would he go? How could he hope to find her? To console himself, he played a game in which he divided his rations, some for him, some for her. He broke a Hershey bar in half and wondered if Makiko had ever tasted chocolate. But the game turned bitter. Now that he was safe, the thought that she was in desperate straits tormented him as badly as any caning from Ushimi.

On the afternoon of two days until rescue, a prisoner in the guard tower shouted that someone approached on the road leading to the camp. Robert and others sprinted to the fence, hoping that the rescue force might have arrived early.

A half-dozen Japanese in civilian garb hiked up the road, dust lifting from their feet. Robert stared, heart thumping, hoping that Makiko was among them.

But his hopes sagged when he didn't see her. The group drew close to the main gate, four women accompanied by a couple of elderly men. All looked as if they hadn't eaten a good meal in weeks. Two of the women shouldered a litter pole between them, a food parcel dangling beneath, its parachute neatly folded and tied into place.

Mancinelli ordered for the gate to be opened. The older of the two men shuffled on his *geta* sandals to the gate's threshold. He made hand signs to the prisoners.

Robert welcomed him in Japanese.

The old man appeared relieved. "We beg pardon," he said, "but this landed close to our home." The two women with the litter advanced and set the parcel beside the gate as if it were a fragile prize.

"What do they want?" Mancinelli asked.

"It's ours," Robert answered. "They're returning it."

A prisoner said, "I wish those bastard guards would've been as considerate."

Robert considered the malnourished state of these Japanese. "I'm thinking they should keep it. They need the food more than we do."

"Tell them to bring us Major Tanaka and Sergeant Ushimi first," Emery snapped, "then we'll give them all the food we can spare."

"At ease," Mancinelli barked. "Tell them we'll trade information for the parcel."

Robert translated, and the old man replied, "*Hai.*"

He invited the Japanese into the yard and ordered coffee to be brewed. Mancinelli brought a map of Japan he had pilfered from Tanaka's office. He unfolded the map on the ground and anchored its corners with rocks. Mancinelli, Robert, and the Japanese knelt around the map.

Hoping for a miracle, Robert asked the old man if he knew anyone named Makiko Asakawa. Robert felt safe asking because none of the other prisoners were as fluent in Japanese. The old man said no. How about Hiro Asakawa? Yumi? Again, no.

The old man turned to the map. "American troops have already landed here, here, and here." He pointed to Tokyo, Hamamatsu, and Kagoshima.

"What about fighting?" Mancinelli asked.

"There has been no resistance."

One of the women wept. "We have suffered so much. Endured the unendurable. Tokyo firebombed to cinders. Hiroshima, Nagasaki demolished by atomic fire."

Robert translated the incredible and appalling words.

Mancinelli asked, "Atomic fire? What does she mean?"

Robert and the old man began an exchange. As the explanation sank in, Robert realized with growing unease that a terrible weapon had been unleashed. He explained to the others, "Hiroshima and Nagasaki were each destroyed by one atomic bomb. Thousands were killed in an instant. Many more tens of thousands perished in the days afterwards from horrific burns."

"You asked me about your friend Makiko," the old man said grimly. "Japan is one vast wasteland. If I were you, I would forget ever finding her. Go home, American, and enjoy your victory."

23

November 1945

For Robert, returning "home" was a process of waiting. Waiting.

Waiting at a repatriation center in Tokyo for a troop ship to sail back to America.

Waiting on that ship as it steamed first to Manila and then to Oahu.

Eager to get home, Robert appreciated that the weeks at sea allowed him time to work on his soul, to reflect on what he had gone through, on what he had lost, and to box up the worst of his memories and forget them. He composed two letters, one that he wrote to his parents, telling them: *I'm alive and safe. The weather here is nice. The food could be better. I'm on my way home. I'll write again after I land in California. God bless. Love. Your son.*

The other letter obsessed him, though he never mailed it. He spent hours thinking what he could write to Makiko. His brief time with her floated in his memory like a flake of ash in smoke. What could he tell her? How could he pretend to make sense of what they had been through? Was he simply tormenting himself into thinking she was still alive? When he actually sat down pen in hand, his prose always disintegrated into mush; he'd apologize to her about what she and her family had gone through as if the damned Second World War was his fault. At the heart of his misery was his refusal to accept that she was gone forever.

While on the ship and in the processing center at Hickam Field, Robert felt stuck in limbo between yesterday and tomorrow. Impatient to get on with his life, he stewed in angst because a troop ship and Army bureaucracy only moved so fast.

He tried to find solace in the Bible, but it was during the final leg across the Pacific when he finally buried his self-pity. If the weather allowed it, the nurses brought disfigured veterans—mostly amputees but the worst were those with cleaved faces and missing jaws—topside to get sun and fresh air. Within months Robert would be settled into civilian life, but for these unlucky bastards their war wouldn't end until they were lowered into the grave.

Though still cool to his place on this floating purgatory, at every breakfast Robert's pulse jumped when he read on a chalkboard the miles remaining to California. On the last day the ship hummed with a palpable gaiety. Men staked places on the bow for the rights to be first to see America. As the coastline materialized in the haze, shouts of joy collapsed into blubbery tears, and men pledged to be forever industrious and virtuous, to honor what they had suffered and in the memory of their fallen comrades. Ignoring, of course, similar promises when they had landed in Hawaii and spent their back pay on

booze and whores in Honolulu. If anything, Los Angeles offered even more opportunities to renege on their vows.

After disembarking in Long Beach, Robert was bused to
the Redistribution Center at Santa Ana Army Air Base. As
a returning POW, he was given the option of an accelerated
demobilization or he could remain in service. He claimed he
was an only child and had sickly parents who needed his care,
which was true. But equally important was that he was tired of
war, tired of marking time, and ready to start fresh.

Three weeks after New Year's, 1946, Robert mustered out.
It was time for a momentous shift in his life, and he proceeded
resolutely into what was next.

***

The Chief passenger train chugged into the LaSalle Street
Station in central Chicago. Like the other returning veterans,
Robert had already left his seat to crowd against the closest
window for a view of his hometown. His breath fogged the icy
cold windowpane and even though he was 30 years old, like
an impatient schoolboy he kept wiping the glass clean, only to
fog it again. When the train eased to a halt, he hustled to the
car's vestibule, and AWOL bag in hand, he was the first out
the door.

Even inside the train station, the frosty chill hit him like a
slap. Back in Los Angeles, the temperature was a balmy sev-
enty-plus degrees and he hadn't bothered asking for an over-
coat, which he now regretted. Striding across the busy station
platform toward the exit, he threaded his way around knots

of passengers and welcoming acquaintances. By the time he reached the taxi stand outside the station, all the cabs were gone or spoken for. Rather than wait, he continued for the trolley station and boarded the first car heading his way.

Crowded hip to hip against the other trolley passengers stood veterans in uniform, officers and enlisted. Robert overheard grumblings about work and trivial slights—being late to wherever, the rising price of whatever—which amused him with the pettiness amid so much plenty and convenience. During the last few days of the war, his existence had been one of disease, starvation, abject brutality, and constant death. A bowl of gruel, a day without diarrhea, surviving long enough to lay one's head down at night became a miracle.

At the stop closest to his parents' home, he climbed out of the trolley and immediately missed the warmth from the crush of bodies. The winter air bit his bare knuckles. A cold breeze traced icy claws around his face and collar, and up his sleeves and trouser cuffs. He scrunched his neck into the collar of his shirt.

He hadn't been at this intersection in years, and his memory had no problem shifting landmarks from an encyclopedia of details accumulated during his wartime travels. The Jamesons' red brick house at the corner. Cracks in the uneven sidewalk. Elm and ash trees towering over the street, their tangle of leafless branches scratching the sky.

He sniffed coal and wood smoke and was instantly taken back to his days of returning home after school. The aroma meant a hot meal, a warm bed, and sanctuary, same then as it was this afternoon.

Continuing down the street, he spied the back end of his father's Plymouth poking from around the corner of his house. Frost dulled the sedan's windows. Robert no longer had a key to the house, but his father's car was here, which meant he should be home. In a letter to Robert, his father mentioned that because of his mom's illness he'd been given a sabbatical from the ministry, and Robert wondered how his energetic father coped, spending so much time away from the pulpit and his flock.

A Christmas wreath still hung on the front door of the house. Gauzy light filtered through the curtain of the living room window.

Stepping onto the front porch, Robert caught his reflection in the door window and noted the weary set of his eyes. Out of habit, he adjusted his hat and went through the motions of tidying his uniform, rumpled from the long trip on the train.

Then he knocked.

Footfalls approached the door. The curtain in the window shifted, then the door was flung open.

At the sight of his father, Robert struggled with mixed emotions. Behind his beaming smile, his thoughts churned with dismay at how old and weathered his father looked. Once radiating with vitality, his wrinkled ruddy face resembled an apple that had been left too long in the pantry. Liver spots dotted his temple, and his proud mane had thinned to the point that Robert could see the waxy peelings on his mottled pink scalp. Once exceptionally neat about his appearance, even when doing chores, now a fraying sweater sagged on his stooped shoulders and shabby trousers wadded over the tops of stained carpet slippers.

But the fires inside his father's spirit still burned, and his eyes shimmered with warmth. Wrinkles framed an enormous grin. Large hands reached over the threshold and clasped Robert's shoulders with reassuring strength. "Son, get in before you catch your death of cold."

Stepping inside, Robert kicked the door closed with the heel of his shoe. He dropped his bag and clasped his father in a bear hug. They laughed and slapped one another's backs.

"You're home, son," the old man's voice faltered, "you're home." He relaxed his embrace and held Robert at arm's length. "Why didn't you call? I would've had a pot of coffee ready."

"I wanted to surprise you."

His father slid an arm over Robert's shoulder and walked him into the living room. His gaze ranged over the uniform. "Why so many decorations?" he asked, then added jokingly, "I told you to stay out of harm's way."

"I tried, Dad."

His father halted and pointed to the wings above Robert's left breast pocket. "Nonsense, you have to volunteer to earn these." His attention dropped to the ribbons below the wings. "Why so many? What did you do, Captain Campbell?" The accusing tone glowed with pride.

His eyes cut to an embroidered insignia above Robert's right breast pocket. "What's that?"

"Shows I was honorably discharged. Technically I'm no longer in the service but with rationing and shortages, civilian suits are still scarce, and this patch allows me to walk about in uniform. Don't be too impressed, though." Robert's finger traced over the insignia—an eagle with wings spread across a golden circle. "We call it the ruptured duck."

He removed his hat and sent it spinning onto the sofa. In his wartime letters home, the censors wouldn't allow him to discuss his missions. After his plane had been shot down, the military only informed his parents that he was missing in action. After repatriation, in his letters home he didn't share details about losing the airplane or his ordeals as a POW, mostly because he saw no point in rehashing something he was trying to forget. At some point in the future he might share that he'd been awarded a Distinguished Flying Cross, a Bronze Star, and a Purple Heart. But today he would focus on the reunion with his parents and his return home.

To change the subject, Robert asked, "Where is Mom?"

The gloss of joy in his father's expression faded. "She's in the bedroom." He gestured down the hall. "Go on ahead. If she looks asleep, don't be afraid to wake her. Meanwhile, I'll make that pot of coffee."

Robert paused by the open door to his old bedroom. His bed and dresser were still there, but aside from that his room looked as plain as a dollar-a-day hotel room. During the war his parents had taken in boarders and so Robert's belongings had been packed away. Curiously, he didn't miss them; they belonged to another life.

In the hall, another door opened to the left, to what was his father's home office. A small, unkempt bed crowded the floor, leaving barely enough space to reach the desk, itself piled with books. Dog-eared journals, pencils, and pens littered the bed and the desk, implements for scribbling sermons he might never preach. Wadded underclothes covered the seat of the desk chair, with trousers and shirts in need of ironing draped over its back. More clothes spilled over the rim of a laundry hamper, and shoes gathered dust under the edge of the bed, along with a box of rags and cans of shoe polish. The messy, scattered belongings made his father look like a transient in his own home. All of his life Robert remembered how affectionate his parents had been to one another; now they didn't even share a bedroom.

The door to the master bedroom was closed. Robert knocked on it gently, heard no reply, then cracked it open to peek inside.

His mother lay on the large bed, her frail body a collection of sharp angles beneath blankets and a quilt. She was propped on pillows, head tilted forward slightly. Time and disease smeared the features of her once handsome face. Dark bags pulled at the bottoms of her eye sockets. Robert winced at the sharp odor of medicine, urine, and bleach. Bottles of pills and elixirs were clustered on the nightstand, and a bucket and washcloths waited at the foot of her bed.

Her head rocked forward and back ever so slightly with shallow breaths. He slipped into the room, padded over the carpet runner on the wooden floor, and eased himself onto the bed beside her. His weight on the mattress caused her to shift, but she remained asleep and oblivious to his presence.

He patted her graying hair, dry and crinkled as desiccated straw. "Mother," he whispered, then repeated it a bit louder.

Her eyelids fluttered open. Her orbs were clouded like old marbles, and they swiveled to find him. Her uncertain gaze lingered on him and slowly, a smile struggled to find purchase on her pale lips. Withdrawing an arm from beneath the covers, she lifted a trembling hand toward him. The sleeve of a baggy nightshift hung from her arm, and the excess cloth made her seem even more diminished.

Her quivering fingers touched his shoulder. "Robert, my baby," she whispered, croaking the words. "You're home." She hadn't called him "baby" since he was four.

Robert clasped her hand, careful since she felt brittle. Touching her skin was like touching cold parchment. Now that she was awake, she winced uncontrollably, her head began to tremble, and he regretted disturbing her.

He was about to ask, "How are you doing?" but the answer was obvious. She was dying. Day by day the multiple sclerosis gnawed on her nerves and chewed on her vitality. The disease had withered her into a palsied caricature.

Waves of pity smothered him. During the war he had seen so much tragedy, and it often overwhelmed him into a numb despair. But in his mother he could see the totality of her life as he knew it, a wise and robust lady who had both cajoled and championed him into being a better man, only to be condemned by fate to deteriorating as this wizened, wasted old woman.

During the journey home, across the days and miles, he kept dreaming of this return. He pictured an idyllic world, one of hopes and triumphs, where disappointments faded under the promise of a better tomorrow. But he was yearning for a place that never existed, and looking at the emaciated body of his dying mother, he was made aware that the world kept turning, bringing with every rotation the good and the bad.

A knock on the door broke the moment. His father beckoned from the hall. "Coffee."

Robert smiled at his mother and patted her hand, but her gaze had retreated into some lost corner of her mind. Eyes bulging with tears, he tucked her arm back under the covers and stood. He bent forward to kiss her cheek, but her head was already nodding in slumber. Backing away, he joined his father, who closed the door, in the hall.

In the kitchen, the aroma of freshly brewed coffee teased Robert's spirit. He waited at the table while his father filled two steaming mugs. He brought a creamer from the refrigerator. Covered dishes and pans were scattered on the table and the counter by the sink, meals brought by the church's congregation.

Robert poured creamer and spooned sugar into his cup and stirred. The simple act of sitting at peace in his home and helping himself to a hot serving of coffee still seemed foreign and magical.

"What now, son?"

"What do you mean, Dad?"

"You. Your life. Work. A career. A family. Everything you've put on hold because of the war."

Robert set his cup down, annoyed, angry. "Shouldn't we be talking about Mom?"

His father stared at his cup and then at the window over the sink. "She's in God's hands now. You saw her. She could leave us in a matter of days. There's not much time except to thank the Lord that she blessed our lives."

The cold analysis surprised Robert. But who was he to protest? His father had been with her throughout as the illness ravaged her body and mind. He had spent many nights resenting her fate, arguing with God how such a good wife and an obedient servant to Him had been rewarded for her faith with such a cruel and humiliating disease.

"What about you, Dad? What's in your future?"

"I'd like to have my own church again. Stewing alone in your own thoughts isn't good for anyone. From the book of First Peter, *we must use our gifts to serve one another.*"

"What kind of a church?"

"Something small that wouldn't challenge these old bones too much. Like the one I had in Oglesby. Those were the best years. We didn't have much, but at that time life was rich with contentment and optimism."

Robert chuckled softly. He could recall plenty of times back then when his parents chafed at relying on the charity of others to get by. His father longed for a place that no longer existed.

"When would that be?" Robert asked.

"At the appropriate time. When God wills it."

This was his father's way of saying after Robert's mother died, to avoid mouthing the awkward and the distasteful.

His father laced his fingers on the table. "But what happens to me, it will be as God decides. What about you? Are you going to take advantage of this GI Bill?"

Robert nodded. "I'm thinking graduate school."

"Engineering?"

Robert nodded again.

"Which schools?"

"Dad, I just got home. Let me get used to being a civilian."

"What about flying?"

"I've had my fill. Let someone else take the controls."

"And then?"

"Maybe return to California. When I worked with Douglas Aircraft in Santa Monica, I got used to the sunshine, the landscape, the sea, the openness."

His father smiled wanly, and Robert detected a trace of envy. Then the familiar command returned to his expression, and he said, "Go, son, and make your mark on the world."

***

Robert and five other pallbearers stood beside his mother's casket. They waited for Pastor Hendricks to finish the Benediction; then they would lift and carry the wooden box out of the church.

Tucked inside a pocket of his borrowed suit coat, Robert carried his acceptance letter to grad school. He had applied to several programs and just this morning had received a firm yes from the University of Illinois at Urbana-Champagne.

The congregation rose from the pews to wait in the foyer and the front stoop. The wall of mournful faces parted, and the pallbearers ambled solemnly out of the church to shuffle down the steps to a waiting hearse. With the funeral director guiding them, they lowered the casket onto the bed of the

Cadillac and pushed it forward on the rollers. The director eased the rear door closed and bright sunlight splashed across its window, dazzling Robert.

He blinked, stepped back, and wished for the day to end, for the sorrow to let go. He tapped the coat over his left breast, felt the letter in his pocket, and thought about tomorrow.

Time marches on, and it was leaving behind his mother.

What about Makiko? The sorrow ebbed back, turning into shards of heartbreak and loss. Would a future without Makiko be worth having?

24

February 1949

Robert slipped from the cocktail party hosted by his boss, Ernie Jacobson, and took refuge on the balcony deck. Jacobson owned a split-level, ranch-style house in Manhattan Beach, and the deck afforded an impressive view of the waterfront and the Pacific Ocean. The party had grown claustrophobic with its gossip and drunken chatter, and Robert needed space and fresh air.

A wooden table occupied the deck, and Robert eased himself into one of the matching chairs that faced the water. A breeze lapped against the canvas awning spread over the deck.

A half-moon hung above the horizon, and its silver light scattered diamond-like sparkles over a tranquil sea. Stars burned translucent behind the clouds. The surf splashed rhythmically, hypnotically, pulling Robert's thoughts inward.

As he promised himself, he had plunged into his career, earning a master's in mechanical engineering from the University of Illinois, and finding a great job with Northrop working on the F89 Scorpion jet interceptor. He was appreciated by his colleagues, he owned a nice house in nearby

Hawthorne, he lived where he wanted to live in California. Robert had kept every promise he had made to himself. Except one.

He could not forget Makiko.

Her memory came to him at random moments, like an unexpected shower of electric sparks. When the sparks first trickled over him, he would try to ignore them by immersing himself in the task at hand. But her memory would only build up and then drench him with alternating sensations of happiness and regret.

He sought hard to make peace with what had happened between Makiko and himself. He had managed to find her—in the middle of war-ravaged enemy country—during the most brutal aerial bombardment campaign in history. And now she was gone.

Dark, spectral images tainted with pain and remorse intruded into this recollection, and he blotted them out, preferring to focus on his brief reunion with Makiko.

The glass door along the rear of the balcony slid open. The strains of "Little White Lies" brought him to the present. He became aware of a cool gust and the smell it carried from the sea.

Dolores Pollard stepped onto the balcony and closed the door, muting the song. She pulled taut the woolen wrap over her bare shoulders. "I knew I'd find you out here," she said.

Robert twitched with embarrassment. He lifted slightly from his chair to greet her. She scuttled across the deck in her low-cut, yellow pencil dress. Approaching the table, she pulled a chair adjacent to his and sat.

"I didn't mean to be impolite," he said. "It was getting stuffy in there and—"

"Don't bother telling me." A plastic cigarette dispenser in the shape of a steamship rested on the table. She reached for the dispenser and upon pressing a life-preserver button, a Newport popped out the stack. "You, me, the only singles in a party full of married couples, I knew the score. Betsy was trying to fix us up."

Which was true. Robert may have been an engineer but that didn't mean he was a social dullard. Whenever he met Betsy, Jacobson's wife, she always asked why he wasn't yet married, so meeting Dolores at this party was no coincidence. Truth was, Robert liked being with a woman, and even dated a few, but his thoughts kept circling back to Makiko. Feeling as though he was hedging his bets and not being honest, he backed away from commitments.

Dolores clasped the cigarette between two fingers. Since the lighter was on his side of the table, without her asking, he scooped it up and held it to her. Bringing the cigarette to her lips, she angled toward the lighter. He flicked it on and a yellow flame ignited, encompassing her in its sphere of light. Her face and the top of her breasts shined bright, and her blonde hair glowed like a halo. Her cheeks hollowed as she drew the flame, then she tilted her head back to exhale the first plume of smoke. Menthol.

Robert extinguished the flame, and the darkness collapsed to the orange dot of her cigarette's ember. She inhaled again, and the ember flared bright to outline her face in red. A cloud of her smoke gathered over the table, until the breeze whisked it away.

"I don't blame you for heading out here," Dolores said. "I felt like a goddamn cow at the fair. Everybody giving me the eye, wondering if you were getting lucky."

Robert chuckled. "What about you getting lucky?"

She leaned back into the chair and with a dramatic flourish, expelled another jet of smoke. Elbow propped on an armrest, she let her cigarette dangle to one side.

"I haven't gotten lucky in a while." She toed out of her pumps and let them clatter against the deck. She crossed her legs, the nylon stockings rasping. The sound drew his glance to her hips, her curves dimly lit by light filtering through the blinds behind them. The skirt hiked up her thigh, revealing a garter and the banded top of one stocking. He traced the curve of her leg to her foot and back to her thigh. Cheeks heating in embarrassment, he turned his attention back to the surf before she caught him ogling her.

Dolores dragged an ashtray to her edge of the table. The ember made her eyes glitter like red metallic buttons. "Betsy said you're from Chicago."

"Yeah, Chicago."

"I'm from Chicago, too. Up near Lincolnwood."

"I know the place. Small world, no?"

"I guess." She took a puff and exhaled another blast of menthol. "My girlfriend invited me to another party. Over in Venice Beach. I know the place is slum central, but it's a wild crowd. Can't help but have a great time."

"Why didn't you go?"

"Betsy. I owe her a favor. So here I am." Dolores tweaked her mouth into a grin and cast a conspiratorial look toward the door. "We could both leave."

"To the other party?"

"Well, yeah."

Robert wouldn't mind a change of venue. He could only stare at the sea and mope for so long. But heading out with Dolores might start something he wasn't willing to pursue.

"I have an early start tomorrow so I have to bow out."

"Tomorrow's Saturday. What do you have going on?"

"Catch up on work." Actually, he was planning on sleeping in. Alone.

Dolores tapped her cigarette over the ashtray and shook her head. "You engineers."

They sat quiet, the cadence of the surf filling the silence between them.

Dolores squashed the butt of her cigarette into the ashtray. "So what's eating you?"

"Nothing."

"Bull. Something's on your mind."

"Just stuff. Life. You know."

Dolores adjusted her wrap. "*Life*. You bet I know."

"There are some things I can't shake."

"How old are you?"

"Thirty-four."

Robert didn't push to ask her age.

She volunteered anyway. "I'm twenty-eight." She popped another menthol from the cigarette dispenser. "Don't get me wrong, I appreciate Betsy's agenda. Trying to set me up. A woman gets close to thirty and is still unmarried, she's practically a spinster."

"You don't look like a spinster. Fact is, you look very nice."

"Thanks."

"Girlish."

"Now you're pushing it."

"Sorry."

Dolores groped for the lighter and put a flame to the Newport.

The glass door slid open. Perry Como poured forth. Betsy shuffled backwards over the threshold, her slender figure ensconced in a tight sweater and stirrup pants. "Hey kids," she announced over her shoulder. "I was worried you two were bored stiff with my shindig, and here I find you out here together. *Wink. Wink.*" She exaggerated the facial gesture, grinning.

Once clear of the door, she carefully turned around, three highballs clasped in her hands. She set the glasses on the table and handed one to Dolores and another to Robert. "I assumed you were getting thirsty." She clasped the third glass and held it between Dolores and Robert. "Cheers."

Robert reluctantly picked up his glass and clinked it against the other two. He had stressed to Betsy that he didn't drink, but she operated under the premise that alcohol was a great social lubricant and a fuel for romance. He brought the drink to his mouth. It smelled of fresh lime juice and rum. Just to be polite, he gave the drink a taste, smiled, and set the glass on the table, unwilling to indulge.

From inside, a wave of laughter. Perry Como gave way to Gordon Jenkins on the record player.

Betsy cupped the highball to her chest and braced her hips against the balcony railing like she was modeling for an ad. She pointed to the left. "The place next door sold. Hard to believe, but in a year, every empty lot on this hill will be gone."

"Seems that all of Southern California will be paved over," Dolores said. "I was with a friend just last month in Pasadena. The orange groves we used to drive through have disappeared. Bulldozed for new developments."

"Why is that a bad thing?" Betsy replied. "It's not like there's a shortage of orange trees around here. Housing though, is what we need. And more highways for all the cars."

More housing. More cars. More things. The thoughts irritated Robert. It seemed like the Second World War—the great victory over fascism and bloodthirsty nationalism—had been about making the world safe for materialism. The great land of tomorrow was simply full of newer and shinier stuff, heaped on top of last year's new and shiny stuff. Better living through planned obsolescence. But don't worry about it because you can buy your way into happiness. Don't have the cash? No problem, we've got EZ credit.

Faces loomed behind Robert's curtain of cynicism. The crew of his doomed Privateer. Paulson. Emery. Phillips. Hayes. Alvarez. Smith. McPhearson. Commander Miller. What had they died for? Why had he been spared and left to stew in survivor's guilt?

"Hey, there you are." Jacobson's big cheery face jutted past the sliding glass door. He limped out. Jacobson had taken a

Mauser bullet to the hip at Anzio, but if misgivings about the war festered within him, he hid them well behind his perpetual grin. Jacobson's bubbly enthusiasm only stoked Robert's dejection, as if he wasn't worthy of accepting at face value what life had given him and moving on with gratitude.

The problem was that California and its sunlit vistas hadn't delivered on their promise to make him happy. But he knew that happiness welled from within, so he couldn't blame the state. Or Los Angeles. Or his boss and friends. Their job wasn't to make him happy. That was his responsibility.

Another face appeared at the door, Willy Owens, an engineer on Robert's team. A woman's face popped up next to his. Janice, his pretty wife.

"I guess the party's moving out here," Owens noted. He and Janice joined Jacobson and Betsy. Two more couples followed. Jacobson let them pass and then poked his head back through the door. "Hey, turn up the volume."

Margaret Whiting singing "A Tree in the Meadow" effervesced out the door and across the deck. Janice snapped her fingers in rhythm.

Owens helped himself to a Newport from the dispenser and shared a light with Dolores. As he winked and turned away, she glanced at Robert and rolled her eyes.

Ice rattled in cocktail glasses. More cigarettes were lit. Betsy and another wife settled into the other chairs at the table and held court like royalty. A coterie of guests filed out of the house, and the conversation rose to a raucous level.

"A pool. You gotta have a pool. It'll do wonders for your property values."

"You can't live in California and not drive a convertible. I've got the sweetest ride too, a Mercury Eight. Sports enough chrome to blind the sun."

"Sure, it's a promotion, but unless it comes with a corner office, you're selling yourself short."

"I want this new music player with...get this. No vacuum tubes. Nothing but transistors. Sure it'll cost a bundle but it's got transistors, that's the future."

"Frank Sinatra is a has-been. He's done. Through. You won't hear of him again."

"Trust me, land around the Salton Sea is worth gold."

The maelstrom of gaiety and chatter didn't draw Robert in, only pushed him away. Feeling breathless and smothered, he tried to stand and offer his chair to one of the women when Jacobson clapped his hand on Robert's shoulder.

"Don't you go anywhere," he scolded playfully. "You already ditched us once."

Robert eased back into his seat. Although he had barely touched his highball, another was thrust into his hands.

Hips bumped into his chair. Arms reached over him for the cigarette dispenser. Tobacco ash drifted across his face, and he batted it away. Rude jokes and laughter swirled around him. He felt the tug of the party's undertow, to fit in, to have fun, and he splashed against it.

His body tensed and he fought the urge to jump from the chair and catapult off the deck. He saw himself racing across the beach, stripping off his clothes as he ran, and diving naked into the ocean. Then swim. Swim. Swim.

Swim until he reached Japan. He imagined himself climbing the rocky shore of Yokohama and sprinting to the house where he and his family had lived. He would find Makiko waiting for him, not the young girl of his childhood, but as the woman he had left behind. Rather, that fate had torn from his arms. Upon their embrace, the dream dissolved into a smile.

When Robert looked up, Dolores had excused herself. Owens took her place on the empty chair. He slumped against Robert, one arm perching across his shoulders.

"That Dolores is some hot dish," Owens said, his breath polluted with booze and tobacco.

"I suppose."

"Suppose?" Owens chortled. "Man, I don't know why a single guy like you isn't all over that." He unyoked his arm from Robert and reached for the cigarettes. "Me? I'd tap her in a minute." He leaned close and punctuated his whisper with a toothy leer. "Wife or no wife."

The banter backfired and Robert's melancholia returned, sharp and toxic as before. He surveyed the party guests and his two hosts, their merriment, their obsession with possessions and status, and decided then and there that he didn't want any of it.

So what did he want?

Love, he answered. *Love and a life with Makiko.*

Would he ever find her? Suppose he did, and she had been disfigured by the war? Horribly scarred? An amputee? Would he still be infatuated with her? And if she had married? What if she was dead, what then? Would he chastise himself for wasting his life and bypassing opportunities? Or would he burrow deeper into his funk and blame himself for her death? Punish himself that he didn't try hard enough to protect her?

He needed answers.

Gazing through a gap in the crush of bodies, he looked west toward Japan. What was to stop him from looking for her again? Why couldn't he settle the issue once and for all?

His job, for one.

Couldn't he ask for a leave of absence? If that didn't pan out, then simply quit.

How about money?

He could sell his house and car. How long did he expect to look for her?

Until he had a definite answer. Only then would he at last let Makiko go.

But he didn't want to let go. He wanted to hold her close.

Again.

25

June 1951

Robert left San Francisco aboard a Pan Am Boeing Stratocruiser and arrived in Honolulu. From there he flew on a Lockheed Constellation to Manila and then on to Tokyo. He noted how many times in his life he had retraced this same route across the Pacific. Thankfully, now the voyage took hours instead of days.

During the trip he fought to rein in his expectations. What fueled his hopes was the conviction that he would find Makiko despite not knowing her whereabouts. He pictured her surprise at seeing him and imagined the heat of their bodies in the crush of their embrace. Robert's pulse raced at the thought, and he grasped the sensation so it lingered in his mind. The reunion transmuted into a serene image of himself and Makiko lounging in bed, enjoying tea and sweets. To complete the picture he saw a Shiba Inu springing onto the bed and nuzzling them for affection.

When he had decided to return to Japan, he wrote letters to the Japanese Methodist Church and asked about Hiro Asakawa and the congregation Hiro and Robert's father had ministered to. The church replied that many of their records had been destroyed during the war, and like many other Japanese institutions, large and small, that tiny church had ceased to exist.

This correspondence took time. Months and months. Years.

The lack of encouraging news dimmed his expectations. Robert wasn't sure how he'd react when he arrived. Certainly, he had watched with sickened fascination the newsreels of occupied Japan. Cities demolished to rubble. Heaps upon heaps of apocalyptic ruin. He studied the footage of desperate, tattered-robed civilians—visibly chafing in humiliation as their plight was recorded for posterity—lined up for handouts. He hoped to catch a glimpse of Makiko (she was alive!), yet at the same time he didn't want to see her reduced to such a wretched condition.

When the Constellation winged over Tokyo harbor, he peered out the window. The ragged coastline welcomed him with its familiarity. Ships traced white wakes across the blue waters below. As the airliner descended, he observed blocks and blocks of new construction and a vista that, from this high perspective, teemed with bee-like industry.

The next morning, he traveled by train to Yokohama with a pile of newspapers and magazines on his lap. Although he intended to peruse them and acquaint himself with local current events, he spent the trip gazing out the window at the passing landscape.

The speed with which Japan rebuilt itself impressed him. Swaths of new concrete rose along the busy streets. Miles of electrical cable crisscrossed the sky. But at the moment when he reassured himself that the ugly past had been banished, the train rumbled through acres of forlorn destruction, the shells of buildings softened by years of erosion.

In Yokohama he paid for two nights' stay in a hostel. Traveling light, he carried only one bag and left it with the clerk.

Downtown Yokohama bustled with commerce. Everywhere, signs and posters advertised business and products. Flocks of people crowded the sidewalks, their numbers swollen by clusters of American servicemen. Traffic clogged the streets: small three-wheeled trucks, tiny electric cars, and swarms of noisy motorbikes. Exhaust tainted the air. He headed to the waterfront and paused at the very spot where his father had bought him yokan from a street vendor, twenty-five years ago.

The breeze brought a sharp ocean smell mixed with the odor of coal and diesel smoke. He studied the harbor, the dozens of ships either cruising over the water or berthed at the piers. The port thrummed with activity. Sadly, he had to admit, much of the shipping had to be war material bound for Korea. Another war? He recalled what an aging Civil War veteran had once told him—that every war was merely practice for the next one. Closer in, along the rocky beach, remnants of the old bombed-out pier littered the water's edge.

Turning from the harbor, he flagged down one of the ubiquitous taxis, a motorized rickshaw. Sunglasses masked the driver's eyes. He looked about Robert's age and Robert wondered what had been his experience during the war. The driver kept quiet, the motorbike's engine putt-putting blue smoke out the exhaust. When Robert recited the address of his destination in Japanese, the driver smiled appreciatively.

Robert climbed into the passenger's seat: padded boards fixed between two narrow wheels. A flimsy canopy provided shade, and its sides were folded back to allow an unobstructed view of the streets. Its engine whining, the taxi lurched into the street and proceeded up the same route Robert had memorized during his childhood.

As in Tokyo, Yokohama was checkerboarded with alternating stretches of construction and neglect. Curiously, the farther away from the central business district, the fewer people he encountered. It pained him to recall that American bombing had drained the city of its populace, either killed outright or through evacuation. Entire communities had been pulverized, the ravaged piles silent as deserted crypts. Deeply superstitious, perhaps the Japanese needed to let the ghosts of those many dead rest a bit before reclaiming their neighborhoods.

The taxi strained up the bumpy, uphill road. Robert's memory of Yokohama layered on top of what now existed, and a too-familiar melancholy returned.

While he recognized few of the buildings, he remembered the layout of the *chome's* jumbled streets. They were getting close, and he sat up straight to look over the driver's shoulder. The taxi rolled to a halt along what passed for a sidewalk. Mostly it was a narrow uneven ledge between a long flat building and the road. He was sure this was the correct address from the tug of memories that pulled at him like gravity.

But everything looked altered. The door he faced should have led into the Asakawas' home. But it was a different door, wider, and made of tarnished, battered steel instead of wood. To his left, he should have seen the gate into the little court-yard. Beyond that, the rectory and the window to his old bed-room. Then, the entrance to the chapel.

What stood here was a long warehouse. He climbed out of the seat, paid the fare, and the taxi droned away. He studied the building.

He looked for a sign to describe what occupied this space, but the dingy clapboard wall was blank. Approaching the door, he pulled it open and stepped through.

After removing his sunglasses, Robert let his eyes ad-just to the relative darkness. For a moment, the interior was bathed in shadows and objects silhouetted across windows on the opposite wall. The humid air smelled of rotting produce. Gradually, Robert could discern about a dozen men, working shirtless, their torsos glistening with sweat as they lifted crates onto tables. They paused and stared at him.

Another man hustled from a room to his right. He was short and dressed in a stained white shirt over blue trousers. Robert introduced himself in Japanese and bowed.

The man was taken aback by the display of native courtesy. He responded in kind and stated that he was the foreman.

"I'm looking for the home of Hiro Asakawa," Robert ex-plained. "It used to be here."

"A lot of things used to be in this neighborhood," the fore-man said.

The reply dismayed Robert. "How long has this building been here?"

The foreman shrugged. "It was already here when I started working three years ago."

Robert looked around. Flies buzzed his head. Discarded pieces of cantaloupe, plums, and cabbage smeared the concrete floor. Forgotten details about the Asakawa home bloomed in his mind. The kitchen. The *ofuro*. The front room. The pictures on the wall. But it was all gone.

"There used to be a Methodist Church over there." Robert pointed to the far wall.

The foreman yelled to the workers. "Anybody recall a Methodist church that used to be here? How about a man named Hiro Asakawa?"

Most of the men had resumed work. A few shook their heads. One replied, "I know a Hiro Asakawa."

Robert perked up.

"He lives the next block over. With his new bride."

New bride? Robert's spirits dimmed. "The Hiro I'm looking for is an older gentleman."

"Then it's not him." The worker lost interest in the conversation and stacked crates on a handcart.

Robert bowed and dismissed himself. A confusion of memories swirled around him. Outside, he blinked and panned the street, the familiarity transmuting into a feeling of dislocation, like he'd stepped through a hole in the universe and found himself in an alternate reality, unmoored from his past.

Spirits tattered, Robert walked up the street. He stopped at the next corner, discouraged by how much the landscape of his childhood had changed. He visited the site of District Four Intermediate School Seven, and unfortunately, and unsurprisingly, it too was gone, replaced by warehouses similar to the one he had just left. A locomotive whistle drew him to the train tracks, and he stood beside them to orient himself. Using them as a reference, he sought without luck the ball field where he and Kaito had played that one last time before Robert's family was kicked out of the country. What had happened to his Korean friend? How sad that last get-together had been, but now its memory glimmered with bitterly sweet nostalgia.

He patrolled the neighborhood for the rest of the afternoon, hunting for relics from his past. When his stomach rumbled from hunger, he hiked down the sloping road toward the central business district. Weighed with despair, he felt out of place, like he was searching for a location that only existed in his mind.

He stopped in a noodle shop adjacent to the hostel, but he was the only non-Japanese patron and this underscored his alienation. After a quick dinner, he retreated out the door. But the night was young and he didn't look forward to holing up in his hostel and festering in a despairing funk. So he plunged into the shuffling chaos of the crowded streets. American servicemen were out in force, drawn to neon lights flashing *Drinks, Dancing,* and *Girls, Girls, Girls!*

Never one interested in ribald entertainment, Robert instead searched for a quiet place where he would be surrounded by his own kind and have a chance to regain his emotional equilibrium. He wandered though clusters of Japanese civilians and Americans in khaki or white uniforms. Teams of Shore Patrol kept vigil along the sidewalks, batons in hand, ready to pummel disorderly sailors and GIs into submission and drag them to the brig.

Robert found a nightclub that appeared more restrained than the others. No tipsy GIs loitered at the entrance. He waited in the packed foyer until a Japanese man in a tuxedo—the maître d'—escorted him to the one empty seat at the bar. Perching himself on the stool, he ordered a Coca-Cola and tried to lose himself among his compatriots.

Layers of cigarette smoke veined the air. A jazz combo, all Japanese musicians, mangled the lyrics of American top hits. Soldiers slouched around small cocktail tables, their blouses undone, ties slack. Alcohol-besotted boasts salted the lively conversations. Though deciding this wasn't his kind of place, Robert couldn't look down his nose at any of the young soldiers and sailors. After all, he had served shoulder to shoulder with their older brothers. These kids were simply blowing off steam before heading out to fight the commies in Korea.

The lights dimmed and the combo began a riff that heralded a change in entertainment. Robert swiveled on his stool to watch a spotlight follow the maître d' to the small dance floor in front of the band. With a pronounced Japanese accent he shouted in English, "Welcome to the Yankee Rhythm Club, the home of cold drinks and beautiful girls."

GIs whooped and clapped. Cigarette embers dribbled from cigarettes.

Beautiful girls? Robert looked around. *What girls?*

"And now," the maître d' announced, "put your hands together for the Flower of Yokohama. Asuka!"

The spotlight shifted to a curtain at the left of the band. The curtain parted and a young, pretty Japanese woman slunk into the glare, her sequined outfit dazzling. GIs whistled and stamped their feet.

The combo started a raucous tune, heavy on the saxophone. Asuka sashayed to the center of the floor. The band picked up the tempo and she matched the cadence with every bump of her hips and the sinuous writhing of her arms and torso.

As he forced an uncomfortable swallow, Robert realized he was in a strip club. He slid off the stool, but a wall of GIs penned him in. The only avenue to the front door was across the middle of the restaurant, right past Asuka. He couldn't help but look at her.

She let her skirt fall to the floor, revealing matching sequined panties. Robert's cheeks flamed, and he lowered his gaze.

A hand slapped his back, and a ruddy-faced petty officer chided, "Whatsa matter, pal? You don't like girls? Whaddaya? Queer?"

"No," Robert protested. "It's that—"

Ignoring him, the petty officer gawked at Asuka. He pounded his hands together, shouting, "Yeah. Yeah."

She now gyrated topless.

Robert's nerves shrank, and he struggled to look past her.

Which proved impossible. She whisked off her panties and strutted before the circle of men, wearing nothing but high heels and a saucy grin.

The GIs held out bottles of beer and took up the chant, "Bottle. Bottle." Some of the bottles had dollar bills and yen notes stuck in the necks. A wave of bills fluttered to the floor.

Asuka pumped her hands, gesturing for more money. Wadded bills bounced around her feet. She nodded to a cue from the band. She made another circuit and snatched a bottle from an outstretched hand while the GIs howled in delight.

The maître d' pushed a chair to the middle of the floor. Asuka danced around it, still teasing.

The ruddy-faced petty officer leaned against Robert. "Oh man, you're in for a treat."

Asuka faced the GIs, propped one foot on the chair, and flashed her crotch. Robert shuddered with revulsion. She sucked on the neck of the bottle and winked at the men, who bellowed in lecherous approval.

Someone yelled, "See me after the show, *mama-san*."

She grasped the bottle and bending forward, guided it between her thighs.

Robert knew what was next. Sickened, he closed his eyes. A chorus of roars and laughter shook the air, rising to a deafening volume until Robert felt he was inside a volcano of debauchery.

The petty officer yoked his tattooed arm over Robert's shoulders and shouted, "Ain't this some twisted shit? Shows what happens when you lose a war. Most of the girls in these joints are widows with no one to take care of them. But Yokohama is full of horny Americans ready to spend the dinero!" The petty officer let go and resumed clapping.

A horrific vision stabbed Robert. That of Makiko on the dance floor, parading herself for dollars. Robert shut his eyes to purge the image. The cigarette smoke, the bawdy cheers, the vibrato wail of the saxophone congealed into an oppressive mass that made the air impossible to breathe. Dizzy, gasping, he leaned against his barstool to keep from buckling.

The song ended with a flourish, followed by a tide of applause. Robert opened his eyes. The spotlight clicked off, and Asuka's spectral form disappeared behind the curtain. The house lights brightened. GIs mobbed the bar and the restroom.

Robert saw his opportunity to leave. He bulled through the milling crowd, ignoring drunken challenges to his shoves. He stumbled out the entrance, nauseous with disgust.

A rainy mist traced across his heated face. He gulped the cool, moist air. Refreshed, he braced against a wall, and tried to focus on the blur of streetlights and people and their reflections on the wet pavement. The image of a naked, dancing Makiko returned to torment him. He bent forward and convulsed with dry heaves.

He had invested everything he had to regain the memories of his youth and find the woman that he loved. Instead he found himself cast as the fool in a carnival of shame.

***

The spectacle poisoned his plans to spend another day in Yokohama. For years he had dreamed of returning to the city and now he couldn't get away fast enough.

Stage Two of his plan was to visit the farm camp where Hiro had sheltered him. Robert couldn't remember its exact position, only that it was along the northern shore of the Tama River and east of Okutama.

He bought a map and traveled by train to Hamura. He rented a Meguro Z1, strapped his bag to the motorcycle's rear fender, and with a cloth helmet yanked over his head, started on his quest. The road had been much improved since he last traveled over it, in the back of an Army truck as a prisoner-of-war. At the time, never had it crossed his mind that he would ever come back.

The Meguro's tires hummed over the asphalt road. Air heated by the engine's cylinder brushed around his ankles. The sun baked his arms and the back of his neck. The odometer marked the kilometers as he motored past Miyanohira and Futamatao. If he reached Kiro, he would've gone too far.

He slowed to scrutinize the landscape. But even at this reduced speed, the lush riverbanks and verdant hills fused into a green blur. In one moment he thought he recognized a landmark, then the next, he'd dismiss it.

Worse, he was going backwards compared to the last time he'd traveled this route. Coasting to the shoulder, he halted. He lifted his goggles and used a handkerchief to wipe dust and sweat from his face. A truck whooshed past, its sound fading into the silence. Looking to the front, and then over his shoulder, the road stretched into the lonely distance. The river flowed by, a tranquil sheet of water. Japan was such a crowded country and yet at the moment, Robert felt like he was the only man alive.

What was he looking for? He closed his eyes and tried to reassemble the faded memories.

He remembered his last day at the camp, when he had crept from his hideout in the chicken coop and snuck around the houses close to where the camp trail forked with the river road. The trail approached the road at an obtuse angle with a rounded corner where vehicles cut to the left.

Robert adjusted his goggles and started back along the road. He slowed at every instance where a path opened in the brush. These tended to intersect at right angles, but each time the way up the wooded slopes didn't appear at all familiar.

He pushed on, trying to remain positive, telling himself that every dead end meant he was closer to his destination.

On the right shoulder he spied where tires flattened a mound of dirt, as if the vehicles had cut across a corner. Was this the camp trail?

Slowing, he veered toward the mound. Sure enough, a trail forked at a sharp angle to the right. A thicket obscured the trail where it progressed up the slope. But after so much disappointment, he didn't bother to kindle his hopes.

He drove fifty meters up the trail and the moment it curved to the left, he was smacked by déjà vu. The motorcycle stalled beneath him, and he realized he'd let go of the throttle.

Up ahead, he recognized the stump where Hiro used to sit and rest. A rectangle of open ground behind the stump marked where the shed used to stand. The trail narrowed and continued up the hill, the same trail the camp's women had carried him down from where he'd been found, the same trail he and Makiko had hiked up, their last night together.

To the right, Robert noted where the brush was growing back to reclaim where the humble structures once stood. He extended the Meguro's parking stand and rocked the bike back so it stood upright. He removed his goggles and helmet, stuffed his gloves into the helmet, hung it from the handlebars, then dismounted.

Approaching the remains of the cottages, a chill poured over him and the hairs on the back of his neck stood on end. All this time, he had felt lost from the past, and now, in an instant, he was firmly planted at the nexus of the past and the present.

He wandered about what remained of the camp. It wasn't much, mostly a few support poles and discarded boards like the bones of a carcass picked clean. A profound sadness pressed upon him that he was alone at this homecoming, this reunion of the then and the now.

But what did he expect? That Makiko and Hiro would be waiting for him, picnicking, needling him for his tardy return?

Then, as if struck by a magnetic pulse, he was pulled to where the chicken coop had been. It was now scattered pieces of moldy lumber. Three poles marked the southern wall. Robert walked to the spot where he lay those many years ago. He stared at the ground and saw himself on the tatami mats, delirious with pain, then the hours of ennui between Makiko's visits. He remembered Yoshi, Takara, and the puppies. He scraped his shoe across the dirt, hoping for more evidence on which to pin his memories.

Nothing, not one chicken feather, not one carpenter's nail.

A thought knifed into him.

Was it still here? It...his watch?

He returned to the Meguro and retrieved a screwdriver from the toolbox on the frame. He then knelt at the center pole. Using the screwdriver, he dug around the pole, pausing to scoop dirt, and clear a hole. A foot down, he clawed through the earth until his fingers hooked something metallic. Lifting his hand, the Elgin dangled from his fingers.

Heart thumping in triumph, he wiped away dirt. The wristband had rusted. Moisture dotted inside the crystal. The hands pointed to 9:23. He held the watch to his ear and listened.

Dead.

He tried to wind the stem but it was stuck. No matter, it was a miracle to have found the watch. At least he hadn't hallucinated his stay here.

An approaching engine brought him to the present. A Toyota convertible grunted up the trail, the gleam of its emerald-green fenders softened by road dust. As he stood, he pocketed the watch and screwdriver and wiped dirt from his hands.

The car halted beside the Meguro. A woman with a scarf over her hair and large sunglasses climbed from the passenger's seat. A pleated western-style dress, blue with white polka dots, draped her slender form. Robert could tell she was Japanese, as was her companion, the driver. He too wore sunglasses, and the sun reflected through the thinning hair on his broad head.

New car. Fancy clothes. Whoever these people were, Robert observed, they had money.

She regarded the motorcycle and then approached Robert in a direct manner considered rudely forward by the Japanese. She asked in fluent English, "You have troubles?"

Robert chuckled at her choice of words. *Troubles? Plenty.*

"I am fine," he replied, switching the conversation to Japanese.

At this, she bowed, and he did so as well.

"Is there a problem with me being here?" he asked.

"My family bought this property," she replied.

"From whom?"

"The government."

"Am I trespassing?"

She smiled. "Not unless you're here to cause a problem."

"Nothing like that. I was here during the war."

"This spot?"

He nodded.

"Why did you come back?"

"I'm looking for Honchu Farming Camp 27."

She glanced about. "It's gone."

"I can see that. But what happened to the people who lived here?"

The driver walked to them. A fedora shaded his face. He buttoned his sport coat, smoothed his tie, and stood protectively close to the woman. Both of them wore expensive, fashionable shoes.

"He wants to know about the camp," she said to him.

"It was evacuated."

"To where?"

"All over. Osaka. Kobe. Nagoya. Hiroshima."

Hiroshima? Please no. Robert's heart turned ice cold but he needed to learn more. "Are there records? I'm looking for a family."

"The evacuation was done very informally," the man explained. "By that time of the war, everything was executed with much expediency. So much chaos. So much destruction. I'd be surprised if you found any documents."

"Is there someone in particular you're looking for?" the woman asked.

Robert didn't mention Makiko's name for fear of jinxing his chances. So he said, "Hiro Asakawa."

The woman pursed her lips and shook her head. She looked at her companion. He also shook his head.

The man cleared his throat. "I'm sorry to broach this, but if you've come this far, to this place, and still not found your friends--"

The blood thumping in Robert's ears drowned out what the man said, but the thought washed over him with grief and resignation.

How much of his life was he going to expend in search of phantoms? Back in California it had been easy to pledge himself to forever scour the countryside for Makiko. But here in Japan, it was as if she, her father, her mother, Kaito, all of them, had vanished like they were stones dropped into the deepest trough of the ocean. The futility of his search burdened his heart like an anchor.

Robert bowed and thanked the woman and the man. They watched him climb back on the Meguro, don his helmet, goggles and gloves, and crank the engine until it sputtered to life.

He twisted the throttle and headed back to Hamura, this time determined to put the past completely behind him.

26

October 1951

Robert was back at his job with Northrop Aviation. He had moved into a small apartment in Huntington Beach to be close to the water. Spending his time off along the water's edge counterbalanced the bustle of his engineering job and an increasingly crowded Los Angeles. Setting his life on an even keel had gone easier than he had thought. The way he eased back into his former life was interpreted as a cosmic signal to move on.

He sat on his bed and bent forward to tie his shoes. Then he would finish his AM cup of coffee and hustle out the door to work.

The phone on his bureau rang, jangling his nerves. He glanced at the clock on the nightstand: 7:42. Calls this time of the morning were always bad news. Good news waited for a more sensible hour.

He rose from the bed and picked up the handset. "Robert Campbell speaking."

"Mr. Campbell," a woman replied, her voice sounding distant and scratchy, "this is Annette Squires. I'm a nurse with the Wesley Memorial Hospital in Chicago."

The words jerked a knot through Robert.

"Just to make sure I'm speaking to the right person," Squires continued, "your father is Jack Campbell?"

That knot inside Robert turned into ice. "That's correct."

"I'm afraid I have some bad news. Your father was admitted last night for treatment."

"What kind of treatment?"

"Seems that he fell. Apparently he had an attack or a seizure."

Robert ran what he just heard through his mind again, and his thoughts lurched in confusion. His father might have been old but he was in splendid health. The last time he had seen his old man, he appeared spry, alert. Robert opened a drawer by his elbow. Inside lay a stack of recent letters from his father and none of them mentioned any sort of medical condition.

"Mr. Campbell?"

"Sorry. How bad was he hurt?"

"He suffered bruising to his forehead and split his lip. In that regard, he's doing fine."

In that regard? "Is there another problem?"

"I'm afraid so." Squires' tone darkened. "The doctor ran blood tests to diagnose what had prompted your father to fall." The line went silent with a foreboding pause. "We've discovered he has pancreatic cancer."

The floor swayed beneath Robert's feet, and his guts sloshed like he'd been thrown about in a storm. He leaned against the bureau.

A ghastly thought bloomed in his mind, an idea so morbid he didn't want to give it substance by speaking it, but he had to. "I've heard when someone is diagnosed with pancreatic cancer it's usually too late."

"I think it's best that you speak with the doctor about this. If you'd like his number, I can pass it along."

"Hold on, please," Robert said. He hunted for something to write on and plucked one of his father's letters from the drawer. He snatched a pen from his shirt pocket. "Okay."

She gave him the number to Dr. Harold Pearlman.

"Could I speak with my father?" Robert asked.

Squires said to wait a moment. The phone thumped as she set it down. Robert heard muffled conversation and a type-writer. The phone thumped again. "Mr. Campbell?"

"Yes."

"Your father has been given medication and is asleep. Let me pass along the number to his nurse's station. If you can, please call this afternoon, around five Chicago time."

Robert took down the second number, and Squires signed off. Robert set the handset in its cradle and eased himself back onto the bed. He knit his fingers, leaned forward to prop his elbows on his knees, and stared at the floor.

He felt vulnerable, so very mortal. Grief washed through him, scrubbing him of substance, leaving him hollow.

When he had lost his mother, he witnessed her passing in degrees as the multiple sclerosis slowly ate her nerves. Her loss didn't come so unexpected; in fact, her death was almost a blessing as it ended her years of suffering.

Now it was his father's turn to leave him.

Tears wet Robert's eyes, and he blinked them back. He pushed against the grief, fortifying himself for the task ahead. Thoughts cascaded through his mind.

He had only been at his new job for a month and now he had to ask for a leave of absence. He shrugged. What choice did he have?

Since he had planned to stay in Japan for an extended time—and didn't—he still had plenty of cash in the bank for these new expenses.

He rose from the bed, slid the envelope from the bureau, and stared at the names and numbers the nurse had given him. He wondered about the utility of making any calls. What worthwhile information would Dr. Pearlman share? At most, he could relay how much time he expected Robert's father to live. Robert also harbored reservations about calling his dad. He imagined his voice, denying that receiving a death sentence from cancer was as bad as it seemed.

Robert saw another door in his life closing, and as his gaze ranged about his tiny bedroom in this tiny apartment, he felt cold and alone. His mother was gone. His father had one foot in the casket. With no siblings he was the last Campbell in this branch of the family tree.

The loneliness became freighted with remorse. Robert thought back on all the times he could've spent with his father. He could've gone to see him instead of wasting his time going to Japan in search of Makiko.

The open drawer beckoned him with its collection of letters. In the closet sat a shoebox with more letters, correspondence between him and Makiko since the beginning of their long-distance exchange. More regrets. More pain. Why did he keep these letters?

***

Robert called work, spoke to his boss Ernie Jacobson, relayed the news, and was granted time off. He next called a travel agent to book a flight to Chicago. As Robert packed, the agent called back and said all seats were filled until late tomorrow afternoon. Robert decided to take the train, calculating that if he left today he would not only beat the airplane, he'd save on the fare. During the train ride, Robert tried to bury himself in a novel, but his mind wandered. He spent most of the trip staring out the window and drifting in and out of sleep.

Arriving in Chicago, he took a taxi to the hospital. As he hefted his Pullman and AWOL bag to the front desk, he realized how road-weary he must have appeared. He removed his fedora and raked back a shock of unruly hair. After getting directions from the receptionist, he left his luggage at the front desk and proceeded to his father's room.

On the way up in the elevator Robert felt the tension ratcheting tight. What would he say to his father? What words were there to blunt the jagged reality that Jack was dying?

The door to his dad's room was ajar. Robert knocked and eased it open. The room was white upon white, relieved by the ruddy pink face of his father sitting up in bed, a Bible on his lap. He was staring at the door. Those familiar gray eyes brightened, and his face wadded into a crescent of wrinkles around his grin. "Son."

Robert paced across the shiny linoleum to his father's bed. The old man's cheeks were flushed, looking redder than usual. A taped bandage covered his forehead and his lower lip was bruised and swollen. Aside from that, he looked pretty good, discounting the fact he was dying of cancer.

His father closed the Bible and offered his hand. Robert clasped it, noting its unusually cool touch. "You look good, Dad."

"As well as can be expected. Have you spoken to Dr. Pearlman?"

"Not yet. I have his number."

"I don't imagine he'll surprise you with a new diagnosis. I guess you'll be staying at the house. Do you have the keys?" His father pointed a crooked finger to the nightstand. "I've got my things here."

Robert tapped his trouser pocket, making its contents jungle. "I brought my set."

Jack settled back against his pillows. Just this small amount of excitement had drained him. He closed his eyes and breathed deep.

Robert scooted a chair close and sat.

His father turned his head and stared. "I guess we should talk about arrangements."

As in funeral and estate arrangements. "That's all right, Dad. We'll have time. Later."

Instead they talked about the Cubs and discussed Harry Chiti's batting average and Paul Minner's pitching. Like every conversation between Cubs fans, the dialogue ended with, "There's always next year."

A nurse stopped by with a tray of small paper cups containing his father's meds. He gulped down the pills. Resting his head against the pillow, he closed his eyes. His breathing softened, and he looked frail and diminished.

In the quiet, the tick-tick of a clock seemed to count the remaining time of his father's last days. The air in the room became unbearably claustrophobic. Robert felt the weight of memories and the inevitability of his father's demise pushing upon him. Breathing took effort. He stepped out of the room and dashed for the elevator.

Returning to the front desk, he made an appointment to see Dr. Pearlman. The receptionist scheduled him for five that evening. Robert decided he had time to go to his father's home, bathe, change into fresh clothes, and return. Maybe he could stop by a barbershop for a haircut and a shave. The change in ambiance would help clear his head and soothe his nerves. He retrieved his luggage and used a payphone to summon a taxi. Outside, he inhaled the fresh air and took in the clouds and open sky.

***

Robert found Dr. Pearlman waiting in a narrow, cramped office in the staff physicians' area. Dressed in a doctor's smock, Pearlman was sitting at a long desk heaped with folders. A mop of thinning hair crowned his large head, and spectacles sat on his long pointed nose. He flipped a stack of forms and jotted notes with his pen. A marked-up calendar and framed diplomas hung from the wall facing him. Blinds lowered over the windows turned the room into a tight, isolated cave.

Pearlman noticed Robert. His chair squeaked as he turned to welcome his guest. Pearlman lifted from his chair, his beak-like nose and short stature reminding Robert of a white bird rising from its nest.

The two men exchanged introductions. The doctor's hand was soft-skinned yet quite firm. Pearlman gestured for Robert to scoot in so he could close the door.

"What can I expect regarding my father's condition?" Robert asked.

"Nothing positive, unfortunately," Pearlman replied. "Your father's cancer is already at stage four."

"What does that mean?"

"The cancer has metastasized into the other organs, specifically the lymph nodes. Pancreatic cancer can be especially aggressive."

"What about this new radiation treatment I've been reading about?"

"It's too late."

"How long are we talking about?"

"Five months. Six. Maybe eight. Your father has a robust constitution."

"And there's nothing we can do?"

Pearlman shook his head to acknowledge the inevitable. "The best course of action is make your father as comfortable as possible." He plucked a brochure from a pile on his desk. "These are the hospital chaplain's services. He can help prepare you and the rest of the family."

"It's just him and me," Robert said. Out of politeness, he took the brochure and glanced at it. "Rather ironic."

"How so?"

"All his life my father was a pastor and a missionary. He's well acquainted with helping others cope with their final days. Now it's his turn."

Pearlman kept quiet.

A knock on the door broke the silence. The door cracked open, and a nurse tipped her head in. "Sorry to disturb you, Dr. Pearlman, but don't forget your staff meeting with Dr. Zimmer." She tapped her wristwatch.

"Time to pay homage to the head surgeon," Pearlman said. "Is there anything else, Mr. Campbell? I know this is a lot to consider, and as you think of new questions or concerns, please don't hesitate to schedule another visit."

Robert thanked him and left. A moody darkness overcame him, a despair so tangible he could hear it as a hum and taste a rancid flavor. He headed to the elevator and rode it to his father's floor.

As he proceeded down the hall, he spied a small girl waiting in one of the chairs outside his father's room. She looked to be about six years old. Her feet dangled past the seat, and head down, she was absorbed in a book. Long black hair obscured her face. Robert wondered who she was and what was she doing alone in the hall.

At his approach, she raised her head to regard him.

Robert halted, stunned by her appearance: high cheek-bones, large inquisitive eyes, a tight mouth with a plump lower lip, a smooth complexion. She not only looked Japanese, she was a double for Makiko when she had been this girl's age.

Curiosity chased away his despair. Taking a chance that she was Japanese, he asked in the language, "Good afternoon. How are you?"

The girl smiled. She folded the picture book on her lap and slid off the chair, her blue skirt bunching around her legs. She smoothed the skirt and bowed. "I am fine, thank you for asking. How are you?" she asked matter-of-factly, seeming nonplussed that he had addressed her in Japanese.

Her confident charm made him chuckle. He returned the bow. "I am fine." He offered his first name and she gave hers. "Fumiko."

"Where did you learn Japanese?" she asked.

"I lived there many years ago."

Without hesitation, the girl said, "My grandfather is visiting his American friend. He used to live in Japan."

"Who's your father's friend?"

"His name is Jack Campbell."

Another wave of astonishment overcame Robert. "Is your grandfather Hiro Asakawa?"

"Yes," the little girl nodded, pleased.

"And your mother, Makiko?"

"Yes. Yes," Fumiko replied, making a little hop in excitement. "How do you know?"

Robert grew dizzy. *Makiko was alive?* He felt himself grow weightless even as his heart pounded in joy.

Then a thought knifed through his mind. If Makiko was Fumiko's mother, then who was the father? The question lodged inside of his throat and he found himself choking.

Someone inside the room hobbled to the door, asking in Japanese, "Fumiko, who are you talking to?" It was an old man using a cane. A Japanese man. Hiro Asakawa.

"Robert!" Hiro exclaimed. He bowed.

Robert faced him. His mind spun in confused circles. Overwhelmed by learning that Makiko was alive, that she had a daughter, and now seeing Hiro in the flesh, Robert put a hand on the wall to steady himself. The years collapsed into one blink. "What are you doing here?"

Hiro shushed him and closed the door. "Your father has just gone to sleep." In a lowered voice he explained, "I'm here visiting the American Methodist Church. Back home we wish to rebuild our own churches, and I've been sent as a liaison." A broad smile bubbled on his face.

"But...but...how did you know my father was here?"

"I asked about him at the Chicago office and they told me the news. It's sad to learn about his condition, but I am pleased to have found him after all this time."

A jumble of thoughts bubbled inside Robert. "I was in Japan just a few months ago, looking for you and Makiko. I tried to find you both but it was like you had vanished. I feared the worst."

"Forgive me," Hiro replied, the smile fading as if the war had been his fault. "There was so much turmoil. The letters I had sent to your father were either returned or lost. Makiko and I lost track of one another as well. When we managed to reunite, I learned I was a grandfather." Hiro beamed at the little girl.

"And Makiko? She's alive!"

"Very much so. She remained in Japan to complete her studies. You know she wanted to become a doctor. I brought Fumiko with me to give Makiko a break from her duties as mother. And we've practiced our English, haven't we?" He smiled at her.

"Hot dog," Fumiko said, reflecting his smile.

"I see," Robert said, his delight with her precociousness cooling into anguish. He had survived calamities that should have crushed him, yet at this moment, he felt like a petulant boy, small and powerless, unable to cope with the truth that Makiko lived—after bearing another man's child no less—and that he had lost her.

"Yumi?" Robert suddenly thought. He remembered that she had suffered from tuberculosis and—his heart chilled—that she was supposed to go to a sanitarium in Hiroshima.

Hiro closed his eyes and swallowed. "She did not survive."

"I'm sorry."

Hiro opened moistened eyes and offered a stoic smile. He tugged Robert's sleeve and led him to the chairs. Both men moved like their bones hurt. After they sat on adjacent chairs, Hiro clasped Robert's hand. "Let us dwell on the present, kind friend. You're wondering about Makiko, no?"

Robert didn't meet Hiro's gaze, afraid for what he might learn.

"This is what happened," Hiro said. "Makiko told me she met a man in the last days of the war, Fumiko's father, and he was killed. Like so many Japanese women, Makiko became a widow."

Robert parsed Hiro's words. *The last days of the war.* Robert and Makiko had been torn apart from one another barely a month before the end of the war. In the hectic remaining weeks before the surrender, she must have found another man. So soon after her tender moments with Robert? He had carried a torch for her, a torch that helped him endure imprisonment, starvation, and torture. A torch he nurtured for years after the war. A torch whose constant heat reminded him of her. A torch that just minutes ago had flared bright as ever, and now sputtered and cooled into dead embers.

So many thoughts twisted and untwisted like a nest of snakes inside his head. All Robert could manage to say was, "Oh."

27

April 1952

Two weeks ago, Jack had returned home. He waited for the end in the same bed Sarah had died in, the same bed they had shared for decades as husband and wife.

Robert held his father's hand. The old man had lost a good forty pounds in the last two months. What remained of his hair were diaphanous threads that lingered across his pink scalp, flaked with dry skin and mottled with blue and purple veins. Liver spots dotted his temple and the back of his bony, corrugated hands. His eyelids were papery wrinkles nestled in deep, shadowed sockets.

But most heart wrenching was the gradual loss of his vitality. It was as if his father's spirit were a photograph fading under the sun. His thin, cracked lips parted and a slow, raspy breath rattled from deep in his throat. Robert leaned from his chair and searched his father's face for clues to what made him uncomfortable.

The rasping breath faded. His eyelids opened to reveal eyes that dimmed and lost their spark. His hand went limp. The cadaverous head sagged into the pillow, and Robert knew that his father was no more.

He rested the dead hand on the mattress and picked up his father's tattered Bible from the nightstand. Turning to the bookmarked page he read from the Book of John, Chapter 14: 1-4. *Let not your hearts be troubled. Believe in God; believe also in me. In my Father's house are many rooms. If it were not so, would I have told you that I go to prepare a place for you? And if I go and prepare a place for you, I will come again and will take you to myself, that where I am you may be also. And you know the way to where I am going.*

Robert sighed and let a pang of loss wash through him. He closed the Bible and returned it to the nightstand. Rising from the chair, he headed out of the bedroom, then down the hall to the kitchen.

Elaine Ross, a volunteer from the church, was at the kitchen table, drinking coffee and working a crossword puzzle. She glanced at Robert, and upon reading his face, closed her magazine. Her broad face wilted into an *I'm so sorry* expression.

Robert said nothing and eased himself onto a free chair at the table. She stuck a pencil behind her ear and hurried to the bedroom. He thought about pouring himself a cup of coffee, but he had already sat down and the percolator seemed so far away.

A moment later, Ross halted noisily at the phone nook in the hall. He heard her dial and ask for the family doctor to come by and pronounce Reverend Jack Campbell dead.

***

Robert sat in the living room of his father's house. He'd been staring at dust motes floating in a shaft of morning light, his mind flitting randomly over the events in his life. Childhood. Growing up in Japan. The war. His search for Makiko. Coming home. The loss of his parents.

The program from his father's memorial service lay on the end table at Robert's left. A cup of cold coffee sat on the program, along with a donut that he hadn't even tasted. He still wore his funeral clothes from yesterday, and as his mind ranged over the emptiness of the home, he listened and heard nothing but the relentless click of the mantle clock. He realized he was alone in the house. The wake had lasted all night and the last of his relatives—cousins he barely remembered from childhood, and a string of oddball aunts and uncles—were gone, but he couldn't be sure when they had left.

Though the mantle clock kept ticking and the dust motes did lazy patterns, it seemed as if time had stopped. His war ended almost seven years ago, plenty of time for him to saddle up and ride straight and true into the future. But it seemed he was on a carousel, spinning through an unceasing cycle of hope and regret.

He might have been alone but he didn't feel lonely. The death of his father brought back memories of his mother, of the family, the recollections vivid as a Technicolor movie.

But it was time to tend to the affairs of the dead and transition to the affairs of the living.

Robert rose on unsteady legs. He raked both hands through his hair. It felt greasy. His fingers scraped the day-old beard on his cheek.

The first priority was taking care of the estate, which his father had outlined in his will. He hadn't left much of an inheritance. A preacher didn't earn much, but frugal living had paid for the house and the Plymouth and kept him out of debt.

Robert shambled to his room, shrugged out of his coat and tossed it on his bed, along with his tie and shirt. When Hiro had told him that Makiko was still alive, Robert wanted so desperately to grow wings and fly to Japan. But his father was ailing with no one to take care of him, and Robert couldn't risk leaving him to die in the arms of strangers. So he stayed in Chicago as the dutiful son and tended to his father.

Robert and Makiko instead reached one another through a drawn-out exchange of letters. Mail delivery between the U.S. and Japan still took two, three weeks, one way. That meant an answer to a question took at least a month.

He opened the top drawer of his bureau and fished out a shoebox. It contained every bit of correspondence between Makiko and himself that he had managed to keep. Robert thumbed the letters, organized by postmark, from most recent to the first letter Makiko had mailed to him in 1930. The images on the stamps jittered like random pictures of a flipbook.

During the latest round of letters, he had asked a lot of questions. How was she doing? How far along was she in her studies? But the big question festered inside him, and he feared asking it because the answer scared him. Who was Fumiko's father?

For her part, Makiko hadn't broached the subject of Fumiko. What was she hiding?

She passed on Hiro's regrets that he had to return to Japan and couldn't spend time with his good friend, Jack Campbell. Plus, Hiro noted, he wasn't in great health either and should the worst happen, he didn't want to be far from what was left of his family.

And something else echoed behind her words, a haunting vibration that seemed to resonate from a deep well of melancholy. Again, what was she hiding from him?

He replaced the lid of the shoebox and set it back in the drawer.

Pen and paper in hand, he walked to the kitchen, brewed a fresh pot of coffee, and sat at the table. He drafted an outline of his tasks for the immediate future. This chore could have been done weeks ago, but this time procrastination worked in his favor. It seemed the longer he delayed, the longer death waited to claim his father.

Robert wrote a heading: Sell the house. Under that he listed the implied tasks. Inventory the belongings. Decide what to keep in storage, sell the rest. The house was in good shape but could use a little attention. Make repairs; patch and paint. Sell the car. Cash in his father's life insurance and bank the money. Robert needed to finalize his expenses and tally his cash. Besides his previous savings, he had earned money as a teacher's assistant at the university.

He reviewed his notes and the columns of numbers scrawled across three pages. Satisfied that he had a firm understanding of what he had to do and what money he would have at hand, he wrote one final task: *Go back to Japan.* He underlined it. Then underlined it again.

He sat and composed a letter to Makiko, sharing that he was on his way to see her.

***

In late June, Robert arrived in Tokyo. After clearing customs at the airport, he headed to the Edo Chrysanthemum Hotel. He carried in his coat pocket a telegram from Makiko, his last correspondence from her; in terse staccato prose, she mentioned that she was looking forward to seeing him, and that she was grateful he had timed his visit to coincide with the break in her residency.

Robert spent the rest of the day and the night pacing about the hotel, fearing that he was yet again wasting his time. The next morning, he woke up drowsy with flight-lag, but forced himself to down several cups of coffee and boarded the tram to Kita, a ward within the greater Tokyo metropolis.

Makiko lived in a ten-story apartment complex overlooking the Arakawa River. Robert stopped in a market and bought housewarming gifts. For Fumiko a packet of yokan, for Hiro a book of poetry, and for Makiko, a bouquet of daisies, cherry and plum blossoms, all made of silk.

The apartment's façade was in a bold, futuristic style, concrete rendered in swooping lines, a jarring architectural break from Japan's classical past; a metaphor, Robert surmised, for the nation's rebirth. A doorman greeted him in halting English and bowed again when Robert asked for directions in Japanese.

He was guided to the elevator, which he rode to the eighth floor. When the door pinged open, his heart skipped a beat and his legs wouldn't move. Two older women, one in a western dress, the other in a kimono, stared at him, waiting politely for him to exit. Robert excused himself and continued to Makiko's apartment. He followed the unit numbers and, finding her place—his stomach churning—knocked on the door.

Hiro answered, beaming. Bowing, he invited Robert in and shuffled backwards in his slippers as he leaned on a cane. Robert demurred and remained on the other side of the threshold. He handed Hiro the gifts. "The book is for you."

The old man smiled and bowed again. "Thank you. I take it the flowers are for Makiko?"

"*Hai.*" Robert scanned the tidy, cramped apartment. A table and a futon took up most of the front room. Bookcases brimming with medical texts crowded the walls. The opposite side of the room opened to a small kitchen with a sink, cabinets, and a two-burner gas stove. Light poured through a sliding glass door that allowed access to a narrow balcony. Children's clothes hung from a clothesline stretched across the balcony.

Robert kept waiting for Makiko to appear through the door at his left, which he guessed led to the only bedroom in the tiny unit.

"I am so sorry for your loss," Hiro said, interrupting Robert's thoughts. "Your father was a splendid friend and an honorable man."

"He thought the same of you."

"*Hai,*" Hiro replied, the one word hanging in the air, sad and forlorn.

"And Makiko?" Robert asked.

"Shopping with Fumiko. Please, come inside and wait."

Robert stepped onto a mat and removed his shoes. Hiro hobbled on his cane to the kitchen and slid the bouquet into an empty glass pitcher on the counter. They chatted briefly about Robert's flight and his impressions of Japan.

The front door clicked. Robert's pulse hitched.

"Makiko," Hiro announced.

As the door opened, Robert felt himself rising from his chair as if buoyed by his expectations and desires. The last six and a half years focused on this long-delayed reunion with Makiko. Always he'd thought it best to not give in to false hopes, to not delude himself about the true relationship between Makiko and him. But he couldn't help growing brittle inside, as he peeled away the armor and exposed his raw longing. He waited, unsure, anxious.

Makiko stepped in, face downcast as she shepherded Fumiko through the door. Robert instantly catalogued every detail of Makiko's appearance. Her face had grown more slender, her brow more angular. Her glossy black tresses were drawn back and pinned with colored sticks, but errant curls dangled over her ears to emphasize the sweep of her elegant neck. A rosy tint colored her cheeks, and her thick lower lip looked as invitingly succulent as he remembered.

A loose white blouse printed with red and blue flowers draped her trim torso, and the hems of blue *monpe* pants hung past her knees. A string bag heavy with groceries hung from one hand. She kicked off her canvas slippers.

He waited for Makiko to lift her head and acknowledge him. She nudged Fumiko in and then raised her eyes. They momentarily met his and appeared huge and deep. He wanted to plunge into them and lose himself within her. He kept his face plain as he waited.

She bowed and said simply, "Robert, welcome. You're early."

He bowed in return, and although his heart threatened to burst with joy, he kept his reserve. He wanted her to explode into a smile, to laugh, to engulf him with happiness. He wanted her to rush from the door and crush into him, to reassure him that he hadn't been a fool for clinging to the promise of their mutual love.

Her eyes paused on him, as if measuring him, and her mouth didn't bend past a polite grin. His heartbeats faltered with disappointment, and his posture sagged a little. There was something behind her eyes holding back. She clung to her formality like it was shield.

This train of emotions whipped past in a flash, and in the aftermath he was left brooding over what to do, how to feel.

She returned her attention to Fumiko, who was kicking off her sandals and had noticed Robert's shoes on the mat. The little girl jerked her head up and bounded from the doorway, arms raised, and she started chattering, "Look, Mama. It's Robert. He's come from America. Just like you said." Launching herself against him, she clasped his waist with a tight hug.

Makiko crossed the room and emptied the bag on the kitchen counter: cans of stewed tomatoes, plums, apricots; an onion, small packets; and a package wrapped in butcher paper. "I was expecting you to arrive later."

"I apologize if I inconvenienced you," he said. Fumiko squirmed against him.

Makiko turned and leaned the small of her back against the edge of the counter. Four short steps separated her from Robert. He hunted for a signal from her, some nuanced gesture to cue him into her thoughts regarding them. He had traveled half the world to be here, and it still felt like the widest gap of the journey had yet to be crossed.

The sparkle that he wanted to see in her eyes didn't appear. Rather, her gaze seemed to close up, to retract, like she was pulling into a shell.

Robert's doubts widened and deepened the moat that kept them apart.

What was she not telling him? What terrible secret was she guarding? When Fumiko pulled away from him, Makiko's gaze tracked her daughter as if she couldn't look Robert in the eye.

Why was that? Perhaps a fallen soldier wasn't Fumiko's father. In the stillness of lonely nights, Robert reflected on Fumiko and wondered if she wasn't instead his daughter. If so, why had Hiro lied? Why wasn't Makiko forthcoming? If Fumiko was their little girl, shouldn't that bond pull them together?

Then an ugly thought slithered from his imagination. Perhaps Makiko had been raped by a Japanese soldier, or worse, by an American of the occupation forces.

Whatever the reason, if Robert truly loved Makiko, then he would have to accept the truth and move on.

***

Makiko thanked him for the bouquet. They celebrated his visit with crackers, yokan, and tea. Sensing tension between Robert and Makiko, Hiro made small talk to keep the conversation going. Fumiko shared the progress she had made in her coloring books, captioned in either Japanese or English.

Late in the afternoon, Makiko and Robert fixed dinner together. The package of butcher paper contained chicken, which Robert sliced and seasoned for grilling. Makiko cleared Fumiko's laundry from the balcony. She asked Robert to light the hibachi on the outdoor table. Once the coals were good and hot, he arranged the chicken on the brazier. Makiko boiled noodles and a vegetable stew that she ladled into bowls.

While they ate and acted grateful to be united, the unanswered questions hung over them, heavy and oppressive. In the evening, Hiro and Fumiko retired to the bedroom to sleep on Makiko's bed, and Robert and Makiko sat on the balcony. A haze diffused city lights that shined through the creeping twilight.

***

To Makiko, Robert looked exactly as she had pictured him. Still tall, broad shouldered, with a modest, youthful waistline. Gray hair salting his temples seemed to be his only concession to the passing of time. An optimistic smile lingered behind his eyes, an optimism she didn't want to encourage.

She knew her reticence was unfair to him. She had never known a better man, and she was honored and flattered by his attention. She wasn't stupid. His longing for her was obvious. Like him, she wanted to tumble into a life of contentment and pleasure.

But she couldn't. Why did she deserve any true happiness?

"I still have your letters," she said. "Want to see them?"

"Later. I'd rather spend this time with you."

Tears crept into her eyes, stinging. She tried not to acknowledge them, to ignore them, to let the sadness pass and allow the tears to evaporate in stoic indifference. But Robert was beside her, and his presence called her to open up, to shake loose the grief plaguing her existence.

But that grief had grown deep, twisted roots in her soul and it kept her planted in the ugly past. Makiko began to weep, and each pained breath only stoked the despair until she broke into a fit of sobs and slid from the chair to crumple against the balcony floor.

Robert's strong hands tried to lift her, but she brushed him away as if to not drag him with her into the abyss.

"Robert," she cried, "I want to love you, but I can't let myself. My heart was shattered by the war and its nightmares. All my schoolmates are dead or crippled. My spirit was maimed by the devastation and ruin I saw in Hiroshima and in Tokyo. The suffering didn't end with our surrender." She clutched her fists and clenched her eyes to withstand the agonizing blows. "I am a Christian woman and my cries for mercy went unheard. God Almighty hadn't just forsaken us, he had cursed us to damnation."

Robert stroked Makiko's hair. His touch soothed her. He again clasped her arms and she let him haul her upright. She braced against the balcony railing and stared with rheumy eyes into the nightscape. "The years have not dimmed the pain. We have built anew, but I cannot forget the faces of the dead and dying. Why was I spared?"

Another wave of sobs wracked her body, and when they passed she managed, "I was pregnant amid so much devastation and even with so little to spare, others did without to help me give birth to a healthy baby." She hung her head. "It's a debt that I can't repay in a hundred lifetimes. I live shrouded in regret. I've always wanted to be a doctor and now throw myself into my studies as a way to appease the guilt."

Makiko had never admitted this, and the cathartic words drained through her. The sorrow ebbed, leaving her mind light and clear like a fever had broken. She gathered herself. A humiliating clump of snot and slobber bubbled from her nostrils. Robert handed her a kitchen towel. Averting her eyes, she thanked him and wiped her face.

"Fumiko is yours," she whispered.

"I hoped so." His tender reply warmed her.

"Forgive me for hiding the truth," she said. "I knew what I had to write in my letters to you, but my heart wouldn't allow it." Makiko climbed back into her chair. She wrung the towel between her fingers. "I lied to my father about her, but I'm sure he suspected. We fool ourselves into believing that a lie makes the unsaid truth easier to bear."

"Yes," Robert replied.

They remained quiet and attuned their nerves to the calm-ing clockwork bustle of the city below them. A boat glided down the shimmering river. Trams and cars crawled like earthbound fireflies across the patterned array of buildings and streets.

"We owe a better future to Fumiko," Robert said. He reached for Makiko and draped his muscular arm over her shoulders. "And to each other."

This time, Makiko leaned into him, wrapped her arms around his chest, and wept.

28

June 1952

Robert and Makiko talked until late into the night. Years later, looking back on this moment, he couldn't recall any specific topics they had discussed. He did remember a lot of laughter. When their conversation became punctuated by yawns, they decided it was time to sleep.

To give them privacy, Hiro slept in the bedroom, on Makiko's futon with Fumiko. His usual bed was the futon in the front room. She extended the futon, covered it with a sheet and blanket, and arranged the pillows.

Sitting on the futon, Robert removed his shirt, then peeled off his socks. He watched Makiko as she wandered about the front room and the kitchen, preparing the futon and gathering the dishware they had used for tea. He admired her youthful, deliberate manner, and the way her hair shined. He so wanted to touch and embrace her.

Makiko turned off the lights and lay on the blanket. She kept on her blouse and *monpe* pants. Still in his trousers and t-shirt he stretched beside her, both of them lying face-up. Night air circulated through the open balcony door.

Their shoulders touched on the narrow futon, and her presence seemed to draw all the loose ends of his life together. They clasped hands. A profound happiness flowed through Robert, and a great peace calmed him. Any anxieties he may have had about reconnecting with her disappeared. He wanted to hold this moment forever. Just to be here, knowing that she felt the same about him as he did about her, made all his trials and tribulations worthwhile. They had triumphed over life's random and cruel turns and were at last ready to continue the journey together.

Fatigue set in and Robert grew sleepy. He had one more thought and asked, "When do we get married?"

She twisted his fingers. "Just like that, *when do we get married?* Where's the romance? The courtship?"

He pulled free of her grip and rolled on his side to face her. "All right. Makiko, will you marry me?"

She rolled onto her side and they studied each other in the darkness. "And if I say yes? Where's the engagement ring? Don't tell me I've been waiting all these years only to have you show up empty-handed?"

"I'll buy you the ring tomorrow."

"In that case," she teased, "you can wait for your answer."

***

Robert woke to the sound of water running in the bathroom. He blinked himself to consciousness and pushed upright. Morning light diffused through the glass of the balcony door. Makiko stirred and sat up. She smiled at Robert and brushed hair behind her ears. They good morning-ed each other.

The bedroom door cracked open. Hiro peeked out. He acted chagrined to have found Robert and Makiko on top of the bedcovers and still dressed. Perhaps he thought they would have indulged in conjugal activities and made up for the lost time apart. Hobbling on his cane, he said, "*Ohayou gozaimasu*," and mentioned that Fumiko was still asleep.

Makiko retreated into the bedroom. Not expecting to spend the night, Robert hadn't brought toiletries. Standing at the kitchen sink, he rinsed his mouth and washed his face. Hiro handed him a comb and Robert ran it through his hair. Now was the moment of truth. "I have something to tell you, Hiro."

The old man had filled a kettle and set it to boil on a stove burner. "What is it?"

Robert glanced at the bedroom door, now closed. Neither he nor Makiko had discussed how to tell her father, or their daughter, the truth about Fumiko. Perhaps they should have, but after the years of evasion and doubt, Robert decided, why wait? How would that revelation change anything?

"Fumiko is my daughter," he said.

Hiro pursed his lips into a tight grin, and he shook his head as if disappointed in Robert. "Please, do not think you are surprising me."

"If you knew, you could've said so before," Robert replied, crossly. "Why didn't you say something when we saw each other in Chicago?"

Hiro placed tea in a ceramic pot and set it on the table. "We Japanese are masters in discretion. If Makiko hadn't told you, then she had good reason not to. Why was it my place to make such an announcement?" Hiro relaxed his weight off his cane and lowered into a chair. "But no matter the circumstance, I am fortunate to have a healthy granddaughter."

Makiko returned, having changed into a fresh blouse and pants. Her face was pink from washing, and she smelled of lilac soap.

Hiro and Robert kept quiet and she glanced at each of them. "What have you two been talking about?"

"Robert told me about Fumiko."

Makiko skewered Robert with a brief scowl. "I was hoping we could discuss that together first."

"Why wait?"

"Why wait?" she replied. "Like my opinion doesn't matter?"

"It's not that," Robert apologized, "It's that—"

Hiro tapped his cane on the floor. He laughed. "Your first quarrel."

The kettle began to boil. Makiko fetched it and poured steaming water into the teapot.

"You two still have much to discuss," Hiro said. "Makiko, why don't you pack a few things and spend time with Robert in his hotel. Get more reacquainted with each other."

Robert felt his eyebrows rise. Although it was obvious he and Makiko had previously had relations—Fumiko was proof of that—Hiro remained religiously conservative and should have frowned on premarital sex.

"What about Fumiko?" Makiko crossed the room to stand next to Robert.

Hiro smiled. "I've been watching her while you've been at school and at the hospital. What's another night?"

Makiko folded her hand into Robert's. "When would we tell Fumiko the news?"

"We can tell her whenever *you* want," Robert answered. "I'm curious to see her reaction."

"I doubt she'll want us to leave her behind when we go to your hotel."

"About that," Robert demurred. After all this time away from Makiko, now that they were finally with one another, he wanted a formal acknowledgement of their life together. "Why don't we get married first? Then we can spend time together during our honeymoon."

Makiko glared at Robert.

"What's the matter?" he asked.

"Honeymoon?" Her expression eased and turned playful. "Remember that question you asked me earlier? When we were on the futon?"

"The one regarding a ring?"

She pulled herself against him and said, "The answer is yes."

29

May 1953

Robert, as groom, waited at the front of the worship hall in the First Methodist Church of Yokohama. He stood beside Hiro, who like Robert was dressed in a tux with tails, and white tie. Although Hiro, Makiko, and Robert did not belong to this congregation, the newly built church stood in the same ward where they had lived before the war. Exchanging their vows here would be a symbolic way of reclaiming their past.

A smattering of guests sat in the pews. Some were friends of Hiro from his church in Kita, others were parishioners from this congregation.

Makiko entered from the foyer, and all eyes turned to her. She was clad in an *uchikake*, the traditional Japanese wedding kimono, this one covered in birds of golden brocade with red swoops on a cream-colored background. Her hair was gathered beneath an elaborately coiffed wig adorned with mother-of-pearl and red-lacquered *kanzashi* combs and hair sticks. She stepped lightly in new *tabi* socks and formal *zoki* sandals. Fumiko followed, wearing a white satin, Western-style girl's dress with a frilly skirt. She carried the wedding rings on a silk pillow.

Hiro balanced his Bible on the crook of his cane. An ordained pastor since before the war, he was honored that Robert asked him to preside over the ceremony.

At the rear of the church, a three-man musical ensemble in traditional formal costume played "*Kiyari-uta*." Eyes downcast, Makiko walked solemnly up the center aisle toward Robert. Fumiko trailed behind her. The congregation stood.

To Robert, Makiko appeared strangely doll-like in her wedding costume. Still, he asked himself how he had been so lucky to have found such a thoughtful and beautiful woman to be his bride. He didn't resent the long interval they had spent apart. Both of them had to bridge years of sorrow and heartache. Perhaps the absence from one another during those trying episodes had been a blessing. Perhaps the turmoil each had to endure would have torn their relationship into tatters. Hopefully, they were now on the leeward side of the mountain, with nothing but good tidings ahead of them.

Makiko halted two steps from Robert and Hiro. Fumiko circled to the left and waited. The music stopped.

Makiko lifted her gaze to her father and bowed. He bowed in return. She pivoted slightly and bowed to Robert. He bowed to her. She straightened, her expression plain, which only highlighted the sparkle in her lively eyes.

Robert extended his hand and Makiko took it. Together they turned, faced Hiro, and bowed as a couple.

Hiro nodded in acknowledgement. Chin held high, he wanted to project a commanding presence, but his eyes misted with emotion. He opened his Bible, cleared his throat, and began. "From Genesis 2:18. *And the LORD God said, it is not good that the man should be alone; I will make him a help meet.*"

***

March 1954

Robert and Makiko rested on a blanket stretched on a grassy bluff. They gazed upon Ise Bay, its silvery waters turning orange with the reflected glare of the setting sun.

Fumiko sat cross-legged on a corner of the blanket. Looking upward, she tugged a string connected to her kite floating aloft. The breeze rustled the kite's rainbow-colored paper.

The family dog, a Shiba Inu named *Rabona*, meaning rowdy, lay beside Fumiko and stared up at the kite as if it were a bird he was expected to catch.

Further down the bluff, a group of amateur photographers readied their cameras. One of them took pictures of Fumiko's kite.

With an unlady-like grunt, Makiko—rather, Dr. Makiko Campbell—rolled to her left hip. Her coat was unbuttoned, and her dress stretched tight across her swollen belly. Eight months pregnant with their second child, today was the first day of her maternity leave from the hospital.

Robert reached for a straw basket on the blanket. He collected their picnic items: wooden cups, a thermos bottle with tea, empty cans of fruit juice, bento boxes picked clean.

He had taken a long weekend from his job at Yamaha Motors in Hamamatsu, where he worked as an engineer and trainer in the Deming process of quality control. Yamaha were still converting their machinery from wartime tooling, and their goal was to begin manufacturing motorcycles.

Setting the basket to one side, he shrugged into his coat and stood, careful that he didn't step into Fumiko's kite string. The wind buffeted his hair and lapels. He offered a hand to Makiko.

Propping herself on both elbows, she looked up at him. "Are we leaving?"

"I'd like to get back to Tahara before it gets dark." They had rented a cottage in the village for their brief vacation.

Makiko raised a hand to shade her face from the sun. "The car has lights. How long will it take us to get there, anyway? Fifteen minutes at most?"

"We could stop and get something to eat."

She glanced at the picnic basket. "We just ate."

"Some fresh tea, then."

"Why the hurry to leave?"

"You look uncomfortable," he answered.

"I am uncomfortable. And I'll be uncomfortable no matter where I am." She patted the empty spot next to her on the blanket. "Now quit fussing over me and sit down. Let's enjoy the sunset."

Robert relented and sat next to her. She moved his arm and scooted close to lay her head on his lap. He stroked her shoulder.

"Have you decided on a name for the baby?" she asked.

"I thought we were watching the sunset."

"We are. But that doesn't keep us from deciding on a name."

"I thought we had decided," Fumiko interjected. "Ichiro for a boy. Katsumi for a girl."

Robert mussed Fumiko's hair so it fell over her eyes. "Your job is to fly the kite, okay?"

Fumiko scrambled to brush her hair back, and she inadvertently jerked the string. Her kite danced and shifted position.

Expecting the kite to fall, Rabona jumped to his feet and sat directly in front of Makiko, blocking her view of the sunset. She raised one leg and levered him aside. When she brought her leg back down, he jumped over her knee and reclaimed his spot.

"He's as stubborn as you are," Makiko said to Robert.

"Stubbornness is what brought me to you."

"And stubbornness is what made me let you stay," she replied.

"Why do you guys always talk that way to each other?" Fumiko asked, her attention divided between her kite and her parents.

Makiko brought Robert's hand to her lips and kissed it.

Robert placed his hand on her shoulder and pressed her into him. He looked across the bay toward the sun as it sank delicately behind the serrated horizon around Matsusaka. The sun's rays poked radiant beams through the clouds, which faded from orange, to red, to purple. Light sparkled on the water like coins.

A rich glow suffused the bluff. Rabona's reddish coat took on a golden cast and the yellow color spread to Makiko and Fumiko. Robert took on the same hue. It was as if they had all been dipped in precious metal, an omen promising a future of opportunity, good fortune, and happiness.

30

I chiro and I stare dumbfounded at what we've learned. Our lives seem insignificant and petty compared to the odyssey our parents endured to find one another.

We started with the letters between Mother and Father, and then sifted through the other correspondence and military records to fill in the blanks of their history.

Both of my parents were heroes on opposite sides of the great catastrophe known as World War II. My kind and empathetic father had been a courageous bomber pilot. My brainy mother, the physician, had as a young woman suffered through the terrors brought to her homeland. She was one of the first to arrive in Hiroshima to attend to the wounded and dying. Our father returned to Japan to marry our mother, and they remained to help rebuild the country.

They loom like giants in my thoughts, and I am overwhelmed with regret that I never heard this story firsthand from their lips. How much more of their remarkable adventure is lost, now that they have passed on?

Ichiro picks through the documents layered around him. Several hours ago, he removed our father's jacket, folded it reverentially, and placed it on top of Mother's kimono.

Between us stands a paper bag from a sandwich shop down the street, stuffed with the empty wrappers. Some time after seven last night, Ichiro had volunteered to make a dinner run. That he offered to pay foreshadows the changes I feel rumbling in us both.

I remained behind, too engrossed in exhuming revelation after revelation about my parents' lives. I've propped Mother's bridal portrait before me. Rarely did I see her wear traditional Japanese dress. In the wedding kimono and with her hair styled and combed, she looks exotic and beautiful, and I can see why Father was so taken with her.

I slurp the last of my Pepsi. It's diluted with the melted ice. My watch says a quarter past three in the morning and though it's pitch black outside, the attic feels like a sanctuary, cozy and secure.

My legs have cramped but I'm too intimidated to make a move, convinced that I must first do something dramatic in homage to my parents' legacy.

"Makes you feel kinda small, doesn't it?" Ichiro shares.

Small about so much in my life. Staring at Mom's portrait, I rub the wedding rings on my finger and ask myself, do I love Eric as much as my mother loved my father? We learned that our father still pursued our mother even when he was uncertain about the circumstances that had brought me into the world. For her part, Mother had been betrothed to a Japanese sailor who never returned from battle.

So if my parents could bury the past, so could Eric and I. Eric came to me recently and confessed he had made a mistake. He was miserable without me. At the time, I dismissed him, arguing that he should've seen those consequences before sleeping with his co-worker. But the truth is that I too am miserable without him.

"I'm going to Japan," Ichiro says abruptly.

The announcement slaps me to the present. I stare at my brother.

He's folding the wrapper from his straw into tiny squares. "Dad was brave. Mom was brave. Why can't I be as brave?"

"Brave about what?" I ask, hoping I know the answer.

He scoops Father's military jacket into his lap. "About who I am. Mom and Dad overcame so much to be with one another. Now I understand their sacrifices. I am as proud to be Japanese as I am an American."

Even after tonight's harvest of secrets, Ichiro's declaration leaves me reeling. "Is this the opportunity you've been waiting for? Ever since you were a small boy, you've been acting like you've been hiding from yourself."

Ichiro gives me a hard look and holds up a hand. "Don't psychoanalyze me." His eyes remain steady on mine. He sighs heavily. "Well, there you have it. I'm going to Japan."

"To do what?"

"Learn. Understand even more about where I come from." His expression softens, like he expects me to congratulate him.

"What am I supposed to say?" I ask. "Are you asking me permission to go?"

"Of course not." His brow furrows and I can tell he's still wrestling with the weight of his confession. He places one hand on Dad's jacket and reaches with the other for Mom's kimono. He gestures with his chin to the letters and photos scattered around us. "Why did they hide this from us?"

"I don't know." From the pile of photos, I select a snapshot of the four of us, outside during a family trip to a park. I was eleven in the picture, Ichiro was two. I turn the photo over and discover a haiku in mother's kanji script.

This pleasant moment
we count our special blessings.
Future bright, past behind.

The words tug at me, and my eyes get moist.

Ichiro asks, "Fumiko, what's wrong?"

I wipe my eyes. "I think I found the answer why they didn't share their past." I start to read the poem aloud, translating to English.

Ichiro interrupts. "Is it written in Japanese?"

"Yes."

"Then read it in Japanese."

His terse reply takes me aback. As I read, Ichiro hunches forward and his brow furrows in concentration. When I'm done, he reaches for the photo. I give it to him and watch as he reads the poem, mouthing the words, then flips the photo over to study the image. Since he was a toddler at the time, he is probably unaware that this snapshot had ever been taken.

"We're their special blessings," he says. "They wanted us to live in the present and didn't want to burden us with their past."

"Does this make you happy?" I rest my hand on Ichiro's shoulder.

He shrugs me off. "Don't make this sound trivial. This is about much more than me being happy." He blinks into space. "My eyes are finally open."

I hold my tongue. My brother is seldom this forthcoming about anything.

He regards me. "What about you? When are you going to be happy?" He moves his hand from the jacket to my knee. "And I want you to be happy." He pauses. "With Eric."

I turn my head. I didn't think my turmoil was so obvious.

Something skitters on the floor between the letters and the footlocker. A spider halts, wary about what we're going to do. Ichiro and I exchange a look. We each smile as we remember the story about our grandmother. He uses a letter to nudge the spider, and it races into a gap in the floorboards and disappears.

Ichiro puts the jacket back in the footlocker and stands. "Okay, enough with the testimonials before we start crying and sing *Kumbaya*. It's your decision, sis. I've made mine." He sounds unburdened, lively.

"Look, Kyle—"

"It's Ichiro," he snaps.

I nod to acknowledge his newly found pride. "Ichiro, now what?"

"I already told you. Once we've finished settling the family estate, I'm going to Japan. What are you going to do?"

I stare at Mother's bridal portrait. In the amber light, her eyes seem to shift and her painted lips tweak just a little. At this time of the morning and lacking sleep, I believe I'm hallucinating. But there's no mistaking the comforting energy radiating from her picture.

I pick up the letter my father wrote to Mother, the one letter that broadcasts his emotions across the years, just as it had back then, when it broadcasted his sentiments over an ocean.

My parents didn't let a world war stop them.

I make my decision. Eric and I should try again.

I reread my father's letter.

Makiko,

I trust this isn't the last letter that I write you. It's my hope that we will be together forever, as husband and wife.

Love, Robert

The End

Kirk Raeber is an emergency room physician. He has always had a strong interest in World War II history and especially in the war in the Pacific. He served in the US Navy and was stationed in Japan for one year. The World War II saga is his first novel. He lives in California with his wife.

Mario Acevedo is the author of the bestselling Felix Gomez detective-vampire series, which includes Rescue From Planet Pleasure from WordFire Press. His debut novel, The Nymphos of Rocky Flats, was chosen by Barnes & Noble as one of the best Paranormal Fantasy Novels of the Decade and was a finalist for a Colorado Book Award. He contributed two stories for the award-winning horror anthology, Nightmares Unhinged, by Hex Publishing. His novel, Good Money Gone, co-authored with Richard Kilborn, won a best novel 2014 International Latino Book Award. Mario lives and writes in Denver, Colorado.

CPSIA information can be obtained
at www.ICGtesting.com
Printed in the USA
FSOW02n0722110917
38617FS